Praise for Ferdinand Mount's

Fairness

"Deft and wicked . . . as much fun as pink gin."
—*New York Times Book Review*

"Mount writes the sort of fiction you just want to sink into, like a hot tub or a Pawley's Island hammock. *Fairness* is funny, touching, picaresque, decked out with eccentric characters, improbable, artful and, rarest of all, unfailingly entertaining."
—Michael Dirda, *Washington Post Book World*

"*Fairness* is certainly the funniest and probably the best novel of the year."
—*Philadelphia Inquirer*

"There may be something of Ford Madox Ford in the skill with which Mount reveals the enormities and tragedies lurking beneath plausible surfaces."
—*National & Financial Post* (Toronto)

"*Fairness* sets a standard of excellence that few English-language novels of our new decade will attain."
—*St. Louis Post-Dispatch*

"Mount has crafted an elegiac comedy of decline."
—*Seattle Times*

"Melancholy though the novel's general outlook may be, its dark comic vision brought joy to my heart."
—Katherine Powers, *Boston Globe*

"Mount is a deep and subtle writer, and if you have not read his novels before, I can only urge you to do so. He is much the best English novelist of his generation, and *Fairness* is his best novel yet."
—A. N. Wilson, *The Spectator*

"A quick, witty read with resonance."
—*Baltimore Sun*

Fairness

FERDINAND MOUNT

CARROLL & GRAF PUBLISHERS
NEW YORK

FAIRNESS

Carroll & Graf Publishers
An Imprint of Avalon Publishing Group Incorporated
161 William Street, 16th Floor
New York, NY 10038

Copyright © 2001 by Ferdinand Mount

First Carroll & Graf cloth edition 2001

First Carroll & Graf trade paperback edition 2002

Library of Congress Cataloging-in-Publication Data is available.

ISBN: 0-7867-0992-8

Printed in the United States of America
Distributed by Publishers Group West

Contents

The lines from 'for Anne Gregory' are quoted by kind permission of A.P. Watt Ltd on behalf of Michael B. Yeats

'... only God, my dear,
Could love you for yourself alone
And not your yellow hair.'

W. B. Yeats, *For Anne Gregory*

'Take a beryl stone and hold it in a clear sun, and so that stone will take heat of the sun and then with tinder you may get fire.'

John Wycliff

The Ville

In the morning when it was low tide the old women in black came in their black boots to dig up shellfish – winkles, cockles, I don't know what. They swung big buckets under their arms as their caber-thick legs stumped over the crumbly tarmac road through the withered sea-grass. When they came to the skimpy shelter of the bushes, they sat down to have breakfast. The ham was so thick in their baguettes I could identify it from two hundred yards and could see the steam coming off the coffee when they unscrewed the thermos. After breakfast they squatted in the bushes and hoisted their black skirts in unison, great white rumps bared to the branches of the bushes – tamarisks were they, such frail protection from the wind blowing up the Channel. Sometimes I fancied I could smell their shit, although it was impossible to open the little round window with its violet and yellow strips round a hexagon of clear glass. I fancied, too, that on a clear day I could see across to the other side and pick out the high ground where the clinic was perched in the fir trees. It was a couple of years since my father had taken me away, but I imagined the timetable would not have changed much. Just about now my fellow asthmatics would be yawning and scratching their way through their breathing exercises. There was an exquisite sense of liberation from all that as I myself yawned and scratched, although what I had stumbled into might seem like anything but a liberation.

'You'll take Brainerd and Timmy to the beach from nine-thirty to eleven-thirty, and they must spend at least an hour with Monsieur.

Remember to tell Monsieur about Brainerd's special exercises. It's so wonderful you can speak French.'

It was a strange house with a little turret on the corner nearest the sea and a pointed red-tiled roof and the occasional fake timber cutting across its cream roughcast walls. The house stood alone on a scruffy road which petered out beyond it and led nowhere, not even to the beach. Were there once other houses on the road, since demolished or bombed to nothing in 1944? Perhaps there had been a whole row planned and this was the model house which had found no buyers and the developer had lost heart.

The Stilwells had rented it for the summer, at a sickening rent they said, but then you know the Ville, in August it's like Park Avenue. They always called the resort the Ville. No one else then, the early 1960s, seemed to use the term. Perhaps it went back to before the war, Mrs Stilwell had come as a little girl with her mother, the legendary Buzz Nielsen (Buzz was usually a boy's nickname but she was as feminine as crêpe de Chine). There was money on both sides, Mrs Stilwell told me, such old money, by our standards of course, by yours we're all nouveau.

I liked the way she went on. She didn't expect to be interrupted but she wasn't relentless either, and she would answer anything I asked her. And the way she put her long bony face round the door and said, Are you receiving guests, that was nice too. With her brindled copper hair swept back and tied with a black bow she looked like an early President on an American stamp. Her fluttery gestures and her bubbling talk came out awkwardly but made me take to her more. She smelled of fresh flowers, and she wore flowery skirts that swirled when nobody else's did. How could she get up so fresh each morning? I could barely raise the energy to kneel on my bed and look through the stained-glass window at the cockle-gatherers lifting their skirts. Dr Maintenon-Smith, the self-styled Napoleon of Asthma, had pronounced me cured, yet there were days still when I felt my breath come quick and shallow, and I retreated into my old solitude, that light-headed state in which the rest of the world seemed not hostile but hazy, insignificant, like the fret which blew up along the beach without warning, first blurring all outlines and landmarks into a pearly grey, then blotting them out altogether as the damp shuffled down into the lungs and the foghorn began to boom from the lighthouse out beyond the rocks.

Jane Stilwell had taken me on as a tutor, thinking my delicate state would make me sympathetic to Brainerd's needs. These were more complex and more obscure than mere asthma. He was an invalid child of the Victorian sort, subject to spasms and fainting fits which they couldn't put a modern medical name to. Someone with my background would be sensitive and understanding when he had one of his attacks.

She was wrong. Being an old hand, I simply thought, Here he goes again. His Bambi teeth seemed to stick out further over his blubbery lower lip and his eyes filled with tears as his whole wimpish body shook.

'Do you want a pill?' He glared at me, to let me know that his condition was too appalling to be put right by anything so trifling. When the shaking had ceased, I asked if he would like to go to the beach.

'Do you think he should? Maybe he should rest?'

'He needs some air in those lungs,' I said with unusual authority.

'And Monsieur would do him good.'

'He would.'

'I don't like Monsieur.' Brainerd had emergency recourse to speech. At the best of times, which this wasn't, he had a drawn-out wailing voice that suggested that his patience had been tried too far.

'I don't like him much either,' I said. 'But his exercises are OK.'

'His exercises are crap.'

'Brain*erd*.' His mother's tolerance suffered an abrupt caesura when confronted with bad language. Anyone who was well enough to swear lost all invalid privileges.

'So they are crap.'

'Brainerd Stilwell, you will put on your sweatshirt and sneakers and go straight to the beach this minute.'

We set off with Timmy, doe-eyed, taciturn, dawdling behind us, not because he didn't want to go – he was a docile boy – but to wait for tempers to ease. He kept a little apart to give Brainerd a yard or two's start in case of trouble.

We went through the rickety glass door that led to the little garden with its beige gnomes glued to the cement balustrade and out through the gate to the beach. On fine days Brainerd would set out his collection along the balustrade, finds from the beach mostly: Coke tins, Seven-up, bottles of Pschitt lemonade and Orangina, queer-shaped bottles of local cider. These items, carefully spaced along the cement parapet, looked as if they were on show in a gallery. Brainerd fussed over them but refused to discuss the project, fearing mockery. When the fog came down, he would scamper outside and scoop them up in a couple of carrier bags he kept for the purpose. The scooping was unceremonious, just like anyone chucking empties into a carrier.

We idled along the smooth stumbly shingle, kicking stones, slipping on the seaweed bubbles. The first ragged wisps of mist began to float towards us. 'There's a fog, it's bad for me, we must go back,' Brainerd wailed. The thin wisps thickened into trailing scarves and then into a damp suffocating blanket. The noise of traffic from the far-away promenade faded and then was obliterated. Even the gravelling thump of the sea was lost to us. All we could hear was the sound of our breathing and the rasp and slither of the shingle beneath our sneakers. We met an elderly couple going for a walk, and they loomed up at us with a menace which drove Timmy to cling to my trouser leg.

We trudged on, beginning to lose all sense of distance. 'We've gone too far,' Brainerd wailed, 'we've missed it', and I was inclined to agree with him. But we hadn't.

The bars came at us out of the mist, nearly twice my height and only a couple of yards away so that I could see how black and wet they were from the mist. Beyond the bars, I could already see the children huddled under the orange awning rigged up in the far corner as a shelter. The lower bars had netting on the outside to stop the smaller children escaping but the upper levels were open, and the nimbler ones would roost up there for most of the period, now and then spinning round the uprights or curling their toes round the horizontals and hanging like bats. But these perches were now untenanted. Monsieur had his entire troupe corralled under the awning. I could see his brown bald head juddering as he barked instructions. He was always clad in white from head to toe, T-shirt, tracksuit, sneakers and on very wet days, not today, a flat white cap. He jogged over to unlock the gate, which was at the children's height, so he did not bother to make the necessary crouch to come through it and barked at us from the other side of the bars:

'Vous êtes en retard.'

'Nous pensions, à cause du temps, vous savez ...'

'Ça s'élèvera.'

His leatherbrown face had all expression tanned out of it, though his cracked voice was full of ill-humour. He shooed Brainerd and Timmy through the gate into the stockade – 'Allez, allez'. But Brainerd stopped, never missing an opportunity to display willpower, and with some dignity entrusted a fresh acquisition to me, an Orangina bottle, a squatter version of the standard model, perhaps an earlier design (Brainerd himself was indifferent to rarity, accumulating two or three examples of a common item without being fussed). I watched the two boys stumbling across the sand towards the awning past the vaulting horse and the hanging rings and Monsieur's other instruments of torture. Then my eye wandered back along the beach the way we had come, to see if there was any prospect of the weather lifting as Monsieur had promised.

To my surprise, at that moment the thick mist was suffused with a very faint gleam, and slowly the air began to move past me, leaving cool dew on my cheeks. The strands unravelled and went gliding on down the beach, as though gathered by some spectral force. The white outline of the breakers returned and with it the sound of the surf on the shingle. That peculiar world without sensation dissolved and all my senses seemed to tingle, as when feeling comes back to a frozen limb.

The mist was light and summery now, trembling with the refracted rays of the sun behind it, so that the two figures coming the way we had come seemed not so much obscured as shimmering. At first I thought they were two children. There was so little difference in their height and the taller of the two was stalky and slender like a child. But something about her walk – I could see it was a girl now – seemed grown-up and assured. The smaller one was a dark boy, as dark as she was fair, with a tousle of black curls and a quick jigging way of getting along, which made her pace seem deliberate by comparison. She was pale, extremely pale, and had a severe look, not so much reproving perhaps as severe on herself.

'Bonjour, M'sieu'. Je regrette que nous sommes en retard.' She spoke with one of those confident English accents, quietly but with no fluster and not much apology about it.

'Don't worry,' I said, 'we only just got here ourselves.'

'Ah I'm sorry, I thought you were – that must be him over there.'

'It is,' I said.

She allowed me a pale smile, neither friendly nor unfriendly, just recognising the facts of the situation. She went to the little gate and finding it locked called Monsieur. He trotted over and let her in. She scarcely had to duck, she was so small, but then had to come back to pull the dark boy through. He grizzled in what sounded like French with some sort of accent but eventually allowed himself to be handed over to Monsieur.

She shut the little gate behind her and came and stood beside me, leaning against the bars, and rolled a cigarette.

'I'm Helen. I'm working for the Farhadis.'

'Faradays?'

'Farhadi. They're Iranian. Close friends of the Shah and all that.'

'Ah.'

I told her my name and my employer's details.

'Are they rich?'

'Very.'

'So are the Farhadis: super-rich. They've got a bodyguard and two Mercs.'

'Can't match that. I don't think anyone wants to assassinate the Stilwells.'

'Not even you?'

'Not yet. I quite like her.'

'Ah.'

'No, I don't mean that. Where – where do you come from?'

'The lower-middle class. Or, middle-lower-middle to be more precise. My dad's a radio engineer, but he works for the BBC, so that puts him up a notch.'

'I didn't mean that.'

'I expect you did. You can always hear an English person listening out for your vowels.'

She spoke in a gentle flat way, and what she said did not sound as sharp as it might have. Now that she had brought the subject up, I started to listen to her voice, but as far as I could tell she might have come from anywhere. She was plainness itself, an unearthly kind of plainness, though. There was nothing remarkable about the way she looked either – five foot one or two I suppose, jeans and an old T-shirt – nothing remarkable except her hair which was golden, a milky gold, so that at first I thought its colour was muted by the mist, but even now that the sun was coming out it was still the same colour. Cut short, nearly straight except for a careless curling at the ends – perhaps that was the mist frizzling it. She might have meant it to be a no-nonsense cut, but that milky gold defied any such intention and the wayward hint of the curling made it difficult to keep my mind on anything else. Standing beside her, smoking one of her roll-ups, I felt not shy, as you do when close to a person who is generally supposed to be beautiful or alarming, but pleasantly inconspicuous, as you might feel if you were doing some household chore in the background of the Annunciation while the angel was passing on the news in the matter-of-fact way that a genuine angel would have of doing things, but still your eyes can't drag themselves away from the golden flicker of the angel's wingtips.

'The Thames, just below Sunbury, is the answer you wanted. Tell me, is this concentration camp really all right?' She jerked a finger at Monsieur who had shooed the children out from under the awning and was now putting them through the usual warm-up exercises.

'No casualties so far. I usually get through a chapter while they're in custody.' I tapped the book under my arm (*Moby-Dick* – I was finding it uphill work).

'Oh, *literature*.'

'You're against it?'

'I'm a chemist,' she said.

'You could be a literary chemist, like, wasn't Goethe a sort of chemist?'

'I'm not interested in the history of science. That's why I did science, to get away from history.'

'You going to be a scientist?'

'No, I'm not good enough. But you wouldn't have asked that question if I'd been doing history, you wouldn't have asked me was I going to be a historian.'

'No, I suppose not, but why does that matter?'

'Because it shows you think of science as the sort of subject which only trolls and grey people do.'

'No, no, I don't.' This conversation began to annoy me, partly because she was at least half-right, but also because it was not a topic that appealed to me, not here as the sun slipped out of the cloud and the blue came back into the sea. But she went on.

'My real interest is biochemistry, but it's all, what's the word people like you use, all "stinks" to you isn't it?'

I indignantly denied it, which made her smile. Though her lips curled at one side to show that this was a superior smile, the expression seemed put-on as though it was the way you were meant to smile when you had said something sarcastic but what you had said was only the sort of thing you might be expected to say and had no real force or feeling behind it. No, on second thoughts, put-on was not the right way to describe her, she did not seem affected. It was more that she had some still, reflective quality which was indifferent to her words, like a tree unstirred by the rustling of its own leaves.

We were interrupted by a violent yowling from the stockade, like a cat being stepped on.

'Brainerd, bound to be.'

Monsieur came through the little gate at a storming crouch.

'Il a tombé, votre garçon. Il est idiot,' he spluttered.

My charge was lying in the sand in the foetal position, clutching his ankle.

'Monsieur made me go up too high.'

'C'est pas vrai,' Monsieur shouted.

'He did too.'

'We'd better take him home,' Helen said. 'You take him under that arm, and he can hop on the other leg.'

'I can't hop.'

'Yes you can, Brainerd,' she said, and he shut up. She was engaged now and spoke in a voice of command, not loud, but in a way that seemed to commit her whole person and so carried conviction. As we swung Brainerd over the sand, she even knew a song about hopping which he consented to join in after a bit.

'Is it all right to leave your own – whatever he's called?'

'Oh Tariq will be OK. Monsieur will be so scared of trouble he'll make sure nothing happens to him.' Her refusal to be impressed by Monsieur's parade-ground manner was itself impressive. She seemed to possess a certainty about how other people would react. Perhaps that was the secret of action, to rely on stability of motivation, to believe that the same stimuli would always produce the same reactions. It was fear of the erratic and unpredictable in others that produced my own hesitancies. To get anywhere in life, you had to make the same presumption of regularity about people as you made about the natural world. And it was pleasant to be caught up in her certainty. We swung along through the lingering mist-skeins with a high cheerfulness. For a few minutes, even Brainerd forgot that he was the invalid of the century.

But then the drag of the shingle on his sneakers revived his self-pity.

'I can't walk,' he said.

'Yes, you can, Brainerd, lean on my arm.'

'Carry me.'

'You're too big to be carried.'

'In war they carry people when they're wounded.'

'This isn't a war.'

'Carry me.'

There was an impasse in the lingering shimmer of the mist and all I could hear was the shingle sliding off our beach shoes. Then over the top of the bank, I saw Bettine's little stall which wasn't usually there so early in the day and so posed no temptation until the afternoon beach trip. Brainerd saw it too and his eyes gleamed at the sight of the giant pink cardboard lollies and the white hatch with Bettine's homely face peering out.

'Can I have an ice-lolly?'

'Of course you can't have an ice-lolly at eleven o'clock in the morning.'

'I can too. When we went to the minigolf Dad gave us an ice-lolly.'

'Your mother says I mustn't give you ice-creams because it's bad for your skin.'

'I can't walk. Look.'

Brainerd dug his toes into the pebbles so that only the laces of his sneakers were visible, hunching his shoulders to complete the posture of misery.

'Brainerd,' Helen said, 'your mother hasn't said anything to me, so would it be all right if I gave you an ice-lolly if you promise to walk all the way home without complaining?'

For an instant, Brainerd's natural instinct for contention tempted him to point out that this was a phoney argument, but wiser counsels prevailed.

'Yeah,' he said, 'strawberry and chocolate, with nuts.'

Behind us as we stomped up the slithery bank, we heard a wailing. 'It's not fair. I want an ice-lolly too.'

'Timmy, you haven't hurt your leg.'

'It's not fair.'

'Timmy, come on.'

'If I hurt my leg, will you buy me an ice-lolly too?'

He laid himself down on his side with great care as though about to go to sleep on the shingle and then felt his ankle, wincing extravagantly before he touched it.

'Timmy, don't be silly.'

Brainerd, by now reaching up to receive the lolly from Bettine's plump hands, turned round with a grin of triumph to contemplate his brother writhing on the pebbles.

'Oh all right then,' I said and picked Timmy up and carted him over to the little stall.

Brainerd's face creased in despair.

'It's not fair, *he* hasn't hurt his leg.'

'When you've made an exception, you have to stick to it, otherwise you lose your authority,' Helen said.

'Who said I ever had any? Anyway, you shouldn't have made an exception in the first place.'

'It's not fair,' Brainerd said, 'I can't walk.'

'You promised, Brainerd,' Helen said. 'Timmy's too young to know about promises, but you promised.'

'Carry me,' Timmy ordered, waving his red lolly, 'I'm tired.'

'No, you're not, Timmy. You're a very lucky boy. You've had an ice-lolly and you haven't hurt your leg and you're walking home.'

'It's not fair,' Brainerd said again, but it was little more than a mumble for the sake of it, a musing sort of utterance not a clamour for action. And he let himself be half-carried along the shingle between us, carefully shielding the lolly with his fingers as he nibbled away with his buck teeth.

It's not fair: somehow the phrase twitches in my memory as I write it down and it takes me a minute or two to track down why. It was the philosopher W.R. Scrannel (1911–66) who used the phrase in one of his legendary lectures, or Scrannelogues as his disciples called them (I am not sure why I describe him so formally here, I came to think of him as almost a friend though an alarming one). After he had said it, he paused, one of those caustic pauses that kept his audience on the edge of their seats, before repeating the word 'fair' and adding with that sudden briskness of his that in the history of this little word lay the history of the past thousand years. All the beauty in the world, everything that *Homo sapiens* was capable of falling in love with, had once been expressed in that simple epithet. When we saw someone who was fair – him or her, there was no distinction of sex in it – the world was flooded with meaning. But now what were we left with? Fair shares for all. What once made the heart beat faster and constituted the best reason for being alive was now all about income tax and waiting lists. From irrational adoration to the rational distribution of resources, that was progress.

Now that I piece his words together and recall the derisive rasp in his voice, I see that he could not have said all this in a lecture because it wasn't really philosophy and it must have been over one of those feverish teas in his house at Pigotts Hill with his wife and daughter that he gave his version of how the world came to be disenchanted.

'Oh God, what's wrong with Brainerd? The ankle, oh he has such weak ankles.' Jane Stilwell enfolded her son with passion. Her copper mane seemed to lasso his neck. In the dim light of the sitting-room, made dimmer by the stained-glass turret window on the corner, I became aware of two shadowy presences behind her, one so huge that he seemed to be as big as the china cabinet next to him and likely to unhinge its rickety glass windows and do terrible damage to the little figures of Norman peasantry which trembled on its grimy shelves.

'These,' she said, her eyes full of tears and with the limp figure of Brainerd sprawled across her bosom, 'these are the darling Wilmots – Dodo and Tucker.'

The huge man waddled out towards us, a distance of some six feet, but even so his progress was stately.

'I'm Waldo, Dodo to my friends who think I'm extinct,' he said putting out a hand the size of a small turkey. His wife, who looked eerily like Jane Stilwell down to the Presidential queue at the back of her hair, said, 'Hi, I'm Tucker.'

Helen shook hands with them in a brisk fashion, as though they were about the hundredth people she had had to shake hands with already that day. I could not help gazing on them with wonder. Dodo Wilmot was two hundred and fifty pounds or thereabouts but with the weight evenly spread, so that he was huge first and only fat second. He was a legend, Jane told me, had made millions in anything there was to make millions in, real estate, hogs, farm machinery and, above all, minerals. He enjoyed a monopoly on the import of sponges and had came close to cornering some other soft commodity – what was it, cocoa, soya beans? – but not close enough, so that when the positions closed he was nearly bust. But minerals, that he was famous for.

'Whadya say your name is?' he enquired but more gently than the words implied, then repeated our names and said again, 'Hi, I'm Dodo,' before relapsing into a contented silence.

At this point Helen woke up to who he was. 'Have you decided where to start digging next?' she said. To me this sounded too quick off the mark, a jump into something which needed more acquaintance, but Wilmot was not disconcerted.

'No, young lady, we haven't. They wanted me to take out a whole bunch of leases in Africa some place, but I've played that game before. I told them, you find me the rock, and I'll pay you a fair price, but I'm too old to go digging again.'

'What are you doing, Waldo Wilmot, going on about goddamned rocks when there's a poor child lying here with a broken leg?'

'Charles'll take him down to the hospital in the wagon, honey, and tell them to bill me.'

'I won't hear of such a thing,' Jane said.

'I don't think you'll have to pay,' Helen said, as they wrapped

Brainerd up in a blanket and I helped to carry him to the car with Jane scurrying along behind.

'Well, isn't that great?' Wilmot seemed at peace with the world. He said goodbye to Brainerd and turned back to Helen with benevolent curiosity. 'How come you know so much about my little business?'

'I'm a chemist, and I'm particularly interested in geology and metallurgy too.'

'Well, we'll have to see if we can find you a job. We need some attractive scientists in our company. Most all of them are bug-eyed monsters.' He laughed, and to my surprise she laughed with him, not in the least offended, but hadn't she said her particular interest was biochemistry?

He patted the seat beside him in the dark corner of the little sitting-room, and talked to her, about his new project from what I could catch as I bustled about at his wife's direction, collecting her racing glasses and telling Françoise the maid to look after Timmy. Now and then I glanced at them sitting side by side, Wilmot with his bulk turned towards her, his huge paw emphasising some key point in his spiel while she sat facing front, as though resisting some entreaty which he should have known better than to try.

'Hey time to go,' Wilmot suddenly called out to us. 'We got the other car out back. You come racing too, Helen, and we can talk rocks.'

'Sorry, I can't, I'm afraid.'

'You not a horse person, Helen?'

'Not really.'

'You look like you have a real nice seat for a horse. I can always tell.'

'Not me,' Helen said. 'Anyway I've got to pick up Tariq. Mrs Farhadi's taking him to have his verrucas done.'

'That wouldn't be Minna Farhadi, would it? We're best buddies with the Farhadis from way back.'

'Yes, that's right.'

'He's a terrific character, Farid. He tried anything on you yet?'

'What, oh no, so far he's been very polite, rather formal really.'

'You just wait, Helen, believe you me. It's only a matter of time.'

'Dodo, can it.' Mrs Wilmot threw in this reproof with leisurely disdain. She did not sound annoyed.

'She's from Texas, my wife, she's old-fashioned, can't get those southern Baptist preacherfolk out of her mind.'

With her chunky gold bracelets and scarlet and orange silk shirt and her great flounce of hair the same brindled copper as Jane's, Mrs Wilmot did not look like someone whose head was buzzing with old-time religion, but you could never be sure. Church historians were now coming to the belief that far from being marginal ascetics the early Christians had been well-dressed, middle-class family people, many of them comfortably off.

The other car was a modest Renault. Wilmot enveloped the steering wheel, his bulk spilled over the seat, the hand-brake sprouted out of the dashboard and burrowed deep into his belly. By shifting his massive left shoulder through the open window, he allowed enough space for his wife to breathe in the passenger seat.

'Oh Dodo, why did you tell Charles to take the wagon?'

'This is a fun car, Mother, a real fun car.'

Inland, the mist lingered. It straggled about the midget poplars and the stream which wound along the little valley behind the town. We passed timbered farmhouses, and crumbling walls and gable-ends with fading ads for St Raphael and Cinzano, and orchards of that deep damp green they had even in midsummer, the apples with only the faintest flush of red on them. Wilmot drove slowly, stopping for every peasant on a bicycle or clutch of hens at a farmyard gate. Each time he braked he exclaimed with a slow exhalation of pleasure, 'Well, isn't that great?' His delight sounded so easy and natural that there was no condescension in it. He just seemed to like slow things.

In a dusty little village smelling of manure, we turned sharp left at a slate-hung belltower with a clock chiming noon on it, and began to climb the gentle hill above the village, doubling back on ourselves, towards the sea.

The air became clear, the sky blue. Over the tops of the hawthorn hedges, beyond the pine trees and the slate roofs of the little town, I could see the pale line of the beach, and I could see the sea. 'Isn't that great?' Wilmot said. He turned the car down a gravel avenue between perfectly clipped lime trees. We fell in at the tail of a queue of limos gleaming in the breakthrough sun. Gliding down this kempt avenue towards the glinting sea, we seemed to have chanced on the road to an unsuspected sort of heaven, one which was no distance at all really but you had to know the way. At the end of the avenue, the ground fell away and spread out below us and we saw the white rails curving round in the shape of a frying pan with the stands at the end of the handle: a row of green-and-white pavilions with flags fluttering above them and the white oval of the paddock rails behind. 'Isn't that great?' Dodo sighed.

'It says Owners Car-Park Right,' his wife said.

We got out, and I heard the car's springs sigh their relief as Dodo decanted himself on to the grass.

'Firm,' he said digging his heel into the green turf. 'Going's good to firm. They'll go a hell of a gallop. You OK? Did I drive too fast for you, you look like you just saw a ghost.'

Which I had, three ghosts, to be exact. For there standing together leaning with their backs against the paddock rails, mulling over their race cards, were the companions of my father's youth, the drinking companions of his middle age, today in light summer wear and straw hats rather than British warm overcoats and soft brown hats, but still with that laconic unhurried air of racing men.

'I know that face. How are you? How's your dear father?' Boy Kingsmill removed his panama with a mock flourish to the ladies, smoothing his tarmac hair with the other hand almost at the same time, as though the smoothing was also an accepted part of the greeting process. 'Well, this is a pleasure,' he said as he passed round our little party, with that obsequious foreknowing way my father loved to dwell on – *Boy can't buy a box of matches without making the woman behind the counter think all his past life has been a preparation for that moment.* Boy might have been camping out on this patch of downland for months in the hope of catching a glimpse of me. When Jane came panting up to our little group a few minutes later (there turned out to be nothing wrong with Brainerd's ankle by the time they got to the hospital), he bent over her hand and bussed it lightly.

'What a darling blazer.'

Jane Stilwell liked to praise other people's clothes. She did it with a special little whoop in her voice as though she could hardly believe her eyes. Hard to say what had caught her fancy here – the full sun on the heavy gilt buttons, the thin almost tropical texture of the cloth, the suggestion of fade about the purple-blue.

'Boating jacket, officers for the use of.' Boy held out his sleeve for her to stroke. 'The bluebottles, the *mouches bleues* they called us over here. Our lot got badly cut up in the bocage. I was laid up with a broken ankle at the time as luck would have it.' Boy waved a hand, introducing his two friends. 'You remember Captain O'Neill?'

'Yes, of course,' I said.

It must have been twenty-five years at least since Frogmore O'Neill and my father had competed on the scales to see who could make the weight for the ride of a lifetime, on Ampersand, the surest sweetest chaser of his day. But Froggie was long past all that. Popping out of his crinkled linen suit, he had even more the look of a frog in a children's story. Something magical like a pearl or a registered letter might plop out of his letterbox mouth.

'Putting up a few stone overweight these days, I'm afraid,' Froggie said patting his paunch and removing his cracked panama from his sweating brow.

'And Cod, you remember Cod Chamberlayne, the punter's friend?'

'Now then young man, I don't cross the frigging Channel to be made game of.'

'On the rails back home, Mr Chamberlayne is an institution,' Boy explained.

'Ought to be in an institution if you ask me,' Froggie said. 'And so should anyone who bets with him. Best thing the French ever did, keeping out chaps like you.'

'I am 'ere on 'oliday, ladies and gents. I intend to make a study of the Pari-Mutuel though I can't see the fun in it myself.'

'You're a bookie,' said Dodo Wilmot. 'Well, isn't that great?'

Cod bowed, acknowledging this tribute with some grace. He too had grown monstrous, the fishy quality of his features now almost blotted out by blubber, although the pout of his mouth and the dull cold eyes remained gadoid. He wore a long smock-like jacket of cream linen almost down to his knees and a dung-coloured straw hat pushed back off his brow. With his sheeny chestnut walking-stick he had the unbuttoned look of an Impressionist painter walking in his garden.

'Well now, let's go get a drink and you fellows can tell us what to back.' Wilmot was captivated by these decayed rogues. Like a small boy following a parade, he waddled behind them between the dwarf box hedges to the paddock bar.

As I ambled along behind, Jane Stilwell gripped my arm and called me by my name.

'Yes,' I said, startled.

'Your father's friends?'

'Yes.'

'I'm sure they're really interesting people, great characters.'

'Yes.'

'But if I were you, well, perhaps it's not for me to say this, but I wouldn't spend too much time with them.'

'They're my father's friends, not mine.'

'You don't mind me saying.'

'Not at all.'

'Great. I just thought.'

'That's fine.'

Her breath smelled of peppermint and something else – lavender was it? She looked pale in the sunlight, and her eyes were somehow bright and tired at the same time. If she had not gone on so, I would have told her that to spend more time with the three of them was the last thing on earth I wanted to do.

'Will you take a glass of wine?' Boy asked her.

'Oh shampoo, great.' She grasped the glass in her slender fingers. The timid fizz of the bubbles in the straw-coloured champagne seemed an infinite luxury.

'What's this? Pretty Poll? I prefer the Widow myself, doesn't make my guts ache.'

'I thought the only thing you minded, Cod, was, Is it a magnum?'

'Now then, now then, I'm 'ere to enjoy myself, don't want any aggravation.' And it was with some serenity that Cod looked out across the course to the roofs of the little town and the sea beyond, his long coat flapping slightly in the breeze and him sighing, almost to himself, 'This is the life.'

Perhaps it was. The racing season had such a reassuring rhythm to it, as one meeting succeeded another, steeplechasing gave way to the flat, and two-year-olds became three-year-olds. The passing of time lost its terror – no, the passing of time was the point of it. Would this one train on, would promise be fulfilled, would it be as good as its parents? Such questions, so pregnant with sadness when you applied them to people, were part of the sport when it came to horses. Nothing tragic except sudden death, the little group that hid the vet taking out the humane killer. But that usually happened off in the country, well away from the stands.

'We always come for the Grande Semaine. There's no place like the Ville.'

'Nowhere like it. I'm so sorry, I didn't catch your name first time, but it's wonderful you've come along, Mr Wilmot.'

'Well isn't that nice of you, sir. Dodo please, call me Dodo.'

'Dodo, we need more chaps like you. This place –' Boy paused for inspiration '– this place needs people who've got racing in their blood.'

'You're right, there, Boy, damned right. Now you know the form here, what are we going to do for the Grand Prix, what's the word?'

'Well, the talking horse is Cornichon but –' and here Boy paused again, perhaps for dramatic effect ' – I've got a feeling that this just might be the day for Ormolu.'

'Ormolu ...' squinting at his racing paper – 'they don't rate it here.'

'They've been holding it back for this race.'

'Ormolu ... OK you're the professor.'

'There may be some late money for it but I reckon it'll still work out at fives or better.'

As Wilmot hoicked out his wallet, Froggie gave Boy a fierce little punch in the ribs and whispered into his ear, a spluttery kind of whisper. Boy listened with his usual serenity and muttered something back which failed to satisfy Froggie who stumped off down to the Pari-Mutuel with his letterbox mouth clamped shut.

'Hey,' said Wilmot, flipping me a banknote in his huge hand, 'you get yourself a piece of the action.'

It was a ten thousand franc note.

'Oh that's too ... thank you very much.'

'Let's go. I can see them coming out of the paddock.'

I queued behind him to place the bet. He had taken his jacket off and fat spilled over his snakeskin belt like a heroic soufflé. As he waited, he sang to himself in a sweet, high Burl Ives voice.

'Allez-vous en, milord ...'

After I had put the money on Ormolu, I stood on the little grassy rise behind the PM, watching Dodo waddle from queue to queue, placing the maximum each time I supposed, like some great beast moving along the water-hole in search of the sweetest water.

'I stuck ten on the nose, Mother,' he reported to his wife.

'Oh Dodo, we'll be washing dishes in the Crécy before the Semaine's out.'

'Ayez confiance en moi, chérie.' His French had a nice throatiness to it, and when he turned to me, his whole mien had a winning docility, the glinting specs, the great loose linen suit and the little snakeskin shoes flickering out from under the flappy turn-ups. I was enchanted, by him, and by the ten thou.

'Ormolu? You folks must be crazy. Cornichon will walk it.' Jane Stilwell was amazed, and distressed too. 'I'd better go get some of your money back.'

'Honey, it's too late. We had a tip.' This was Mr Stilwell, a neat little fellow with a strange leathery skin and a mouth which pursed up before he spoke which wasn't often. During the pauses which tended to follow his sparse remarks, his face would relax, look almost serene for a second, before tightening up when someone began to answer him. If someone, usually his wife, broke in before he had finished, he would frown even if the breaking-in was only to say yes, yes, I couldn't agree more.

But by then Jane Stilwell was back off down the grassy slope to the PM, her skirt swirling in the breeze and her high heels flicking out sideways as though she was trying to throw mud off them while she ran.

'I reckon she'll just about get home by a neck,' Dodo said, and we laughed, all except Mr Stilwell who said, 'It's too late, she shouldn't have gone,' and pursed his lips after he had spoken as well as before, a sign of displeasure.

There was something foal-like, awkward yet free about the impulse and the way she ran, the lollop of her hips and her arms and legs like sticks. And a furtive fondness for her came over me, a kindly feeling as though I was fifteen years older than she instead of the other way round.

'I got a mille on,' she panted in triumph.

'Great girl,' Dodo Wilmot said. 'You'll save our bacon' – although judging by the size of the notes he had been thrusting through the window, she wouldn't have saved a tenth of it.

Cornichon's jockey looked like a Chicago hood, even had a scar running across his swarthy cheek. 'Hippo Rossi, he's a Corsican, all the Corsican jockeys are bent,' Froggie said as the squat little man in his yellow silks was given a leg up. 'Looks like a sour lemon, don't he?'

'Is it a good idea to have a bent jockey?' Jane asked.

'Might be, might not. He must have jocked off Jean-Claude. Jean-Claude's down to ride him in *Ville-Sport*.' Froggie looked worried. 'Cod, did you know about Hippo getting the ride on Cornichon?'

'There was a bit of argy-bargy is my understanding of the matter.'

'About what?' Jane asked.

'Never you mind, madam, it don't signify. 'Ippo can ride a bit.'

And as they came round the tight bend, their boots flicking the quickset hedges, it seemed as though Cornichon's jockey was riding the hardest of any, his lemon cap burrowing into the big chestnut's mane his knees up to his chin and his elbows working like pistons. In the lead two furlongs out, he gave the horse half a dozen furious whacks, but it was no use. Out of the pack of following horses appeared the pink and green colours of Ormolu, and with a relentless, smooth motion passed Cornichon and ran out a comfortable winner. My father's old companions threw their straw hats in the air, failed to catch them and then scrabbled for them on the ground, still chuckling their triumph.

'It was a work of art. You'll never see anything like it in all your born days and you can tell your dad I said so.' Cod Chamberlayne was still chuckling as he clapped his old straw hat back on his sweating brow.

'Formidable,' said Dodo Wilmot. 'Atta Boy. You're a genius, sir.' He bowed at Boy Kingsmill, who raised the hat he had just put back on.

Boy looked intolerably beatific. His eyes were half-closed, his lips were moist and parted in something which was less like a smile than an expression of sexual rapture.

'I can't understand it,' Jane said. 'That horse had no form at all. Dodo –' But Dodo had gone off to collect his winnings. I could see him at the back of the queue on the payout side of the PM, a huge blob of contentment in cream linen. When he returned, he was still stuffing wads of notes into his deep pockets, so that his jacket bulged at the sides.

'We'll have some fun at the gala, I'm telling you. You folks coming along?'

'I'm not much of a one for dressing up,' Froggie said. 'I'd better look after this old fool.'

'Now, now then, who was it 'ad to carry you all the way from the Silver Ring bar to the car-park at 'Aydock?'

'I'd love to come,' Boy said.

'Minna and Farfar will be there. It'll be a swell party.'

The weather set fair from that day on. Helen and I met daily at the cage after Monsieur had done his worst and walked on a couple of hundred yards with our charges to where the sands spread and the shingle shrank back towards the road and the villas beyond and the big hotels.

When the children were bored with digging holes and flicking sand at one another, Helen showed them the flora and fauna of the beach which she had collected while her charge was with Monsieur. She spoke to them in her serious way, as if they were on a school trip, making no concessions. They imitated the seriousness, squatting either side of her like assistants on an important scientific project. Sometimes Timmy would stand behind her to get a better view, idly pinging the strap of her green swimsuit against her pale shoulder. She showed them how to tell the seaweeds apart: the stubby fronds of the oar-weed, the twin pods of the bladderwrack, the single pods of the knotted wrack, the great flat leaves of the *Laminaria saccharina* (so-called because you could get sugar out of it), and the red dulse which poor people in Scotland ate, and the Irish moss or carragheen which you could make jelly out of. And then the living things, the mussels, the cuttlefish, the limpets, and winkles and periwinkles, which Brainerd collected in one of his tins and then had difficulty getting them out again.

I lolled on my side, only half-listening, affecting boredom, or rather genuinely bored as I had always been in botany, biology whatever this was, yet unable to stop listening and even taking in a good deal.

Brainerd and Timmy somehow sensed my fractiousness and disapproved of it, sending little frowning looks in my direction when I idly popped the pods on the bladderwrack. How priggish children were when it suited them, as her sternness did. I liked her sternness too. She seemed out of place in that easy decade. 'I can see you're not a 60s person,' she said, but she wasn't either. It turned out I was a year and a bit older, nineteen to her eighteen, but it could have been five years the other way round, just the opposite of Jane in fact. Even then I knew about girls maturing earlier in every department, but in the years since that first summer I never seem to have made up the deficit. There she is, coming out of the mist towards me, quite thick mist sometimes and she's not always as calm as she was then, far from it, but somehow she's still ahead, further into life, and her hair still the same milky gold.

In the evening on the beach, the shore wind brought down the scent of the little grove of pines to the rise beyond the harbour. Through the hexagon in the middle of the stained glass I saw the sea turn grey and violet as the dusk gathered and the lights came on along the promenade. My hands struggled to tuck the end of the bow tie behind the loop. How easy it had seemed when my father stood behind me and guided my hands. Through the thin wall with the clumpy nosegays on it I could hear the Stilwells bickering as they dressed – or rather the bubbly stream of her talking with occasional dry little responses from him. You might think they complemented each other perfectly, except that they were not happy.

I gave Brainerd his supper: french fries and a cheeseburger, with two scoops of pistachio and chocolate ice-cream to follow.

'You look like a real waiter.'

'Don't spill, Brainerd.'

'You look neat. If you're good, I'll give you a tip.'

The air outside the Casino was full of the smell of the pines, and the scent of the women getting out of their limos. It was a starry summer night, one of those nights when the fullness of the skies overwhelms you and you twist your neck to look for the Plough or the Pole Star.

'Look, there's Farfar and Minna. Don't they look great? And there's your friend.'

The three of them glowed like fireflies as they got out of the

Mercedes and clunked the doors behind them. For a moment, they stood apart from each other, as the chauffeur drove off down the ramp. Farid Farhadi was nearest the great glass doors of the Casino, his brown face gleaming with impatience, his burly body almost bursting out of his dinner jacket, sleek and jumpy as a sealion at feeding time. His wife and Helen were outlined against the sea, Mrs Farhadi in a glistening silk dress, rose or purple – it was hard to tell in the half-light – and scintillating with jewels. Helen in a plain dark-blue dress with a ballet skirt. She looked like a severe fairy.

Farid Farhadi greeted us as we climbed the shallow semicircle of steps to the glass doors, swooping at each of us in turn with a moment of intense cordiality, kissing or shaking hands at a terrible rate as though some appalling fate would engulf us all if any greeting took longer than two seconds.

'You', he said, 'must be the *tutor*,' looking at me with marvelling eyes, with the voice of one who has discovered some secret too rare to be credited.

'Well, more of a nanny really.'

'How wonderful, *quelle chance*. The opportunities . . .' With one sweep of his arm he brought Helen into the circle. 'You know our Helen, of course. She is –' he paused for an instant to convey the impossibility of finding the words – 'we just love her' – this descent into a fine simplicity undercut only fractionally by Helen's businesslike Hallo again, the sort of Hallo again you give someone who has come for a second job interview.

'Avanti, avanti.' He shooed us into the high marble salon with a frantic urgency, leading the way with quick little steps, not quite a strut. Nobody else in the huge room seemed to share this bright hurry. The other diners moved at a leaden pace with a thick glaze of tedium on their faces, and also a peculiar modesty such as you might put on at a funeral while trooping out to the graveside and taking care not to trip over a tombstone or crowd your fellow-mourners. We passed through the gaming-rooms, the deadened hush broken only by the weary calls of the croupier and the faint rattle of the wheel spinning, more suffocating than any funeral.

'It's all fixed,' Helen hissed to me.

'Is it? How do you know?'

'It's run by the Corsican Syndicate.'

'Surely you don't need to fix roulette. The house wins anyway.'

'It's fixed,' she said fiercely. 'Farid told me.'

We came into a smaller room which had girls in skimpy gold and white dresses off one shoulder selling exquisite trinkets from behind little gilt tables: tiny leopards and elephants sculpted in semi-precious stones, sprays of flowers in gilt and enamel, miniature crystal phials of Dior and Chanel scent, exquisite corsages of real flowers. When a guest pointed to one of these confections, the salesgirl would hold it against her bare shoulder so that the purchaser could see how it sparkled against the flushed ivory of her skin.

'Oh Dodo, handbag-fillers.'

'Your handbag is too damn full already, Mother.'

As we regrouped in this fragrant saloon, Farhadi came up to Helen and with an almost explosive *empressement*, as though this might well be his final action before he was carried off by a thrombosis, said: 'There, please, for the darling of all our hearts.'

He thrust something at her and she took it with the resigned manner of a nurse receiving a scalpel from the surgeon.

'What is it, Helen, do let's look.'

She held it up with the same dutiful mien and we stared.

It was an orchid, a waxy exotic bloom with purple and yellow spots on its recurved trumpet. The pale fleshy stalk disappeared into a brown rubber bulb.

'There, it will keep for a fortnight. You simply refill the bulb.' Farid took it back from her and then pinned it at the vee of her dress, so that the bulb was out of sight down her front.

'It's lovely, thank you.' It was impossible to tell whether she genuinely liked it or thought it an evil monstrosity.

'Farfar, you are too much,' Jane said.

'And where is *my* orchid?' Mrs Farhadi asked.

'My darling, at Chantilly you have a whole conservatory.'

We came into the dining-room which looked even larger than it was because of the long gilt mirrors between the windows. The waitresses were standing at attention beside the tables. They were dressed as jockeys with miniature peaked caps perching on top of their bubble curls, like Harpo in *A Day at the Races*.

'There you see, the Wildenstein colours, and Aly's and the old Boussac silks and those, I think, must be Jeanne Schlumberger's. It's so enchanting, isn't it?'

'They do it every year,' Jane Stilwell said, 'last year they still had Ed Pereira's colours although he shot himself two months before.'

Till quite recently, I had kept the menu, then lost it in some move or other, but even now I can almost recite it by heart:

Timbale de queues de langoustines
Turbot aux herbes
Sorbet aux fraises des bois
Escalope de foie de canard au Calvados
Le château de la Belle au bois dormant

The wines were:

Chassagne-Montrachet (I forget the year)
Lynch-Bages 1947

and I think the champagne was Krug.

But it was Sleeping Beauty's castle I dreamed about, for years afterwards, with its spindly turrets of silver and gold sugar, its gooey battlements and the creamy succulence of its inner courtyard of ice-cream soused in some divine liqueur – Grand Marnier, Jane said. No, Kirsch, Mrs Wilmot said, bet you ten dollars it's Kirsch, and the two brindled copper heads, which might have been made of the same spun sugar as the castle, appealed to the waiter who smiled and didn't know.

At the end of the table sat Helen next to Jean-Claude Robinson, the number three jockey in France according to Dodo, the one who should have been riding Cornichon if he hadn't been displaced by Hippo Rossi.

'What happened, Jean-Claude?'

'They want 'Ippo to ride, 'e ride, 'e lose. *Tant pis.*'

And he shrugged his shoulders with a smile which said I'm not telling you the half of it.

'Why Robinson?'

'My grandfather emigrated from Newmarket. There are plenty of us 'ere, Smith, Jones, Robinson, all French now.'

He ate scarcely at all: a couple of crayfish tails, a mouthful of fish, and then sipped a glass of champagne.

Together at the end of the table, he and Helen looked like a miniature king and queen whose grosser courtiers we were. Helen ate hugely, taking great mouthfuls of French fries with her duck liver.

Farid Farhadi talked all through dinner: how he had been helicopter skiing – you mean the helicopter *skis?* – 'No, no, they drop you on some isolated mountain and you schuss down through virgin powder, such bliss. Gianni Agnelli took me, the *avvocato* you know, he only goes on the mountain with the chopper now. And then down to the bottom of the ocean, the Great Barrier Reef, you know it? Once you have dived there, it spoils you for anywhere else, I went to Jamaica last winter, I did not put my toe in the water, I was spoiled. You must know the Reef, Professor.'

No, I did not know the Reef, or the Mountain, or the Quartier, or the Canal, or the Faubourg, or any other of the geographical features which had graduated to this singularity. But I didn't mind, as another turret of Sleeping Beauty's castle melted on my tongue, and the unexpected warmth behind the tingle of the champagne tiptoed down my throat. It was as in a dream that I watched the neat figure of Jean-Claude go up to the little stage to receive a tiny gold whip for being the top jockey at the meeting despite losing the ride in the Grand Prix.

'It's his third *cravache*, he's such a darling,' Jane said.

As he came back to the table, he waved the whip in a shy little gesture of triumph and passed it to Helen who waved it too but more as though it was a sceptre, part of her regalia in this miniature gilded kingdom.

'What do you think of Bowyer?' Dodo asked me.

'Who?' I was still looking at Helen and the jockey.

'George Bowyer, the Admiral.'

'Never heard of him, I'm afraid.'

'Never heard of him? The guy who lost a leg on the Glorious First and was awarded the Gold Medal when Collingwood wasn't? And Collingwood never forgave him, but then Collingwood was a mean bastard, though he didn't do too bad at Cape St Vincent. He was in the

Hector then. But Bowyer was the better sailor, he'd have taken over from Nelson at Trafalgar, not Collingwood, if he hadn't lost that goddamn leg. You interested in naval history?'

'Not really, as a matter of fact.'

'And you from a seafaring nation, that's great.' Dodo forgave me with a big slap on the back and threw back a huge glass of wine. Even his glass seemed to be bigger than mine.

Then the little woman in the black dress which looked so worn came on. She had to pull the microphone down to bring it level with her head (or perhaps this was a bit of business to remind us how small and frail she was) before she could begin to sing her hits, sounding throatier, more resonant still, than when she had first sung them, as though all the drink in her life and the brutal lovers and the suicides attempted (and some succeeded) had combined to add more power to her voice, so that while the rest of her body shrivelled into a rusty old concierge the voice went on growing.

'Quand tu me prends dans tes bras.'

'Oh *no*,' Jane shrieked, as though it was the most extraordinary thing in the world for her to choose this number. Whoop went Dodo Wilmot, and Farid clapped, for the first time looking a little bored.

When her act was over and she had slipped away behind the curtain, I could not help thinking of the rest of her evening, the scrawny thug in the belted mac who was waiting to beat her up and demand money from the management, the bottle of scotch on the dressing-table amid the swabs of cotton wool smeared with make-up, and that image, too, part of the enchantment, even if her publicists had touched it up a bit, so that she seemed to be fleeing a tough reality into the gala's golden light, backing on to the stage and reminding the lucky ones what they had all got away from, for the time being anyway.

'Let's go to the Boudin.'

'Oh Dodo —'

'Yeah, we'll go to the Boudin.'

Swept along in the umbrous comfort of the Wilmots' limo, I scarcely noticed where we were heading except that even the limo's springs could not conceal the fact that we were bumping over some roughish cobbles. Wilmot started talking about Nelson's admirals again. He seemed to have a real grudge against Admiral Collingwood. I imagined that the Boudin would be as grand as the Casino, perhaps lined with pictures of elegant nineteenth-century ladies sitting on the beach turning their parasols. But when we got out, we were on the quayside of the shabby little port across the river from the Ville standing outside a dull café front which scarcely seemed to have any lights on, though the door opened to us instantly. Rain was falling, softly, and I could smell the pines above the port.

Inside was a long narrow room with dirty brown walls hung with pictures and photographs of people making and eating black pudding, white pudding and other offal products. There were pictures of girls with garlands of black pudding round their necks and beaming chefs holding silver cups and wearing silver chains with their prizewinning *boudin* displayed in front of them. And here and there, as though to show fair play to the provider of all this, there were coloured engravings of pigs: pigs in sties, pigs rootling in the forest, pigs with bows and rosettes tied to them at agricultural shows, pigs of enormous size filling the entire picture frame. It was a sort of shrine.

'Isn't it great, the Boudin?'

We sat on banquettes facing each other at opposite sides of the room. The gangway between the two lines of tables was narrow and made narrower by a giant black and pink porcelain pig snuffling in a lead trough which stood on a metal stand surrounded by brass vases of flowers, blotting out the Farhadis and the Wilmots, at least until Dodo's huge babyface rose above the flowers like some pasty sun.

'Hey you guys, lighten up over there, we're having ourselves a party, not a wake.'

Something came through the air and caught me a light stinging blow on the cheek. I picked it up. It was a bread roll. Soon a couple more followed and now the Farhadis rose into view above the hydrangeas and started throwing as well. At the end of our table Boy Kingsmill got up and with a seraphic smile on his face began throwing the bread rolls back. A nervous little waiter pushed a huge basket of rolls down the table and then ran for cover.

'Hey, you a Member of Parliament?'

'That's right,' said Boy raising his arm to launch another brioche. 'Leicester Central, Conservative.'

'Great. You must be used to this kind of thing.' Wilmot raised his balloon glass to his mouth while flinging a roll with his other arm. He had a graceful baseball arm, which sent the missiles skimming at head height. Mrs Farhadi threw with a jerk of her elbow which made it look as though she was hitching up her dress. I threw a roll back. At my side Helen sat pale and silent, not even bothering to dodge as the bread rolls mostly passed over her head.

'Time for the heavy artillery.'

Dodo drained his brandy glass and threw it high in the air down to the far end of the room where it smashed into a picture of pigs playing musical instruments. Another glass followed, and another, and the room was filled with the sound of broken glass and the pictures were taking heavy casualties.

'Farfar, you just gave me an idea back there in the casino. The ladies need some flowers, flowers for the ladies.' And Dodo started picking armfuls of flowers out of the vase and throwing them around with a great sweep of his arm.

'We need some more glasses.' He was up on the table, quite nimble for his size, and began waddling down the line of tables picking up glasses and throwing them as he went with Farhadi aping him a couple of yards behind.

'Now jump, baby, jump,' and they leapt across the narrow path down the middle of the room which turned out to be not narrow enough for Wilmot, so that he crashed to the ground with his head almost severed from his shoulders by the edge of the opposing table. Unmoved by this setback, he scooped up three or four glasses from the table and began throwing them back at the side he had come from.

'Waldo please.'

'Isn't that great when she says Waldo please? I like a woman who pleads. You look dry my friend, I don't like to see a dry politician.' He took the brass vase, empty now, and raised it high above Boy's head, then with a solicitous, almost baptismal motion poured it over the sleek tarmac of Boy's hair. His victim stood unflinching with eyes closed and the seraph's smile on his lips. Then with the same solicitous reverence, Boy himself took the next brass vase and poured it over Wilmot's bristles. The two stood dripping face to face delighted with themselves and then bowed to one another and to the rest of us before Dodo rampaged on down the middle of the room chucking everything that was left at the walls, glasses, plates, knives, forks, before collapsing in a heap on the bench at the end.

'I'm going home now,' Helen said.

She got up and picked her way through the broken glass round the giant pig which had lost one of its ears in the mêlée.

'Don't worry, dear, he does this every year,' Mrs Wilmot said. 'He always pays afterward, you know.'

Helen said nothing and marched out of the door.

'You better go with her, it's not a very nice area.'

As I came out into the drizzling night, the café owner was sobbing in the street, with his few strands of hair flopping down his cheek.

'I can get home by myself, thank you,' Helen said.

'Mrs Wilmot said I should come.'

'You don't always have to do what other people say, you know. You didn't have to throw those rolls. It encouraged them.'

'I didn't know they were going to go on like that.'

'You didn't have to do it.'

'At least he'll pay for the damage, his wife says.'

'*Pay.* Can you imagine how long it took to collect all those pig things?'

I fell silent. She walked fast and angry and I had to hustle to keep up with her, but felt I ought to go on talking, silence seeming to confirm my complicity.

'I was surprised at Farid,' I said. 'I wouldn't have thought –'

'Surprised? Why? That's just the sort of person he is.'

'Have you still got that flower?'

She unpinned the orchid from her dress and held it up. In the bleaching light of the street lamp, it looked like a surgical specimen.

She threw it into the water, where it floated, still and evil-looking with the lamplight winking on the rubber bulb.

'He is a disgusting person, my employer. Do you know what he said to me?'

'The darling of all our hearts, yes I was there.'

'No, not that. Just afterwards, when we were coming into the dining place. He whispered into my ear, would you like to suck my cock?'

'Oh.'

'Charming. They're all charming.'

'So, what did you say?'

'I said no.'

'I expect that was the right thing to say.'

She snorted a kind of laugh and told me she was going home tomorrow because she wasn't going to stand for that sort of thing and anyway she had already done her month but I could come and see her in London if I liked and I said I would.

It wasn't the same after she had left. Although we had only just met, she had already become the focus of the whole show. Her neat still little person caught my eye even in the gilded halls of the casino where there were so many other sights for gawping at. And when she spoke in that quiet spelled-out voice, she instilled silence around her. I noticed that even Dodo Wilmot, or perhaps particularly Dodo, paused a fraction before taking up something she had said. Somewhere within his elephant body there was some high-frequency receiver not installed in other people who looked more sensitive, and he had to let her vibrations die down before he began transmitting.

The morning after the Boudin, he came down early, looking babyfresh as though he had never touched anything stronger than milk and a good deal of that.

'Not on your trapeze today, Brainerd?'

'There's no Monsieur on Mondays.'

'Where's your collection? I don't see anything out there ...'

Brainerd glared. He resented all enquiries on the subject. 'I only put it out after lunch,' he said. An obvious lie. Most days you could hear the clank of the Coke tins and the grating of the Orangina bottles on the cement balustrade first thing after breakfast.

'Sorry, I didn't know about the gallery's opening hours. Well, we had ourselves a ball last night, didn't we, I've just been along to give M. Pingeot a couple of tickets for Chantilly, turns out he's a racing man.'

'Waldo, a couple of tickets – I mean, do you think that's quite –'

'Jane baby, what do you think I did with my winnings? Believe me, the old Boudin's going to be so refurbished you wouldn't know it. Yes, that was quite a party.' He relapsed into beatific contemplation, before turning to me: 'I was wrong. It was the *Excellent* Collingwood had command of when he engaged the *Santissima Trinidad* at Cape St Vincent, not the *Hector*, he was transferred to the *Hector* the year before, when Bowyer left the *Honfleur*.'

'Ah,' I said.

'I checked it out when I got home. She got away.'

'What – who did?'

'The *Santissima*. She was to windward.'

'Ah.'

'Outgunned him anyway. Those Spanish four-deckers were really something.'

'They must have been.' I began to feel as if I too was rolling about in a high sea, nausea, headache and a curious sensation of evisceration combining to decrease my interest in naval history, never a major subject as I had already conceded.

He looked at me with tender concern, blinking a bit behind his glasses.

'I diagnose a touch of gala flu, my friend. You stay here in this darkened room and let Miz Stilwell take care of you.'

'Oh Dodo,' Jane said, 'leave the boy alone,' but she put her hand upon my throbbing forehead. Her fingers felt cool and separated, like so many little cold compresses.

'How about Massa Stilwell, OK is he? Sorry about the flying glass.'

'John has gone to the doctor.'

'Well, tell him Hi from me and tell him too to duck next time.'

'Dodo, I'm afraid he expects an apology.'

'Well, you just apologise for me, you're hells good at that kind of thing. Tell him I wouldn't want to hurt a little bitty hair on his head, specially since there's so few of them these days – no, no don't tell him that. I better run along before I cause any more ructions.'

And he waddled out with a debonair wave of his great paw.

Silence fell in the sitting-room. How stale and dusky was the light coming through the stained-glass window in the corner turret (the one just below the window I watched the beach from). It might have been half-past seven in the evening, not just before midday. Outside, now that the coast was clear, I could hear the scrape of Brainerd's tins on the balustrade.

Jane was sitting next to me at the table, slowly writing a shopping-list. She was wearing a pale blue beach shift over her dark-blue swimming costume – the straps were just visible through the thin material. She put down her pen and looked at me.

'You mustn't think we're all like that. Dodo just gets a little – uncivilised when he's got a load on.'

'No, I enjoyed it really,' I said – which I had in retrospect, though this was not to be admitted widely, certainly not to Helen, but Jane was all right, I could admit things to her. Why was this? She was much older and my employer. I just could.

She put her hand in mine. 'How white your teeth are.'

'No they aren't,' I said.

'Yes they are.' She stroked my forearm very slowly, so that the hairs stood up. No, I thought, no, not –

She half-rose from the chair and turned towards me, expectant, her face extraordinarily pale. In appalling slow motion, as in a film where the projector had broken down and you became aware how primitive is the artifice of frame succeeding frame, if anything getting slower still, her lips parted, not smiling, and approached mine until there she was. It was a moment, not of truth, although that too no doubt, but of intense excitement and cold detachment, as cold as though I was watching her, watching myself from the other side of the universe. Even as I too came forward, flushed with the undreamed-of thrill of it, my mind was galloping with a giddy regress of thoughts: I've chosen to do this haven't I, *this* and not *that* – *that* being to pull back and upset my coffee-cup on purpose and the whole thing to be forgotten in a fluster of getting a cloth to mop up – and *this* is an extraordinary thing to do, to be a nanny (male) and get off with your (female) employer, or perhaps it isn't extraordinary at all, perhaps everyone in my position does it. It's a sort of Cherubino story, perhaps Cherubino was really a sort of nanny-tutor. But wasn't it a much odder thing, definitely much odder, to be thinking in such a detached way when this amazing thing was happening, not to mention the other obvious thought to be thought, that all this would land me in hellish trouble, if found out which it almost certainly would be. If Mr Stilwell had been so indignant about a little bit of flying glass, how would he react to this? But meanwhile there was this to be got on with, and it was wonderful too, the speed of her unzipping me, her nimble fingers with the pale long nails so cool against my skin. No, she said, as I tried to do the same for her, you can't do this, Brainerd will come in, but the sly fingering and the surprising pathways were ecstasy enough for the time being. The slither of damp lycra under my hand and the smell of the cooling coffee on the table and my head still hammering in the dark room and outside the sound of Brainerd moving his Coke tins up and down the balustrade. It's so dark in here, she said, I like that.

It lasted four days exactly.

Every minute, every second of it was felt separately and yet with a longing for the next one. A year or so later, in a Scrannelogue I heard Scrannel deride some other philosopher, fashionable at the time, who liked to invite us to split up time into an infinity of nano-seconds and ask ourselves what reason we had to think that the next nano-second would follow the one we were now experiencing. This was a futile exercise, Scrannel said, since every instant could be imagined or described only if you knew all about the one before and the one before that, having lived through them, and among the things you knew about them was how incomplete, how pregnant were the motions observed in them: the boot about to kick the ball, the last note of the phrase about to be sung, the glass half-raised to the lips – all these motions could be interrupted no doubt but the impulse to interrupt, that too would be present in the previous second and so on. No, it was not senseless to imagine that the world might stop now in the next instant, just like that, but to imagine such a thing was already to start thinking about the causes of such an event, just as it was if one were to imagine one's life coming to an abrupt end in sixty seconds' time (Scrannel had himself only a year or so to go when he gave this little talk and, as I say, his voice, never short on asperity, had already taken on that nasty rasp).

At first I thought how brilliantly Scrannel had destroyed this sterile fancy, but then I recalled the four days with Jane and how the time had felt just like this, not stretched out but chopped up into an infinity of moments, precarious, unconnected, compact with dread and longing.

On the surface it was not like that at all.

Every morning I took Brainerd and Timmy to Monsieur, then I walked back along the road in the sleepy morning sun (there was no mist at all that week) trying not to look as if I was hurrying. About half-way back, Mr Stilwell in his hired Deux Chevaux would come puttering along on his way to play golf and he would wave and I would give him a traitor's wave back.

She would be sitting in the darkened room with a fresh thermos of coffee, so that this is what I think of still when I smell fresh coffee. And she would hold out her thin arms as though I had been away for a long time. It was so quick, the quickness was part of the delight, and over so soon.

We lay like sardines packed on the narrow hard settee. 'I'm sorry,' she said and paused, giving me time to say there was nothing to be sorry for. 'We can't, you know, go the whole way.'

'Doesn't matter,' I muttered.

'John has this condition now, I owe him that much.'

'Condition?' I asked, wishing I hadn't.

'It's a very rare condition, I'm not sure of the medical name for it, but it's an inhibiting factor, that's what he told me. He feels really bad about it.'

'I'm sorry.'

'Well, it's not your fault, but that's why.'

'I quite see,' I said, which I didn't. She had awakened no pity for Mr Stilwell, not then at any rate. Now I feel a certain kinship with those people who have no natural power to awaken sympathy and being dimly conscious of this start actively repelling it, but at the time I felt nothing for him.

She was relieved to have explained the situation, got it out of the way or into the open or both. All the same, what she said could not help cooling the air. Any mention of Mr Stilwell was liable to have that effect in ordinary circumstances, and here in the darkened room with our pulses beating so fast that it was hard to tell whose heart was whose, his name stopped us flat, so that in a couple of minutes she was sitting upright unscrewing the lid of the thermos and pouring me another cup.

It was not that our intimacy had gone. We now had a shared secret and, as a result of that, something which could be called an arrangement and when she put her arm round my neck and stroked my damp shoulder under the shirt it seemed as though we had known each other in this way for years.

'Your teeth *are* white,' she said.

'No they aren't. Yours are. American teeth always are.'

How odd to be talking about teeth. But then what did people in our situations talk about? Their childhoods usually, and so did she. She had been raised in Connecticut in a lovely old house with creeper all over it. The garden ran down to the Sound where they went skinnydipping and it would all have been great except that when she was eight she overheard her father, who was kind of a banker though what he was banking was mostly his own money, say how can I have such an ugly daughter and soon afterwards he was up to a bottle of scotch maybe two a day and having electric shock treatment which didn't do much for him and she was the only one who could still talk to him because her mother had given up and eventually went off with the little realtor with the hair brushed across his skull who was trying to sell the house, and then he had a stroke in his study though he'd never studied anything in his life, and the money began to go and everything else went too, so she failed to get into Bryn Mawr and went to work in New York, in a little dress shop next to Saks, and then John came along and he rescued them really, all of them, her mother who had been left by the realtor and her brother who wasn't too bright and her father who was still in St Joseph's and didn't recognise anyone now.

She talked on in her bright jumpy way and I listened, suffused with deep contentment from head to toe, idly watching the sun straggle through the stained glass and on to her pale features with just a little colour still in her cheeks. A few seconds later, I was grateful that we were sitting decorously at the table like this, because the doors blasted open and the doorway filled with Dodo Wilmot, who was so full of news he started speaking before he had got properly into the room.

'Guess what, no you won't, though I had my suspicions, the whole thing was too goddamn neat. The gendarmes have nabbed your pals. *Regardez.*'

And he flung down a copy of *Ville-Sport* upon the table. Together we leant forward and read: *Scandale de la Grand Prix: 3 stoppeurs anglais arrêtés.* 'What's a *stoppeur?*' 'Chap who stops a horse, must be.' And there was a fuzzy picture of Cod Chamberlayne, Froggie and Boy coming down the steps of the police station with a gendarme in front of them.

'What a bunch of comedians. Seems they or some buddy of theirs gave Hippo Rossi a bundle to pull Cornichon, and Hippo got loaded and blabbed. Some people just can't hold their liquor.'

Dodo was enchanted, he guffawed and banged the table with his huge fist as though applauding some terrific cabaret act.

'But he was riding the horse flat out, wasn't he, hitting him with his whip again and again.'

'Jane, that con was just belting thin air. If you know the trick of it, you can make it look like you're riding the shit out of a horse when in fact you're telling him whoa, whoa, what's the hurry, *où est le feu*. I always thought that tip was too good to be true. Still, the money's in the bank now – well, to be precise it's in Pingeot's bank, so there's no great harm done. We just did our little bit to increase the velocity of circulation of the currency, like they taught us back in Economics One.'

'What will happen to them?'

'Oh Hippo will deny it now he's sober, say they misunderstood him. There won't be any other evidence. The vet will find something wrong with Cornichon, burst a little blood vessel, strained his back, something not too serious, nothing the trainer could have spotted. Gus's friends will get a polite warning and a little encouragement to leave *la belle France tout de suite*. Hey, what's up with you guys? You look like a bunch of celery in the moonlight. Nobody's going to arrest you, Jane, you're in the clear, you backed the wrong goddamn horse. Come on out and get some fresh air. Jesus but it's dark in here.'

And we walked out on the shingle, with Dodo stumbling on ahead of us, cackling and belching with laughter like a schoolboy. I could feel the light breeze ruffle my neck and begin to dry the shirt on my back, the sweet ache at my loins fading now. Beside me, Jane raised her face, letting it draw in the sun and the air.

That was the second day.

The third day we went for a picnic with the boys.

Jane parked in the corner of a cornfield above a low crumbly cliff with the beach beyond. The soil was rocky, and there were more poppies than corn. The wind was strong, and we moved about looking for the perfect place, but as soon as the rug touched the ground, it began to flap about. We walked on with the heavy baskets until the field stopped and we came to the beginning of a row of villas along the cliff. The first villa was derelict, windows and doors all smashed in, but at the bottom of its garden there was a beaten-up old wooden summerhouse with a verandah and a railing of logs nailed together in a rustic criss-cross pattern.

'This'll do, it's out of the wind and there's no broken glass or anything.'

So we sat on the verandah of this clapped-out pavilion, looked out at that milky wallowing sea as the owners, who had so carefully nailed PROPRIÉTÉ PRIVÉE above the door, must have done on summer evenings and no doubt thought how fortunate they were and how much they deserved their good fortune.

I looked down at her, lithe and brisk on all fours setting out the picnic on a red-and-white cloth: pâté, ham, baguettes, tomatoes, Camembert and Anjou rosé for us; Nutella, pretzels, Ritz crackers, strawberry cheesecake, Hershey bars, Pschitt for the boys.

'The man in the shop said this was the best pâté he had. Pâté de grives. I said what's grives and he made flapping motions so I guess it must be something like a pheasant.'

The pâté was an evil greyish colour and we took nervous dabs of it on our bread.

'Tastes like old birdshit.'

'Mm so it does. Hey I've got the pocket dictionary in my bag. No . . . oh how sad . . . it's thrushes. Think of all the songs we've missed.'

'Must take hundreds of them to make this much.'

'Took thousands of my francs. Let's bury it. Timmy, Brainerd, we're going to bury the poor thrushes.'

'That's yucky. You shouldn't have bought it if you didn't know what was in it.'

'Well, do you know what's in Nutella?'

'Yeah, chocolate, and nuts.'

I scrabbled a shallow grave in the stony soil and gave the pâté decent burial. After lunch, the wind dropped and the boys trotted off down the field to the low rocks above the beach. We gulped the wine down, quickly as if it was medicine. Our lips were still wet when they touched. The buttons on her shirt came undone as easily as though they were the buttons on mine. Again that double sensation of being at a huge distance, like when you are drunk or semi-conscious and your mind seems to be hovering above your body, and yet at the same time a sense of utter intimacy and intermingling, so that her heartbeat and her trembling might have been mine. With the detached part of my mind, I wondered what I felt or ought to feel for her as a person, and with the other part retorted that we were beyond all that or perhaps hadn't got that far. Below us, I could see Timmy walking solemnly, processing almost along the bottom of the field with behind him Brainerd holding a large stick. Every few paces, Brainerd would raise the stick in the air and brandish it two or three times. I could not imagine what ritual of humiliation or servitude they were acting out. There was probably more morality in it than there was in the two of us. Her thin sleepy smile had no anxiety or guilt, no whisper of past or future, only the unshadowed present.

'That was in memory of the thrushes,' she said.

'They deserved a good send-off.'

'They surely did. You all right?'

'I'm fine,' I said.

'I'm all right too. I'm trying a little British understatement.'

'You're very good at it.'

'I don't think I'll be able to keep it up for long, I'm liable to go over the top, you know.'

'I'll go with you.'

'Will you? That's nice.' We lay on our backs side by side, feeling the dusty slabs of the verandah against our shoulder-blades.

'Oh look at that.' She stretched out a dozy arm and pointed at a dusty object the size of a grapefruit lying just inside the door of the summerhouse. I got to my feet and picked it up. It was a crude wooden carving of a goblin. The broken jagged base suggested that it had been a knob on a gatepost. Even through the dust and plaster, I could see his sour, disappointed leer.

'He's a voyeur obviously. Lies in there spying on courting couples.'

'Do you think lots of people come up here for that sort of thing?'

'I'm sure they do,' I said. 'They probably book at peak times.'

'How sensible of them. We must come here more often.'

'We must.'

'Can we take him with us? It would be neat to have our own private voyeur.'

'Wouldn't he get bored with just us?'

'No, he'll get fond of us.'

I dusted down the horrible mannikin and gave him a rub with my handkerchief. For the first time, a twitch of melancholy. I put him in the picnic basket.

And so ended the third day.

Something about the picnic, perhaps just being in the open air, perhaps the wine and the sensuous ambience of the afternoon, had left me with a scalding restlessness, a kind of impatience that I didn't know what to do with. At the start, I suppose, our coming together was so startling – to both of us probably – such a windfall that it didn't need thinking about. But now that simple acceptance seemed inadequate. The thing had lost its innocence if it ever had any. The goblin propped up on the table in my room seemed to be jeering me on. To what? To make something more of it was the nearest I could come to describing the dissatisfaction that had come over me like a rash. All through the long slow dinner – mostly taken up with Dodo Wilmot explaining how he handled mineral concessions in the Third World – the dissatisfaction nagged at me.

'I didn't sleep, not properly,' I said the next morning, when we were alone in the darkened sitting-room.

'Nor did I, not a solitary wink,' she said, looking not displeased. 'I expect you felt the same as I did.'

'What ...'

'You know, that we have to talk.'

'Yes,' I said, wishing suddenly never to talk about anything ever again.

'Oh you are so dear. You don't want to talk, do you? You just want to go on having fun, don't you?'

'No, it's not ...'

'Well all right then. I'll be your plaything. Tomorrow we can be serious.'

I wasn't sure whether she was on the verge of laughing or crying. There was a frantic tremor in her voice which sounded as if some more violent feelings might be unleashed unless I did what was the only thing I knew how to do for her. And although doing that calmed her body, her mind was clearly unappeased. She whispered thank you to me, but there was a touch of irony, irritation, even, about the thanks. And the thanking irritated me too. Oddly enough, though, it was only in these fractious moments that I became fully conscious of what it was that I really liked about her, the awkward zest of her conversation, the way she ran down to the Pari-Mutuel, the way her laconic calm would, quite without warning, break up into raunchy chuckles – all that came clearly into view only when it was under threat, like a hazy landscape that sharpens its outlines when a storm is brewing.

The mist was there again the next day, Friday. Brainerd was mutinous and whiny, Timmy looked white and tired, sickening for something, but both were sent off to Monsieur regardless. Brainerd talked in a dull undertone to his Action Man all the way along the beach. This neutered mannikin was at present kitted out as a deep-sea diver. Perhaps Brainerd's undertone was to show that he was talking to someone who was hundreds of feet under water. As I dropped off the boys at the cage, the bars dripping in the mist once more, Brainerd thrust the diver into my hands with instructions to leave it in his room.

The staircase wound up the back of the house, a dark and airless spiral, smelling of polish and old cabbage. Even when the light was on upstairs at the far end of the landing there was still a risk of losing your footing on the narrow treads. As I was going up, there was a brisk clatter of footsteps on the landing above, and she came skipping down the stairs in that eager getting-on-with-things way of hers and ran straight into my arms. I held her tight, the whoosh of her copper hair swirling across my cheek, the deep-sea diver gripped in my hand just visible over her shoulder.

'Hi,' I said.

'Well, hi,' she said, and at the same moment that I realised that it wasn't her I heard more footsteps behind me and twisted my head round to see Jane's white face peering up at us from the bottom of the stairs, but only for a second because in no time she was gone and I heard the door bang behind her.

Tucker Wilmot stepped back out of my arms and, not much discomposed, began smoothing her hair.

'It is kinda dark here, isn't it?' she said.

'Yes, I'm very sorry.'

'No call to apologise to me. But perhaps –' She pointed in the general direction of downstairs.

'I'll go and find her.'

'You do that. But I'd wait a coupla minutes. I was just going to fix myself a cup of coffee. You want some?'

'Oh yes.' We came downstairs into the hall where a bulbous candelabrum of Murano glass gave a dim light.

'You mind me asking, but have you got some kind of thing about dolls and stuff?'

'What? Oh yes.' The light shone upon the diver's little imitation-brass helmet.

'Because yesterday you had that goblin, and today –'

'It's Brainerd's.'

'Right. On second thoughts, you better get after Jane and have the coffee later.'

'Yes.'

'I'll take care of that diver for you.'

'Thank you.'

Out on the beach, the mist was blowing aimlessly, thinner now, drawn out in grey snotty skeins. The sea beyond was darker, a dull gun-grey slopping half-heartedly against the shingle with a lazy slap. Not a human being, not a dog nor a seagull to be seen. I trudged for a few hundred yards towards Monsieur's cage, then thought no, she would have gone in the other direction, towards the little port. But for all I knew she might have gone inland instead, up towards the hotel, even perhaps to find her husband who played bridge in the *salon de thé* on dull mornings when golf would be no fun. I walked on without much hope of finding her, nor indeed much hope of convincing her of my mistake. The embrace had been intense. In my agitation I even fancied that perhaps Tucker had begun to respond. She certainly seemed not to be at all resentful, if anything quite cheered. All the same, the darkness on the stairs might be a saving grace. Jane might not have seen all that much, might be prepared to accept that it was just a chance collision. No good saying I'd mistaken Tucker for her in the darkness, I knew that much. Nobody wanted to be mistaken for anyone else.

I trudged on until I was nearly at the last breakwater before the beach expired on the low crumbly rocks. Here the mist was thicker, paler. I could hardly see the sea beyond, could hardly see anything, but then there was nothing much there, and only the cry of the gulls beyond the rocks picking over the garbage that came down from the harbour.

My eyes were already tired from peering through the mist and so I did not see the figure coming across the rocks until she was ten yards away. She was soaked, hunched and shivering, and slipping and skidding upon the wet seaweed and the tideworn purple rocks. Her great flounce of copper hair had shrunk into lank and sodden hanks, making her face seem more white and bony still.

'I'm so sorry,' she said. Her eyes were as red as a mongoose's and her teeth chattering. 'It was too cold.'

I began to explain but she kept saying it was too cold. Then I tried to put my arms round her and her mood changed in an instant. She thrust me off with a flailing fist.

'Go right away now. Go away. Go away.'

'Yes all right but I must explain ...'

'Just go, fucking go now. Can't you understand?'

'But I don't want you to think ...'

'Who gives a fuck what I think? You want that peabrained bitch, you have her. She'll —'

'I don't want her, I don't. It was a mistake, can't you —'

'It certainly was a mistake, a big mistake. Get out, get out now.' She was sobbing so fiercely and shivering so much at the same time that it was hard to make out what she was saying. Then she went from anger to misery again, from rage against me to pathetic babbling apologies for how she always messed everything up, she couldn't even drown herself properly and how she'd let everyone down, she'd chosen this part of the beach because she didn't want the children to see her but she didn't realise how shallow it was, she walked miles out and it was still no good and anyway how could she have thought of doing anything like that when she had Brainerd and Timmy even if she was no good to them or to anyone else.

'Look,' I said, 'we just bumped into each other on the stairs. That's all it was. I don't even know her properly.'

'You don't know me either, do you, not properly? Don't know and don't much care either. Well, I don't blame you.'

'It was a mistake, a mistake.'

'It was a crazy idea, the whole thing in the first place. I don't know why you went along with it. You're probably hard deep down, don't give a damn about anything much. Poor Tucker, doesn't know what she's let herself in for.'

'She hasn't let herself in for anything, it was a mistake.' My voice up to a shrill yelp now.

'Never mess with the help, that's what my mother used to say. She wasn't right about much but she was right about that.'

'Look, I'd better leave.'

'Yeah, that's right. Easy for you. Just walk away. Forget the whole thing. Oh yes I spent the summer in France, with some Americans, quite amusing really, the wife wasn't bad.'

'Please don't, please.'

She was quiet for a bit, and the only noise was the squelch of my shoes on the shingle and the sound of her sobbing. About a hundred yards from the house, we met Brainerd and Timmy slouching back from Monsieur.

'Mom, you're all wet. Why're you wet?'

'I fell in the water, honey, off the rocks.'

'That was dumb.'

'Yes, real dumb.'

She clutched the boys to her, crouching down to their level. They wriggled away at the squelch of her wet shirt, but she held them tight and they moved along as a crablike threesome. The boys had come back early because Timmy had thrown up.

The turret of the villa looked full of menace against the bruised sky with the foghorn still sounding out to sea. I wished I had never come and had instead spent the summer picking raspberries with some cousin who had a small fruit farm in Perthshire and needed help. Why had I come? It was only now that the end was so obviously in sight that I fully admitted to myself that what had decided me was the woman at the agency saying when I hesitated: 'Oh but they're so *rich*, you'll have such a good time.' There had seemed something entrancing in the prospect, a kind of freedom. Even if I had to work a little for the privilege, I would be in the company of people who didn't have to, something of their carelessness might rub off on me.

'You go play outside while I get some dry clothes on.'

'But Mom, we've been outside the whole morning.'

'You go play.'

There was a figure seated at the end of the table in the sitting-room. Even in the dark, there was no mistake about this one. Mr Stilwell sat upright like no one else, spreading the impression that those around him were suffering from sloppy posture if not curvature of the spine. But for preference he sat alone, like now, and that is always how I think of him. He was wearing the blue blazer and the lilac Lacoste polo shirt, his usual costume for bridge.

'Why honey, you're wet,' he said to Jane who was fleeing upstairs. She was at the turn in the stair before he had finished speaking, and invisible, half-audible, flung back a curt 'Fell in'.

'Fell in?' he repeated as she disappeared from view. 'In the sea?'

'Yes,' I said. 'The rocks are very slippery.'

'Never heard of anyone falling in the sea, not fully clothed. In a pool, yes, but not the sea.'

'It was misty too.'

'Right. She better have a hot bath, catch pneumonia else.' He paused, as though pondering whether to pass on this advice directly, decided not to, then paused again before moving on to another topic, no doubt the topic he had been thinking of before she appeared.

'Tell me,' he said, 'if you have a piece of real estate in England and you find oil underneath it, or coal, what's the legal position?'

'You mean, who does it belong to?'

'Yup. Is it yours or Her Majesty's?'

'Well, I think it belongs to the Coal Board if it's coal. Perhaps you get some kind of compensation.'

'Is the Coal Board a separate legal entity from the Crown? Would the royalty be negotiable or on a fixed percentage?'

'I don't know.'

'Interesting,' he said. 'Dodo's going into Britain offshore, for oil, that is. The offshore coal's just about played out. It's gonna be huge, the North Sea, I understand, as big as Kuwait.'

'Really, how amazing.'

'You didn't know that. Not many people do.'

There was a pause lasting a decade or two.

'How come Jane got so wet? If you slip on the rocks you might get your jeans wet, but she looks like she's into total immersion, and she's a good Episcopalian.' There was something rather charming about his slow dry little smile, even if it came only in response to his own jokes.

'They're quite deep, those rock pools.'

'Is that so?'

'This may not be the best moment,' I said, 'but I'm afraid I've had some bad news from home. My father, he's not well, nothing too awful, but I think I ought to ...'

'Go see him,' he supplied after another year-long intermission. 'How'd you hear?' By now I had got the hang of him and knew that this was not a suspicious question but merely part of his craving for practical information.

'There was a letter at the Post Office. I had my mail sent Poste Restante because I didn't have the villa's address.'

'Probably get your mail quicker that way. Good idea.'

'I could get a train tomorrow.'

'How'll you go? Change at Rouen and take the Havre boat? You may not believe this, but it could be quicker by Dieppe.'

He didn't say anything about how much they would all miss me. He was a truthful person.

As I packed my bags, I looked out of the window through the hexagon of clear glass. It was low tide, the sand as pale as Helen's skin, the sea an uninsistent lilac-grey, the sky motionless. The women in black were stumbling over the shingle talking to each other in hoarse voices. I could hear the clank of their buckets as they walked out over the huge wet sands.

Minnow Island

'You can't get across from that side. You have to go back to the station
and walk over the bridge into Middlesex.'

'Back to the station?'

'Yes. You're in darkest Surrey. We don't speak to people over there.'

She was quite close. The channel between us was narrow and the
tide was right out, only a sluggish trickle in the stony river-bed, so I
could see tyres and oil-drums and old boots though they were all
covered with an evil brown sludge. The tall weeds guarding the island
were coated in mud up to the high-water mark. The river seemed
depleted, without hope of refreshment. Helen was looking down from a
rickety wooden balcony on the bungalow roof. The bungalow was
faced with clapboarding painted a brownish-black colour, much the
same colour as the mud. The balcony had the look of a bridge on some
decrepit little galleon that had only just managed to limp back into
port.

It was a warm day for September and quite a long way round. The
first drops of sweat were gathering on my brow as I crossed over the
railway bridge and heard the grimy green SR trains below charging up
with that peculiar zinging chung as though impatient to infect the
sleepy suburban platforms with their surplus energy. Beneath the great
ironwork bridge the river was already busy with pleasure cruisers and
young men rowing their girlfriends down to the pubs in Twickenham
and Teddington. Another quarter of a mile up the towpath on the
Middlesex side and there was a high skinny footbridge spanning the

broader channel over to the island. She was waiting just the other side of the bridge, fair and tiny just as I remembered her.

'What made you think you could get across from that side?'

'The map makes it look as if you can walk straight over.'

'Not unless you're Jesus Christ you can't.'

The air was heavier on the island in among the willows sweeping the ground and the bosomy poplars whose leaves were shimmering and rustling though there was scarcely a breeze. There was no road on the island, only a winding footpath of crumbling tarmac between the bungalows, shacks and chalets scattered through the undergrowth at odd angles to one another, refusing to present a front even to the narrow path. Something secretive, yet also provisional, not so much that I felt there was a danger of eviction (though that might be a risk too), more that one morning the people living in these makeshift dwellings would suddenly declare they had had enough and move on. The more ramshackle places looked as if they could be taken apart and loaded up on a lorry to be reassembled somewhere else. The link fencing was heavy with bindweed and sticky sweetheart.

Some of the little gardens had runner beans in full flower giving still more protection from the outside world. By the front doors of these hutches there were improvised devices, for bringing supplies over the footbridge she said: wire trolleys attached to bicycles, little detachable trailers knocked together out of wood and hardboard and painted green or pink with flowers, and a peculiar sort of hod with bars running round it and a harness, this last locked to the porch – the island was full of locks, heavy padlocks on the sheds, lighter Squires and Chubbs on the bikes, there was even a wheelbarrow locked to a rose-trellis. Was the isle a warren of footpads, the lack of motors and its tiny, primitive jungly atmosphere for some reason provoking thievery?

'Oh yes, put something down in this place, turn round and it's gone and they're off the island in a flash.'

Yet it also seemed like a place to squirrel things away in. Having to cross two bridges and go into a different county to get to it made me feel as if I had burrowed right to the core of things. But then again, this sense of impermanence, the restless, fidgety feel of the place, and the never-stopping rustle of the leaves.

'Have you always lived here?'

'Oh no.' She thought the question extraordinary. 'We never stay in the same place, not for more than a couple of years. Dad sort of exhausts a place.'

He too was waiting, just by the front door of the little clapboard bungalow which on that side was painted a dirty royal-blue, the colour of an upturned boat. An intense slight upright man, very dark-faced, not at all like his daughter to look at except for the motionless upright way he held himself, like a chessman about to be moved. His face was fixed in a frown, not so much of irritation as puzzlement, as though he had just heard a strange noise which he couldn't quite identify but which he knew needed attending to. His dark blinking eyes had the same intense uncertain look.

'Ah there you are then.' I expected him to start with a question and his quiet firm voice came as a surprise, a cool, rather pleasant sensation. 'Martin Hardress,' he said as an afterthought.

'Sorry I'm late, went along the wrong side of the river.'

'It's like the Boat Race, you have to choose the Middlesex station. Come on in.'

I could hear the north in his voice, but only just. In the north they would probably have thought he had put on a bit of a southern accent. Following him in, I noticed again how slight he was. The immaculate faded jeans seemed to be keeping themselves up.

The door opened straight into a little study lined with bookshelves with no books in them. Instead, the shelves were filled with old telephones with boxes beside them, mostly tin and wood painted khaki, the brass bits beautifully polished.

'Field telephones. That's the oldest one there, Boer War issue. I've been collecting them for years. The Science Museum have offered me a fair sum, but I'm not biting, not just yet anyway.'

Over the desk there were half a dozen framed certificates which I peered at: Twickenham Show Best Kept Pony – Helen Hardress (Bouncer); General Certificate of Education, Advanced Level, in the following subjects ... On the side wall more certificates: Lower Thames Gymkhana, Showjumping Intermediate, First Prize; Eventing Junior Team, First Equal.

'You told Wilmot you weren't horsy.'

'I just wanted to shut him up. Anyway it was years ago. One night I'm going to creep in and smash the lot. It's so embarrassing.'

'You'll only set off the burglar alarm, Hel. I've just rewired it and connected it to the police station. You'll be arrested on suspicion of stealing your own certificates. You have a burglar alarm?'

'No, afraid not,' I said.

'You're quite right. Lot of trouble, especially if you connect up to the police. What do you think of the police these days?'

It was impossible to tell what answer he expected or wanted, or even whether he would be interested in the answer. I said something about them being all right in the country, but a bit dodgy in London.

'Quite right,' but even when he said quite right it still wasn't clear whether he really agreed. Not that he seemed the least bit insincere. It was more as though his brain had moved off in some other direction and he was having trouble in trying not to appear distracted. No doubt all sorts of people have that problem a good deal of the time, most conversations not being on the subject you would have chosen if you had a free hand in the matter, but his manner was so intense, that you couldn't stop wondering what was going on in his head.

'Ah here's Helen's mother.' His voice suddenly lost all its flatness and almost throbbed with relief as if her presence had been secured with enormous difficulty, perhaps by means of a parachute-drop, although there had been a clatter of crockery from next-door ever since we had come into the study. She was tiny too. It would have seemed odd if she hadn't been. I was already learning to live with my Gulliver-in-Lilliput role, trying not to bump into the field telephones or stoop too obviously (bending the knees a fraction helped more than you might expect).

'Oh,' she said, 'coming all this way and getting lost at the end of it, I'm so sorry.' She had a boat-shaped face, prettier than her daughter's, but ruffled by anxiety to such an extent that it was hard to believe that my journey could possibly have provoked so much worry. But then she began to describe how she had overcooked the leeks and her face was overwhelmed by the same shattered look.

'I'm sure they'll be fine, Min,' he said, but in his distracted way which wouldn't have reassured anyone, let alone her.

'They're horrible, overcooked leeks, horrible aren't they, don't you think so?'

'Please, Mum, no clutchpaws.' Mrs Hardress's hands were already curled into little nests and shaking slightly, a squirrel who couldn't remember where she hid her nuts.

As we went into the kitchen, I felt more and more like the intruder from the oversized world, gross and clumsy, who has strayed into a more delicate realm. The kitchen had a low window looking out through the drooping grey-green willow branches to the river, so that we might have been in the entrancing lair of Mole or Ratty. I half-expected to be served elderflower wine and to nibble at raw carrot-tops. But the food was hearty, an aromatic beef stew, a blackberry-and-apple crumble, and a fragrant Rhône wine. The Hardresses all ate and drank hugely, as though their frail exterior was some kind of brilliant trick which they did not have to keep up when they were among themselves.

'What do you think of the BBC?'

I couldn't think of anything useful to say on this one either.

'They're bastards to work for, that I can say with some authority. Total bastards. I'm not sure how much more I can take of being messed about, I'm thinking of going freelance, giving it very serious consideration.'

'Oh don't start on that, please don't. I mean it's mad, do tell him it's mad, won't you –' She couldn't think of my name or didn't like to use it and the little squirrel paws went into a clench and began drumming against the edge of the table but lightly like the percussion introduction to some menacing theme tune.

'Don't, Mum. You don't know it's a mistake. I mean lots of people make more money freelance, don't they, Dad?'

'It's a gamble, Hel. This isn't a country for freelances, it's a country for arse-lickers.'

'Martin, please.'

'Well it is, in the BBC all you have to do is shove your tongue up the nearest available arse and you're made.'

Discharging this advice appeared to give him some sort of ease and he passed round the wine with a smile which was on the sly side, as though he had not just offended his wife but also surprised himself, not being the kind of person who talked like that. In fact she did not really seem to mind the language, being more upset about the thought of his giving in his notice.

'I'm sure it can't be as bad as that,' she said. 'I mean when we met that head of personnel or whatever he was at the Christmas party, he seemed quite a mild-mannered man.'

'Oh him, he's a cipher, it's the people higher up. They just tear up the rule-book whenever it suits them. Take the new rules on waiting-time, a total travesty.'

'Well, can't the union stop it then, if they've broken the rules?'

'The union, they're a bunch of complete wankers, worse than the management because they think they're doing you a favour when they bother to do their job which is about 2 per cent of the time. Come on, let's go outside while the sun's still out.'

We walked across what had been the lawn before the long willow branches had swept the grass off it. We had to draw the branches apart like curtains to thread our way over the bare ground, dodging the yellow and white smears of duckshit. Moorhens and mallard were dabbling in the river. The tide was rising now and the water beginning to lap at the roots of the tall daisies on the bank. The sun came out from behind a tree and flooded the narrow channel with golden light. We stood on the bank transfigured, a little drunk, eyes closed against the sun, letting the light wash over us.

'On an afternoon like this,' Martin Hardress said, 'you don't want to be anywhere else.'

'Really, Dad? I thought I heard you saying this was the last year you were going to spend living like a water-rat.'

'That was February, Hel. Oh that wire's gone again.'

Where the bank fell away, a chain-link fence dropped down towards the water. Beside it a floppy sapling had been prevented from collapsing into the water by two wires fastened to the fence. One of the wires had snapped and the flossy-headed tree was yawing away from the fence and bobbing at the river, its bright leaves now sinking below the surface, now splashing and twisting on top of the rising water.

Helen and I walked with Martin Hardress back towards the far end of the bungalow below the rickety balcony. He opened another blue door into a little room, dark to our sun-dazzled eyes. He switched on the light and we were in the neatest little workshop imaginable, big steel vice gleaming on the workbench, teeth shining on the small circular saw let into the end of it and what looked like a lathe under a protective plastic hood. All along the walls spanners, files, wrenches, hammers, pliers, drills and bits, T-square, pigeon-holes, all purpose-built.

'This is the centre of Dad's universe.'

'Don't be so patronising, I scarcely get a moment to myself in here these days. Now where's that wire?' He went through a pantomime of searching, but he could have found the wire blindfold and the clippers too. While he fussed around gathering staples and rubber treeguards, we wandered out of the workshop and into the bright afternoon. I looked back through the open door: the bent figure scrabbling around under the hot artificial light seemed like the creation of a fevered mind, a goblin blacksmith in some intricate myth of virtue and struggle. The willow branches waving across the low clapboard made it hard to estimate the size of the house. Like burrows in children's stories or adults' dreams, the Hardress house was both minute and endless, each room opening into another with a glimpse of another one beyond that. And although the rooms were small, they were not as small as they first looked and each one contained a surprising amount of furniture and implements. I had a sudden longing to see the field telephones properly.

'You're extracting the michael. Nobody's ever wanted to look at them.'

'No really, I really do.'

'Oh all right then. I mean I'm happy to.'

He looked at me with gratitude still laced with suspicion.

We went back through the house, on the way passing through another unsuspected room, a little sitting-room full of chintz and books and tapestry pictures of things you wouldn't have thought of making tapestry pictures of, like the winding-gear of a mine and the New York skyline, all in vivid colours, especially red in unexpected places. Min's sideline, he said. In the corner, there was a tapestry frame and some shelves with assorted wools laid out on them. The picture on the frame was half-finished and looked to be of some power station of the heroic age, Bankside possibly or Battersea.

'She won't sell them, could make a mint.'

'Aren't they horrible?' Helen said. 'Actually I rather like them, to be honest. I always take one back to college, reminds me of home.'

'You'd call it kitsch, wouldn't you?' He looked at me, the suspicion fully operational again.

'Umm. No I wouldn't, I don't think. I mean, kitsch means sentimental, doesn't it, and they aren't sentimental at all.'

'Does it? Is that what it means?'

'It's not a word I use really.'

'Gone out of style has it? I suppose to say kitsch nowadays is probably a kitsch thing to do. You just can't keep up.'

I cannot now recall the technical details of the lecture he gave me on field telephones, how the device had evolved from a simple echo chamber linked by wire, to a wind-up transmitter using electric current along the line, then to real telephony and increasingly sophisticated techniques for finding frequencies, the introduction of bakelite in the late 1920s, then scrambling, then miniaturising, and all the various improvements in making them transportable and packable and even elegant. It was his technological exuberance that was utterly seductive. His enthusiasm communicated more than was in his actual words, so that as he was describing, in dry enough terms, how the Boer War had accelerated certain technical improvements, I visualised men with sunburnt legs and puttees covered with veld-dust lying behind some kopje and barking panic-strewn instructions into the primitive lacquered wooden mouthpiece, the sweat running down through their Kitchener moustaches.

'People take things for granted, don't they? Forget all the effort, all the brilliance that went into each little step forward, all they remember is the upper-class twits who got shot up the arse because they went the wrong way. I bet you can tell me half a dozen names of guys who copped it at Rorke's Drift or Ladysmith and you can't remember a single important figure in modern military technology. Probably your grandpa won the VC.'

'Da-ad.'

'Marconi,' I said.

'Except Marconi, anyway he was a con artist.'

'Maxim, Gatling, and was Sten a person?'

'Guns are easy. It's all on the same principle. I'm talking about communications, about something difficult, something which requires imagination. Organised violence is so childish, childishly simple. You ever read military strategy, it's about as complicated as six-year-olds playing tag. Then Sir Marmaduke brought up his left wing – kids' stuff. No, I'm not a pacifist. They're all hypocrites because they're so bloody aggressive and bad-tempered.'

'And you're so sweet-tempered and nice?'

'Just impatient, Hel. There's a difference. Impatience is a virtue.'

'Alexander Graham Bell,' I said.

'Took you quite a time, didn't it?'

He looked at me with his bright dark eyes and his mouth twitched in a grim smile, instantly suppressed as though it might damage his reputation.

'Well then, what did you think?' She walked with me back to the station.

'Of them, your parents? Oh they were –' I paused before the word, not because I couldn't think of it (it had come straight to mind) but because I didn't quite like to use it – 'impressive.'

'That's an odd word to use.'

'It is.'

'Like you might say of a flower display.'

'Yes I know, but they were.'

'You're not being –'

'Patronising, no, I thought you'd think that.'

'Well then, say what you mean by impressive.'

'It's as though they were trying harder than most people.'

'And that impresses you?'

'Yes it does,' I said.

'It doesn't make them easy to live with.'

'Didn't say it did.'

'In any case, you hardly saw my mum and she was in a cooking panic most of the time, and Dad was moaning on about the Beeb.'

'Yes but even so you –'

'No, I think you're right. I've always been kind of aware of it, I suppose, I was mystified by other girls' parents just seeming to take life as it came and not minding about things.'

'And you minded too?'

'Still mind. I don't see any point otherwise. If you just adjust to things as they are, you might as well not be there. Oh there's the train. See you. 'Bye.'

The kiss she gave me was quick and light, a moth grazing my cheek. Her greetings and goodbyes seemed to be abrupt, almost brusque. I might have flattered myself that it was because she was brimming with emotion which she was scared of spilling, but I only had to watch her walking down the platform and out through the side door of the little station to see that she was quite calm.

That winter it often came back to me, the golden afternoon by the river and the field telephones and Mrs Hardress's tapestries and the inturned intensity of their lives, which seemed neither happy nor unhappy but simply thoroughly lived – though how could I presume to imagine that on the basis of a single afternoon and several glasses of Rhône wine? But there was no doubt about my own feeling which was a sort of puzzled envy. It came upon me strongly when I squeezed into an armchair in somebody's small sitting-room with two people I didn't really know and others I didn't know at all crouched on the floor. We were watching the Boat Race in an apologetic haze. Nobody had anything better to do on a chilly March afternoon. Then I heard the commentator saying, 'And Oxford have won the toss and chosen the Middlesex station.' The magic phrase had an extraordinary effect on me. I shivered and then blushed too, so that the good-natured girl on one arm of the chair asked was I all right and perhaps I was sickening for the flu.

The afternoon on Minnow Island came back again a few months later when an elderly barrister said 'I'll tell you something' in tones which meant here comes a piece of sage advice. 'The truth is,' he said, 'nothing matters very much and most things don't matter at all.' Depends who you are doesn't it, I could hear Martin Hardress saying, it only comes to the same thing if you're all right to start with.

The barrister – Pettifer, Pettigrew, some suitable name like that –

had been standing just inside the door of the reception room at a hotel, a frowsty room down a side passage with SHERIDAN SUITE on the door. It was Jane Stilwell who had said to me, 'Oh you must know Petty, he's so charming, everyone says he's the most charming man in London.' I didn't know him, but this turned out to be unimportant, since his charm turned itself on without outside assistance. If there had been a contest for Best Use of Two Cubic Metres of Hotel Space, he would have walked it. And until he blew his cover with the *mot* about nothing mattering much, he was helping to put off the awkward moment in a fashion that was better than painless.

The awkward moment came up, though, soon enough.

'Oh so you have met, isn't that great?' Mrs Stilwell looked first at the two of us together with a hostess's impersonal pride, then at me.

There had been a formal goodbye before I left the Ville, refereed by Mr Stilwell. Jane had been wearing a dark-green ribbed jersey and had looked even whiter in the face than she usually did. She had kissed me on the cheek maternally, and we had shaken hands which made it seem even more like the end of a bout which it wasn't clear who had won.

She had written me a letter:

This is the only letter I'm going to write to you, although I'd like to write every day 'cos [I wish she hadn't written 'cos] *that's the next best thing to seeing you. But I've made a mess of my life and I don't want to make a mess of yours too. You have such wonderful things ahead of you, such a brilliant future. Besides I owe John a hell of a lot and he owes me nothing and I don't want to go deeper into debt from the emotional point of view. You know how much I love you and will always love you. And you know how I could go on for pages, because you know how I can go on. But I won't. Jane.* **X**

The letter was on paper of a thick creamy weave and stood up to being carried around in my wallet for weeks.

Then, contrary to her promise, a second letter arrived, also short (perhaps she was one of those people who found it a struggle to get over the page).

Darling, I said I wouldn't, but I'm so miserable without you. Our four days together were the greatest days of my life and it eases my heartache a little to be able to say that to you. I know it had to end, but the way I ended it was wretched and foolish, and so awful for you that I am ashamed every time I think of it. I didn't mean to upset you darling, not for all the world. And I just want you to know that I shall never forget and hope that now and then you will think of your Jane.

Now here she was in a little black dress and a swirly gold brooch pinned to her breast. She glowed in that pale alabaster way she glowed after we lay in the abandoned villa.

'Oh you do look well.'

'I am.'

'That's great. It's wonderful to see you.'

There was a danger that we would go on batting these stilted greetings back and forth without ever thinking of anything more substantial to say, but an interruption diverted us.

'Well there you are. Jane said she might get you along. Dodo Wilmot. Blast from the past.'

He did not seem quite so huge now a couple of years later – perhaps memory had inflated him. And the look on his babyface was keener, less bemused. In his dinner jacket, the only one there, he had a certain massive authority.

'Not quite the old Boudin, is it? Don't worry, I'm on my best behaviour, isn't that right, Jane? She's so lovely, isn't she, I bet she looked just the same in high school. Did you ever see Vivien Leigh in *That Hamilton Woman*? I saw that film five times, it was Winston's favourite film, she could have been Jane's sister though the colouring was different than Jane's. Time for a little music.'

He waddled over to the piano in the corner of the room, sat down and riffled a few chords to attract attention, then ambled into 'You're the Top' and two or three other Cole Porter songs, singing in his surprisingly light Burl Ives tenor.

'He's awful, Dodo, he *will* flirt and with Tucker not here he insists on pretending he's my beau. But what can you do, he's our oldest friend.' Jane patted my hand, a light cool pat like a cook testing whether a mousse has set. 'It's so great to see you and say sorry in person.'

I couldn't say anything. My throat seemed choked and I tried not to cry, at the same time annoyed with myself for being so soft. Only then was it clear how dry and solitary my life had been up to that point, and although this episode (you could scarcely call it a relationship) was over, it had been not an initiation so much as a release.

'Night and day you are the one. Under the moon or under the sun,' sang Dodo Wilmot.

'Met Cole a couple of times at Eden Roc, years ago,' the charming barrister, Pettifer/Pettigrew, said in my ear, in a front-row-of-the-stalls whisper. 'You'd be amazed how modest he was, awfully amusing too. Delightful fellow. Basically queer of course.'

'Night and da-ay . . .'

'I think that *is* enough,' Jane said. She went over to the piano and whispered in Dodo's ear, but he caught her by the hand and with his other hand launched into 'We're a Couple of Swells', and so she had to join in, which she did, cracked, out of tune, hopeless. And I stood beside Pettifer/Pettigrew with my eyes watering.

'You all right, old chap?'

'Must be getting a cold.'

'Redoxon, that's the only thing, always works. Redoxon, or Vitamin C, same thing. Pills or powder, they both work.'

Near the door, talking quietly to another neat little man, was John Stilwell.

'Hi,' he said. 'You went by Dieppe Jane tells me, quicker than you thought hey?'

'Yes it was.'

'Thought so.'

I was half-way along the corridor, more or less pulled together again, when I heard light running footsteps behind me and felt a clutch at my elbow.

'Here,' she said. 'Don't forget, ever. He'll remind you,' and into my hands she thrust a knobbly brown paper package. She was gone as quick as a child who has just to touch base before running back to where she started: thin legs flying outwards and the lollop of her hips, like when she had run down to the Pari-Mutuel to put her money on the wrong horse. The curve of the hotel corridor had an airless finality.

In my damp palm my fingers explored the unforgiving contours of the carved goblin.

'What is that thing?'

'Jane gave it me, as a souvenir I suppose.'

'It's repulsive isn't it, but then souvenirs usually are. It looks quite studenty on that bookshelf though.'

It wasn't clear why Helen had asked to come and see me, but as soon as she had climbed the stairs to my freezing attic in Back Buildings, it seemed obvious that there was no particular reason and didn't need to be. She had a natural friendliness which somehow tended to be overlooked because of her upright motionless figurine of a body. Her open cheerful way of talking did not translate into her body language, so that she gave the impression that she might be thinking severer thoughts which she was reluctant to bring to the surface.

'Do you know who I've got downstairs? My dad.'

'Why didn't he come up with you?'

'He's so silly. He said he'd just drive me down here because I've failed my driving test again and it would be a ghastly surprise for you dumping himself on you after he'd bored you stiff last time. So he's sitting in the car reading Bertrand Russell.'

Mr Hardress was in the driver's seat frowning at the book propped on the steering wheel as though it was an impenetrable manual of some kind, perhaps the owner's handbook.

'The conquest of happiness, my aunt fanny,' he said, after only the briefest hallo. 'Hasn't a clue. He ought to stick to philosophy. That *History of Western Philosophy* is a marvellous book, I thought so anyway, you probably thought it a bit juvenile.'

'Haven't read it, I'm afraid.'

'I expect it's only people like me who bother with it. They think we aren't up to the real thing, so they give us the kids' version.'

'That's rubbish, Dad. What's stopping you reading the real thing?'

'Ignorance, my dear, sheer bloody ignorance.'

He gave us one of his grim smiles. There was a paler, more withered look to him or perhaps it was just that the sun was not shining as it had on Minnow Island. ('Is your mother called Minnow too?' I had asked Helen on the way back. 'No, Minerva. Her father taught Latin, wasn't at all keen on Dad, not the kind of son-in-law anyone would fancy really although he must have been good-looking.') With the two of us in our raincoats peering in through the car window, Hardress must have looked to passers-by like someone being questioned by plain-clothes police.

'All right then,' Helen said to me, 'you tell him what he ought to be reading, give him a reading list as though he was a mature student just starting.'

'Oh I couldn't,' I said.

'Go on,' he said, 'you can think of them over lunch.'

In the dank pub by the canal we had flabby Cornish pasties and beer that tasted of the disinfectant the pub smelled of, and Hardress talked non-stop as though he had just returned from a long solitary journey and had a huge assortment of things he wanted to unburden himself of.

'Full of anger my father was, poured off him like sweat. When I was growing up, I took him at face value, thought it was all anger about injustice, poverty and that, which it was, but it was just anger too, kicked the cat, kicked his bike (we didn't have a car), kicked Her too, always called my mother Her when he was in a rage. I used to think that was the drink, she said it was, everything was blamed on the drink in those days, quite right too usually. I've inherited a lot of all that, but not the politics, not actively anyway, I'm more interested in the logic of action. Take Suez.'

'Oh Dad.'

'No I'm not going to say what you think, about it being a pathetic reversion to imperialist aggression, though it was. What I couldn't understand was why, having started, they didn't go through with it to the bitter end, or, to put it another way, why they ever thought they could get away with it. Trouble was they didn't have the balls, you needed a real pirate like Churchill to pull off a stunt like that. Well what have you got for me, sir?' He took the scrap of paper on which I'd written down while he was talking the only books I remembered being told to read.

'*The Concept of Mind*, G. Ryle, *Sense and Sensibilia*, J.L. Austin, *The Truffles in the Wood*, W.R. Scrannel, well, that'll do to be going on with. Are you sure about the Truffles one, doesn't sound like philosophy to me.'

'Afraid I haven't read any of them myself yet.'

'I'll send in my exam paper before the end of term.'

'I expect they're terribly dry. Everyone complains about how sterile philosophy is at the moment.'

'Do they now?'

He was not at all put off by the prospect, excited if anything. And before the month was out I got a letter in exquisite handwriting, neat and clear, not taught like my coarse italic, but the outcome of a natural dexterity.

Thank you for recommending those three books. They are just what I hoped they would be, especially the dryness of them. I think it is right that philosophy should try and clear away the language muddles and category mistakes (see I'm picking up the lingo already) so it can't help being a bit dry. It isn't for philosophers to tell us how to live or what to believe. That is for us, otherwise what the fuck is the point of it all? I especially liked the Scrannel book. As you will recall, if you have read it by now, the point is that bad philosophers spend their whole lives in the pursuit of certainty which in most cases isn't something that you should be looking for (except for mathematics etc). All you have a right to expect is varying degrees of probability according to what field you are in, but most of the time there are no truffles in that particular wood, and you're wasting your time looking for them. (Funny isn't it about truffles being a delicacy. I had them once in France and they were like rubbery licorice only without the taste. Must be because they are so hard to find.) Anyway, how dreary life would be if bit by bit you could ink in the certainties until there was no terra incognita left on the map. Uncertainty is the only refreshing thing, and so I found your books very refreshing and not dry at all. It was a pleasure to come and see you with Hel. My wife says I hang around her too much but she's got a mind of her own and she doesn't mind telling me to piss off when she wants.

On the subject of uncertainty, I've certainly got a basinful of that with this new freelance lark. It's quite something being your own boss. You begin to realise what a soft option it is being a wage-slave. Well, we mustn't weaken.

Yours sincerely Martin H.

PS Would you like to come with Hel to the Asses Night Out

(=Association of Sound Engineers Annual Ball). We've got four tickets and somebody's got to share the agony.

It was surprising from what little I knew of him that he should even think of going to a ball. I imagined him dressed in old jeans, refusing to eat the haute cuisine, perhaps even bringing his own sandwiches. But there he was, waiting for me as I got out of the taxi, a bright showy little figure in a dinner jacket, his hair now cut short, almost down to bristles, which made him look like an actor in training for some demanding part that required spiritual concentration and a lot of interviews.

'There you are then. Welcome to the evening of a lifetime.'

Behind him, there was Min in a mauve dress which was billowy but at the same time gave her a vulnerable look as though she had been surprised with no clothes on and had wrapped herself in the nearest curtain.

'Evening, Ted. Lionel, how come they let you in? Boris, I don't believe it. Min, have you met Boris the Beast of Borehamwood?' He bobbed from side to side on the shallow steps of the Ballroom entrance, acting like a frantic greeter. His colleagues responded to him cordially enough but with a hint of surprise, perhaps even caution as though there might be some catch in it.

'Don't see much of the lads these days. No great loss I suppose, bunch of cowboys really.'

He led us into the huge ballroom. There must have been a hundred tables, a thousand people milling about in search of their places. On the floodlit platform at the end, two men in grey uniform were fiddling with the microphone that sprouted out of a spangled lectern with a scarlet-and-gold coat of arms on it. In the smoky half-light, it seemed about half a mile away.

'Just like a bloody Nuremberg rally, except that the sound always goes wrong. I think they do it on purpose just because we're who we are.'

A toastmaster in a scarlet tailcoat told us to be upstanding for the grace and a man in a dinner jacket with a purple vest intoned in a dolorous chant: For all thy great gifts O Lord we give thanks, for the gift of speech and music and the power to transmit those precious sounds across thy globe, and we ask thy blessing on the broadcasting industry and all who labour in it, and especially on these thy servants gathered here tonight, and for what we are about to receive may the Lord make us truly thankful.

'Stupid prat, who let him in? They're 95 per cent atheists in this room and the other 5 per cent are off their trolleys.'

'There's always a grace, dear.'

He still sounded jovial enough, but something about the set of his lips suggested that his fragile calm was beginning to fray. A waiter bent across him and began distributing bread rolls with a pair of flimsy tongs. Martin Hardress caught his arm and pinned it down on the table.

'If,' he said, 'if I'd wanted a clip round the earhole from your little tongs, I would have asked you first, wouldn't I?'

'Yes, sir.'

'But I didn't, did I?'

'No, sir.'

'So I think you can take it for granted that I didn't want a clip round the earhole and that your little tongs are surplus to requirements.' Keeping the waiter's arm pinned to the table with one hand, with the other he removed the tongs from the waiter and carefully bent them double, then handed them back. 'Now, would you hand round the bread properly?'

'Oh Dad.'

'They've got to be told. Just because this is a cutprice do, they think they can treat you like dummies.'

The trembling waiter fled, dodging between the closely packed tables with the bread basket clasped to his bosom.

'Now we haven't got any bread,' Helen said.

'Oh don't you worry, it will descend from heaven. I'll just go and ask that bishop to organise it.' He made as if to rise from his little gold chair, but when his wife pulled at his jacket he sat down quite meekly and permitted himself one of his grim smiles.

'Will you stop it, Dad?'

'Oh there's nothing to stop. It all stopped dead years ago. This country's just one huge full stop. Look at Bryan there, BBC Assistant

Director Engineering in brackets, don't forget the brackets because in brackets is where he belongs.'

'Dear, it was really nice of Bryan to send us the tickets. They did their training together, you see.'

'Martin, great to see you, and Min, you're looking gorgeous. So glad you could come.' Close up Bryan was larger. He had fulvous tufts of hair in his ears and a nice rueful smile.

'Thank you very much for the tickets,' Min said. 'It's a lovely occasion, it really is.'

'Well, what are friends for? Alas, duty calls. I must look after our guest of honour and between you and me he takes some looking after. See you later and we'll have a proper natter.'

As the Assistant Director passed on, leading the celebrity to the top table in a cloud of assorted aftershaves, Martin raised his eyebrows.

'Well that's what success does to you. He used to be all right, old Bryan. But that was years ago.'

'When we lived in Petersham, they used to come for picnics. That was when he was still married to Thelma.'

'Ditched her, then ditched the next one. She's got a health food shop in Chobham now.'

He relapsed into a gloomy silence and ate with a slow, suspicious chomping as if engaged in the task professionally.

'We're selling Minnow Island, you know, if we can find a buyer. Looking for a flat, something smaller, nearer to Martin's work.'

He scowled at Min. It was not clear whether he wanted this news kept dark or he wanted to release it himself. Yet his good humour seemed to be returning. Without any encouragement, he began talking, with that light fluency that seemed to come to him now and then like a patch of sun moving across a lawn that was in shadow most of the day.

'I've been thinking again about uncertainty and that Scrannel fellow. Of course it's all very right and proper that you shouldn't look for certainty where you've no reason to find it. That's absolutely right, and as soon as you've grasped this a whole lot of nonsense just melts away and you understand just how many millions of people have wasted their lives looking for something that isn't there and that if they stopped to think honestly for a moment they'd know wasn't there. But then of course you can't stop. Once you've started breaking down the old certainties or at any rate the old pursuit of certainties, what's left?'

Preceded by only a faint crackle on the mike, a Yorkshire voice broke into our seminar, one of those gravy-rich voices which now and then rumbles off into the noise of a load of gravel being tipped out into the road. The celebrity was off.

You would not have thought him a comedian, he was tall and muscley, looked as though he had just jumped off a tractor. His manner was loud and distracted at the same time. His act was a man being heckled by his wife from the next room or upstairs: the man's voice a weak, tremulous alto, the wife a rich, confident baritone. Have you got your sandwiches, the wife said. No, no, I don't want any sandwiches. They're cheese and pickle. I don't like cheese and pickle, the pickle gives me wind. No it doesn't, don't blame the pickle, it's in the blood. Your mother was just the same, give her a pickled onion and she was a one-woman hurricane, Hurricane Gladys, she caused a lot of damage in Florida, did Gladys. My mother was a good woman, loved all God's creatures. She were a right little St Francis, that woman, preferred the budgie to her own flesh and blood, hush, she'd say, listen to Winston, he knows, you know. Should have called it Goebbels, that bird . . .

Martin Hardress shut his eyes, put his hands behind his head and leaned back as blissful as someone taking the sun in a deckchair. The grim lines returned when the celebrity started handing out the awards. There was a special award to Bryan for distinguished service to the broadcasting industry.

'If that means he's screwed every trainee producer he's crewed with, he really deserves it, it's that hangdog look that pulls them,' Hardress said in his dry distant voice which didn't really seem to come from him, not least because his lips scarcely moved, so that I felt like looking round the table to see who the ventriloquist was. He seemed to occupy his body only at intervals, when he felt like it. But if he was keen on the subject, as when he talked about philosophy, he seemed to be all there, trembling with life.

By now we were quite drunk, like the other thousand people in the ballroom, who were beginning to glisten and paw each other. A band began to play theme tunes from radio shows – 'Music While You Work', 'The Archers', 'Down Your Way' – and then there were foxtrots and quicksteps and sambas and cha cha chas and even a veleta. And although the steps of the veleta were beyond us, there was a tipsy stateliness about the other couples that carried us along. Helen clasped my waist with fierce little fingers and looked mock-stern. There was not the tiniest spark of desire between us but we were both in love with the cosy intimations of our childhoods that came with each new number. Glenn Miller now – 'Little Brown Jug', 'In the Mood' – then a salute to Irving Berlin: 'Cheek to Cheek', 'I Won't Dance, Don't Ask Me', 'Smoke Gets in Your Eyes'.

When we got back to the table, Martin Hardress seemed to have taken against something his wife had said. She was twisting her hands together as though trying to dry some small article hidden in them. Quite without warning, he stood up placing himself so close to my chair that I couldn't sit down.

'There's something you should know,' he said, 'And I think we ought to get it quite clear. You've got to look after my girl. Properly I mean. If you let her down, if you treat her like Bryan would, I'll kill you. That's straight, it's not meant as a joke.'

'But we aren't, I mean, I haven't any –'

'You can say anything you want tonight because we're all pissed, but don't forget what I'm saying to you, don't think I'm not serious. You can't just waltz away from this one. This isn't a joke.'

'I didn't think it was.'

'Martin, please.'

'So that's understood then.'

He sat down and looked immensely sad. His wife came and sat next to him and took his hand. Helen and I spoke in an undertone, scarcely able to hear one another, as though we were alone with her parents in a small room and didn't want to disturb their concentration. We pretended to argue about the name of the last tune and how you spelled veleta, and then, more quietly still, about how soon we could go home.

Three or four days later Helen rang.

'I don't know why I'm ringing you because we don't really know each other that well, but he's gone and we're desperate and we can't think what to do or who to talk to.'

'Gone? Your father?' I didn't really need to ask, but I did for form's sake.

'Disappeared the morning after the party. Didn't take anything at all that we could see, just a raincoat because it was raining.'

'You've tried his workplace, the BBC and so on?'

'Yes, and not only was he not there, but they hadn't seen him for months, even this independent production company he used to do stuff for. Apparently they'd had some quarrel and he'd said he'd never touch them again and all that. I can see him saying it.'

'So what was he working on?'

'That's the awful thing, I don't think he was working on anything. We looked at his bank statements and there'd been no money coming in, not for months. So we don't know where he went during the day. And so Mum's twice as desperate because of him keeping all his troubles from her, unless of course they weren't troubles and he'd got a glamorous second family somewhere like that man in the papers, but it doesn't sound like him. I mean he could barely cope with one family – and a midget family at that. So we don't know what to do next and I don't expect you do either, but it would be great to have a bit of company because the police aren't exactly sympathetic. You can tell they just think he's done a runner and perhaps he has, but they ought to pretend, don't you think?'

The rain was coming down hard and I took some boots with me on the train and felt as if everyone could guess where I was going, although the boots were in an M&S carrier bag. Somewhere not quite hidden in the gloom and concern was a twitch of excitement, the sensation of the cold ledge of reality beneath the trembling fingers.

'Going hunting, are you?'

'What?'

'In those boots. Off to watch the fox get torn to pieces?'

It was hard to tell how young the man was. There was a tawny fuzz edging his pale chin. The carrier bag had sagged like an old woman's stockings round the ankles of the boots, so that their glabrous green tops sprouted naked and unashamed.

'No, why should I be?'

'Or fishing then. You look more like a hunting type, though. Either way, we're after you, don't you worry.' He blinked at me with his mild eyes. He might have been asking what the next stop was.

'Are you a saboteur?'

'Who said I was? Got to get off here. Just watch it, that's my advice.' He did not give me the time to say that this was one piece of advice I had taken to heart long ago.

When the grubby green train rattled into the little station, for some reason I took the wrong turning just as I had on my first visit and found myself on the other side of the river looking across at Minnow Island through the rain. There was no sign of life inside the house. Under the dark skies, it seemed a miserable shack shivering in the wind under the leafless willow branches. Why had I made the same mistake? There was something wilful about the error.

She was waiting on the far side of the footbridge, as before. In a sou'wester rainhat this time and boots, Christopher Robin effect but somehow not childish.

'They've searched the island already. It's not very big really. But you might see something they missed. A fresh eye.'

She led the way down the path past the locked chalets and the dripping chain-link fences with the withered tendrils of bindweed clinging to them. The air was grey and steamy, the rain coming down harder. I looked at the blank shed-doors, jaunty lime-green and blush-pink, desolate now.

'They've been through the sheds, have they?'

'But they're all locked.'

'One could have been unlocked and he gone in it, to shelter from the rain perhaps and then it got locked by mistake.'

'Do you believe that?' she said.

'No. But they ought to look.'

'They still think he's gone off with a woman. Anyway it's difficult because half the people here disappear in the winter. I think some of them are on the run.'

There was still that calmness about her, which might have made the police think she was not much bothered. She said, 'Excuse me' and held out a photograph to a woman coming towards us, and no one would have guessed she had been crying.

'No, I'm afraid not, I mean, I know the face but I haven't seen him recently. Your father, is he? I heard something about it, what do the police say? Never there when you need them, are they? Mind if I take another look?'

This time she gave the photograph a lingering, almost sensuous gaze, not like her first hasty embarrassed glance.

'Nice-looking isn't he, yes, I've seen him quite often now I come to think about it but not for quite a few weeks now.'

She had a shopping bag in one hand and some stuff for the cleaners under the other arm, but she seemed reluctant to move on. My impatience turned into a lurching, sickening apprehension that he was certainly dead, and almost certainly very close to us, perhaps within touching distance. The rain's chill fingers tapped on my shoulder as though they were his. I turned aside to hop over a low fence and try the door of a wooden shed. Locked of course, but there was enough slack on the chain to open the door an inch or two and peer in: an old mower, a folded-up garden seat.

The woman stood startled, no doubt about to say something about trespassing, but then Helen snapped open the garden gate of the nearest chalet and began banging on the door and, when there was no answer, pressing her face to the little porthole window. I hopped over into the next garden on my side, not bothering to go back to the path. The shed here was bigger, more like a garage, made of creosoted planks with an asphalt roof. The catch on this one was loose and I yanked it off with one tug. Inside there was a rickety workbench and tools and bits of wood piled up any old how – a painful reminder of the sweet order of Martin Hardress's workshop, but that was all there was. As I closed the twanging aluminium door behind me and tried to make the catch look as if it had come off of its own accord, I heard Helen behind me cracking on to the next chalet. We were driven on by a shared frenzy, she by a kind of terror that was almost exuberant, and, well, I didn't know quite what I was doing, except that it seemed necessary to be ruthlessly active, though why this would help it was impossible to say, still less why I had this feeling that Hardress was so close to us at that moment.

The woman stood still on the path, her mouth open but never quite able to form the words 'You can't do that'.

On we went down the path banging doors, trying windows, lifting up tarpaulins. Eventually we came to the river bank. The path was churned up into deep mud and I remembered about the boots in the carrier bag which had been flapping and niggling at my calves as we ran along.

'Oh no, you're not going to try the river,' she said, as I stopped and put on the boots.

'It's just the mud.' I waved a vague helpless hand at the morass which led along the bank to the bungalow hidden in the dripping trees.

'The mud,' she repeated with listless contempt, then fell into my arms and had a proper cry. We said nothing but gave up the silly search there and then and slithered along the path. The police had promised to start a full-scale operation by the weekend, Min said. The superintendent would be there, and possibly divers although they were on another job at present. February was always a busy time.

But the police search came up with nothing either, and that seemed like a score to Martin who, wherever he was, would obviously prefer not to be found.

It was four weeks, more perhaps, before a boy and his dog scrabbling in the undergrowth on Leith Hill found him. The dog was a half-dachshund, they told her, an enterprising mongrel combining wriggle and tenacity, which was why he was the only dog to penetrate the thicket of box and holly and bramble half a mile from the nearest path. Not that even the paths were much frequented now, it being a raw March and a thin wind coming up the gully which was narrow though it had a great view. I could see most of Surrey, a cold grey-blue shimmer stretching to the curve of the earth.

'That's not the Thames, is it? I was wondering if we could see Minnow Island from here.'

'No, we're facing the other way. Anyway, you couldn't because of the South London hills. For a scientist you don't seem to know much geography.'

She had insisted on taking me. She wanted someone to come with her, as a witness. He wasn't there any more. As soon as they had found him, they had cut him down and manhandled – the right sort of verb in the circumstances – him down the hill to the car-park by the Wishing Well café which was as close as the police van could come. The coroner was a little testy about this and complained that the usual scene-of-incident drill had been skipped. There were no photographs taken, no reliable sketch maps made. Helen thought that even the police had been too horrified to leave him there above them with his scuffed sneakers tangled in the tops of the sodden bushes. But it was not hard to imagine his blackened face and lolling tongue and the thin wind keening around his rotting skinny body, the unseeing eyes staring out over the Home Counties.

'That branch up there it must be, you can see where the wire has rubbed.'

'How did he get up there?'

'Oh he showed me the trick of it once, he showed me a lot of funny things. How to hang yourself without having to stand on a chair and kick it away. Helpful hints for dutiful daughters. You make a kind of rudimentary pulley and then a running noose on the other rope. You need two ropes.'

'You didn't have to come,' I said.

'Yes I did. You've got to see everything.'

She wriggled through a place where the brambles had not yet choked the box bushes, perhaps the place where the dog had got through, there wasn't that much difference in size between them. Her fair hair, short as it was, snagged on the brambles and she had to disentangle it with her free hand. The other hand held the posy she had picked from the garden, not much to be had at that time: a few wet narcissi and the scant white blossoms of some shrub that smelled of disinfectant. Not snowdrops, snowdrops were bad luck in a bunch, though it was difficult to visualise much more bad luck.

She came back without the posy.

'I left it at the foot of the tree. Thanks for coming.'

Going to Leith Hill wasn't only like a Sunday visit to the cemetery to lay flowers, though it was that obviously. There was also some kind of dedication in it, a commitment to carry on her father's — what? Not work exactly, he seemed to work only to earn money or to fill in time. To carry on his impatience is the best way I can describe it, his serious impatience. It was the word he had used too. Impatience is a virtue, he had said.

She had rented a ground floor in Fulham, a little red-brick house which was all bay window and at the back a patch of garden with a few cabbage stalks, running down to the District Line. Upstairs there was an old lady, a controlled tenant whose rent was still reckoned in shillings, but I don't think I ever saw her properly. A faint scurrying overhead, a glimpse of carpet slippers already almost out of sight on the tiny half-landing, that was all. Perhaps she thought if she was too visible they would put her rent up. But then it was a quiet place generally. Even the trains scarcely rattled the window although they were so close, perhaps because the track was on a high grassy embankment.

'Does sound rise, like hot air?' I asked.

'What a silly question,' Helen said.

'You don't know the answer, do you?' I persisted.

She laughed.

She was sitting cross-legged on a little rag rug in violent reds and greens, which her mother had made, having given up the tapestries because they reminded her of Martin. With a bent wire fork in her left hand, Helen was idly toasting a slice of bread. There was a toaster but the element had broken. On the rickety table was a pile of science books – mostly about nutrition, food hygiene and other subjects connected with her thesis – and butter in a blue-and-white striped dish with plates to match, and Tiptree's jams, and a sponge cake which her mother must have brought up from Minnow Island on her weekly visit to see Helen and take in an exhibition to cheer herself up. I too had taken to dropping in on the way from work. At the time it didn't occur to me that Helen's place was then the nearest thing I knew to a home (my father was still alive, but visits to him had their tensions).

'You will come again, won't you?'

'Come where? Here?'

'No, idiot, to Leith Hill.'

'Do you really want to, isn't it too painful?'

'Well, I don't want him to be forgotten. And I can't exactly go to the crem.'

'Surely when you go home, you must be reminded of him all the time?'

'That's different. I want to pay my tribute, is that the right word?

And you've got the Morris Minor, and otherwise it's two changes and then a bus.'

So we set off again in the little black car with the maroon folding hood.

It was a cold day but we both preferred to have the hood down, so we must have looked a cheerful couple, both pink-cheeked, her golden hair swept in the wind as we drove along the South Circular, and I thought how odd our mission would have seemed to other people if they had known, but then no doubt plenty of them would be on odd errands too.

I parked the car at the Wishing Well café, and we walked up the path that led diagonally across the hill with the great grey-blue view of the downs unfolding as the slope turned away to the north. Then we stopped to catch our breath before the last steep climb, off the path proper up a muddy sheep-scratching to the little thicket of box and bramble and the tree half-hidden in the middle. It was a sycamore. I was aware of our feet scrunching on the withered leaves, smaller here than the leaves on the sycamores in the valley because the wind had stopped the tree growing. Now that I looked at the upper branches, they seemed hardly high enough to hang yourself from, but then he had been no height at all, only an inch or two taller than his daughter. This time she did not wriggle through the brambles, but simply placed the little bunch of flowers as near as she could get to the tree from the edge of the thicket, in a place where they would be out of the wind.

'Somebody's bound to pinch them,' she said, as we were going back down to the Wishing Well for tea.

'You don't mind that?'

'Not really. Perhaps it's better than them withering up there. You don't have to come again, you know.'

'I'll miss the tea.'

The Wishing Well was a dismal green prefab chalet on the edge of the beech wood. You wouldn't have expected them to serve fresh lightly browned scones with proper clotted cream and strawberry jam. The cream tea was a relief after the sound of the wind rattling the naked brambles. All the same, I don't think I could have borne to do it again. Later on, she would still go by herself but at much longer intervals, she told me, once or twice a year perhaps.

Anyway, in no time at all, the same day in fact, I had something else to think about, something which left me shuddering with humiliation, still does really, for the memory of one's own humiliations is bred to last.

The telephone was jangling as I was unlocking the door, the noise vibrating against the low ceiling as though trying to escape to some place it would be attended to.

'Where've you been?'

'Out, down to – well, with Helen in fact, to a place called Leith Hill to –'

'I've been calling for hours, I'm in London.'

'You do sound quite close.'

'Close, is that all you have to say?'

'No, no, I mean, that's great, I've only just got in.'

'Can you meet me tonight?'

'Yes, oh yes.'

'At the Sheridan, at eight? Just you.'

'Yes of course, who else do . . .' But she had already left me with the dead whirr.

Jane was standing just inside the door of the hotel room and opened it as soon as I touched the bell so that I staggered straight into her arms and the terrible twenty minutes began. Well, to be exact, the first five were glorious, everything I had dreamed of, the clothes falling off us, her fingers daring, clutching, stroking and the wonderful smell of lavender. All this had happened before in France but this time I knew there would be no holding back at the last. She was so direct this time, even harsh, in her words too, murmured, almost grunted, chivvying herself on. And when I abruptly failed, quite without warning, as though some connection had been switched off, she too growled to a halt like a car braking.

Even in my haze of wretchedness, I had room to be startled by how angry she was.

'Did you come here to humiliate me, deliberately, do you hate me that much?'

'No, no, please I'm sorry.'

'Or am I so disgusting that you can't bring yourself to do it?'

'No, I'm really sorry. I've just had –'

'You thought, I'll make that stupid old bitch pay for holding out on me.'

'No of course I didn't.'

'Well you can get the fuck out of here, and take your little prick to show that Miss Goldilocks of yours, it's more her size.'

She began crying as I put my clothes back on. When I was dressed, she embraced me in a blind, wild enfolding and muttered how sorry she was and I muttered how sorry I was and she told me to get out all the same because she was no good to anyone. Despite this clumsy patching up, the things she had said before did not go away. I shut the door behind me very gently as if I had committed a murder and did not want to attract attention.

If she had not lost her temper, possibly I would have written to her, told her what I had been doing that day, and how there was nothing between Helen and me, but the hurt was too raw and Jane too much to cope with.

So it was Helen I heard from next.

'Sorry to lean on you again. But this odd thing's been happening and I don't like to talk to Mum because she's still so upset about Dad. And the women at college would make the wrong sort of fuss.'

'What is it?'

'Two or three nights a week something horrible gets delivered, a dead rabbit on the doorstep, or a nasty picture through the letterbox – a photo of Auschwitz or a horse being shot. You never know when exactly or which night it's going to be, so I lie awake almost all night, then while I'm asleep it comes. I'm going fairly crazy, as you can imagine.'

'You sound amazingly calm.'

'I can't help sounding calm, sometimes I wish I could. It's so boring having this voice that sounds as if I don't care about anything.'

'I could wait outside and see who it is.'

'How? He'd see you.'

'Not if I was sitting in a car.'

'Would you really? That would be fantastic.'

There was also the possibility that it might make me feel less useless. For the first time in weeks, life seemed to have regained its savour. I bought a sleeping bag from the army surplus stores, checked whether the old thermos leaked and bought a new one when I found it did. Thick socks were important, Helen thought. She offered to share the vigil, but it seemed necessary that she should return home in the normal way, perhaps show herself at the window and turn out the light, in case the pervert liked to watch these things first before depositing his evil gift.

The first night, a moonlit Wednesday, it was impossible to find a parking space within a hundred yards of her front door.

'And I can't see round the corner either, whichever way I face.'

'I'll lend you a hand mirror.'

So I sat at the end of the darkened street holding up the mirror across the passenger seat. Sometimes the moonlight caught it and the empty street took on a dreamlike quality. Sometimes as I rested my weary arm, I caught sight of my own tired panicky face, like an animal that has been chased to the edge of a cliff. But nothing happened.

The next night I fell fast asleep almost as soon as I took up position.

'In fact, you've been wasting your time,' Helen said. 'I've been looking back in my diary and it only happens on Monday and Friday, so we're due for one tonight.'

That night I parked the car early and then took Helen out for an Italian meal. We sat silent most of the time, like an old married couple. Then she went back on her own, and I had another glass of wine and followed half an hour later. The night was dark, with rain at about midnight and the trees dripping on the car roofs after the rain had stopped.

Just after three-fifteen, a small man in a raincoat walked along the pavement on Helen's side with brisk skippy little steps. He went fifty yards past her front door, then turned round and came back again. He looked both ways and began to go up Helen's steps. I reached him just as he was turning round after leaving something wrapped in newspaper on the doormat. He wriggled a bit as I grabbed him by the hem of his raincoat which flapped open to reveal some kind of greyish uniform.

'Let me go.'

'What are you doing that for?'

'Doing what for?'

'Leaving that thing on the doormat.'

'It's nothing to do with me.'

'I saw you put it there.'

It was about now, a minute or so after grabbing him, that I realised it was a chauffeur's uniform he was wearing and in the same instant I realised whose chauffeur he was.

'No you didn't. I was just looking to see what it was.'

'Did somebody make you do it?'

'You're her boyfriend, aren't you? That's what it's all about.'

'Who paid you?'

'Nobody paid me.'

'Was it a woman – a woman with her hair tied back?'

'Well, if you know so much, why do you ask?'

'Look, please don't do it again, she won't know you haven't done it. Just don't, that's all. I promise I won't –' but before he could hear my stammering offer of immunity, he had shaken free of my grip and was off down the street, the soles of his polished shoes slapping the pavement in the silent dawn.

I bent down and picked up the package on the doormat. Inside the rolled newspaper were some pieces of offal already leaking through the paper and smelling vile. I put them in the dustbin and rang Helen's bell and explained.

'Why do people do such things?'

'It is peculiar, I agree. How do you say to someone, here's this disgusting bit of tripe or whatever, go and leave it outside this address after midnight and don't let it drip on the seat? Still, I expect he's paid pretty well.'

'I didn't mean him, I meant her,' she said. 'Even if she had any cause to be jealous, how would it help? If I really was going out with you, it wouldn't frighten me off. The opposite, I think. In fact it'd be more likely to scare you off her, wouldn't it?'

She looked at me, not accusingly, for there was nothing to accuse me of, but in a musing hypothetical way.

My mind had drifted a little, to fix on the little rat-faced chauffeur, now presumably half-way home, probably wondering what he should say to Jane the next morning: had a bit of bother last night, madam, I would advise desisting from this course. For some reason, my imagination gave him a Jeeves-style voice although in reality he spoke old-fashioned flat cockney.

'*Would* it scare you off?' Helen repeated the question.

'Well, it certainly wouldn't make me any keener to see her again,' I said. 'Being mad isn't attractive, is it? That's the sad thing about it. You can be much worse things, like cruel, and that can make you more attractive, but not mad.'

'So you think she's just mad, do you? Did you think she was just mad when you were, uh, working for her? When she was all over you, did you think this is a madwoman assaulting me?'

Helen was cool but friendly, like a doctor talking me through my symptoms.

'No, not at all, well, I suppose I wasn't what you might call thinking much. I was overwhelmed really.'

'Poor you' – now there was a sardonic edge – 'overwhelmed by a woman half your size and twice your age.'

I was suddenly depressed by Helen's contempt. She didn't seem to see that it was really quite easy to go mad.

'Anyway,' Helen said, 'what exactly did she see in you? I mean, you're quite tall, but otherwise . . .'

'She said I had white teeth.'

Helen jumped up from the armchair she had been sitting sideways on and clasped my jaw firmly to pull it open, like someone checking a horse's age.

'White-ish,' she said.

'I think she was, well, I suppose rather lonely somehow.'

'Spoilt is the word you're groping for. Had everything done for her since she was nought. Never had to worry about where the next dress or sports car was coming from, or come to that, boyfriend. I bet she expected them to queue up, so she could moan about never finding true love. Then she could have a breakdown and go to a shrink and be all anguished and interesting. They're all the same underneath.'

'Who are?'

'The rich.'

'How the same?'

'Oh smarmy and considerate when you first meet them – except the ones who are openly shitty of course – but that's only the surface, or the opening gambit. When it comes to it, all they're doing is deciding what they want and then demanding it and usually getting it, sometimes in the nicest possible way, but usually not, specially not if they're meeting any resistance.'

'All of them?'

'All the ones I've met which isn't many, not compared to your vast acquaintance. Certainly all the ones at "the Ville".' She gave the phrase inverted commas as big as mudguards.

'The rich are never idle when they're feathering their nests.'

'Mm, must be a quote. Who said it?'

'My friend Moonman.'

'Oh you mean the one who does that funny magazine? What's he like? Is he a laugh?'

She brightened at the mention of Moonman (Gerald to his mother I dare say, but nobody else). This surprised me as I hadn't put her down as a reader of *Frag*, which had just started and was then full of japes and jollities, not yet having acquired the serious satirical purpose indicated by its title – the word GIs in Vietnam used for shooting an unpopular officer in the back.

'No, not a laugh really. He's solemn and strange like a dodgy sort of priest, except he's an atheist like you.'

'I think I'd admire him, admire what he's done, I mean, starting something.'

'You like *Frag*?'

'Haven't read it yet. But it's a good thing it's around, don't you think?'

She stopped and smiled and I realised how seldom she asked for my opinion or even asked to have hers confirmed. I didn't mind that. She seemed like someone who ought to have opinions. The opinions wouldn't need to be ferocious or dazzlingly original. Helen was just opinionated, if you could use that word without being offensive. Anyway it gave me pleasure to hear her give them an airing. It was like overhearing someone with a good voice start singing without much thought of who might be listening. You didn't want to break the spell by starting up yourself.

'Why are you staring at me like that?'

'Was I? I'm afraid that's what happens to my face when my mind wanders. It freezes.'

'Well, don't let it, or it'll get slapped. It's rude to stare, especially when I'm giving you the benefit of my views. Anyway, I can stare back. There, isn't that disconcerting?'

'Yes,' I said.

'That's what you look like.'

'Sorry.'

But her stare was not really disconcerting. There was something quizzical, even unconvincing about it as though she had just told an obvious lie and was daring you to challenge her.

'Oh all right then.' She came towards me and gave me a big luscious kiss on the mouth. A fraction later, no more than a couple of seconds, she placed my hand on her left breast, firmly so that I could feel the lace of the bra through her shirt.

Outside, a delivery van changed gear on the corner and the rain was dripping on to some flat roof now and then, erratically as though a person thinking of something else was idly playing a hose upon the asphalt. And behind that the gentle unappeased murmur of London at night. My hand began to stroke her, somehow remotely as though it was burrowing of its own accord.

'No,' she said. 'Not now. It's been too much already tonight, don't you think?'

Written down, her words sound tentative, almost inquiring, but the way she said them was final. Not this night meant not any night, ever. Nobody wanted to prolong a duet with a Cherubino who was too late. If you were too slow to realise you were in love with someone until after she had just told you that you hadn't a hope in hell, then you deserved everything you didn't get. Perhaps if Jane hadn't – no, you couldn't blame other people for the opportunities you had missed. I should have fallen in love with Helen the moment I first saw her coming towards me on the beach. Could there be a 'should have' about such things? Yes there could and I should have.

'Anyway my life is complicated enough as it is,' she said.

'Yes,' I said, thinking that her life was probably quite simple, certainly the bit of it which didn't include me.

'But anyway, thanks again.'

Curiously her thanks, plain almost curt, affected me even more than the kiss, because they seemed to come from somewhere nearer her heart and what I liked most about her was that plainness. Right from when we first met, when she accused me of looking down on people who did science, that was what had got to me, the direct response which fell just short of being rough though it was challenging in a friendly way, like a stick tossed for a dog to run after. That, and how fair her hair was.

'Come and see me at Woodies.'

'What?'

'The Woodland Institute of Food Science, place I'm doing my training at.'

Woodies and Padders

There was a man crying by the gatepost. Not convulsive sobs, just crying quietly like a drizzle that keeps on all day. He looked up at me and I could see the tears on his cheeks and running on to his frayed collar. He raised his hand to me in salutation, then checked it half-way as though someone had told him not to.

'There's a man crying at your gate,' I told the man in uniform standing by the glass door of the little domed building.

'He'll be from next door. They often cry when they let them out. This place used to be part of it, still is, if you ask me. When they talk about Woodies down the pub, it's the funny farm they mean, not us.'

I looked at the brown door-plate behind him which had WOODLAND INSTITUTE OF FOOD SCIENCE in cream lettering, then under it a couple of other names painted out.

'Proper madhouse here, too,' he went on. 'Who did you want to see?'

'Helen Hardress.'

'Ooh you lucky man.' The porter or whatever he was, a slight austere figure in sky-blue uniform who didn't look at you when he spoke, gazed up at the sky, standing with his hands clasped behind his back like an airman in a British war picture. The huts attached to the little building which must once have been the hospital's sports pavilion had a wartime look too. Perhaps the whole place had been some hush-hush research establishment for the duration before becoming a hospital again.

The porter went to look for Helen. I peered through the big window at the dripping trees which came close enough to brush the flat tops of the huts. Beyond the huts some kind of boiler house or laundry was emitting steam from an old brick chimney. The steam was swallowed by the mist so quickly that I wondered whether it wasn't an illusion and there was nothing coming out of the chimney at all.

'Here's your boyfriend, Helen. I've told him he's got to behave himself on company premises.'

'Piss off, Dave,' she said.

'Going down Trotter's, are you? Mine's a pint.'

'Get it yourself then,' Helen said, as she opened the glass door and let in the damp air and a little whoosh of leaves.

At the end of the short avenue of scrubby sycamores, fifty yards long at most, the crying man was waiting, still crying.

'And how are you today?' Helen asked.

'Very well,' said the crying man, 'very well indeed.' He had a light voice, like the way people talk in old musical comedies. When he spoke, you wouldn't have known he had been crying at all.

'Is he all right there?'

'That's where he likes being. The nurse comes and keeps an eye on him now and then but he won't go back to the hospital till dark.'

She had to shout the last words because the traffic was so noisy. The little avenue opened straight on to a bit of the North Circular where the lorries were changing down so they could slalom through the next roundabout, then jamming on the brakes when they found they couldn't. At the roundabout we went off to the left and crunched across the broken tarmac of a huge car-park, almost empty. Behind the car-park there was a field with the mist still breathing through the thistles and a couple of shaggy ponies cropping the grey ectoplasmic skeins. At the end of the car-park stood a big half-timbered pub with its lights on, the Jolly Highwayman, with a creaking sign depicting some olden footpad of the North Circular.

'But what do you actually do – two ploughmans please, yes, and a pint of bitter and a half of lager – what's the lab for?'

'We test things, like how much preservative do you need to put in to make some pickle or ice-cream last x months. Or how little you need, to be more precise.'

'Couldn't they cut out the additives entirely?'

'I knew you'd say that. Have you got any idea how many people die of food poisoning each year? Because that's what happens if you don't put in any preservatives. Stupid people go on eating it long after the sell-by date. That's the trouble with your marvellous organically grown produce. It just goes off.'

'I didn't say anything about organically grown produce.'

'No, but that's what people like you think. Just because Woodies is funded by a company which happens to make a profit, you –'

'Oh,' I said, 'I thought it was a government thing, I didn't realise it –'

'It's Swiss,' she said firmly.

'How are you today, young lady? Mind if I park myself here' – but he was already sitting down, this man, thirtyish, narrow-faced, dark and pale, could have worked for an undertaker's, had a huge crevice in his forehead as though some small meteorite had dented it. 'Still poisoning the populace, are we?' He grabbed my hand across Helen's lap, kissing her lightly on the cheek as he leant across. 'Don't think I've had the pleasure. Tolly d'Amico, with an apostrophe, all the way from sunny Italy by way of Trotter's Corner. Tolly, short for Tolomeo, Ptolemy to you lot.' When he smiled, he didn't look like an undertaker's mute at all, or only an undertaker's mute off duty having a quick cigarette behind the hearse and sharing a macabre joke with his colleagues.

'Didn't think you'd be in so early', said Helen.

'Thought you were safe, did you? Don't worry, Tolly always gets the girl in the end. What's your line then, mate?'

'I'm in the civil service.'

'Tax, customs, anything of that type?'

'No, no.'

'Thank God for that then, otherwise we might have had a conflict of interest.'

'So what do you do?'

'What don't I do? What would you say I did, Helen my love? How would you describe my occupation?'

She laughed kindly but without enthusiasm. 'Oh he's a sort of villain.'

'A. sort. of. villain. Oh thank you *very* much. That's all the gratitude I get for all that lager not to mention those cherry brandies I've poured down you.'

'All right then, you say.'

'I am a trader, my love, that's what I am.'

'Same thing,' she said.

'Same thing? You mock the ancient calling that has made this country great. This country is a nation of traders, isn't that right, sir? Napoleon said it shortly after he captured the Balls Pond Road. Now the moment you've all been waiting for, it's my round, comes up every ten years so don't miss your golden opportunity.'

She pushed out her glass for a refill. How easy she was anywhere, with anyone. Yet she didn't put herself out at all. Sometimes you had the feeling that she wasn't much impressed by people. She clocked in who they were and what their line was, but they didn't make much impression on her. That was what put men on their mettle, especially the men who were used to making an impression.

'And you?' She turned to me for the first time. There was quite a queue at the bar now and Tolly d'Amico was at the back of it. 'What are you doing?'

'You mean, at the office – it's too boring to –'

'No I mean, outside. What's your life, who are you seeing?'

She enquired calmly, almost as though it were her professional duty to put such questions. Yet the questions touched me greatly, touched me more perhaps because she didn't love me and never would and realised that I knew this but that it didn't stop me hankering. What she did make me realise was how lonely and shut up in myself I had become. It was in scenes that should have been brimming with warmth and intimacy – squashed on a sofa at a party, three-quarters drunk – that the desolation visited me most sharply. Sitting at my desk or trudging down a street in pouring rain, I was better protected against the brusque onrush of despair.

This discovery had led me to seek out places where my own melancholy would be somehow muffled, outgloomed, by a kind of atmospheric inoculation. Taking a short cut home from Stamford Bridge, I found myself following part of the crowd through the gates of the Brompton Cemetery. As our glum cortège (the team had lost to Derby County) padded through the sodden leaves, I paused by the monument to Sir Augustus Harris, manager of the Drury Lane Theatre, with the sorrowing figure of a woman carrying a wreath looking like she had just flunked her audition. Then a tomb with a colossal white lion on it which was John Jackson, champion pugilist of all England, friend and sparring partner of Byron. Gentleman Jackson. He could lift half a ton, write his own name with a six-stone weight attached to his little finger. The most perfectly proportioned man who ever lived. Statue erected by public subscription.

So I had wandered, on that afternoon and others, through these avenues peopled by dead merchants and their unfailingly worthy and charitable consorts, by monuments to acrobats and music-hall stars and singers – Richard Tauber and his melting tenor voice finished up there. Then a weird ambition seized me to visit the other 'hygienic cemeteries' which had been built around the city's skirts to scoop up the swelling population of Victorian London – Abney Park with its Egyptian gates, Nunhead and Norwood, the great rolling expanse of Kensal Green, the precipitous dark avenues of Highgate with their sudden steepling panoramas that took my breath away, and, dimmest and saddest of all, the obscure tumultuous deathscape of Tower Hamlets cemetery. There was slum crowding even in the afterlife. As I passed through the little lodge in Southern Grove – nothing less grovelike, less southern – I came upon a spectacular scene of frozen mourning, tombstones jostling against one another at every height and angle, extended from the earth not so much by the prospect of some Stanley Spencer-style resurrection as by the pressure of the noxious gases building up below. Here I was happy.

Then the fever really took hold of me and I had to see other cemeteries too. Bunhill Fields, of course, with Bunyan and Defoe and all the other great Dissenters, and the Tottenham Garden of Peace, then the Jewish burial grounds, Kingsbury Road, where all the Reform Jews were buried because the Orthodox wouldn't lie alongside them, and the Spanish and Portuguese Jews down the Mile End Road, and the jewellers and bookies up at West Ham. And I kept a little notebook for epitaphs and oddities like the one to George Cruikshank in Kensal Green about how he had struggled for the cause of temperance for forty years, or the one to the champion rower Robert Coombes with his boat and his Doggett's Coat and Badge thrown over the keel and the legend 'Fare thee well my trim-built wherry, oars, coat and badge, farewell'.

Some, not all of this I described to Helen and Tolly d'Amico.

'They must be very picturesque, those places. You want to know where they bury us lot? As far away as possible. We had to go out to Ilford to find a plot for our Auntie Elsa. Not like in Italy, wonderful cemeteries they have there, beautiful family chapels with your own key, so you can be private, have a picnic of a Sunday. Now tell me something, Gus, you did say your name was Gus, we like to have pictures of the deceased on the tombstone, a photograph, or something to jog your memory. You don't do that, do you? Now why is that?'

'Don't know,' I said. 'It's odd. We do for famous people, sculptures not photographs, but it's the same principle. But for ordinary people we don't, perhaps we –'

It had been in my mind to say something feeble about how perhaps we were less keen to be reminded of our nearest and dearest when I became aware of Helen's frosty expression.

'I think they're horrible places, cemeteries,' she said.

'Well, I suppose that's the point of them really, to give you a shiver of mortality. They're meant to be horrible.'

'And you crawling around them all day, that's just creepy. You're sort of exploiting other people's grief – no, not exploiting it, wallowing in it.'

'I suppose so but –'

'Anyway, they're a disgusting waste of money. Think of what you could do with the land. In the train you go past acres and acres of those places with their fake greenery and their grotty little chapels when it could be green fields or hospitals or housing, I don't mind which.'

Tolly said soothingly: 'But Helen my love, if the family wants to grieve –'

'It's all sentimental rubbish, so undertakers can screw gullible people when they're defenceless. I'd like to see every one of them dug up.'

'You can't stop people believing in the hereafter, my love.'

'Yes you can. Or if you can't, you should bloody well try. I'm going to the loo.'

Helen got up. She seemed to be shivering, or perhaps she was simply shrugging on her coat as she clambered over my legs, but there was no mistaking her rage.

'I like women like that, not afraid to give you the benefit of their opinion,' Tolly said. 'But perhaps you hadn't seen her like that before, on her high horse with a force ten gale behind her.'

'No, I suppose not.'

'You wouldn't probably.'

'Why wouldn't I?'

'Dunno.'

He smiled, not unfriendly but a patronising touch about it, as though he had a perfectly clear idea of why I failed to provoke Helen's passion but was too nice-mannered to say so.

'Anyway, it was me who set her going then,' I said.

'That's true. She doesn't care to hear the D-word. It's something you don't talk about in polite society, like sex and money. Still, what else is there? Tell me something, what exactly do you think I do for a living?'

'You said, or she said.'

'Trader yes, but trader in what?'

'How should I know?'

'Have a guess.'

'Mm, something to do with ... no, I really don't know.'

'You were thinking, is it cars, or is it scrap metal, but you didn't like to say, did you?'

'Oh all right then, I give up.'

'Property.'

'Is that any more respectable?'

'No, it isn't, not after the activities of P. Rachman Esquire. He's a bad boy, that one.'

'Is that the business you're in, winkling and all that?'

'Certainly not, wouldn't touch it, much too dangerous, you never know when some old lady's going to have a son-in-law with violent habits. No, I'm in the mathematical end of the business, reversions, well it's more of an art than a science really, no malice in it at all, but what there is is lots of death about it, because half the time you're making an educated guess about how long some fellow's going to live and your guess needs to beat the actuary who's just going by what his slide-rule tells him. Ah, here we are.'

Helen came back, patting my shoulder as she clambered over me. Sat down, undid her coat, then took Tolly's hand which was resting limply on his knee and placed it on her thigh, just below the hem of her tight skirt which had ridden half-way up or more. Shoulder pat for me, high thigh for Tolly. Perhaps that was what each of us deserved.

'So I expect you go to church every Sunday, probably sing in the choir,' she persisted.

'I'm tone-deaf,' I said weakly.

'Ah so you *do* go to church.'

'Didn't say I did.'

'Didn't say you didn't.'

'Oh Helen, give over, stop persecuting the poor boy.'

'He can speak for himself, can't you Gus?'

She used my name purely as an offensive weapon. Like many other people.

'Short for Augustus is it then?' said Tolly trying a diversionary tack.

'No, Aldous.'

'Aldous, that's elegant. Family name is it?'

'No, it's after Aldous Huxley the writer' – only Tolly's forceps would have extracted such an admission.

'My namesake was into geography. Thought the world was flat like a dinner-plate. Some people say I take after him.'

'Ptolemy didn't think the earth was flat, he thought the earth was the centre of the universe, just like you think you are.'

'Ooh, back into the knife-box, Miss Einstein.'

'So why do you go?' she said. 'You can't really believe all that stuff. I mean, it's not even a question of science having exploded it. Most of it was quite unbelievable in the first place.'

'I haven't even admitted I go to church, let alone whether I believe in it, or what I believe in, if anything.'

'Surely one must follow from the other, doesn't it?'

Her lips were parted in a frozen kind of expression, not a smile exactly, more like the expression on a not very good statue, an angel designed to express ecstasy but the effect not coming off, so that the face seems uncertain, neutered of emotion. This, I was beginning to see, was the way she looked when she was angry and unwilling to show it.

'No, it doesn't follow,' I said.

'Why not? It's a total contradiction. If you go to a special place once a week and stand up and chant "I believe in such and such" and you don't believe in such and such, that's pure hypocrisy, I'm sorry, but there isn't any other word for it.'

'Why do you mind so much?'

'All right, unlike you I don't refuse to answer a simple question. Because my father brought me up to be an honest atheist, that's why.'

'Atheist or agnostic?' Tolly put in a surprise question. He was losing his temper too, and the meteorite crevice on his forehead seemed to be convulsing as though about to give birth to a tiny alien.

'Atheist.'

'How can you be so sure? You can't prove a negative.'

'If there are good reasons for not believing all the hypotheses so far advanced, man with a long white beard and that, then there are good reasons to call yourself an atheist, because there's no plausible hypothesis left to remain in doubt about. Of course, evidence could come along to prove anything that we can't now conceive of, like that pigs can fly, after all. But you wouldn't say you were an agnostic about flying pigs, would you?'

'So you have to either believe or not believe?'

'You either go to church or don't go to church, because you can't get up and say I sort of half-believe in Almighty God, and I'm in two minds about the Holy Ghost.'

'You seem to think I spend the whole time asking myself all these great questions.'

'You mean you avoid even thinking about them. That's worse still because that means you must know what the answers are and you just don't dare face up to them.'

'So you know all the answers.'

'So do you.'

'Do I?'

'Yes you fucking well do' – her voice louder and sharper now – 'you know perfectly well that God isn't even a question worth asking any more, the whole thing is –'

'Oy, turn it down a bit there, some people are trying to have a quiet conversation.'

With startling speed, Helen jumped up and twisted round, kneeling on the seat so that she was looking over into the next booth and, rather more quietly than she had spoken about God or the Holy Ghost, said:

'Well, you'd better go and have your conversation somewhere else then.'

'You're drunk, young lady.'

'You're ugly.'

'Look, I'm going to have to speak to the landlord.'

'See if I care.'

'Don't care was made to care.'

The other half of this conversation turned out to be a sturdy elderly midget in horn-rims who moved with some agility towards the bar.

'Time to go, folks,' Tolly said.

I knew how sad, not even sad, sad has dignity, how pathetic my outings every Sunday would look to an unsympathetic observer. For I did not seek out beautiful churches where the singing might be superb and even the sermon might be bearable for an intelligent modern person. That would be a cop-out. My preferred haunts were scruffy brick barns of the 1860s, their great eastern rumps hoisted to the traffic and their grotty, garbage-blown porches crouching amid the laurels in some desolate crescent where three-quarters of the residents were still in bed sleeping it off and the rest were out washing their cars. As for the clergymen – the Rev. Alan Dickholm BSc, priest-in-charge of St Aidan's (they were trying to close it down and wouldn't make him a rector), was typical: former research officer at Farnborough, whistling speech-defect no doubt contracted from excessive exposure to wind tunnels, his mind a pretty fair wind tunnel itself, sermons drawing on TV news stories, usually the items towards the end of the bulletin, the ones about pets and floods. Yet he stuck to King Edward's prayer book and King James's bible, both of which he read from very slowly and with a merciful absence of expression. So for me sitting in the pitchpine pew behind the pillars, listening to his slow whistling voice and the roar of the traffic behind him, a degree of serenity was achieved but not a serenity which could easily be explained to Helen.

After a year or two the bishop shut St Aidan's – an average congregation of fourteen was scarcely up to quota – and my custom had to be taken elsewhere. All Saints, Scuttle Alley, was an instant wash-out. Father Prout-Mahony, with his sweet squashy face and his belchy breath, had a bunch of virtues which might shortly waft him aloft if he didn't lay off the Jamesons, but clarity of diction was not among them. He gabbled through his Mass so quickly that even regulars found difficulty in keeping up with the responses. The next one I tried, Terry Briscoe, Your Parish Priest, as it said on the board outside St John's, Fakenham Gardens, wasn't too keen on 'taking' the service in a taking, authoritarian way and would sit in some remote corner of his church, accompanying the hymns on his electric guitar (perhaps he needed to be over there to be close to the power point), while selected children went up to the lectern to read prayers of their own composition. The assorted idiosyncrasies of these incumbents managed to provoke all my principal vices – snobbery, impatience, pedantry – without offering much in the way of balm until I happened upon the Rev. James Moonman.

His church, St Columba's, has gone now, its fabric so much deconsecrated hardcore beneath the dual carriageway, but when it was standing, St Col's was a dear little Victorian gothic box, with a miniature green spire, modelled on the Sainte-Chapelle according to the flyblown but exhaustive leaflet by the poor-box, and chocolate-and-blue tiles and a series of glowing windows all round the church telling the story of how the faith came to Iona: the mountains a sumptuous purple, the fields bright green and the saints stepping out of silver boats from an azure sea. Mr Moonman, very old, smelly and unkempt with a fringe of bristles along his jaw, read in a precise, old-fashioned voice with a peculiar snorting sign-off effect at the end of each passage, a sort of 'Haugh!', strangely pleasant. It was quiet in St Columba's. Mr Moonman's congregation made the average turn-out at St Aidan's feel like a football crowd. My fellow worshippers, mostly elderly women, sat well spaced out and made little or no noise, even when the prayer book instructed them to respond. When Mr Moonman went 'Give peace in our time, O Lord, haugh,' there came back only the most delicate of rustles, barely classifiable as human speech. Mr Moonman also made no effort to heat his church, so that even on a mild spring day there was a midwinter chill in the pews. And it is with a shiver – a pleasurable shiver – that I remember that sensation of utter coldness and peace experienced those Sunday mornings in St Columba's – the coldness deepening and entrenching the peace.

Belief didn't come into it at all, would have spoiled the effect.

Impossible to explain that to Helen. How could you sit there, I could hear her saying, if you didn't honestly believe? Impossible to convey that the words 'honestly believe' represented a state of mind that was beyond me, in fact not one that greatly appealed even if I had been capable of it. In some moods, to believe in anything – certainly not just the truths of religion – seemed to me a most peculiar ambition, which made me think of an argument that Scrannel had once elaborated.

We have been taught, he said, for several millennia that belief is something that comes naturally to us, that to have beliefs is part of a proper person's normal equipment. This conviction about the necessity of having convictions is so taken for granted that we do not stop to wonder whether it is odd, whether there may even be something a little touching, or touched, about it. Even the word itself betrays a certain poignancy: belief is originally, after all, only 'be lief', be dear, be lovable. So this word which is now employed to describe our grandest intellectual projects, about the origin, nature and destiny of the universe, is the same as that which we once used to describe our humblest, most intimate, most personal passions. We needed it then, not to state, quite coldly and impersonally, that such and such is the case, but rather to state that so-and-so is a darling, and we want to hug her, or of course him, and bind her to us for ever – which I cannot resist pointing out is what most scholars agree is the root word of religion, *religo*, I bind fast or moor. So religious belief simply means huggy hug. It is an old ambition, perhaps our oldest and a lovely one some think, to clasp the universe, to return to those comfortable moorings in the womb from which we were so rudely untied, but it isn't exactly what we think we are doing when we embark on our grand explanations of how the world came into being. How cool and objective we mean to sound, how hot our hearts.

There was another reason why St Col's drew me and held me. When I had first seen the board outside the church with the tiny lettering on a piece of paper rather ineptly pasted over some earlier inscription, announcing that the Rev. James Moonman MA was temporarily at the helm, I wondered whether it might be the same man who had been the vicar in the next-door village when I was a child, the father of Gerald Moonman the editor of *Frag* magazine and Lytton Strachey lookalike. The Moonmans of my childhood were said to be rich, by the standards of vicars anyway, but to keep chickens in their kitchen, or perhaps in the larder. I never got inside their house to test the truth of this but remember once biking past it and seeing Mrs Moonman standing on the gravel sweep in a large blue cloak like a nurse's and hitting her son deliberately about the face for refusing to get on a pony that was standing quite docile a few yards away. Moonman too was standing docile as the blue cloak swirled and another blow fell on his cheek. Delighted by the spectacle, I took my feet off the pedals and stood astride the bike on the verge the other side of the road. Moonman himself had turned his face to the skies and seemed seraphically indifferent to his mother's assault. He did not utter a word. Frightened of being caught snooping, I pedalled on.

The stooped elderly man in a cassock came out of the church and reaching the pavement looked up at the skies to inspect the weather. It was the seraphic indifference with which he turned his long face up to the lowering clouds that brought back to me the incident of Moonman and the pony. This was indeed Moonman's father, and the slow, even languid way he moved was like his son and so was the quickness of understanding which took you aback, so that you thought the languidness must be a pose to conceal some cunning plan rather than a natural physical attribute.

'Gus,' he said before I had a chance to say a word, 'what brings you here?'

'I was just passing.'

'Passing here? Well I suppose people do pass this way. There are pavements. I am standing in for a friend who is on a mission to convert the natives in Rhodesia. He returns next Christmas when he has converted them and I can then go back to Norfolk.'

'How is Mrs Moonman?'

'Dead, I am sorry to say. She was never the same after we had to sell the house. You remember Tussocks?'

'Yes of course.'

'We had to sell it. She entrusted all her money to a rogue and he spent it or lost it in some imprudent speculation, we were never quite sure which.'

'Do you see Gerald much?'

'He does not see me. He disapproves of me, you know, doesn't care for all this' – Mr Moonman waved his hand at the grimy brick pinnacles of St Col's and its mottled green spire on which a light drizzle was now falling, to which in proper Moonman fashion he paid no attention, his earlier interest in the weather now having disappeared.

'That's sad.'

'It is, although at my age there is a certain satisfaction in being disapproved of. Gerald distrusts people, you know, rather a useful gift if you intend to be a *journalist* – he gave the word three full syllables and a faintly French pronunciation – 'and if one is to distrust people one had better start with one's father, don't you think? He gets it from his mother, although of course in matters of money, in which I may say she was keenly interested, she was trusting to a fault. But then we all have our blind spots, in many ways they are our best spots, do you not think so? Being too perceptive can be a burden, though it is not a burden which my parishioners are often called upon to bear. But I still have Bobs.'

'Ah yes,' I said, at a loss. A faithful dog perhaps, or even the pony, though it would be old by now? Perhaps he kept the pony in the kitchen now that Mrs Moonman was no more. Or could Bobs be the last of his poultry, some mouldy cockerel chosen to accompany him from Norfolk?

'He's taking me to lunch at his club. Not something I look forward to as greatly as I ought. I am always delighted to see the dear boy, but – ah there he is now.'

A small red MG, not in its youth, the hood repaired with sticking plaster and a dent in its front bumper, came over the brow of the hill, quite a steep brow, and pulled up by the laurels. The young man who got out was unmistakably part of the Moonman range but an economy model, four or five inches shorter with a face squashed upwards to make room for an Adam's apple of memorable size to repose on a red-and-yellow cravat. The tweed jacket, green with a widely spaced brown check like the ground plan of the prairie states, grubby twill trousers and scuffed chestnut brogues completed an ensemble that must have been a planned riposte to Gerald Moonman's get-up – long beard, flowing black cloak, black boots, and a general air of belonging to some extreme Hassidic sect on bad terms with its rivals.

'Sorry, Dad, club's shut, so it'll have to be spag bol at the old Salerno.'

'What a pity,' said Mr Moonman looking cheerful – although like Gerald he never looked melancholy exactly, despite his costume and his languor. Rather, at moments of particular satisfaction, a lightness of being seemed to take hold of him, as though he might if he wished levitate, casually and with no fuss, and hover a couple of inches off the floor until his mood changed.

'The new chef's an absolute ace, he does amazing things with tarragon. Hallo, a blast from the past. Remember me, Baby Bobs?'

Nowhere in the files could I dredge up any recollection of a chubby younger brother.

'*Much* younger,' said Mr Moonman, as usual squinting effortlessly into my mind, 'Bobs would have been little more than a baby. An afterthought. A blessing of course,' he added after a pause.

Bobs was paying little attention, being already occupied in pulling back the MG's hood and pressing down the bits of sticky tape loosened by this manoeuvre.

'My dear Bobs, isn't it a little . . .'

'Don't be soft, Dad, it's almost stopped. A bit of air will give your tubes a good blow-through.'

'Air yes, but this' – he turned his palms to the sky, suggesting an incident in some parable.

Bobs did not answer but opened the passenger door and tipped his father into the low bucket seat roughly but not without affection. Mr Moonman's untidy grey hair, already lank-tressed from the rain, was smeared across his forehead and his spectacles were pushed half-off, his nose having caught the edge of the windscreen getting into the car. With his cassock twisted about him, he looked like the victim of some multiple pile-up wrapped in a blanket by the emergency services.

'So nice to have seen you again,' he said, 'do come to St Col's one Sunday if you care for that sort of thing.'

The little car achieved a few unconvincing revs before breaking out into a convulsive growl that reawakened all the life-enhancing uncertainties of early motoring.

The farewell smile Mr Moonman gave me, turning as best he could in the confines of his seat, kept me under his spell and drew me back to St Col's.

Even Bobs seemed to bathe in his father's glow a little, so that when he rang me up, his voice, which wasn't at all like his father's, being quick and yappy, not reflective or sonorous, still made me think of Mr Moonman shuddering with mock despair as Bobs put the MG into gear and they went off up the road in a spurt of mud and leaves and gravel.

'You seemed interested in cars,' Bobs said, 'I thought you might like to have a drink at the Clutch on guest night. There's usually some quite interesting chaps.'

'Did I?'

'Did you what?'

'Seem interested in cars.'

'You asked me whether I had the A model or the B.'

'Did I?'

'Oh well, perhaps it was somebody else. But come anyway.'

So I did, though I knew nothing about cars and cared less.

'You a member?' asked the voice on the intercom from the second floor in a bleak alley off Regent Street.

'No, I'm a guest of Mr Moonman's.'

'Who?'

'Moonman. M.O.O. –'

'I can spell. He's on the stop list. Hasn't paid his sub.'

'Well, is he in there?'

'Not if he hasn't subbed up, he can't be, can he.'

'Can I come in and wait for him then? It's cold out here.'

'Can't help that, mate, I didn't invent bloody November.'

'Well, if he does turn out to be up there, could you tell him I'm waiting down here.'

'Suit yourself.'

For the next five minutes I stared vacantly at the supercilious plaster mannequin wearing a silver fox stole in the furrier's window, then felt a slap between the shoulder-blades and turned round to face Bobs. He was wearing exactly the same outfit as on our first meeting, down to the cravat.

'You should have gone upstairs and had a drink on me.'

'They wouldn't let me in.'

'That's appalling. Have to speak to the secretary. Been a lot of complaints about Brad lately, I believe he's got wife trouble, but he oughtn't to take it out on the guests.'

His face under the street-light was pale and furrowed with concern – unlike his father or his brother, neither of whom ever showed anxiety, certainly not on behalf of anybody else.

I wondered whether this was the moment to alert Bobs to his subscription problem, but he produced a gold key out of his pocket and thrust it in the door with a flourish of his wrist, as though this wasn't an ordinary key but one which demanded a certain manly skill.

The walls of the stairs were painted with big black parallel lines wiggling round the corners in imitation of a Grand Prix circuit. Leaning out of spectator stands or crouching behind straw bales, there were caricatures of racing drivers, and other figures in the game – owners, commentators, engineers, drivers' wives or girlfriends, some of whom looked familiar but I couldn't put a name to. The doorway at the top said THE CLUTCH CLUB. Underneath, the same cartoonist had drawn a man with a moustache falling over with a chequered flag falling out of his outstretched hands.

'Full tonight,' Bobs murmured unnecessarily as he piloted me through the crowd. I had to admit, to my chagrin, that the place had a buzz. The men seemed on the whole rather small, Bobs's height or less, and dressed like him too, quite a few with RAF moustaches which looked stuck on. The women were mostly taller than the men, with beautiful white shoulders and short, spiky blonde hair and startled looks. Great cheerfulness, a sense of belonging to a fraternity that wasn't much interested in what the rest of the world thought of it.

'Let's get a bit of peace and quiet,' Bobs said leading me in the direction of a flashing red arrow with PIT LANE underneath it. Down a couple of steps, there was an area with tables where we took our drinks and sat down.

'You don't need to worry about the girls here.'

'How do you mean?'

'Well some places, I wouldn't touch them with a barge-pole or any other type of pole, if you know what I mean, but here ...'

'Oh good.'

'Clean, absolutely clean.'

'Good.'

'So don't mind me, you just go ahead.'

'How do they know for sure, I mean they don't, well, *inspect* ...'

'Christ man, it's not that sort of place. I just meant they're a nice sort of girl.'

'Ah yes, I see.'

These fine distinctions were beginning to befuddle me. The quick yapping of Bob's voice was not as irritating as what he said might suggest, because there was an unreal quality about it as though he was some alien agent flawlessly trained in accent and intonation but with no grasp of or perhaps even interest in the meaning of the lines he had been fed. It was hard even to tell whether Bobs himself had approached these girls, except that he then said: 'I mean, it's not something I go in for now, not at all. It's more of a phase you go through in your first year, really, isn't it?'

First year of what, I wanted to ask, but then with that habit he seemed to have of answering the question you hadn't asked, he said: 'Not that I'm the university type, not academic at all. Gerry collared all the brains in our family. Unfortunately, brains was all we had after that chap walked off with Mumsy's money. Water under the bridge now, Dad's completely forgotten we ever had any cash.'

This, I noticed, like many other things Bobs threw out seemed to be not quite true, in fact not true at all. He also had a knack, second sight almost, for getting things wrong, even things you might expect him to know about. There was an easy impartiality about his wrongness which stepped up the impression not so much of him not being all there as not being all here, not least when he gave off the air of being in his element, like in the Clutch Club.

'She's something else, isn't she?'

'Who?'

'Her. Over there.'

He pointed to a cluster of habitués by the bar, tightly packed with their arms round one another's shoulders. I noticed that quite a few of the members had a way of gripping their friends like so many steering wheels. On the way through to the Pit Lane, one of them had given my shoulder-blades an amicable kneading before realising we were strangers and mumbling sorry.

Then the scrum parted and in the dim amber light a mop of blonde hair gave itself a brisk shake.

'There.'

'Oh yes, I know her.'

'You know her? How amazing.'

'We were nannies together, in France. She's called Helen.'

'Nannies? Fantastic.'

He was already off his velvet stool and moving towards the cluster at the bar which annoyed me, though there was no good reason for me not to go up to her. Had I been by myself I would have sat there several minutes longer, perhaps even until she was leaving, before making the approach. There would have been a sidelong pleasure in watching her toss her head and drink her drink without knowing that I was there. Had I always had these furtive tastes or were they growing on me as my life became more dull and solitary? Anyway I was the weird one and Bobs going up to say hallo instinctively without consulting me was being natural.

'Helen what?' he asked over his shoulder.

'Hardress.'

'Funny name,' he said, almost as he began introducing himself to her without waiting for me. 'Hallo, I'm Bobs Moonman, expect you've heard of my brother Gerald, he edits that magazine *Frag*, you probably think it's a bit of a rag, but people have heard of him and nobody's heard of me, anyway it's great to see you here. I was just having a drink with thingy here and I thought you two familiar faces ought to get reacquainted.'

'You,' she said to me. 'Well. I didn't know you were a racing driver.'

'I'm not, but then I didn't think you —'

'Tolly is, or was till he did his knee in.'

Coming forward out of the shadow, Tolly d'Amico exuded Sicilian melancholy. The amber light caught the crevice in his forehead so it now looked like a dark amulet.

'Only vintage cars, most of the drivers are twice as old as the motors.'

'He had an Alton Special. I bet you don't know what that is.'

'Nor did she until five minutes ago, when I showed her the picture. There.'

By holding the photograph up to the light, we could just make out a bulbous blue racing car with a younger smiling Tolly standing beside it holding his leather helmet. At the other end of the car there was a dark girl in a beret.

'Who's that lovely totty?' Bobs asked.

'My sister.'

'Go on, give us her phone number.'

'She died seven years ago.'

'Oh God, Bobs does it again. I am most dreadfully sorry.'

Tolly patted him on the shoulder. It was almost a caress, a gesture of solicitude which at once calmed Bobs.

'You never told me,' Helen said. 'How did she die?'

'Meningitis.'

'I wish you had told me.'

'Well, now I have' – but he said it with a gentle opening of his hands like a priest starting a blessing and Helen too became less agitated, though she went on looking at him in a puzzled way.

Bobs had recovered from his gaffe and was chatting to her, standing very close which she didn't seem to mind. He was also talking very quietly, all the yap gone out of his voice as though he had turned off some booster mechanism. I couldn't hear what they were saying and was irritated that I minded this.

'She is irresistible, isn't she?'

'Oh, Helen?' I temporised. We were standing, Tolly and I, by the heavy curtains at the end of the room, a yard or two from the rest of the group. How had we come there? Had the drinks been stronger than I thought, or had Bobs poured more of them down me? He was generous, solicitous as a host. Because he was so vexatious, it was hard to be properly grateful.

'You only have to look,' Tolly said. 'All the men – there.'

'Yes, you're right obviously. It's just when you've known someone for ages, you don't think of them as irresistible.'

'Don't you? Are you sure? Perhaps you prefer not to notice because it is almost embarrassing. I remember with my sister –'

'I'm so sorry about that.'

'No, no, it was long enough ago, I can talk about her now. My mother can't of course, but I can.'

It was plain that he couldn't really, and his grief began to unman me and my knees went wobbly and my eyes filled with futile tears. The heavy curtains enveloped us like mourning robes. The earthlings still chattering around the bar seemed miles away.

'How do you think it would take you, being like that?'

'Like what?' I mumbled.

'Irresistible. Like the other Helen.'

'What other Helen?'

'Helen of Troy. Don't they teach you anything in college?'

'Helen of Troy wouldn't have been like that.'

'No? What makes you so sure? Anyway, the point is, it would make you feel extraordinary, marked out by God.'

'Helen doesn't believe God's around to mark anyone out,' I said.

'By destiny then. You would feel chosen.'

'I suppose you would.'

'So you would be particular. You could take your pick, so you wouldn't give yourself to just anyone.'

'No, I suppose not.'

'But Helen isn't that way, not at all.'

Suddenly I was wide-awake.

'How do you mean?'

'I mean, she lets you do it, just like that.'

'Oh.'

'She enjoys it, but as far as I can see, it's no big deal to her. I don't mean she doesn't you know, or she seems to anyway, but she doesn't make a fuss about it.'

'Oh.' I couldn't think what else to say, my whole, what?, body, being, self was suffused with such a suffocating mixture of lust and humiliation.

'That surprises you? Of course it might be that she's hopelessly in love with me – they say it can be done – but I'm not a complete idiot, I can tell she isn't. She likes me all right, but that's about the limit of it. You've known her a long time. Have there been others?'

'Why don't you ask her?'

He looked at me not without pity.

'That's not a thing you ask a girl, that's an accusation.'

'Well, why do you want to know?'

'I want to find out if I'm right.'

'But if you do find out you're right, it will be upsetting, won't it?'

'Of course it will. But there are things you have to know even if getting the answer is going to be a grief.'

'Well, as it happens, I don't know the answer.'

'You sure?'

'Quite sure. I don't know the name of a single other lover of hers.'

He nodded, looked pleased but dubious, changed the subject, took me back to the rest of the group.

'What have you lot been nattering about over there? Women, I expect.' Bobs was flushed and full of himself.

Tolly d'Amico smiled and said nothing.

That was not something you could accuse Bobs of. He was a one-man information bureau, endlessly forthcoming on any subject you cared to mention and quite a few you didn't: masturbation in public schools, the date of the introduction of the overhead camshaft, the low cost of motor insurance in Denmark, his aversion to goat's cheese, the effect of the Six-Day War on petrol supplies, where he was standing when he heard about Mike Hawthorn being killed which he could remember as opposed to where he was when he heard about J.F.K. which he couldn't, recordings of 'Rock Around the Clock' not made by Bill Haley, the likely date for the introduction of decimal currency and its effect on the prospects of Britain going into the Common Market or the other way round, why Tammy Wynette was a greater singer than who was it now. I cannot recall all the subjects he touched on that evening and on the other evenings that followed.

Why did any other evenings follow, what weakness of will, what pathetic desire for company made me yield to his cheery call, always coming through at some awkward moment, just as the permanent secretary had come into our office and was asking how we were all getting on (I had joined the Department three months earlier)?

'Hi, who did you screw last night, what's the buzz on the Rialto, why don't we meet at the Cri sevenish?'

The Cri! Nobody had called that decayed pleasure palace by any such abbreviation since before World War One, nobody had even been to the place. But there were no inverted commas about Bobs. He had probably read the brochure about the Criterion in its golden years while munching the nuts and olives there with his manic esurience. Other people's slang, whether fashionable or hopelessly moth-eaten, stuck to him like burrs. He accepted every invitation that came his way, invitations that nobody else would have dreamed of accepting and that had nothing at all to do with him. From the Aetherius Society, Chelsea Town Hall, 8 p.m. – Why we can prove that Aliens have landed – Speaker Dr R.P. McKechnie, Refreshments; or the old Waltonians Choral Society, G & S night; or Britons Together, Methodist Central Hall; NATO our shield, General Sir Walter Walker, Admission Free; or Ethical Society cheese and wine evening, Conway Hall, all welcome. Happenings, Be-Ins, vintage car rallies, he went to them all. He had two kits, at least only two that I ever saw: (a) the green and brown jacket with the prairie-states pattern, grubby twills, brogues and the red-and-yellow cravat, the total effect like a down-at-heel Rupert Bear, which he wore for work and to go motor-racing; and (b) an oatmeal jersey with some brutal cable stitch and jeans of the bright blue colour that most people tried to wash out, which he wore for more way-out occasions. At an arts event in a deconsecrated Baptist chapel in the Polish bit of Hammersmith, I saw the jersey being ruined by a beaky-nosed girl with long black hair in a black leotard covered with spray paint entwining herself about him to some incongruously cheerful Beach Boys number while Bobs stood there with that seraphic Moonman look.

'Yes, I picked it up on the hall table at Padders, addressed to J. Devlin, not known at this address, so I snaffled it, might be fun, don't you think?'

This was an invitation to the Polish Dance Society Waltz Night at the Baltic Military Club, wasn't fun at all, couldn't possibly have been for two non-Poles who had no one to dance with and, speaking for myself, couldn't have waltzed if I had. Yet after an hour or so of some 500 per cent Polish vodka, Bobs picked up a stout Polish lady with hair piled high on her head, and whistled her round with some fluency.

'Only thing I can do better than my brother,' he said returning her gasping to her tall sombre mate. 'That, and talking.'

Sometimes he would make me meet him at Padders, his frowsty

second-floor flat in Padstow Mansions. When I rang the bell, even if I had come at just the time he said, he was always having a bath and would have to come down to open the door because the buzzer was broken. If he had a towel, it would fall off and his hairy white buttocks would be exposed as he hurried back up the stairs. Then he would turn round to explain why he was behind schedule and his frothy little genital cluster would bob at me. He had to hurry because the light on the landing only stayed on for a few niggardly seconds before needing to be pressed again, and so if he paused to chat, we would be plunged into dusty dark and the first thing I would see as the light came on again would be his naked bottom scampering on upstairs, white as chalk against the floral encrustations of the wallpaper.

I wondered why the other tenants hadn't bumped into him naked like this or if they had why they hadn't complained, but there was never anybody else on the stairs when I was there and the letters lying on the wooden ledge above the radiator in the hall didn't seem to change. You felt that the dust rising from the brown stair-carpet was the same dust that had filled your mouth and nostrils a month before as you gasped for breath on the landing. It was easy to press the wrong bell in the poor light – the Moonman inked in the No. 3 slot was almost illegible. But none of the others – Brotherton, da Silva, Mr G. Prem – ever answered. Nor were they the same as the names on the uncollected letters – R.P. Sawyer, Serena Bell and Miss J. Johnson. Perhaps they had all left Padstow Mansions years earlier or never lived there in the first place.

'Fantastic new hotel deal we've signed up in Fuengirola, Spanish lawyers gassing all day.'

These claims to be caught up in high negotiations didn't often trip from him. In fact he was almost secretive about his work at the travel agency, once coming close to implying that their contract with some governmental body had a hush-hush aspect.

'Oh it's because he's only a clerk,' Helen said. 'I mean, he's the person sitting behind the desk who makes you wait for hours and then gets the booking all wrong.'

'How do you know?'

'I walked past and looked through the window and there he was.'

'Didn't you go in?'

'No, I didn't quite like to.'

'But you do go out with him?'

'There's no *but* about it. I go out with him. Do you think I shouldn't just because he isn't the boss?'

'No, no, I wasn't thinking of that. It's just that he's ...'

'Such a bore,' she finished for me, 'yes, but you "go out" with him too, or so he says.'

'Well, he asks me.'

'Same with me,' Helen said. 'Asking gets you a long way, doesn't it?'

'Not the whole way. Or does it?'

'I don't answer that sort of question.'

She giggled.

Bobs became a shared secret between us, a joke which was more than just a joke and was somehow liberating – from what I don't know. He was our Puck, a half-cock sort of Puck, but none the less an importer of magic. It was better when the three of us did not go out together, because I could not help catching Helen's eye. In any case, the pleasure came from reporting not from experiencing an evening with Bobs which at the time was exhausting, often edgy. Our enthusiasm for his company was not widely shared. Strangers who ran into him would soon begin to find themselves disconcerted, not quite able to decide whether they were bored or irritated or amused, and on deciding that amused was not what they were would discover that it was too late, Bobs already had their telephone number or had found out where they worked or, worse still, had already lowered the boom, a phrase Helen and I had borrowed from him – 'one of these days the Stock Exchange is going to lower the boom on these inside deals' – and applied to his effortless, perhaps unconscious, technique of shepherding his victim into the corner of the room, then leaning across him or her, usually her, with his hand planted firmly on the opposite wall, which made escape impossible, especially because he was so short.

'Look, the boom's down.'

'You'll soon see the look of panic spreading across her face.'

'It always takes them a bit of time because they think Bobs is going to take his arm away and let them out.'

'Like any normal person would.'

'They don't realise he can stay in that position for hours.'

Tolly didn't care for Bobs's company – he had made that plain enough – but he cared even less for our skittish conversation about him.

'I suppose you'd rather we talked about you instead,' Helen said.

'No, no, I just don't like that kind of talk.' Tolly's voice, normally soft as fur, sharpened to a bark. He looked almost hurt. We had offended against an obscure sense of decency – at least it was obscure to us and he was in no mood to spell it out. His own brand of banter left his fundamental seriousness unaffected. But serious – was that the word for someone in his line of business? Perhaps seriousness was a trickier quality to pin down than it looked, Tolly d'Amico being more serious, by his own lights, perhaps by mine too, than the Rev. James Moonman, to name but one.

That was the last time I was to see Giovanni Tolomeo d'Amico for several years and it was not our happiest meeting. His presence was leaden, even mournful. Bobs was not the only topic he cut off in what seemed to us its prime, and I could not blame Helen for getting up abruptly and saying she thought she would get Bobs to drive her home. She had to make an early presentation to the ice-cream people in the morning. She didn't usually talk much about her work. We had teased her too much. There was something about the idea of it which sparked our fantasy. We imagined Helen bombarding vats of ketchup or cream cheese with a spray gun loaded with chemicals and the mixture then rising to an evil green froth, out of which strange misshapen creatures would clamber, probably flesh-eating and capable of devastating an entire postal district. At the back of the little pavilion didn't they keep hutches full of defenceless rabbits or beagles who would foam at the mouth and fall into contortions when she fed them her experimental compounds? No, she said, it wasn't like that at all. It was more a question of measuring qualities such as acidity, analysing chemical change over time, painstaking compilation of statistical data. There was scarcely any tasting involved at all, even by humans. That was done back at the various factories by panels of volunteers. In any case, working with chemicals your taste-buds soon became unreliable.

But even her serious answers only provoked more fantasies of her dulled taste-buds confusing things like caviar and tapioca, and so she soon learnt to say nothing at all. Referring to the ice-cream presentation must have been the only excuse she could think of to make a quick exit. Tolly jumped to his feet. 'I'll take you. You don't want to risk your life in that draughty old heap. He's a lousy driver anyway.'

'He's going my way and you're so grumpy tonight.'

'I can't help it if you two insist on talking such a load of cock.'

'I don't want a row, Tolly, I'm just going. Good-night. End of story.'

She was gone in a moment, with that unobtrusive quickness she had when her mind was made up.

Tolly kept me back for another drink. He sat with his head bowed like a mourner in a pew. His face looked heavier when downcast, the crevice in his forehead merging into his frown.

'You take these things pretty lightly, don't you, you people?'

'What things?'

'Love, relationships, life – they're just words to you lot.'

'No,' I said. 'What makes you think so? Just because Helen and I were having a crack about Bobs –'

'All right then,' he said, 'I don't know about you, I don't give a shit about you, but her – that's how she thinks.'

'Is it? How do you know?'

'Would you go off with him, if you really minded about me?'

'Go off with Bobs? She's only asked him to run her home because you're a bit ratty.'

'That's what you think, is it? Shows how much you notice.'

'Oh,' I said. 'Really, are you sure? *Bobs.*'

'Yes, Bawbs,' he said, mimicking my drawl.

'Well it's crazy,' I said, 'but even if it's true it doesn't prove she isn't serious, I mean a serious person, not necessarily serious about him. She may be sorry for him.'

'You think that's all right, do you? Going with someone because you're sorry for them?'

'Well it might be, I don't know.'

'No, you don't know. You don't know the half of it. You don't know anything about it at all.'

'No, I don't, I never pretended to. You brought the whole subject up.'

'Yes I did, and now I'm going to tell you.'

'Fine.'

'Listen, my grandfather came from Palermo in 1890, sweatshop in Saffron Hill, made straw hats, Henley Regatta and all that, his wife started a little deli over the other side of the Clerkenwell Road, both of them worked eighteen hours a day for sod all, straw-hat business went belly-up in 1914, no boaters in the trenches, deli staggered on, my dad took it over, chased the girls, so that went phut too. It wasn't fine then, before or since, and it isn't fine now.'

'I don't quite see how —'

'— this connects up? It connects up because when you have to fight each step of the way it teaches you to appreciate life and the facts of life are hard and it's the hardness gives you pride because you've earned it, however little it may be.'

'So your pride's hurt because —'

'Don't sound so amazed. Of course my pride's bloody hurt.'

'But if she happens to prefer Bobs, I know it's obscene, but —'

'Prefer? Who said anything about prefer?'

'I naturally assumed —'

His forehead was glistening and the tiny alien was making the crevice throb.

'She doesn't prefer Bobs, she includes him, she adds him to the list. Is that clear enough for you?'

'Oh I see.'

'And she doesn't mind telling me about him.'

'That's a bit much. You mean, all the details?'

'No, no, she's not like that. But if you ask her a question, she'll give you an answer.'

'Well, if the answer shocks you, you shouldn't have asked the question.'

'Of course it bloody shocks me. I mean a wimp like that especially when —'

'When what?'

I wasn't sure whether his hesitation was a theatrical pause or whether some scruple was detaining him.

'He can't get it up. I hadn't meant to say but she makes me so fucking miserable.'

'Oh,' I said, taken aback and also annoyed to find Bobs a fellow member of my fraternity. 'Isn't that a bit of a consolation to you?' I added, somewhat lamely.

'No it is not. She should get rid of him if he can't, can't be a proper man.' (Even Tolly found this sentiment a little too Sicilian to spit it out without hesitating.)

'Why? What's wrong with being kind to him? Perhaps she sees him as a challenge.'

'He's not a challenge. He's a disaster area and he shouldn't hang around if he can't cut the mustard. And she should have more pride than to let him.'

'Not to mention your pride.'

'You don't understand any of this, do you? You don't think pride matters.'

'I don't think it's the most important thing in life. In fact, I don't think it ought to be that important.'

'You're talking balls, you know that? Because underneath you're just as proud as I am, you're just too fucking proud to show it.'

Tolly stopped talking and laughed, not in a particularly friendly way, but rather to signify that he had run out of anger for the time being and was ready to let me go home.

He was right of course about my own pride, even I had enough self-knowledge to acknowledge that, but he could, I thought, have pushed his analysis one step further and turned it on to Helen. It wasn't because she lacked pride that she let Bobs hang around or had taken him on in the first place. And it surely wasn't that she wanted to clock up a record list of lovers either. That wasn't the kind of pride she had. But there was a variety of pride she did have, although it was hard to describe, and letting Bobs hang around was not unconnected with it. The fact of his being a non-performer and this not putting her off him had something to do with it too. Suppose, though, Bobs had been someone quite different, someone brutal and oppressively virile who insisted on doing something unpleasant and painful to her, she would be just as long-suffering, just as accommodating. Most people would describe that pattern of behaviour as promiscuous, and you would have expected Tolly d'Amico to take that line. Certainly if he had thought like this, he wouldn't have hesitated to use the word, or a ruder one. But he hadn't. Rather, part of his anger seemed to be inflamed by puzzlement as to how to describe what she was up to. He wasn't just angry to discover Bobs as a rival, though that was enough to enrage anyone, he was angry because she was so serene about it. Her openness reduced Tolly and Bobs to the same level. They were like so many volunteers for a research project, into the common cold, say, having chosen to contract this non-life-threatening complaint and then being nursed through all their coughs and snuffles and thanked at the end of it, but none of them could hope to be given special treatment. Her patients would be grateful to have found a refuge from the chaos and unkindness of the world, but they had no right to resent that the patient in the next bed had found the same refuge, though of course they did resent it like hell. How had I got tangled up with these awkward characters with their peculiar secrets and desires? Did other people feel so ill at ease with what the outside world would have assumed to be their friends? When I watched other people in the street or in a bar, they seemed to fit together, even when they were quarrelling. I could imagine their unspoken sense of intimacy, of being right for each other.

'Look, could you come round?'
  'Come round where? I'm not going to the Clutch again, it's a –'
  'No, no, come round now, to the office,' Bobs squawked.
  'Your office? But it's miles away and I've got to –'
  I was about to invent some important meeting, but Bobs's voice was so frantic that I let him interrupt me.
  'There's a call I've got to stay in for at lunchtime, so could you come then, there won't be anyone else around.'
  As I came up the steps from the Underground at Marble Arch, a cold wet wind blew in my face. Outside the sandwich bar next to Go Now, the lunchtime queue was already out into the street, the queuers all with their back to the wind and the wet, so they looked as though they had all turned to watch an accident. Inside Go Now, there was just Bobs sitting behind a dusty festoon of little plastic flags and a plastic name panel which said ROBERT A. MOONMAN.
  'What's the A for?'
  'Ambrose. He's one of the Fathers of the Church.'

'Thank you,' I said coldly. 'Well, what have you got me in here for? It took me nearly an hour.'

'You could always take the Iberia flight to San Sebastian, though it would be quicker to –'

'What –' then I followed his eyes. A large man in an overcoat with hair *en brosse* came out of an inner office and proceeded on out of the glass door, breaking wind delicately as he passed my chair.

'That's the manager, he only goes out for half an hour.'

'How long is this going to take then?'

'Look, this is an emergency or I wouldn't have asked you. Now you may or may not know that Helen and I have been having a thing together.'

He paused, unlike him, as though it was important to clock my reaction before moving on to the next stage. I gave him an unfriendly nod.

'It started as little more than a flirtation but then as we got to know each other better we agreed that we might think about making it a physical relationship, to see if we were suited in that way as well, because often you know that you can get on with someone brilliantly but when it comes to fucking –'

'Do we have to go through all that?'

'I think it's important to understand. Anyway, we slept together for the first time nine weeks ago, just after that Happening when my guernsey got ruined, and it was the bang of a lifetime. Absolutely fantastic.'

He gave me his furrowed look, the one he put on to explain how much faster his car could accelerate if he kept it in third. What I wanted to say was that I didn't want to hear any of this, and that even if it was all true, and I had reason to believe it wasn't, why was he telling me and would he please not mix up the talk about relationships with all the banging and fucking and choose a normal mode of speech, but all I said was:

'So what's the problem?'

'But many of our customers prefer to take the train to St Jean de Luz and hire the car there, instead of changing gauge.'

I looked round to see the *en-brosse* man opening the door and returning, heavy-treaded to his office, from which he instantly emerged once more with an umbrella.

'It was so fantastic that I wanted to see her all the time, not just, you know, when we're all a bit pissed at the end of the evening so I said would she like to come and live with me.'

'What, at Padders?'

'We could do it up together, I mean, it's potentially a great flat. Anyway, she said it wouldn't be fair to Tolly. I said I wasn't interested in being fair to Tolly, because I thought he wasn't right for her. A person like that could drag you down, however strong you are and Helen is strong. I mean, when you get down to it he's really a cheap crook going nowhere.'

'Unlike you,' I said cruelly.

'I didn't pretend my prospects were that terrific, but at least I would give her full commitment which is what she needs because she's really rather an alone sort of person and she's too proud to admit it.'

'And how did she take this analysis of her plight?'

'She didn't lose her cool, not at all, but she did say she thought she was the best judge of how lonely she was and who was or wasn't good for her, but she was incredibly grateful for my offer and of course she'd think about it, but she needed a bit of time. So I agreed to that.'

There were plenty more acid ripostes waiting to be unleashed, but his earnest little-boy look above his ginger tie with silver horse-shoes on it (a new addition to his limited wardrobe) melted me, so I merely asked how I could help him.

'Well, you see, I gave her a month.'

'You gave her a month?'

'To make up her mind in. I promised not to mention the idea for a month if she promised to give me a firm answer at the end of it. So she said all right. And the thing is, the month was up last Tuesday and I've rung her and rung her and I can't get hold of her at all anywhere, so finally I went round to her place and left a note saying how much I loved her and how my offer was as cast-iron as ever and I couldn't live without her. Would you like to read it? I've got a carbon.'

'No,' I said, 'not just now.'

'So when I got back from an airline do earlier this morning, I found a message on my desk saying she was going to ring at lunchtime.'

'That's the call you're waiting in for?'

'Yes, I don't know why she insists on calling me here.'

As it happened, I could see why she might prefer to make her call under constricting circumstances. But all I said was that I still couldn't see why he needed me here to listen in.

'Of course, I don't want you to listen in. That would be quite out of order. I just want your advice, because this could be the most important half-hour of my life.'

'Really?' I said, returning to acid mode.

'You see, I think she's probably going to say no to my offer. And I can see why, she doesn't want to close off her options at this stage. But the thing is, I can't stand it if she says no.'

He leant so far forward across the prune-coloured Formica that his cheek was almost grazing the little plastic flags. Close to tears, I thought, feeling hot and cramped myself.

'So?'

'So what I want your advice on is, if she says no, should I say will you marry me. Might that tip the scales, make her realise how serious I really am?'

'It would certainly show you were serious.'

'Or would it put her off for good, so she never wanted to see me again?'

'I don't know. Why do you have to ask her today?'

'I just know I have to. Can't you see that? If I miss this moment, the whole thing will fizzle out. You must see that if you've got any soul in you at all.'

'I haven't trekked half-way across London to be told I've got no soul. Anyway, she doesn't seem particularly keen to see you at all at the moment, so why should asking her to marry you make all the difference? It just doesn't sound like real life.'

Bobs paid no attention and now began to talk in something closer to a mutter, as though rehearsing the arguments to himself, having given up on me:

'Thing is, to place it on record. Might go either way, of course it might. But I owe it to myself, couldn't forgive myself if I hadn't made myself clear. Would go through life wishing I had. That would be –'

Then the telephone rang. Curious that it hadn't rung before, it was usually impossible to get through to a travel agent at lunchtime. Probably someone asking the cheapest way to get to the Bahamas. But it wasn't.

Bobs's side of the conversation was mostly grunts and half-finished protests, not very coherent, with an occasional Yes, I see what you mean. I heard him try to arrange a time to meet or for him to ring her. Eventually, he put the phone down.

'Well,' he gulped, 'I'm afraid there wasn't much point in dragging you here after all, because as you heard I didn't get much of an oar in, let alone make my famous offer she couldn't refuse.'

'No,' I said.

'She said she was awfully sorry she hadn't managed to get in touch with me recently but she had a ghastly lot of arrangements to do with work that she had to get sorted and then she had to say goodbye to Tolly – which perked my spirits up when she said it, but then I immediately thought it seemed to take a bloody long time to say goodbye. And then she said straight out that she had thought over my offer but she didn't think us living together would really work out. The other thing she was ringing up to say was she was going to Africa to do a job in mining – I would have asked her about that, it sounded dead interesting, but I was too upset – for a couple of years it would be, but I wasn't to think that was the reason she couldn't live with me, even if she hadn't been going away she couldn't, she was sorry but there it was.'

As he broke down into strange asthmatic sobs, not jerky but gravelly like an almost continuous snore, the glass door opened and the *en-brosse* man came in again, belching with equal delicacy as he passed us.

'Let's go out and get a breath,' I said.

As Bobs got up, it looked as though he could scarcely walk, but then I saw he had stumbled over a box of leaflets for Bulgaria The Unusual Destination. In one hand he had picked up a styrofoam cup of potato and chive salad, which I hadn't noticed on his desk.

'That's all I have for lunch now. I thought Helen might like it if I lost weight.'

We stood side by side outside while he ate the salad with a little plastic fork. The rain had stopped which only meant you could feel the damp more.

'Mining,' I said stamping my feet. 'What does she know about mining, unless it's an ice-cream mine?'

'Well, Grabiner, you know, the people who owned Woodies, they went belly-up after that thing about the dodgy vitamin supplements, so she needed a job.'

'Look, I'm afraid I really have to go now.'

'You don't care, do you? Couldn't expect you to, I suppose. People don't care about other people, not really. Anyway, you thought she deserved better. I can see that, don't blame you. You haven't seen how fabulously we got on together, you can't imagine how sweet –'

'I'm very sorry,' I said, trying to cut him off.

'Are you really?' he said, giving me another of his furrowed looks, this one a good deal less friendly. 'I expect you told her I wasn't worth it.'

'No,' I said, 'we never had that sort of conversation.'

'Funny,' he said bitterly, 'it hadn't occurred to me until this very minute, you and Helen probably spent all these evenings together swapping jokes about me. I mean, I can't see what else you had to talk about. You're not interested in science and she's not interested in whatever it is you're interested in. What *are* you interested in, as a matter of fact? I've never heard you start off a subject. You just like to knock, don't you, pull other people's pathetic little remarks to pieces, so I'm sure I wasn't left out. Have you heard Bobs's latest, you wouldn't believe . . .'

The time was past for making a dignified exit. I grunted an incoherent farewell, hoping it looked as if I was shattered by his cruel and unfair accusations, and turned off down the street, disregarding his half-raised hand with the little plastic fork in it.

His misery stayed with me like the damp which rose up against the windows of our office, blurring, then blotting out the trees long before the teatime dusk. The misery had shown how near the surface lay his consciousness of insignificance, which rather destroyed the joke of him. No, worse, it might show him to be superior to those of us who had that consciousness buried several layers deeper.

The whole business left me feeling restless and irritated, with both him and me, and guilty too, in fact mostly guilty. It did no good to argue that even if I had never met either of them Helen would never have gone to live with Bobs in a million years. And it was no good either to protest that it was he who kept seeking me out, which he did again, very late a few evenings later.

'Ah there you are. Thank God.'

He sounded breathless, incoherent, drunk probably, not to be blamed for that, at that time of night.

'I'm glad you phoned,' I said. 'Look, I really am very sorry.'

'No time for that. Please you must come round now.'

'Again?'

'No, this time it's urgent. You –'

Noise of telephone falling on floor. That sounded urgent enough and even if it was a joke he had a right to get his own back.

It wasn't a joke. He was lying on the floor, on a dhurri in violent colours, orange, purple, sickly yellow. He was comatose or nearly, breathing heavily, not unlike asthmatic sobbing. Pills were scattered near his head around his spectacles which I didn't know he wore and a string of amber worry beads. The whole scene was like a photographer's set-up for a thriller-jacket.

'Oh,' he said, waking a bit, 'there you are. Sorry to be a bore.'

Which was the first time he had apologised for that.

'I'll get a doctor.'

'No, no, Helen, get Helen.'

His voice was very faint, not a hint of a yap in it.

'I'll get a doctor *and* Helen.'

He closed his eyes without another word and I began dialling while keeping a watch on him. The breathing was gentle and even, but then I didn't know whether that was a good or a bad sign.

His cheek felt cold and bristly. I went next door for a blanket to put round him. By his bed, in a battered leather frame there was a photograph of Bobs and his brother in shorts, aged about five and fifteen, with their parents either side of them, the father already looking frail and mischievous, Bobs smiling, Gerald glaring. Curious to want to wake up to that every morning. On the chest of drawers a small pottery horse and hairbrushes with R.A.M. in tarnished silver letters on the back, a framed colour snap of a man waving in a blue vintage car, and next to it a sepia school group, the figures already sinking into the ivy-clad wall behind them. As I pulled the blanket off, I slipped on the tribal rug beside the bed and fell face down into the bedclothes. This tiny mishap stuck in my mind, so that ever afterwards I remembered my foot and the rug skidding on the lino underneath and the coarse mouthful of blanket.

The ambulance men came first, jocular, truculent, giving me the impression that they were like lifeboatmen dragged away from their real jobs to bail out this idiot who was entirely responsible for his own plight, not untrue in Bobs's case, but I suspect they would still be like that if you were struck by lightning and utterly blameless. Then, as they got down to the business of putting Bobs on to the stretcher, they suddenly became so gentle that I forgave them. Perhaps the brusqueness was something they were taught, a way of taking command of the situation which then gave them room to be deliberate in moving the patient, and helped to calm the bystanders.

'He'll be all right once we've pumped him. Pulse is good.'

I saw them out into the gathering fog. Bobs gave a brave little wave at no one in particular as the doors closed behind him.

The fog was shifting, sometimes almost white then a murky grey under the street-light and thickening all the time. When I came down to answer the second ring, it was so thick that at first there seemed to be no one there. She came up the steps and it was like the first time we had met when she came out of the sea-fret: little pale face, golden hair, not quite real but strangely definite.

'They've taken him? That's good.'

'Yes, they were quick. Said he looked as if he'd be all right.'

'Oh' – long drawn out, a sign of exhaustion as much as of relief. 'That's good. I'm glad I didn't have to see him in that state. What did he look like?'

'He just looked passed out.'

She gave another long sigh and hugged me against her cold cheek and fast-beating heart. Then sat down.

'It was terrible what I did, I know it was, but I didn't know what else to do. He was so, well, insistent and then –'

She stopped, not to find a word but thinking where to go next.

'We must go to the hospital, now,' she said, briskly as though I had been delaying her.

'Yes, though I don't expect we can help much. They took the pills, so they know as much as we know.'

'That's not the point. We must be there.'

'Yes,' I said, repressing the instinct to say that I knew that too and had only been waiting for her.

In the taxi she said, 'He insisted, you see, and I didn't see why not because he is sweet really in a way, but then he took it so seriously so I knew I had to make it clear, just saying I was going away wouldn't do it because he'd try to come as well or start talking about trial separations and so on, and I didn't want any of that, I really didn't.'

She took my hand and clasped it tight, then burst into tears, which stilled my carping but confused thoughts.

'Sorry to hear about Woodies,' I said, for something to say. 'You don't expect a Swiss firm to go bust.'

'It didn't go bust,' she said sharply, 'they simply decided to concentrate their research in Switzerland.'

'So what about the vitamin supplements?'

'That had nothing to do with it. The press coverage was totally slanted. Anyway it's much more suitable for a hospital annexe.'

'So Woodies is going back to being part of the bin?'

I thought of the crying man wandering up and down the avenue. Perhaps they would billet him in the pavilion now and he wouldn't cry so much. But she didn't want to talk about Woodies.

'You've heard about my new job? I must have told you, I've been telling everyone. I'm going to Africa. Dodo's setting up an amazing project, in the Egerton Hills.'

'Dodo Wilmot? But I thought you hated him, smashing up that café and just paying the man off, you really loathed him.'

'Gus, he's changed, he's much more serious now and the project is, well, I'm not supposed to say anything about it, but it's fantastic. It's going to transform the whole country. Anyway, I don't think we should be talking about it just now.'

'No.'

'Poor Bobs. Oh I hope he'll be all right.'

'So do I.'

'We're really fond of him, you and me. I mean, you wouldn't think it to hear the way we go on, but we are.'

On Edge

'This is a good day,' the driver said and laughed. The way he said it, the bright upbeat on the last two words, made me laugh too and my lungs filled with the air flooding in through the windows of the Land-Rover and I breathed so deeply I nearly choked. The air, everyone had mentioned the air. It was the altitude but not just the altitude, and their hands flapped with the futility of trying to describe it, it's the space, and the sky, you don't see skies like that anywhere else. And in the travel agent's or the queue for the jabs their voices lightened and soared at the thought of it all, like a balloon that has just had an extra puff of gas. They went on about the views too, those huge views that gave you the feeling you were looking at the whole of Africa. And I dutifully looked out of the window and saw that the joy of it was not just the endlessness but that there was nothing to see, nothing at all, no church spire or distant cooling towers, not even a line of hills, but only the unbounded expanse, straw-yellow and parched green plains to start with, then drifting lazily into bluey-green and a mild unassertive blue, quite familiar, the blue of an English summer sea or sky, but motionless as English seas and skies were not.

At first we had come through eucalyptus plantations and fields of young corn with dusty tracks winding through them up to low white farmhouses, but now slowly gaining height we had come out of the farming country on to the high veld and the landscape relaxed into its casual, indifferent self. The great boulders strewn along the ridges looked ready to roll off in any direction. We overtook bulging buses which had stopped, it seemed in the middle of nowhere, to let off passengers carrying cardboard suitcases and old rucksacks who ambled along the roadside before disappearing into the thorn bushes. Now and then there was a village with a petrol pump and a bottle shop. The breezeblock bungalows and occasional cluster of reed or straw huts reminded me of somewhere else, perhaps only of pictures of Africa in travel magazines, but the huge strangeness, that was not so easy to capture on camera and take away. Nor was the pace they walked at, not really an amble or a dawdle, that suggested deliberate slowing down, but a pace that was so quiet and easy I could not help thinking of people back home grinding their cartilages to shreds on city pavements. Everyone noticed the walking too. In fact everyone had just the same thoughts their first day here, but that did not make them seem any less fresh. The opposite in fact, it was a privilege to bathe in the common experience, to shrug off the burden of inventing my own first impressions.

The landscape was changing again, harder, rockier now. No baboons chattering in the thorn bushes, then no thorn bushes. The tawny dust turning to orange and brown scree and ahead of us low mountains with sharp, broken purple crags.

'Nearly at edge now, sir,' the driver said. He had told me he was called Black and he had laughed at that too.

'Edge of what?'

'Egerton East, sir. That's what we call it. Edge.'

The next hill had great stones perilously balanced on either side of the road, huge dimpled balls, dappled here and there with lichen silvered by the sun. A storm gathering over the valley beyond, a dry stony valley with no green or softness, then a vast rift, the far side of it raw orange and a dark rust colour. At the bottom and perched half-way up were little huts linked by some sort of railway or conveyor belt. As my eyes locked on to the scale, I could see that they had gouged out the best part of two low hills and at least half the rift was man-made. Coming down the hill a little more, I could see the real valley: a dry river-bed, broad and stony between groves of gum trees with a red dirt road slashed through them leading to a scrabble of breezeblock bungalows, four or five at most, one of them more like a long barn with a rusty corrugated iron roof.

'Edge?'

'Edge. Very good village.'

'Yes, I can see.'

'First-class water and landing strip.'

She was sitting under a tin-roofed verandah which looked out on a lawn of coarse grass with gnarled old trees full of twittering yellow birds. Beyond the old trees were trees the colour of flame and then a wire fence ten feet high at least. She had her legs up on a pile of logs and was slurping down a yoghurt before she jumped up to say hallo. Baggy beige shorts. She looked about ten years old.

'You'll find it just like Surrey they said, but as you can see, it isn't.'

'It's wonderful,' I said.

'The air, I expect you've noticed the air.'

'Not like Surrey at all.'

'This used to be the D.O.'s house, before independence. Now the government lets it out to Wips.'

'Wips?'

'Wilmot Investment and Prospecting.'

'To which you are –'

'Assistant Geological Adviser, only the G.A.'s got tick-bite fever, so I'm really him for the moment. Look at the weaver birds, isn't it sweet the way their nests swing?'

The breeze rustling through the gum trees sent the willow branches waving. The birds hung on to the nests trailing at the end of them, twittering as though they were about to be swept away for ever.

'Why's the fence so high?'

'Oh leopards, thieves, terrorists – the border's only a few miles away.'

'Don't you mean freedom fighters?'

'Are you going to be like that the whole time? Can't you just enjoy it?'

'Can you?'

'Look, there's no point in having attacks of conscience if you've come to do a job. It's the Africans who suffer most from the terrs in any case. They don't bother us.'

'Well, how do they feel about you carving up their country?' I waved at the scarred further face of the valley, just visible between the trees.

'You're just tired and irritable, I expect it's the heat or the altitude or something. You used to be so nice and puddingy. There's really no point coming all this way if you're going to start lecturing me in the first five minutes.'

Which was true. It was perverse to be breathing in the air of paradise one minute and then without any provocation to start behaving like the sort of person I wasn't and didn't care for. Yet the sight of her sipping the yoghurt, and her legs, pale honey not tanned, so pertly propped up on the eucalyptus logs – she was provoking.

'In any case,' she said, 'they're really pleased about Wips coming here. With the drought they've had the past five years, it's their last hope. We could have gone further up the valley, place where a man with a bucket and spade found emeralds before the war, that's where the G.A. originally advised but Dodo liked the look of Edge. Feels it in his water that this is going to be the mother of all mother lodes.'

'Emeralds, is that what you're after?'

'Could be,' she said nonchalantly. 'Come and have a beer.'

We went into the dark sitting-room with its furniture all covered in hide the colour of dried blood and the framed photos of Victoria Falls and the Matopos hills and the back numbers of the *National Geographic* and the native earthenware jugs and bowls with swirls and criss-crosses all over them, and the fan on the ceiling making a swoopy burring noise. And in the unthreatening darkness with its hint of damp, my annoyance went away and a sudden happiness took hold of me, fresh and cool like the freshness after a squall.

'You'll come into town with me, won't you? We could have another noggin at Ma's after we've done the shopping.'

'Ma's?'

'Mrs McGuigan. It's the, well, I suppose you'd call it the social centre.'

It seemed only a short drive, perhaps twenty minutes down a rolling dipping tarmac road with glimpses of green farmland and clumps of eucalyptus. The country looked tamed again here, and there were neat groups of huts perched above us and men and women walking along the side of the road. Yet only a few miles back Egerton had felt like the edge of the wilderness. There didn't seem to be any clear distinctions in this country, I thought, as Helen stopped the Land-Rover at a crossroads with low white-painted cement buildings and sidewalks shaded by wooden roofs. On the far side of the road, where there were no buildings, women in brightly coloured clothes had set out stalls with produce piled high – water-melons, oranges, tomatoes and familiar vegetables such as cauliflowers and onions, as well as tropical fruits I didn't know the names of. We walked through a gap in the buildings into a leafy square with a sandy garden in the middle. The garden was shaded by banana trees. Beyond the shops there were avenues with tall trees stretching away into the distance, and even a church spire. To come upon this place so suddenly in the bush was unsettling. The heat of the afternoon was pleasant, not shimmery. All the same, the whole thing was like a mirage.

It seemed I had been gazing happily at the sandy garden only for a couple of minutes before she was slinging the last brown paper bag into the back of the Land-Rover and saying, 'Right, let's get a beer.'

Helen led me under the cement arcades into a dark bar, so dark that my eyes didn't focus at all until after she had ordered the beers, and I had the cold glass in my hand before I could make out the woman with frizzy sandy hair behind the bar. She was handsome with large pale blue eyes and she smiled a sardonic greeting as she stubbed out her cigarette. She was sitting on a stool behind the bar in a laid-back sideways posture, as though to make it clear she had as good a right to enjoy herself as the customers.

'My, you are a paleface,' she said.

'You're not exactly bronzed yourself,' I found myself saying.

'Where did you dredge him up?' she said. When she got up to fetch her cigarettes, I thought for a moment from the shape of the green cotton sack she was wearing that she might be pregnant, but then she passed under the light above the rack of bottles and I could see that this was a silly mistake because she wasn't young at all.

'He's an old friend. We were nannies together in France ages ago.'

'A male nanny, Christ you hear that, Frank, this guy's a nanny.'

'You don't have to tell the whole fucking neighbourhood. It's still illegal here you know.'

The voice from the corner of the room was slow with a rough twang to it, which might have been Australian rather than South African or a mixture of both. He was a man with a long brick-red face and a gaudy striped shirt and he gave us a slow salute.

'I said nanny not nancy, you fool.'

'Oh,' he said and paused before saying very slowly, 'I'm an agronomist myself.'

'Alcoholic is the word he's groping for,' she said.

'She makes her customers feel good, you see. That's why we keep coming back to the crummy place.'

'Talking of which, when's your big man coming back?'

'Tomorrow,' Helen said.

'Do you think he'd be interested in my emeralds?' She twirled her necklace of chunky green stones.

'Marie, if he thinks those are fucking emeralds ...'

'Don't call me Marie. Listen, Hel darling, you just bring him along here and we'll show him how the natives have fun. And you can bring Paleface too.'

'Thank you,' I said.

'Treat the place as your own, everyone else does, including those bloody backpackers.'

She jerked a finger at a murky corner of the room where there were rucksacks piled high on top of each other nearly up to the ceiling.

'Where do they go without their ruckies?'

'Search me, it's like where do flies go in the wintertime, one of life's great mysteries.'

Helen drained her glass and tugged my sleeve. The agronomist blew her a slow kiss as we said goodbye and stumbled out into the clear bright light of the afternoon.

'You didn't tell me Dodo was coming tomorrow.'

'Didn't I? He's been in Jo'burg talking to the bank. He's really good at that apparently. Did you get on with him, I can't remember.'

'I let him down on British naval history.'

'Oh, I do remember.'

'And on bread-roll throwing too.'

'Ghastly failure all round, in fact. You must look at the LPs the D.O. left behind, they're an amazing time-warp.'

Back at the D.O.'s house, I riffled through the wire rack: *South Pacific, The Best of Harry 'Tiger' Roy, Mario Lanza Sings, Semprini's Greatest Serenades, Carroll Lewis and the Savoy Orpheans* – and the thought of those lush songs and tinkling ivories singing out over the noises of the African night seemed horribly touching.

'This is the only playable one, Miriam Makeba, isn't she fantastic?'

But somehow Miriam Makeba didn't move me, not like she had in London. I couldn't think why, but she sounded out of place on the D.O.'s blue-and-grey rexine record-player.

'Afraid you'll have to sleep in the guest-house which is a bit primitive. The best spare's reserved for the big boss.'

'Fair enough.'

She led me behind the house through a kitchen garden-cum-orchard, parting branches of the oranges and lemons to clear a path. The fruit, cool and waxy, brushed against my bare arms and legs. Behind the fruit trees there were familiar English things, high-heaped rows of potatoes and runner beans up sticks. The guest-house was a square outhouse with a tin roof, the white paint on the walls so thin that the texture of the breezeblocks showed through. Inside there was a truckle bed, a round rug, a table and a chair. Through the one little window above the bed I could see the top of the hills the far side of the valley.

'Perfect.'

'Isn't it? I sometimes come and sleep down here because it's cooler. It's so close to the fence you hear all the bush noises twice as loud.'

After supper – spaghetti and the local weak fizzy beer – she gave me a candle and a mosquito net. Trailing the net behind me and holding the candle high to keep it clear of the oranges and lemons, I looked like Wee Willie Winkie, she said.

At first it was the noise from the house a hundred yards away, where Black and his family lived. After they were quiet, the barking and snuffling and coughing began, occasionally punctuated by a rustle or a screech or a sudden flurry noise followed by a grunt or a cackle. At first I was sweating and then the sweat went cold and I began to shiver and diagnosed instant malaria. Then I realised for the first time that there was no glass in the window and the little patch of night sky to be seen through it seemed dizzily close. At last I slept.

In the morning I met Black carrying lettuces up the path. Behind him at the door of his blockhouse his tall elegant wife gave a shy wave.

'What would those animals I heard in the night be?'

'Animals? Oh, those just our dogs.' And he pointed to a couple of terriers and a gingery mongrel playing outside his house.

'Just dogs. It wouldn't be a baboon? Or a leopard?'

'Leopard?' He roared with laughter. 'No leopards here any more.'

'And no lions, I suppose.'

He laughed harder. 'To see lion, you must go to the game park. Who telling you these stories?'

'Helen.'

'Miss Helen? She joking you, she great joker. I must hurry to give these lettuce to Miss Brinscombe, she got no water and her lettuce all die.'

At the far end of the path, a white woman in a floppy white hat and a print frock down to her ankles was waiting with a basket.

'Thank you, Black. The D.O.'s lettuces are always first-rate.'

I introduced myself. Mrs Brinscombe's pinched white face looked at me without interest.

'You wouldn't have any eggs to spare, would you, Black? They just aren't laying at Musani.'

'Yes, yes, all eggs you want,' he laughed and sauntered off to the henhouse.

'He's a good worker, Black, when he's not off on a bender. We used to take it in turns to pick him up from the bottle shop, me and Dolly, that's the last D.O.'s wife. If he was really bad, Margaret, that's his wife, would chuck him out and he'd come and stay with our boys. I don't know what will happen to this place after the mining's finished. Go back to bush, I expect. Or one of the fatcats will get it for a song. It's a bit too near the border for comfort. Not many of us left, that's for sure. We used to have six tables at the bridge night. Now you're lucky if you can raise a four.'

She spoke in a flat drone, not peevishly. High on her right cheek there was a mole with hairs sprouting in it.

'If you need a lift to church on Sunday, I'll give a toot as I pass the gate at a quarter past ten. No hymns, the organ's got termites.'

Abruptly she went off to collect the eggs which Black held cupped in his elegant long hands.

There was a roar overhead and I saw a small aeroplane which seemed to be doing a circle round the bungalow. Helen came running out and waved at the sky, then led me off to the thatched lean-to where we had left the jeep.

'She's a cow, that Brinscombe,' Helen said, 'always on the scrounge. Her husband was shot by robbers, most people would rather they'd got her.'

We bumped across a dry watercourse and up through rocky scrub with little tender-green bushes that looked like blueberries, then down into the valley and another raw stony watercourse. Beyond it, a flattened strip of runway beside a long white building with EGERTON E. painted in black on its shining tin roof. The little plane had already landed and two men were climbing out of it.

The taller of the two stood for an instant at the doorway while the other one who had jumped down wheeled over some rusty steps that were standing by the runway. Hunched in the low opening the taller man looked frighteningly large, as though there might be a lot more of him still squeezing to get out of the plane.

Finally he reached the ground and stood looking about him.

'He's probably saying, Isn't that great,' I said.

'Yes, except that, well, he's changed a bit.'

'Has he? How?'

'You'll see, I think you will anyway.'

Dodo Wilmot put out a hand which was as huge and firm as before, but he looked more rugged somehow – he might have lost a stone or two – and for the first time I noticed his eyes as he was pointing out something in the hills: pale, the palest sort of green that is nearly grey. With his great slab of a chin and squat nose and a few strands of hair plastered to his scalp he was no longer a blob but positively ugly with a fine imperial ugliness. Even his walk seemed a little different, carrying a certain authority.

'How's Greg? Make sure Mrs Cardwell keeps him down at the mission for a couple of weeks minimum. You want to treat tick-bite fever with a certain respect. Any of that quartz from One-Tree turn out to be worth a dime? No? That doesn't surprise me. I always said we'd need to go higher up the valley. Well, isn't this great? Remember that night at the Boudin. You certainly had a load on. I thought you were never going to be done throwing up in the canal.'

He punched me lightly on the biceps and I wondered who he was thinking of.

His sky-blue bush shirt smelled fresh, of some flower that wasn't quite lavender. He seemed unquenchable, not really human but not alarming either.

At a fork in the road that I had not noticed on the way down, he put his hand over Helen's left forearm and made her turn the wheel to the right.

'Let's go see the mine. I can't wait ...'

And he began singing 'Big Rock Candy Mountain' in his high light voice that didn't sound as sweet as Burl Ives now that he was singing a Burl Ives number.

The road, not much more than a track here, traversed the side of the stony hill and slalomed down through thorn bushes and reeds to a dry river-bed. Now and then we splashed through a shallow pool and sent the river birds skittering off into the bushes. Dodo took a pair of shades out of his shirt pocket and put them on.

> *'O I want to go*
> *Where there ain't no snow*
> *And the wind don't blow*
> *In my Big Rock Candy Mountain.'*

Helen joined in. I had never heard her sing before. She turned out to sing so flat that I wasn't too shy to add my drone. Sitting between us Dodo kept time beating lightly on our thighs.

We came to the half-eaten hills quicker than I had expected. Close up, they were imposing, the great cliffs and ledges, raw pink with purple zigzags running through the rock and here and there flashes of quartz catching the sun before they were dulled by the next cloud of dust coming up from the cutters working across the lower levels of the quarry. What had seemed from the other side of the valley like an affront to nature now felt like part of some gigantic natural process of crunching and shifting the earth's surface. The noise and the dust were exhilarating. In my ear Dodo was shouting how many tons of rock his new Brenner-Thyssens could shift in an hour. I looked up at the machine just above us edging along a narrow col between two enormous craters.

'Looks dangerous.'

'You're bound to take casualties in an operation this size. Statistically it's safer than travelling by an African bus. And they take damn good care because they know if they lose a machine they're out.'

'And what are you looking for exactly?'

'We are prospectors, Gus, high on hope and low on information. According to the report of the learned geologist and his fair assistant here, these granites are liable to contain mega crystals of quartz, beryl, columbite, cassiterite, you name it. Could find a crystal thirty foot long, weighing twenty tons, beryl especially.'

'Beryl? I remember my mother had a beryl ring she liked, rather watery sort of thing.'

'It's a beautiful stone, colour of my eyes, would you believe. Take a look.'

And he bent towards me, grimacing to open his left eye to the maximum, as though asking me to remove a speck. Almost against my will, I stared into that green-almost-grey iris which seemed not to return my gaze, as if made of glass.

'Ain't worth shit, the ordinary beryl. As a precious stone, that is. Worth a bit if you find the yellow one, that's heliodor if it's a silicate, or cat's-eye if it's an oxide, like my ring' – and he flashed a signet with a tawny gold-flecked stone in it – 'then there's a blue beryl, what you'd call an aquamarine. And of course if you really hit paydirt, there's the green one.'

'Emerald? Is that a sort of beryl too?'

'Sure is.'

'And that's what you're hoping to find here?'

Dodo grunted and tapped his nose.

I looked up into the quarry now obscured by swirling dust and felt myself to be deep in the heart of King Solomon's mines with Prester John himself as my guide. The whole enterprise sounded so high and reckless, carving out these great chunks of hillside in the hope of finding a piece of quartz which was probably only the size of your fist and had happened to turn green a million years ago. But then perhaps once in a lifetime you would find a twenty-tonner and come back to

England with a huge emerald on your pinkie and live in a stucco palace in Kensington where you would die of boredom dreaming of the high veld.

We dodged out of the way of a dusty lorry bumping off towards the tall sheds at the far end of the quarry. My canvas shoes were soaked by the grey and brown slurry that ran in sluggish rivulets down from the quarry to the river-bed. The same liquid slurped out of the corners of the dumper trucks carrying the waste off to the sheds.

'That's where we break up the spoil, damn hard on the grinders but it makes great road metal. The Government don't pay us much, but it keeps them sweet and we'll leave them a few miles of highway you don't break your ass on. Let's go, Helen.'

Dodo laughed and slapped the side of the jeep as though geeing up a sluggish nag. He poked his head out of the window to catch a last glimpse of the swirling dust and the great pink escarpment and the mild blue sky.

'Isn't Africa great? Don't you just love the space?'

He bathed his beryl eyes in the continent. Its whole languorous sprawl might have been made for him. And even I could see the glory of it, the moral romance of the whole project.

That night he told us how he got his start. You could see he had told the story a hundred times.

'We were farm people, had a stretch just east of Rapid City, South Dakota. You ever hear of the Badlands? Well, this land was really bad, topsoil would blow away in the first puff of wind and this was twister country. Anyway my daddy devised this special light plough with a cute kind of ridge-guard to keep the dirt down, got the local blacksmith to run him up a couple, then sold a few to the neighbours, pretty soon he had some cash he didn't need to tell Mother about, so he started gambling. Well, he had beginner's luck, my daddy wasn't much good at poker but the other feller was worse, and he won this opencast mine off him in Saratoga one night. My daddy didn't know a thing about mining either, so he said to me, Waldo you try your luck at it. My oh my, doesn't that look wonderful?'

He paused to let Helen put the dish of steaming spaghetti on the verandah table. The white strands looked naked and off-putting against the dark earthenware dish and seemed grateful to be veiled by the tomato sauce Helen plumped on it.

Dodo's odyssey rolled on. There was a one-eyed engineer who tried to flood the mine because he hadn't got paid, and a Mexican girl whose father tried to shoot him because he wouldn't marry her and a bank that went bust and a quarrel with his daddy who by now had cancer and a drink problem, and he had to sell to a Greek who closed the mine and sold it to a real-estate man for ten times as much but by then he had the bug and he invested in the Dolores which nobody else thought worth a damn but to everybody's surprise –

'And the rest is history,' said Helen. 'Eat up before it gets cold.'

'Why, you are tart, my dear. I guess you must have heard the story some place before.'

He was quite unfazed, tickled if anything to be interrupted. This recital could evidently be switched on and off at will, and after he finished his spaghetti he took it up again without any sense of the flow being broken. In fact, he looked at her with a sort of intent fondness as he began again, as though these were things he knew she would want to be reminded of.

The zing of the crickets and the last chatter of the weaver birds in the branches and the scent of the gum logs and the huge velvet sky – everything around us on the verandah of the little bungalow seemed at once to press in and to lift us out of our skins, so that we were simultaneously floating like weightless men in space and tethered like Gulliver in Lilliput. There must be banal physical reasons for this queer feeling – the long flight beginning to catch up with me, the beer not as weak as it seemed – but Dodo's rambling, bardic narrative had something to do with it, particularly in the way it seemed to bind the three of us together.

When I said good-night and went off down the path to my blockhouse my feet stumbled and my head was so full of the scent of the oranges that I could hardly keep my balance. At least I shall sleep tonight, I thought. And as soon as I hit the truckle bed – I could feel the wire triangles through the old blanket – I was cradled by that extreme fatigue that makes you feel your flesh has melted away and you are nothing but a huddled bag of bones, like a beggar sleeping on a pavement.

But this sleep didn't last and I awoke surprised, alert enough to remember how tired I had been. All around were the usual noises – coughing, barking, rustling – but nothing out of the usual. Then something different: like a cry of pain but somehow hoarse, unfinished. Not a loud noise. Perhaps it came from some way off. But it was definite and insistent. Despite what Black had said, perhaps this was some wild animal on the prowl, if not a lion, at least a hyena or a baboon. How little we ordinary Europeans knew of the sounds made by our fellow-creatures – a cow, a sheep, a cuckoo, that was about our limit. How dull our ears were, how rusty all our senses in fact.

Again the cry, was it more urgent now, or more relaxed? Perhaps it wasn't a cry of pain at all but some exuberant night-call which my inadequate systems decoded wrongly.

I stood up on the bed, still under the mosquito net, the gauze tickling my damp cheek, and put my ear to the open window but the noise seemed no louder. Then I threw off the net and went to the door and let in the cool night. There was no doubt about it now, the noise was coming from the bungalow.

The path did not go straight and I blundered off it through the orange bushes until my bare feet felt the earth of the vegetable patch and the beansticks reared up against the night sky. Pausing to regain breath and bearings, I heard the noise again.

So that was what it was. Perhaps I had really known from the start. But that was the first feeling, horror, of the kind that makes you gulp and wonder whether you will disgrace yourself by some kind of physical collapse. Absurd to describe it in those terms, verging on hysteria. After all, why shouldn't she? But how could she? How could anyone who had the choice? Perhaps he had forced himself upon her – but that idea could be thrown out straight away. Her ability to fend off all comers if she wanted to, of that I was as sure as ever. She had chosen to come out here and she had chosen this, but oh. My feet ploughed into the soft potato ridges as I wandered blindly to the edge of the patch and scratched my legs on the boundary hedge of dry thorn branches. My flapping pyjama shirt caught on the prickles, forcing me to twist and tug like a sheep caught in brambles. Finally I found the gap in the hedge where the path was and exhausted as though I had walked twenty miles rather than twenty yards fell upon my plain bedstead and, to my surprise the next morning, slept sweetly, not like the night before.

The next morning was as beautiful as any morning ever. A tremble of dew on the orange trees, the weaver birds chattering above me, now and then the scarlet swoop of a widow bird or the kingfisher-blue flash of some other species – perhaps it was an African sort of kingfisher. I sat on the step letting the still gentle sun kiss my knees. Perhaps I had invented the whole thing in my sleep. Certainly I felt not soiled or disillusioned but indecently refreshed.

Then from Black's house there came a strange wailing and though it was not really like the noise of the night before – it was obviously a woman's voice and full of misery – it instantly revived the memory in a way that left no shred of ambiguity.

Margaret came running towards me.

'Black is gone, sir. He has gone to kill himself.'

Even as I mumbled some useless reply, it was impossible not to notice how beautiful she was, with a long-legged gawky elegance, and a face that even in her present anguish had a docile and serene quality.

'Couldn't he just be –'

'At the bottle shop or with Miss Brinscombe? Yes I looked already. But her boy saw him on the road walking very bad and saying what he said to me.'

'That he was going to kill himself? But why?'

'He says he is wicked and God is angry with him.'

'Surely God doesn't tell him to kill himself.'

'Yes, I told him that too but he is not very clever.'

I was about to suggest we went and looked for him in the Land-Rover when Helen came down the path. She was wearing a faded print frock which was a couple of sizes too big, making her look like one of those old photographs of an Okie farmer's wife in the Depression.

'Yes, I know, it belonged to the D.O.'s wife, I found it in her cupboard. Dodo says we have to be tidy for church.'

'Church?'

'You'd better come.'

'Why?'

'Don't argue or Dodo will have gone and we'll have to go with

Brinscombe. Hallo Margaret, what's the problem? Black gone off again?'

'Yes.'

'I'm sure he'll turn up, he always does.'

'Yes, miss.'

'Would you like to come with us?'

'No, miss, I better wait here.'

She seemed calmed by Helen's cool confidence. Behind her I could see Dodo backing the jeep out of the car shelter.

'Well, and how was your night?' he bellowed at me.

'Great.'

'Isn't it a pearl of a morning?'

'Yes.'

He didn't need to say it made him feel good to be alive, that was written all over his face. As we bumped along the road back towards the town, I stole a sideways look at Helen, hoping perhaps to see some signs of embarrassment or fatigue. But no, she looked well, very well, perhaps in a way more ordinary because the sun had bleached her hair and her face was going a honey-brown so that she was beginning to look like the girls I had seen trying to change their money at the airport.

The small, scattered congregation in the little whitewashed church at the end of the township exuded no such vitality. Most of them were in their fifties at least, and were neither tanned nor fit-looking, often being scrawny and running to a sluglike pallor like Mrs Brinscombe's. The vicar welcomed us overseas visitors and said he was from Godalming himself, apologised for the absence of music, though he said he hoped to have good news to give us on that subject soon, and then in a surprised, glottal voice read from the *Book of Revelation* the bit about the building of the new Jerusalem:

And the building of the wall of it was of jasper: and the city was pure gold, like unto clear glass.

And the foundations of the wall of the city were garnished with all manner of precious stones. The first foundation was jasper; the second, sapphire; the third, a chalcedony; the fourth, an emerald;

The fifth, sardonyx; the sixth, sardius; the seventh, chrysolite; the eighth, beryl; the ninth, a topaz; the tenth, a chrysoprasus; the eleventh, a jacinth; the twelfth, an amethyst.

'Quite a coincidence,' I said to Dodo afterwards, 'all that stuff about precious stones.'

'Not really, I asked the guy to read that one for us, for luck.'

'And –'

'Well, I hadn't yet signed the cheque for the new organ, so he agreed.'

I was spared having to listen to Dodo's chuckles because at that moment my sleeve was plucked by Mrs Brinscombe.

'Rather poor turnout, I'm afraid. There are usually more at Christmas when the young people come up from the coast. Ah there's poor Geoff Hocking, he's had no water for four months and he's still waiting for his hernia, he used to be such fun. You know, what I wanted to tell Helen was that Black has just turned up at our place, covered with dust. Apparently he tried to throw himself over the top of the quarry but fell into a dumper on the next ledge. That's his story anyway, but you can't really believe a word they say, you'll understand when you've been here as long as we have, probably just spent the night in the ditch and wanted to make a drama out of it.'

We followed Mrs Brinscombe in her pale green Ford Anglia with the rear window that looked as if someone had taken a bite out of it. Quite soon we turned off the tarmac road up a steep track. At the junction a clutch of little signs stuck in the raw earth: MISSENDEN LODGE, JACKS HIGH, MR AND MRS R.B. LOFTHOUSE, DAVE-AND-DI, and, hard to read on a weathered wooden oval, BRINSCOMBE. The bungalow, half the size of the D.O.'s, stuck out on a tawny ridge with a couple of straggly gums behind it. When we got closer, I could see how narrow and precarious its perch was. Not twenty feet beyond it was the high wire fence and then nothing but mild endless sky.

'What a view.'

'You can't eat the view,' Mrs Brinscombe said. 'Roy was crazy to settle up here but it was all we could afford.'

She gave a despairing wave in the direction of the stony paddocks the other side of the track. A little further up the track there were some straw huts surrounded by a low hedge of dry thorn branches. Overhead a large bird of prey was gliding idly on the thermals.

'Isn't that great?' Dodo Wilmot said.

'Oh you get used to it,' Mrs Brinscombe said, but quite fondly, seeming to know what he was referring to and being grateful.

'Ah there he is now the scamp, he hasn't even bothered to get cleaned up,' she said pointing to a dusty figure coming down the track from the huts. But even this she said indulgently, as though Dodo's general praise had tinged Black's escapade too with a kind of magic.

Black was a forlorn figure covered with brown dust from his scalp down to his ragged cotton trousers.

'Sorry one and all,' he said.

We were standing on Mrs Brinscombe's dark verandah which faced away from the view on to the track. And as he came up to us making a lopsided bow of apology as he spoke, Helen ran forward and embraced him in a fierce, wordless embrace, then stood side by side with him and patted him on the back as though he had just completed a marathon.

'Come inside and have a glass of sherry,' Mrs Brinscombe said, going back to her frigid voice.

It was even darker in the sitting-room and there was a smell of damp, odd and depressing after the dry bright air outside. We stood awkwardly, waiting for our eyes to focus after the dazzle. Mrs Brinscombe's knees cracked as she squatted at the polished dark cocktail cabinet with its little gilt railing round the top, guarding a photograph of an angry-looking man with a moustache, who had a spaniel on his knee. Helen handed round the little schooners brimming with the brown liquid which tasted dusty and sweet and made me sad as I gulped it. The other side of the flyblown french windows I could see Black waiting like a candidate outside an interview room. Besmeared with the mud of the mine, obviously he couldn't come in, yet somehow the situation was not satisfactory.

'Could I take Black something?'

'I think he's had enough, Helen, don't you?'

'Something soft perhaps. He looks thirsty.'

Reluctantly Mrs Brinscombe resumed her knee-cracking squat and dribbled out some ancient orange squash into a glass not much bigger than the sherry glasses. Helen took it out to him. For some reason, this simple exercise paralysed us into silence. It was not until Black raised the glass in salutation to us through the windows and gave his great grin that we felt licensed to break out into feverish chatter.

'I see what you mean,' I said afterwards in the Land-Rover.

'About what?'

'About Mrs Brinscombe being a cow.'

'Well, it must be tough for her up there on her own, hells tough,' Dodo said, although I wasn't talking to him. 'That land ain't worth a pitcher of warm piss. And she's good to her people, isn't that right, Black? Mrs Brinscombe looks after her boys.'

'Miss Brinscombe very good to me. She always take me home.'

'You see, Gus, out here folks have to rely on one another. As far as their women go, why, they may not always see eye to eye. But when it comes to helping their neighbour out of the ditch, well, they just lend a hand.'

'I see that.'

'The truth is, you're just a snob,' Helen said. 'You don't like Mrs Brinscombe because she comes from Bexleyheath.'

'I don't know where she comes from, or care.'

'As a matter of fact,' Dodo intervened, 'she's from Keynsham which is a small town near Bristol, it's her late husband who was from Bexleyheath, he was in cement before he came out here.'

'Cement?' I said weakly.

'Top Grade, he was regional manager for Top Grade before they were taken over. Great little firm.'

There seemed no way to explain how none of this mattered because wherever she came from and whatever had happened to her or to the late Mr Brinscombe she could never have been a lovable person, for that too they would have thought mean-spirited, even as I thought she was. And it was hard to argue that they weren't right, because how could you know what she would have been like as a dark slender girl being wooed by a coming young man in Top Grade Cement? The little mole high on her right cheekbone might have lent her a Margaret-Lockwood air of mystery and that voice which now sounded so peevish might have been one of those low far-off-sounding voices which are attractive though it's hard to say why.

'You look hot and bothered, my friend,' said Dodo. 'This afternoon we'll take a swim, after I've had my presidential nap. There's a great swimming-hole a couple of miles downriver.'

'What's a presidential nap?'

'It's the nap the president takes when the other guys are still working their butts off. That's why he always looks fresher than they do.'

The sun was still high as we came over the stony bluff to the little pool kept brimming by a great tawny rock blocking the river. There were willowy branches growing out from the bluff and dipping in and out of the bright water. Helen threw off her shirt and shorts, and walked along the tawny rock. It was hard to pull my gaze away from the white shiver of her bottom and the sway of her whole body as she picked her way flexing her toes on the sharp edges of the rock. As she was slowly lowering herself into the water, the sky was suddenly full of Dodo, planing down from the bluff, huge and clumsy like his non-flying namesake, but also magnificent as his great blunt head crashed into the water, his balls swinging as long and free in the sunlight as a medieval purse of gold. In that brief moment he transcended fatness. He struck out across the pool in an easy crawl – there was not room for more than four or five strokes – and I slipped into the cold water as unobtrusively as a butler refilling the glasses, then hung on to a willow to watch Dodo bob and dive and splash like a porpoise in an aqua show. Even when he hoicked himself out of the pool and stood on the rock shaking the water out of his ears, he still looked – the only word was magnificent. His swelling thigh muscles with the great furry scrotum dandling between them nearly down to his knees reduced his enormous belly to a decent proportion, so he looked not much fatter than a carthorse or a seal, and when he turned to shout something at Helen his furry back, repellent when glimpsed sprouting over his shirt, seemed quite natural. What had happened to the gigantic heap of blubber which had been comic to the point of obscenity back at the Ville? Perhaps he hadn't really lost that much weight but possessed some weird sort of energy, which allowed him to transform his body at will, like an animal that can change shape or colour when it scents danger or opportunity.

'Isn't she lovely?' he said to me as we lay side by side watching

Helen clamber up on to the scree the far side of the pool. 'You ought to get yourself a girl like that,' he added, turning over on to his back, his amazing genitals spilling across him like coins that had fallen out of his pocket.

'Yes,' I said.

'Tomorrow you better take Hel on a trip. I've got the bankers flying up from Jo'burg.'

'Won't you need her to explain what's going on?'

'No, no, this is money talk, not rock music.'

'Right.'

'They came up with the first tranche like lambs, but I always knew they'd take some convincing to go the whole way.'

'What will you do? Show them some crystals?'

'Oh they're beyond that stage. They want to see us shovelling the shit. I'm going to have every one of the BTs cutting away like there was no tomorrow and the dumpers going back and forth like yo-yos. Then when their eyes are full of dust, we show them the figures.'

He laughed and his great seal belly convulsed in time to his laughter.

The sun had gone behind the bluff and I shivered instead of laughing back.

'Better get some clothes on. It cools quick in these latitudes.'

He was still lying on his back and seemed to be looking straight up at the sky. How had he spotted my shiver? Those strange glassy eyes must see sideways, backwards too perhaps. Odd that he didn't want Helen there to show the bankers round. She would look so reliable in a crisp shirt and tailored shorts (she made everything look tailored, even if she couldn't sing or swim).

She clambered out of the water and stood on one of the smaller rocks to the side, briskly rubbing her hair. It was as though she were alone. She had grown thin out here, she couldn't eat the mealie porridge the chuckwagon served at the mine, and at the bungalow she ate mostly fruit and vegetables from the garden when she was by herself. I could hardly bear to watch her, she looked so desirable and so sad. No sooner had I thought this than it seemed a peculiar thing to float into my head. Why sad? Thoughts of mortality I suppose, but something more than that, something special to her or special to her for me. I still had little clue what she was thinking at any one moment, least of all now.

Although she talked in such a down-to-earth style, she remained a mystery, or rather I wanted to keep her as a mystery, quiet and still like an angel in the background of a painting by Piero, which of course she would have rightly ridiculed if I had been silly enough to confide it to her. If she had known what I was thinking, she would have said Haven't you ever seen a woman with no clothes on before.

Dodo chuckled as he pulled on his scarlet boxer shorts, at last tucking away his appalling scrotum.

'Your girlfriend's old man's coming up tomorrow.'

'My girlfriend?'

'John R. Stilwell. He'll be there representing Stilwell Jackson, they're only in for 5 per cent, but their name is bringing a couple of the bigger houses in on their coat-tails.'

'She's not –'

'Seemed to me you and Jane were getting along pretty damn fine.'

'There were no –'

'Don't take it so hard, John won't do anything. He don't care for scandal.'

They must have taken off well before dawn because the sun was still a blood-orange spilling stealthy rays over the grey veld, mist still hanging in the trees and wrapping itself around the great rocks, when their little plane skittered in over the bluff.

'Hey, you guys slumming it today. What's with the Gulfstream, you trade it for a few beads?'

'We didn't like to risk the bigger plane on your dirt track,' said one of the large untidy men clambering down on to the runway.

Behind these Dodo lookalikes, but after a short interval, as though he had been a President waiting for the cameras to get into position, came my former employer, neat as ever, lips pursed tight in his little moue, more reflective than disapproving, as though he couldn't let you have his opinion right away but if you would sit quietly a well-pondered judgement would soon be delivered.

'Two hours ten minutes,' he said. 'There was a slight headwind. Great to see you again, Gus. And Helen, hi, how are you?'

The way he used our names in his tight voice, which was quiet at the best of times and with the noise of the mechanic working on the plane almost inaudible now, sounded curiously intimate, affectionate even, although anyone else would have done the same meeting us again, what was it, seven, eight years after the summer at the Ville. He didn't look older, but I was somehow more conscious of his physical presence, the tanned skin of his narrow cheeks and his dimity little chin, the bony fingers clasped round the handle of his square oxblood briefcase, the long black hairs on his skinny forearm – he was wearing a blue short-sleeved office shirt and as a concession to Africa had his dark jacket hung over his other arm.

'You guys had breakfast?' Dodo asked.

'We brought our own.' One of the large untidy men jerked a finger at the pilot who was handing down large silver metal boxes from the cabin.

Helen brought out our basket of melons and oranges and we sat down under the tin-roofed verandah of the hut which had EGERTON E. on it. The pilot spread a white cloth on the trestle table and unpacked hot croissants and thermoses of coffee.

'Kenya beans, from the company farm. With the losses they're making, it's the least they could do to give us a decent cup of coffee. Honey or marmalade? You Brits just love marmalade, don't you.'

Under its flaky brown outside the croissant seemed almost to tremble as I dolloped on the chunky bitter-sweet marmalade and my nostrils inhaled the fierce aroma of the Kenya coffee. I caught Helen's eye across the table and we nodded in unison together, this time hitting the interval just right as Dodo said, 'Well, isn't this great?'

Brainerd was planning to go to Cornell, majoring in archaeology and entomology. He had had a little trouble in high school, he was not a good mixer, he got that from his father, he took a keen interest in the stock market, well, he got that from his father too, but that didn't make you too popular when you were sixteen years old. Timmy was fine, just fine. And Jane? Jane? Her health had been uncertain, but she was improving all the time.

Just as I was thinking how to probe further without being so inquisitive as to stir up Mr Stilwell's suspicion, Dodo said: 'Right, gentlemen, let's go see some rocks. And you young people go off and enjoy yourselves.'

Helen made a mock-angry face to hide her real-angry face, and she and I helped the pilot put the silver boxes back into the plane. They still seemed very heavy. The pilot said that was because of the cold salmon and the Krug and the Pavlova cake and the other lunch stuff which they were going to have on the way back. Dodo and the bankers walked to the little convoy of Land-Rovers parked behind the hut where the chief geologist, now recovered from tick-bite fever, was waiting for them. John Stilwell, last of the group to cross the stony ground, seemed pitifully slight. Just before he disappeared behind the hut, he gave us a brave little wave like an innocent man being led off to execution by thugs from Security.

After they had gone, we drove off in the other direction, south, to look at rock paintings.

'I expect you'll think they're naff.'

'Why should I, I've never seen any rock paintings.'

'They're not Botticelli, you know.'

'Didn't think they were.'

Her annoyance at being kept out of the mine inspection was still scratching her like barbed wire. When we came up to the place and walked through black-eyed daisies and some other tall flower with fluffy yellow petals and edged round the huge giant's cannon-ball of a rock, and found on the underside the slinky skeletal drawings of elephant and antelope, in rust and black and orange, and as we crouched under the great rock the warm breeze from the enormous plain behind us nuzzling our bare legs, then I thought her sour mood might have lifted but it didn't.

'What are they called, these big round rocks?'

'Dombas, I told you.'

'So you did, sorry.'

'He's a bastard, sometimes you think he isn't, but he is. We're sleeping together, you know. I expect you knew that.'

'Sort of,' I said.

'You know everything, don't you, because you're so bloody sensitive. I expect you're wondering how she could possibly and all that.'

'No,' I lied, 'I hadn't got that far.'

'Well, I'm wondering, I can tell you.'

'It's not a compulsory exercise, is it?'

'I don't do things because they're compulsory. I do them because I want to, but sometimes I just can't see why I ever wanted to.'

She turned away from the paintings, and sat down with her back to them. Even though she was so slight, she still had to bend her head under the overhanging rock. I lay in front of her at the edge of the ledge looking out over the endless veld, listening to her snuffles.

Perhaps she just liked to be obliging, was the thought which occurred to me and which after some hesitation I offered out loud. Not a good decision.

'*Obliging?* You make me sound like, oh, a hotel manager or something – we aim to oblige, madam – that's a disgusting thing to say.'

I tried to explain that it wasn't meant to be offensive. All right, she was a sort of manager if that was the word she wanted, a manager in life's grand hotel and she was merely trying to keep the guests happy, and what was wrong with that?

'So what you think is that I go out with people in a patronising sort of way, because I think they're really cases who need looking after.'

'No, not exactly,' I said, meaning yes exactly, or something pretty close to it.

'Well, I don't think I need your amateur psychoanalysis, thank you very much. In fact, I don't need your advice at all and I don't remember asking for it.'

'All right, I'll just utter sympathetic grunts instead.'

'You do that,' she said.

So I lay quiet, feeling the breeze hump and ruffle the back of my shirt. The position became too uncomfortable and I turned over on to my back with the shadow of the rock keeping the sun off my eyes. We had got up early to meet the plane, early for me anyway, and I began to feel dozy as the sun crept in under the rock and inched up my face.

For a few minutes, I don't know how long, sleep or something like it blanketed my brain, jumbled up my thoughts – something about emeralds, very bright green, and two men in a taxi and a pond that seemed to be steaming, but I wasn't sure whether because it was hot or cold. Then in the flash of a camera shutter – no, click, shutters clicked – there I was awake but having to remain as still as death, not a nerve-ending must be allowed to twitch. Because something extremely strange was happening to me and if I betrayed by the slightest movement that I was awake it would stop happening. That was part of the bargain, though how could it be a bargain since not a word had been said about it and even the thought of it hadn't entered my head.

But it was happening, anyway, and what was even more surprising, though only incidentally, was that the sensation of it made every other part of me feel more intensely: the ache of my shoulder-blades against the uneven rock and the thistle-stalks pressing into the back of my thigh, and the faint, very faint tingle of her breath on my neck. And the sensation did not blot out the little questions scudding across my brain such as why hadn't I heard the szz of the zip being undone, or perhaps that was what had woken me, and why on earth this impulse, this wonderful impulse had come to her. But mostly I thought how cool and strong her fingers were. It couldn't go on for ever, naturally, but each moment was undeserved delight which seemed to accumulate so that by the end I was flooded with gratefulness, though not of course only with gratefulness. She wiped her fingers on the nearest plant and looked at the pearly drops sliding down the green stalks. 'Like cuckoo-spit,' she said. 'Did you call it cuckoo-spit when you were small?'

'Yes,' I said, looking at the way the sun shone through the stalks of the daisies, if they were daisies, and flushed the drops the palest green you could think of, the green of the sea off Weymouth, or no, better, the pale glassy green of a beryl stone.

'Or like a beryl,' I said.

'Too white, no, I see what you mean.'

'That was wonderful, but —'

'But why did I think of it? Well, you looked all right when you were asleep. Not so disapproving. You don't mind being — obliged, do you? Oh, look, that must be them.'

Miles away at the end of the ridge we were on, a little plane was heading south, gleaming silver against the grey-green veld. It seemed to move with drowsy slowness like a mayfly coming towards the end of its time, as though the hot sleepy afternoon had affected the engine. You could just about hear the calm drone in the distance and it came to me only then that what was so unsettling about these vast views was their quietness and that was what made me feel so insignificant. Nobody down below had learnt how to make a loud enough noise to be heard against the gentle day-long breathing of the wind. At which point, a thought struck me: suppose that this amazing, just concluded thing was something she also did for Bobs? A service, in fact, that she provided for all unsatisfactory admirers? One which, come to think of it, was what Jane had preferred, suggesting that I was in danger of being for ever typecast in the Cherubino role, fit to be tickled but unsuitable for any deeper engagement.

It was odd to think of Helen and Jane Stilwell in the same breath. They had always seemed such opposites, the one serious and disciplined, the other frivolous and spoilt. But perhaps Helen had her playful side too, one which the sternness of her life had muffled until now. Even so, *Bobs.*

'We haven't got anything to drink, have we?'

'No, the pilot took it all back with him.'

'You should have asked him for a bottle. I need a drink badly.'

'I'm sorry,' I said.

'Let's go home.'

She led me back along the winding path through the tall daisies, at times almost as tall as she was. The wind seemed to whistle through the dry stalks, but perhaps that was an illusion too.

She drove fast like a rally driver, cutting into the corners and accelerating out of the humps as though she was set on shaking the sweet languor out of my bones. The gum trees went flip-flip past us and the close-sounding rustle of their tops was drowned out by the roar of the Land-Rover's engine being pushed along harder than it cared for.

The D.O.'s compound was full of heat and silence. It was a relief to get inside the dark sitting-room.

Almost without looking what she was doing, she pulled a bottle out of the D.O.'s drink cupboard. The bottle was dark and dusty, which didn't mean it was going to be any good – and it wasn't. She caught me looking at the label as I poured out.

'Don't be stupid. It's just plonk from the Cape. The Rhodies used it for petrol when the sanctions started to bite.'

She snatched the tumbler from me – I couldn't see any wineglasses – and drank half of it in one gulp, awkwardly with her elbow somehow in the wrong place like somebody smoking their first cigarette. Then she sat still in the dark sitting-room on an oxblood settee with the damp mushroomy smell all around us.

'Oh what a mess,' she said.

Being part of the mess, it was hard to see it exactly in those terms. For me the day was still touched with magic, a freakish sort of magic but magic all the same. But it was hard to express that feeling without sounding like a guest saying a phoney thank-you at the end of a party. So I said nothing until the telephone jangled, which enforced silence anyway because the half-dozen houses with a phone in the scattered settlement shared a party line and we had to count the rings to see who the call was for.

'Have you heard?' It was Dodo, breathy, talking quick but loud so I could hear standing next to Helen.

'Heard what?'

'About the crash. They came down at Mosetse.'

'Who?'

'The investors, the money men. I'm on my way. It's a hundred miles to the south, the other side of the border. I'll pick you up.'

'But –'

'You're a nurse aren't you? You've had training.'

'No, whatever made you think that?' she said, but he had already put the phone down. 'Why should he think I'm a fucking nurse?'

'Dunno,' I said, but it was easy to see why anyone could think that.

'I didn't even get my first aid certificate at school. It's awful, isn't it? We must have been almost the last people to see the plane, perhaps we could have seen it crash if we had looked long enough.'

'What good would that have done?'

'No good,' she said, 'I wasn't talking about good. But it would have been – something to see, like when you see an aeroplane droning overhead and you sometimes think perhaps this will be the moment when the engine cuts out and in a ghastly way you're half-hoping it will be. Why is that? You don't wish the people in the plane to be killed, do you? You just want a cheap thrill.'

It was unlike her, this wandering imaginative turn, unlike my idea of her at any rate. Perhaps it only showed how upset she was.

'I don't know what use we could be,' she went on. 'The police and ambulances will be there hours before us if they aren't there already.'

'Dodo feels responsible for them, I suppose.'

'Well, I'm not responsible for them. They chose to come up here in that stupid little plane. Get me another drink.'

We had finished the bottle before Dodo's hoot. He flapped open the passenger door, didn't bother to get out, hardly spoke as we got in. His Land-Rover was the big-engined *de luxe* model and even on the up-and-down patched-up roads it tucked away the miles so that we were soon in unknown country, barren terrain with rocks strewn about and untidy thorn bushes. Now and then there was a muddy patch beside the road and half a dozen mangy cattle with cattle egrets sitting on their humps picking at their fleas. They waved us through at the border bridge, they had already heard about the crash.

We must have gone another forty miles before I asked the question. 'Did they survive, any of them?'

'What do you bloody think? A twin-engined prop falls ten thousand feet on to a rock, what do you think your chances of survival are, a rough estimate will do, I don't need it down to the third decimal point.'

'Sorry.'

'OK, it's a terrible thing, and I'm just grateful for you folks coming along. I'm hells sorry too.'

He put his paw on Helen's knee. She didn't respond but didn't take it away. A baboon, grey and sad-looking in the thickening light, hopped across the road. Helen turned her head to watch it scuttle under the rusty wire fence and into the bushes and I smelled the tang of the red wine on her breath.

'This is all tribal trust land here, beats me how they can make a living off this scrub. They should have brought the Gulfstream. They could have landed it all right on the strip.'

He seemed lost in distress, and I thought I had misjudged him.

We came to some long, low white buildings beside the road: Pius XII Catholic Mission of Masvingo.

'All gone, all gone to Zaka,' cried the African standing by the road, 'I will show you,' and he jumped up into the back without waiting to be asked. He directed us off the road, along an upland track with the stony red earth criss-crossed by little dry watercourses. Over the next hill, we saw it. The last rays of the sun caught the fragments of metal lying half-way up the hill beyond. Below the wreckage at the foot of the slope there were three or four jeeps and vans parked, presumably the nearest point they could get to.

'Damn, damn, damn, oh God, oh God.' Dodo's swearing sounded almost pious.

Just above the jeeps the bodies were laid out covered with blankets. Beside each of them crouching on his knees in the blueberry and heather was a monk in a beige robe. Higher up were Africans moving about the hillside, collecting fragments of the wreckage. At the request of the policeman Dodo clambered up to identify the dead and came down again to tell us that they looked peaceful, it must have happened just like that and their bodies were not much, he couldn't think of the word, and then said 'marked'. The policeman said, in halting English, that they hit the side of the hill and mimed a glancing blow with one hand lightly brushing across the palm of the other.

The head of the mission, a plump Irishman wearing dark glasses although the sun had gone behind the hill, said they would be glad to take care of the bodies in their chapel for the time being until the next of kin had been informed.

'That would be very much appreciated, Reverend Father,' Dodo said.

'And if you and your friends would care to spend the night with us?'

'That would be swell.'

The Irishman hitched up his robe and began to scramble up the hill, calling to his brethren.

'That will do now, boys. Just lend a hand, will you?'

'There is another thing,' Dodo said to the policeman.

'Yessir?'

'The plane was carrying valuable mineral samples, to be analysed down in Johannesburg, you understand.'

'Yessir. Nothing will be moved. We will guard all your property. I will give you chitty.'

'Well, chief, I have every confidence in your officers, but I have strict orders from the government to keep personal control of all mined material at all times. That is the condition of my licence and I want to do the right thing, because you folks have been good to me.'

'Yessir.'

'So what I suggest is that we take those crates you have there down to the mission where the Reverend Father and I can keep an eye on them tonight.'

'Yessir, all OK, sir.'

'They'll be under divine protection down there. No harm can come to them.'

'No sir.'

The inspector told his men to begin loading the square metal boxes into Dodo's Land-Rover. Some were dented and a couple had burst, leaving weird splashes of yellow and pink and grey powder over the heathery hillside, but the bouncy heather and the glancing angle of the crash had preserved most of them. But then they were built to withstand impact. Unlike the investors.

The boxes were so heavy that it took two policemen to carry each one, staggering down the overgrown slope. And when we bumped off down the track, even with the four-wheel drive Dodo could scarcely get the Land-Rover up the far side of the little dry watercourses.

'My God they're heavy,' Helen said. 'Do you think the weight could have – '

'Don't even ask,' Waldo Wilmot said. 'They should have brought the Grumman Gulfstream, takes twice the payload.'

'Was it absolutely essential to take the samples with them?'

'Honey, you want to play the D.A.?'

'I mean, the rocks could have gone down to Jo'burg by truck.'

'Helen, *can* it. These are busy men, they're only in Africa for two days. They can't afford to wait a week for a goddamn truck.'

'Greedy, you mean.'

'What?'

'You said busy, you meant greedy.'

'Is that any way to speak of four decent men whose bodies are bumping down the track behind us at this very moment? All right, so they got a little excited like kids on Christmas Day, they wanted to open their presents. Is that so bad?'

Dodo had a point, I thought. Their impatience was surely innocent, or at worst part of that same restless energy that had brought them here in the first place.

But Helen was unmoved, with that set expression which was the nearest she came to letting anger show.

'And here you are, rushing off with your precious minerals while your friends' corpses bump along behind us, as you so charmingly put it.'

'Look,' said Dodo, 'I have a legal responsibility for these rocks and I have an order from the police chief licensing me to carry out those responsibilities. That's it, so shut the fuck up and let me get us out of here in one piece.'

Our little cortège knocked and rattled its way down the track to the main road and turned right, back towards the mission. It was dark now and the purring of the big tyres on the tarmac and the huge deep-blue sky with every star pricking it so brightly affected me in an unexpected way hard to describe. I felt as though we had been winched up on to a more intense level of reality, or perhaps it was only the wind and the shock and the long drive. The whush-whush of the gum trees passing by and the little huddles of reed huts with their fires burning a hot red in the night and behind us John Stilwell and his fellow-investors – there was no way of denying the awful fact that I was happy.

At the entrance to the mission there were two African boys holding tarry torches to guide us. In the smoky flicker their heads and forearms looked polished and unreal like blackamoor figures in a drawing-room. The main room inside the low plain building contained nothing but a long table and benches and a couple of posters on the wall, one about Lourdes and one about respecting womanhood or the Virgin, or a bit of both. We sat on the benches and the boys brought us bottles of local beer. It seemed odd to be sitting there drinking as the brothers came through carrying the four bodies each covered by a hairy blanket, the same oatmeal colour as their robes.

'They'll take them through to the chapel and keep a vigil there. Now as for the next step, were they Catholics, do you know?'

The Irishman had turned to me and I did not like to say that except for John Stilwell I didn't even know their names. It seemed fraudulent to be caught up in this cortège on such slender acquaintance. But Dodo answered the question for me.

'Catholics, Father? Well, not John Stilwell, or Jack Greenbaum, certainly not him, Fonso Leonard, maybe, maybe not, Des Donovan, that's the pilot, he sounds like a good bet.'

'Well, we don't want to divide up the poor souls tonight, do we?

There'll be soup and millet bread coming through in just a tick and Brother Anthony has some of his sweet and sour pork for us tonight. He's from Hong Kong like most of our brothers. I fear that vocations don't grow on trees in the old country any more.'

Now that I got a proper look at the brethren, I saw that five out of the six around the table were Chinese.

'Please, do engage them in conversation. They need to practise their English and out here we don't get many guests, because of the situation. 'Tis a crying shame that you should come on such a terrible occasion. There is so much to see. We rear our own pigs, you know.'

'Isn't that great?' said Dodo, slurping down the vegetable broth.

After we had eaten, Father Ambrose said we would probably like to see the chapel. He still had his dark glasses on, so it wasn't just the tropical glare he was protecting his eyes against. The bare white-washed chapel was bigger than I had expected and my dread that we would be standing on top of the bodies was needless. The four oatmeal blankets lay in a line in front of the simple altar from behind which came a steady banging noise.

'That's Brother George. He says he'll have the coffins knocked up by the morning, just plain gumwood. Do you want them covered till then? Personally, I don't like to see them uncovered until they're in their boxes.'

'Covered? Oh I see, yes, I'm sure you're right.'

'Good, well, we'll just say a little prayer together.'

He took off his shades revealing a nasty stye swelling over his left eye and intoned a short prayer which we couldn't hear much of because Brother George was still hammering.

'Well now, Bedfordshire I think,' said Father Ambrose. 'I won't expect you up for our early Mass, but don't mind us.'

The bed in the little whitewashed cell off the passage leading to the chapel was fractionally softer than the one at the D.O.'s and I was off to sleep in no time. But the knocking of Brother George's hammer kept me company in my dreams, that and the glow from the fires in the cooking huts, so mysterious in the black night but also so homely, so that they left a queer disoriented sensation as I sped by, reminding me that I was the restless wanderer and they were by their own hearth. It occurred to me as I drowsed off that my dreams might be haunted by the crash or by the four bodies lying under their oatmeal blankets a few yards along the passage, but nothing of the sort came into the rather sedate if incoherent narrative of my dreams, mostly about Pickup minor, a warty boy at school who had been interested in butterflies and moths and who now had become a jockey and appeared to be riding in a race against my father, who won the race except that the stewards, who included Cod Chamberlayne, said that he must be disqualified because it wasn't a real horse and my father said a bookmaker couldn't be a steward and so their verdict was invalid.

The tedium of other people's dreams is an important fact, Scrannel once argued, and one not to be explained away by our selfish indifference to the inner life of others. For the truth is that dreams like all inconsequential narratives are intrinsically without interest, as is shown by the fact that we frequently dream about minor characters in our lives whom we would not dream of — now there's a real Freudian slip — discussing in our waking lives. Nor is it likely that our dreams can be dredged to reveal some significant secret about ourselves. If our dream-life is some intimate psychic sanctum, then surely we would express ourselves there with directness and freedom: a phallus would be a phallus, one's desire for one's mother would be openly and violently expressed. Yet if we are to believe the head-doctors, the dreaming brain is as prim as a Victorian lady covering up the legs of her piano. No, my dear boy, I am well aware that Victorian ladies were not in fact so silly. It is our twentieth-century fantasies about the Victorian age that cooked up this particular legend, and it is in just the same way that the psychoanalysts and the surrealists have imposed their sinister designs on to the harmless and meaningless kaleidoscope of our dreams.

I woke with a start to the chattering of birds and a sense of great anxiety that I had forgotten something of importance. Which in a couple of minutes turned out to be true as it came to me that today was the day of my flight home.

'Helen will drive you back to Edge and get your stuff. I'll finish up here and get the police to run me back. See you back at the ranch.'

Dodo looked large and competent in the bright light of the mission courtyard. In his bush shirt and beige trousers with complicated flaps and pockets, he might have been some US cavalryman come to save the mission from the Indians. For a moment the morning seemed to have washed away the terrible events of the day before. Then Father Ambrose, shades reinstalled, scarcely coming up to Wilmot's shoulder, said he was sure we would like to see the coffins, Brother George would be so gratified.

So we filed back down the passage and there they were, four gleaming gumwood boxes just where the four blankets had been, as though a conjuror had whisked the blankets away and made the coffins grow out of the floor.

Brother George either operated to a standard measurement or had had no opportunity to measure up, for Jack Greenbaum and Fonso Leonard were bulging out of the boxes with scarcely room for their arms to fit in along their sides. As in life, their faces were swollen with discontent. Next to them, John Stilwell looked poised and not at ease exactly but not out of place, rather as if he was standing, neat and uncomplaining, in an elevator designed for one. I didn't have time to look at the pilot before I had to go outside.

'Empty stomach, that's always the problem. We should have given you breakfast first.' Father Ambrose patted me on the back, almost as though to congratulate me. Then he gave me a white cloth to clean myself up with. The cloth had a faint tickle of incense clinging to it. I wondered whether it had some liturgical use. As I was wiping my face, Dodo came up to Father Ambrose.

'You've done a terrific job, Father, I don't know how to thank you. I hope this will cover the cost and leave an itty little bit over.'

He handed Father Ambrose a bundle of notes. On his face there was that same rueful innocence I remembered from when he was describing how he had paid off the owner of the Café Boudin. Here was another little caper that had gone off course and the damage had to be paid for.

Back in the courtyard, we found one of the lorries from the mine and Dodo began ordering a couple of his men to transfer the samples from the Land-Rover.

'Don't want to slow you down, honey, and the boys can take the stuff straight down to the strip. I'll fly down to Jo'burg myself with the bodies tomorrow or the next day. Life goes on.'

He bent down and kissed Helen in a fatherly way which she endured rather than responded to. I could see she was as impatient to get moving as I was, but Father Ambrose was reluctant to let us go – 'You'll have to promise you'll come back and see us on a less tragic occasion' – though in the nicest possible way even behind his dark glasses he seemed less than overwhelmed by the tragic aspect of this occasion.

As we drove away, he waved us goodbye from his low white roughcast kingdom. His enthusiasm was touching.

After seven hours' driving, more than four back to the bungalow and nearly three to the airport, we were dog-tired, at least I was, and I wasn't taking much in, and noticed only that Helen was also carrying a bag.

'What's that?'

'Just some stuff I said I'd drop off at Ma McGuigan's. You go on to Departures, I'll catch you up.'

And she disappeared into the throng leaving me with her bag as well as mine. For a moment, I had a wild fancy that she had landed me with a huge consignment of drugs or arms, but the bag felt like anyone's bag.

'That's great,' she said, running up to me and thrusting her arm through mine. 'They had one ticket left.'

At Sea

'Why'd you say you were dropping your bag off at Ma's?'
'Didn't want to look silly if they hadn't got a ticket.'
'Is that really all the stuff you brought with you?'
'Don't be so bourgeois.'

Beyond the boundary fence, some kind of deer, antelope were they, pranced off into the bush. The aircraft began to taxi and suddenly seemed full of air and light, the light flooding down on to Helen's face. It was something to be part of her impulse, startled by it and exhilarated. By now she was rummaging through her bag, but I still felt the warmth of her arm thrust through mine.

We took off, rising rather effortfully at first, over the scrubby trees, flushing several more antelope out of their torpor and pricking them into a reluctant canter as though they didn't quite believe in us. And as we lifted and turned, a little of the same uncertainty spread through me and put my elation on hold. What exactly was all this, why had she come? To ask such questions seemed insensitive, but not as insensitive as to bury myself in *Moby-Dick*. So I stared at the red and grey swirls of the upholstery on the seat in front and studied the grey bristles on the back of the neck of the man sitting in it.

'Well?' she said.
'Well, what?'
'Aren't you going to ask?'
'Ask what?'
'Don't be dumb, ask why I jumped on the plane like that.'
'I thought you'd tell me.'

'Did you? Well, I won't.'

'Why not?'

'Because it's obvious you don't care. You just think, oh God, I'm stuck with her for the next twelve hours, is there any way I can stop her making a scene.'

'That's absolutely untrue. I'm delighted you've come, I really am, I just don't quite know what to make of it.'

'Are you really, is that true?'

'Of course it is, there's no one I would rather fly across the world with. I do love you, you know.'

It was surprising to find myself saying such things, not that I didn't mean them. The last half-dozen words seemed to come from some part of the brain not in full-time service and were dragged out in a rusty, croaky voice. Anyway, there they were, strange prehistoric sentiments which had not been filtered through the usual channels. And in the silence that followed, there was a kind of inquest going on in my head as to how they had been allowed to get out. Not that I wished them recalled, in fact I was rather proud of having blurted out something which needed blurting.

I had no idea how she would react, not much idea how I would like her to react. Perhaps she hadn't either. The silence was a long one. She brought it to an end by bursting into tears, loud, convulsive sobs which were audible over the engine drone as far as the nearest air hostess whose cherry lips parted in a startled gawp. It was some time before Helen could throttle the sobs enough to be able to speak.

'Oh I am sorry,' she said, 'that makes it much worse, but I expect you're only saying it to be polite.'

'No, no I'm not. But what does it make worse? I mean, I can see —'

'You probably can't see, and why should you? It's only logical you should think I'm just jumping on this plane because you're on it and —'

'I didn't. Anyway, I don't think you really believed I did.'

'Of course, it's nice you are on it. There's no one I'd rather be on a plane with.'

'That makes two of us. But that's not the reason. You just want to get away from him.'

'Yes.'

'That's understandable, in fact it's more than understandable. He's repellent. But he's going away, isn't he? Did you have to leave all this?' Gesturing at the window, with a wild, distressed wave, I saw far below through the cloudless air small dots moving across a straw-coloured plain, with tawny-crusted mountains beyond.

She began sobbing again and muttering, not unkindly, something to the effect that I didn't understand but it didn't matter. I put my arm round her, awkwardly in the confined space, just as we hit a patch of turbulence and so we were thrown against each other like orphans sheltering from the elements. A strange certainty came over me that the antique confession I had just made to her would never lead to anything or be repeated. But making it had locked us into a friendship which was indissoluble because it was more than platonic but not the other thing either. I had heard my father once referring to two of his contemporaries having an *amitié amoureuse* and thought how phoney it sounded – or at any rate reserved for the middle-aged, – but perhaps that was what Helen and I were gearing up for, the last *amitié amoureuse* of the twentieth century.

Now inching back into a kind of tranquillity, I could see that her escape was not so odd. If you woke up to the fact that you had been sleeping with a monster, not only a physical monster but a monster who cared for nothing but emeralds, you wouldn't want to go on working for him, even if he was in a different continent. The mystery was, always had been, why she had ever taken on the job in the first place and why she had then let him crawl all over her. And suddenly, from running on subtle questions of relationships and sensibilities, my brain was full of the vilest images, especially of his great swinging scrotum, and it was a relief when the stewardess asked whether I wanted the chicken or the vegetarian menu. Then we drowned our embarrassment in the Cape Cabernet and she made a fuss when the stewardess wouldn't let her have another bottle.

'Down with Dodo.'

'Down with Dodo.'

We clinked our plastic glasses and I reflected that I knew her no better than on the day I first met her, which was somehow a comfort. She went to sleep and so did I, but later we both woke and somewhere in the midnight hum of the aircraft and the shuffling of blankets, I thought I heard her say, 'This has got to change.'

A raw, cold, dark dawn, a wet runway in a Heathrow January. Helen had stopped lolling against me and was sitting up straight, looking frostily at the other passengers queuing to wash and scent themselves. We said goodbye at the taxi rank. There was a bus, she said, and she'd only collapse again if she came with me.

The roads were empty and even when the light straggled through the dirty grey cloudbank they did not fill up much. Half the petrol stations were still closed, though it was past nine a.m.

'Seems very quiet today.'

'Fucking three-day week, mate, where you been, Timbuktu?'

'More or less.'

'And the bloody A-rabs starving us of petrol, had to queue an hour and a half to fill up.'

The darkened villas seemed lapped in misery, as though they were being punished for being so neat. The taxi-driver, half-laughing, half-snarling, threw me crazy little stories – how a government minister had instructed people to brush their teeth in the dark, how some patriotic old lady had thought it would help the nation if she drove at night without her lights on, how in Lincolnshire a man had suffocated to death trying to run his boiler on chickenshit.

The taxi took me straight to the office, not because I was eager to do my bit but because I was due back in that very day. My suit had been left hanging in the cupboard, plus shirt and tie, and I was just stripping off my dusty Africa clothes when Hilary Puttock surged in, burly, ebullient cyclist, keen student of Ambrogio Lorenzetti and the Sienese school, unstoppable, with the spirit of the service running through every nerve and vein in his body.

'Thank God you're in. The miners are coming out today. I can't think how you failed to clear your leave with me, or rather I can, because there would have been no question of it at a time like this. We've been two men short in the unit throughout the whole business. Riley-Jones is still out with that testicle trouble.'

'I cleared my leave back in August when I got the tickets.'

'In that case, you should have applied for confirmation when you saw how things were going. I've never heard of anyone taking a month off in the middle of a national crisis.'

It is hard writing down Hilary's words to convey the good humour radiating from him, the total lack of peevishness. My colleague, the swollen-balled Ian Riley-Jones, used to do imitations of Hilary announcing various disasters – the Black Death, the Holocaust, Armageddon – to his superiors. As the pile of corpses, the record of beastliness and blood and filth mounted, the fantasy-Hilary would sound ever more cheerful and positive, at the same time increasingly larded with gravitas: the most urgent priority is to improve interdepartmental liaison, I venture to suggest that a steering group at undersecretary level might be helpful, it would be advisable to consult the Pope and the Welsh Office.

Hilary paused and looked at me more intently, taking in my bare legs and grubby bush shirt.

'Why are you trouserless?'

'Just changing. Came straight from the airport.'

'Good man. What I think we'll do is slot you in where Riley-Jones would have been: Energy Supplies Liaison No. 3 Area, essentially the West Midlands. I suggest you base yourself in Birmingham, anywhere but the Midland Hotel, that, I'm afraid, is for G-Ones and Twos only.'

'And what precisely do I do when I get there?'

'Keep the home fires burning, Gus.'

He always signed off by using your name, followed by a grin of quenchless benevolence. But on this occasion he couldn't resist leaving with a quip: 'Oh and don't forget your trousers. They mind about that sort of thing up there.'

The next day Helen called.

'Is it all right ringing you in the office?'

'Yes, of course.'

'I thought it would be quicker like this, you'd want to get off the phone because there'd be important people breathing down your neck.'

'Only the Foreign Secretary and the head of MI5 at the moment.'

'That's all right then. Because I just wanted to say to avoid misunderstandings and things that it would be better if we didn't see each other for a bit. Sorry, can't think of a less corny way of putting it.'

'A cooling-off period?'

'A what?'

'Doesn't matter, that's what we call it in this department.'

'Because my life is too fucked up at the moment and I don't know about yours but I'm too fond of you to want to make it any worse.'

'I'm going away anyway,' I said.

'Are you? That's good. Where?'

'Birmingham.'

'That's nice,' she said laughing.

'No it isn't. Can I ring you when I'm lonely?'

'I wouldn't. I'd only make you feel lonelier.'

'You wouldn't.'

'Yes I would, I can make people feel very lonely even when I don't mean to.'

The last words were swallowed by a kind of sob during which she attempted to say sorry again or goodbye or both and rang off.

She was right about how lonely she could make people feel.

So I set off for the front in the class war of the century, or so it was billed, as I discovered when I caught up with the newspapers.

I established my headquarters in Room 9, second floor back, with a view of the Leofric Laundry, in the Beech Lawn Hotel, Beechlawn Avenue, B&B only £5.25. I ate my other meals round the corner from the Ministry's regional office at the Edgbaston College of Food and Domestic Arts (Hotel and Catering Dept), which did an excellent four-course meal for the absurd price of 70p: Poussin farci polonaise, Délice de sole Mornay, that sort of thing. I don't think I have ever eaten so well and been so kindly served as by Brendan and Sue and the other fresh-faced students breathing heavily as they enquired through their noses whether everything was all right. Where have they gone, those eager cooks? Twenty years on, they are probably pulling overcooked farragos out of giant microwaves for customers who estimate the value of a dish by the number of its ingredients.

Each grimy dawn, looking anonymous in a thick navy anorak or so I hoped, I drove my hired red Escort to see how things were going at some industrial site – a coke depot or a power station or a steel rolling mill (there were no actual coal-mines in my area). They were bleak yet also magical, these excursions. I had the sense of probing to the heart of things, as I steamed darkling along the unlit avenues of Edgbaston, then in stragglier, scruffier streets until the road twisted off into a wasteland of rusted-up railway sidings, scrapyards, tyre depots. Leave the car some way off, in an out-of-the-way spot where it wouldn't get smashed up, then walk the last half-mile to where the police lines started, and I could see the glow from the brazier of the pickets and the great grey outline of the depot beyond. Sometimes, out to the west around Wolverhampton, I could see the hills beyond too, a fainter grey in the blood-orange dawn, Housman's blue remembered hills, Shropshire, perhaps even Wales, and something about that austere scholar's life, its underlying hardness I suppose, seemed in tune with this grim, plain struggle too, although reading Housman you wouldn't suppose we had advanced beyond the horse-drawn plough.

They already had most of the depots sewn up round here. Just a thin line of half a dozen pickets stamping their feet, the police guarding the gates. The first few days, one or two lorries would rumble on through the gates, the pickets jumping aside at the last moment, still jeering as they stumbled, but within a week it was hard to find a place that bothered to try to keep its gates open. And the coke mountains, once as high as the cooling towers the police told me, were now trifling hillocks which had to be kept back for agreed emergency services such as hospital generators. Out in these desolate sites a strange testy intimacy grew up between the police and the pickets and the few others involved, journalists, miners' wives, support demos, mostly only a handful out here. After the fun was over, I would drive back into town and ring the usual numbers to gather information from around the area, balancing the plastic coffee cup and the receiver in one hand as I jotted down figures with the other. Then I would ring Hilary.

'No violent incidents to report?'

'None,' I said.

'Excellent. That seems to be the picture everywhere. I assured Ministers that it seemed unlikely there would be any repetition of Saltley. Comrade Arthur's playing it by the book this time.'

'So far anyway.'

'Good, good. Well, the election will clear the air, and then we can move forward.'

'How?'

'What?'

'How will it clear the air?'

'Well, there will be a new situation. The government will have a fresh mandate.'

'A mandate to do what?'

'A mandate to reach a settlement on the common ground that has already been established.'

'If it's already been established, can't they reach a settlement without an election then? I mean it doesn't seem to make much difference whether they surrender before or after the election.'

'Gus, I have better things to do than argue the toss over the phone about matters which are in any case out of our hands. And I don't want any talk of surrender. Would you dictate the rest of your report to Diana? I must fly to Misc 93.'

He put the phone down, and I could see him shrugging on his jacket over his broad shoulders and clasping his big notebook to his chest as he sailed along the dimpled drugget towards the Cabinet Office. Across the stone floor, medieval in parts, heels clanging – men with a future in the Service often had metal crescents on the heels of their shoes, like horses – then down the long passage with the three right-angled bends, through the door with the winking light above it, green if all was well, and on into the ultimate bunker, Conference Room H, or J, or K, airless, windowless, impervious to terrorist blast or the changing of the seasons. There the feedback from around the nation would be liaised until it was whipped into a smooth verbal mayonnaise, stiff enough to keep its shape, yet yielding to the slightest pressure from an anxious minister. Good luck to them, or good hunting as Riley-Jones swore he had heard Hilary say after the final meeting of the committee to review the presentational aspects of the introduction of decimal coinage.

'How do you make this spinach tart, Brendan, has it got cheese in it?' I enquired, looking up from *Moby-Dick* as Brendan cleared my plate.

'You just grate a little parmesan over it at the last minute. Sue got the idea from *First Slice Your Cookbook*. Excuse me, sir, but have you been to Woden Heath yet, the coke works? It's just round the corner from our home and there was trouble there this morning. I know you said you were looking for trouble, like the song' – and he sketched out the Presley number in an adenoidal drone.

'Well, not exactly looking for it, but thanks for the tip.'

To be honest, which I wasn't, even my few years in the Service having taught me never to confess ignorance unless forced to, and preferably not even then – a lesson people seem to find useful in all departments of life – I had not heard of Woden Heath. But there it was in the briefing notes: small Gas Board coking plant, stocks at 3/1/74 17,000 tons, normal traffic estd 20 lorries per day, reserved loads to Woden District Infirmary only.

Next morning, the streets seemed darker than ever (perhaps they were, didn't daylight go on dawning later well into January, to crush your hopes?). Darker and longer. I felt my way round the west of the city, stopping now and then to look at the map by the light of the torch which had turned out to be essential for these early-morning jaunts. The odd passer-by peered at me, suspicious rather than helpful. Did he think I was a burglar who couldn't find his way home? Finally, I hit the big avenue out to the north-west but soon I had to leave it and peel off into a potholed road which led into broken heathy land, not quite country though once or twice the smell of wet fir trees came to me through the smells of diesel and tar and anthracite and another sharp stinging pungent kind of smell I couldn't pin down. Then more fir trees and the fog drifting through them in thick swathes and oncoming headlights swinging at me through the twists of the road. A sheep, or was it a shaggy goat, suddenly floodlit on a damp tussock, and the fog catching the back of my throat, because the de-mister had packed up and the window had to be kept open. Still hellish dark when I came into a small town, or was it only a straggling continuation of the city? No one about, but a peeling big blue sign the size of a hoarding directed me to Woden Heath Plant – Energy for the Heart of England. Down a bumpy muddy side-road there was the usual array of police vans and, as the night at last began to lift, grey shapes against a black wooded hill beyond. This was the end of every line I could imagine. Beyond here there could be no beyond, and nobody in their right mind would bother to search for one.

But Brendan was right, Woden Heath looked promising. As well as the usual half-dozen pickets there was a knot of people, about twenty of them, standing by the fence but a little apart from the pickets.

'Who are that mob?' I asked the policeman after flashing my ID (always one of the high points of these excursions).

'Come from London. Funny lot, dunno who sent them. We had a bit of bother yesterday, but I reckon we've got them sorted this morning.'

I nodded, as though this was the kind of information that was only to be expected, and walked over to them. They were chanting 'The miners united will never be defeated' in a cheerful but slightly provisional-sounding way, as though this was a chant to fill in time until they received the real message.

A small woman in a bobble hat came forward.

'We've got permission to stand here,' she said.

'*No*, what −'

'God, it's you. I thought you were a policeman.'

'How on earth did you get here?'

'The union sent us, they're spreading support groups all over the area.'

'No, I mean, how ... we only just got back.'

'Oh, Bobs, well, recruited me, I suppose is the word.'

'*Bobs.*' I gasped the word, but it had to turn into a greeting as the familiar figure, barely taller than she was, detached himself from the group and stood beside her.

'Gus,' he ejaculated back, 'I didn't know you were coming. This is great.'

'Wake up,' she said to him. 'He's not with us, he's working for the government.'

'Oh. Yes, of course he is. Bobs does it again.'

And he slapped his forehead with the palm of his hand, his usual gesture of self-humiliation. But as the hand had a grey woollen mitten on it, the gesture looked like a ritual, a knight in armour swearing fealty, and indeed he didn't seem much fazed.

'What are you doing here then exactly? Counting the sheep?'

As he said it, it sounded like a self-mocking description of his own group but the sweep of his mittened hand pointed to a remarkable sight opening out in front of us as the mist cleared the hillside beyond the dark wood and revealed a huge rolling tussocky heathland behind the coke works, with sheep grazing in the patches of wet grass between the withered bracken. Here and there I could see the disturbances of old mine-workings, black and overgrown. At the end of the hill where the fog began again there was a broken-down chimney and the crumbled walls of some ancient kiln. It was a scene of abandonment, as wild as anything I could think of in England, a place for gypsies and corpses down mineshafts and the odd out-of-town coven.

'Counting you lot, I suppose,' was all the lame response I could make.

'We were told not to bring any more,' Bobs said. 'It's a bit of a sideshow here really. They only tried to take a couple of lorries in yesterday because they're so desperate. There's not much coke left here, you see, only enough for the hospital. That's what the branch secretary tells us. Our orders are not to join the pickets, so they can keep the numbers down to six, then we can't be accused of intimidation.'

He then lapsed into silence, which was unlike him because normally he went on yapping to fill the gap. In fact, his voice was suited to delivering this sort of crisp sitrep. If you hadn't known, you would have put him down as a professional organiser of such rallies. Perhaps he was, had been for ages. That was the awesome thought. If even Bobs could deploy such unsuspected competences, entertain such hidden allegiances, lead what could only be called a secret life, then how could anyone know anything about anyone else?

The second shock of the morning had followed so instantaneously upon the first that there had been no time to reflect how extraordinary it was to see Helen here. Until – how long ago was it – three, four weeks, no more – her interests in mining had been rather different. The annoying thing was that I could see her following my still only half-awake train of thought and a titchy smile beginning to form on her lips.

'All right then, I am surprised,' I said. 'Come and have a drink and explain it all when you come off duty or whatever you call it.'

'Sorry. We really ought to stay with the group. We've only just come, so I don't think we should be seen – consorting with the enemy, is that the phrase?'

'Great to see you, though,' Bobs added.

'And you,' I replied mechanically. I debated briefly whether it might be fun to embarrass her by trying a fraternal kiss, decided that the embarrassment would end up on my side, and stepped away, towards the police lines where I belonged.

As I sidled between two large policemen, there was a cheer. The six pickets were standing in a line with their hands linked high above their heads. The rusty spiked gates were being drawn to, then locked with a clang. The support group scampered up to join the pickets and form part of the line with their hands held high. Another chorus, this time jubilant, of 'The miners united'.

'Bit of a pantomime, if you ask me,' one of the policemen said. 'They were only expecting the two loads for the Cottage Hospital and those went off an hour back.'

But still, they had closed the gates.

There was no denying that seeing the two of them there had shaken me up. Helen, it was clear enough, was pleased that I had found her at Woden Heath, in fact she was almost radiant and didn't seem to mind at all that she was under Bobs's wing. At least that was what she appeared to be. He might even be the leader of the support group, from the authoritative way he spoke, and that was a surprise too, because I had never heard him utter political views in that direction, but then nor had I heard him spout the conventional Tory views you might hear in the Clutch Club. True, he was a great one for exploring other people's obsessions and associations. But this wasn't just an exploration, this was a commitment, and even 'commitment' might be too lukewarm a word for the force that had brought them into the wilds of the Black Country at seven a.m. on a January morning. The correct word was 'conversion', or 'conversion experience', as the phrase was now which was superfluous because the essence, the whole excitement of conversion must be the experience, the actual moment of turning, feeling this one throbbing irresistible impulse, compared to which all previous life was muddy error. That truly authentic moment was something to be envied, nothing else in life came close to it. And envy it I did, without beginning to feel that their cause was just or sensible or any of the things I minded about.

At least so I told myself when I stopped in a layby on the way back into the city and wrote down what the police inspector had told me.

Yet that was not the whole truth. What I felt was not simply envy of their moment of surrender to a moral passion. No, the malaise went deeper and burrowed under the confidence every public servant must have, that, whatever the twists and turns of official policy, basically the whole enterprise is well intentioned and decent people may honourably be engaged in it. But what if it wasn't well intentioned? What if there was something mean-spirited lying deep at the core of it, something poisonous seeping into the well, something which couldn't be got rid of except by a great movement of the heart?

Not all of that came to me at once. Quite often I just thought that Helen had been badly treated by a brutal older man and she was looking for the quickest way of taking it out on society and that Bobs was a birdbrain. But then again, as I lay half-asleep between the strangely waxy sheets of the Beech Lawn Hotel, they would whisper to me, Helen and Bobs: Come on in, these moments pass by once and once only and if you let them pass, what's the rest of it worth? All this going through the motions, keeping the show on the road ... how about one sweet sip of the authentic for once?

Authenticity, Scrannel once mused, making me feel each one of the five syllables in turn, a swallow of disgust on the 'auth', a prolonged, exaggerated dental 'ent' and a trilled run on the 'i-city' – authenticity is an odd notion and the pursuit of it is a curious activity, like the pursuit of certainty in the sense that it comes to obsess those who have an insistent cast of mind, but not at all like it in other ways. For one thing, certainty is a destination. If you managed to reach it you would never need to budge again, and your only nagging fear would be that you might not have reached it, that someone else more inspired or simply better informed, God for example, might be able to point out that your situation wasn't certain at all but only contingent, provisional, even transitional, that the piece of rock you were so proudly perched on was fatally porous, or liable to shift or crumble at any moment.

But if you are in pursuit of the authentic, he himself pursued (ignoring, if I remember rightly, that he had only chanced to hear the word used in passing by a prissy young art historian in a bow tie who had come to tea and was in any case using the word in a much more modest sense to apply to a disputed Parmigianino in the Ashmolean), then, Scrannel said, you must be eternally on the wing, you can never stay to prolong the experience, because the moment you linger like the princess in the fairy-story you are turned to stone. What fairy-story? interjected Mrs Scrannel, raising her blue eyes from her tapestry, more to show that she was listening, not uncritically, she herself being a trained philosopher (though, as her husband liked to remark on bringing up this fact – in fact, that was why he brought it up – a trained philosopher is a contradiction in terms, since the purpose of doing philosophy, if it has a purpose, is to untrain). Turned to stone, he repeated, or, perhaps better, to sludge. Ecstasy must be fleeting or it is not ecstasy, because you are no longer standing outside the dreary workaday world but have chosen to settle in a new world which must itself become just as dreary and workaday.

'They closed the gates up at Woden this morning,' Brendan said.

'Yes, I saw them. How did you hear?'

'My brother-in-law's in the force. Handy being out at Woden Heath, he can nip up our place for something to eat after work, and my sister can take the baby to Mum for the day. Says she's never seen so much of them until this strike started. I'd have the Sole Colbert if I were you, Sue's got the mashed really fluffy today. What did you think of the pilaff yesterday? A bit grainy it seemed to me.'

'I would have preferred it softer myself.'

One of the features of the Catering Department was the way customers, waiters and cooks all took part in a continuous exercise in criticism and self-criticism. Perhaps because they were so young, there was not much chef's vanity around. They didn't talk a lot about the strike, although like Brendan many of them must have had friends or relations caught up in it. The Catering Department was, by some unspoken rule, a sanctuary from the ruder world outside, an impression reinforced by the gothic brick façade and whitewashed walls of the former infants' school in which it was housed. And when my mind wanders back to those tumultuous days in which the nation seemed to totter, it is often only to think of those conversations with Brendan about the texture of the terrine and the restrained murmur of the other customers, women come in from Kidderminster to top up their shopping, lecturers from the university bitching about their colleagues, strange single men reading newspapers.

'No lunch tomorrow, you remember, sir. It's an off-day, but Mrs Pocock says this is a good opportunity to hone our sandwich-making skills, so if you don't mind a b.l.t. by candlelight, come along one-ish.'

'How will you cook the b?'

'On the primus. Mrs P's switching over to gas when this is all over.'

And it was all over soon enough, the election, the settlement of the strike, my return to London and that general feeling of – what – failure, sourness, bewilderment. Not a good time for anyone, perhaps not even for the winners. Or perhaps I am projecting my own exhaustion upon the whole nation. I can't remember being so tired before or since.

'Our masters are looking to move the debate on. The view is that it would be helpful to draw a line and enter a new phase.'

Hilary Puttock's neck was still damp although he had showered after cycling in from Dulwich, or perhaps it was the shower he was damp from. His forearms surged out of his half-rolled shirt-sleeves. He brushed aside my mumbled congratulations on his C.B.

'Comes with the rations, as you very well know, Gus. The important thing is to get the message out.'

'What message?'

'The message that Britain can cope. We've had our little domestic differences, but basically this is a vibrant modern economy bursting with ideas and the can-do spirit. Particularly important to get this across to the Americans.'

'Isn't that the Foreign Office's job?'

'Naturally, that's what the F.O. thinks. But Ministers think we need to have someone out there who has been at the sharp end, someone who can tell them about the real Britain.'

'Out where?'

'New York. You'll be attached to the Consulate, of course, but it'll be a roving brief, tariff negotiations, airline route allocations, and above all, presentation with a capital P. In my humble submission, it's the best job around, at your level of course. The other guys in the department will be eating their hearts out. But with your experience there's no other possible candidate.'

'Thank you very much,' I said, my mind wallowing in thoughts of Woden Heath: the broken tarmac, the brooding smell of gas, the little houses petering out into desolate industrial estates and the scrubby heathland beyond with its overgrown disused mineshafts, and the nasal Black Country voices bickering in the clammy dawn.

'When do I –'

'The sooner the better. Sort yourself out a passage, first-class, of course. We don't want to look cheap.'

By that effortless knack of self-deception so necessary to success in public life he really did seem to have forgotten exactly what I had been doing. A month or so of gathering facts and figures and passing them back to the office had been transmuted into a heroic feat of daring and initiative comparable with a spell on the North-West Frontier during the worst of the Pathan wars. All the same, I was grateful. This was a moment to escape. Whatever type of fiasco might be waiting in America, it must be better than the dismal prospects at home.

I looked in at Go Now with a light and skipping heart. Under the pretext of buying a ticket, I had a curious desire to see Bobs again.

'First-class eh? You don't want to waste the opportunity.' Bobs was back to yapping mode.

'How do you mean?'

'You take a cheaper flight and charge them the rate for going first. Everyone does it. No, I've got an even better idea. It's here somewhere.'

He rummaged around the chaos on his desk and came up with a fuchsia-pink ticket folder.

'Free passage to the Big Apple on the *Zephyr*. Heavensent Cruises sent us this freebie for their introductory cruise. Unique, unforgettable, etcetera, etcetera, thank your Uncle Bobs. Don't worry about the paperwork. I'll just send you the receipt for the air ticket and you bank the cheque.'

'Um.'

'Oh come on now.'

The pitying look that creased his little pug face was unbearable. Bad enough to have to recognise him as a friend of the People, especially when the People had won a great victory, which didn't happen often, but to be patronised as a stuffed-shirt by Bobs the fly operator, the man who knew his way around. . . . Well, if there was trouble, it was always possible to pretend the travel agent had sent the wrong bill.

'All right then, if you insist.'

A smile unclenched the pug face.

'She sails in three days' time. From Tilbury.'

It turned out to be Southampton. Bobs and Helen insisted on coming down in the train to see me off, almost as though they wanted to make certain I really did take the boat. They sat opposite holding hands. To an outsider they must have looked well suited, these two small neat figures and both of them so fair. In fact, I imagined the soft-looking woman, fiftyish, sitting next to me must be thinking sweet sentimental thoughts about them, which might be why she had her head cocked on one side, as people do when amused by the antics of children or pets. We were passing through the first chalky downs of Hampshire at the time and I was staring out of the window looking at a great white crevasse with wind-blown beech trees teetering above it, and thinking how odd Helen's life was, and why did she always fetch up with these substandard characters, and why was she still so superior, not in the sense of being proud, but unsullied by these relationships.

'Hurrkudhoulohurddo.'

'What? Sorry?'

'Clokeriddo, eese.'

The soft-looking woman pointed at the window then fell back gasping into her corner seat, in the same movement pulling out of her big floppy bag an orange plastic mask with a tube running from it. She clamped this to her face, and a gentle breathing sound filled the carriage.

As I rose to pull up the strap, I caught sight of the fuchsia-pink Heavensent label dangling from her suitcase on the rack. The label said Mrs George Fitch, *SS Zephyr*. Suddenly the whole expedition seemed not a welcome escape but a ghastly trap, as though all concerned – Hilary Puttock, Bobs and Helen too, for she had said it was a brilliant opportunity – had conspired to get me out of the way.

At the quayside, there was no way of not telling Mrs Fitch we were travelling on the same boat, since the pink Heavensent labels were dangling from my luggage too and she didn't seem to be blind as well as speech-afflicted.

'Oo-oo, uvvy,' she said, or words to that effect.

There was a dreadful inevitability about what Bobs was going to say next. The only hope was that he would wait till she was out of earshot, which of course he didn't.

'It'll be a shipboard romance, I bet,' he said.

She must have heard but, as she was already smiling her sad toothy smile and her expression didn't change, it was hard to say whether she intended to acknowledge Bobs's quip or whether she was still thanking him for carrying her bags. Climbing the steep gangway, I could hear Bobs's endless chatter above the clanking of the cranes and the calling of the gulls, or not so much above as through. In fact, the cranes and the gulls seemed engaged in an admirable but doomed campaign to drown out or at least scramble him.

'Must be all of 10,000 tons this boat, not like the old *Queens*, but they'll look after you very well, it's got two outdoor pools as well as the sauna and every kind of medical back-up, there's even an on-board dentist, you must be down here, C-Deck, no, that seems to be the purser's office, must be this way.'

'Why does he have to mention the dentist? Have you seen her teeth?'

'Oh that's Bobs, Nobel Prize for tact,' Helen said with a forgiving twinkle.

'You can't be really serious about him.'

'Does being engaged sound serious? Or does it just sound old-fashioned?'

'*Engaged.*'

Helen and I were sitting side by side on my bed in the cabin which was comfortable in a hospital sort of way: sickly picture of a bluebell wood on the wall, slithery pink chintzy eiderdown on the bed, pink quilted box for tissues with Heavensent's motif, a rumpy cherub, pricked out on it.

'You make it sound like a line in *Private Lives* or something,' she said.

'Bobs isn't witty enough for a part in *Private Lives.*'

'Well, anyway, that's what we are. He wanted it, I mean, I said why don't we just get married, but he thought his parents would prefer it if we were engaged first, though of course his mother's dead and his father wouldn't notice if Bobs said he was changing sex.'

'You actually want to marry him?'

'Mm.'

'You can't. I remember you saying just after he −'

'That was then. I'm thirty years old now. It's not the 1960s any more.'

'Do you mean you're old enough to decide for yourself or that –'

'The biological clock is ticking on. Both.'

'Even so …'

'You think I could do better. Well, I can tell you, better isn't better, or what looks like better isn't. They lie all the time, sometimes they lie to themselves too, but they always lie to you.'

'Who?'

'Men, all the men I know anyway.'

'And Bobs doesn't lie?'

'I don't think so, not to me, so far anyway.'

She seemed to be near tears and I wasn't so far off myself.

The imminent saying goodbye was partly to blame, and so perhaps was the gentle motion of the boat at anchor, not so gentle when another boat's wash rocked us and the quilted box of Kleenex slid into my lap and I took the opportunity to pass her one.

'Well, I agree you wouldn't, for example, expect Tolly d'Amico to tell you the truth, but in fact he was surprisingly frank about most things.'

'About his wife and three children in Harold Hill? Or about his prison sentence?' she said sharply.

'But surely you took up with him because, or partly because he had this air of criminal mystery.'

'Is that what you think?'

'Yes. You almost said so to me once.'

She gave me an icy stare.

'I don't remember saying anything of the sort, and even if I did sort of half-think that he might have been as much of a villain as he claimed to be, I thought he would have only been inside for fraud or something.'

'And –'

'I didn't think he had been a pimp.'

'That's worse?'

'Much worse and if you can't see it I can't see much point in carrying on this conversation.'

'I'm sorry, of course I see it's horrible.'

'He did five years. At one time, he had four girls running for him, or whatever the phrase is. I got a journalist to look it up in a cuttings library. Tolly wasn't even ashamed enough to change his name.'

'So all the time he was letting us think he was just a dear old property swindler, you were suspecting he wasn't.'

'Well, I was right.'

'And Dodo, how has he betrayed your childlike trust? What's his dark secret?'

'It's not funny.'

'I didn't say it was.'

'You sound very bitter,' she said.

'You seem to be the bitter one.'

'Well, I have plenty of reasons to be.'

'Yes, I know.'

'No you don't know, not all of them.'

'Well, tell me then.'

'I can't.'

'What do you mean, why can't you tell me?'

'I can't tell *you* is what I meant. No, I can't tell anybody in fact. Look, it's time we were going.'

She got up and pulled on her short navy-blue coat, which had a merchant-marine look about it, and shook out her fair hair with that motion of a curtain swirling in the breeze which always meant she was moving on. And once again I had that same feeling I had had for her ever since we first met, which was not at all like the feeling I have had for anyone else before or since, not desire exactly, though not unmixed with desire, but a sense that she was at the centre of life, or of what life ought to be, not because she was a moral example (I could think of several cases where I couldn't say she had done the right thing) but because she had a moral seriousness attached to her in some way, not as a weight or burden, more like a fragrance. Could seriousness be a fragrance? What was seriousness anyway? Going on at things seemed to be the way most people thought of it, not holding back or stopping half-way for second thoughts or a cigarette. Was that always so admirable? Somehow it wasn't a topic I could discuss with Helen. I suddenly thought how much I would have liked to see her father again and have this sort of conversation with him.

These tired and teasing thoughts were brought to an end by a brisk rap on the door. Bobs.

'I've bedded Mrs Fitch down. She's a widow. Husband worked for BP, large bald man like Boris Karloff. Showed me his photograph.'

Bobs looked merchant-marine, too, with his blazer and general briskness. Perhaps he and Helen were a suitable couple after all, and the sooner they settled down together the better for them and everyone else. Deep fatigue swept over me as though I had swallowed some opiate shortly after boarding the *Zephyr* and I found it hard even to follow them up the companionway and wave goodbye from the deck.

As the hooter sounded, my legs began to give under me and I had to hold on to the railing with one hand while making a bravura farewell with the other.

Soon I was swaddled in the *Zephyr's* pink sheets, my nostrils appeased by the scent of Lavender Haze sprayed over the bed. Even the gentle hum of the engines beginning to make way conspired to shoo me off to sleep, one of those sweet and utter sleeps that you awake from bewildered, tumbled back into a world so strange and unsought that you are not sure you aren't still in dreamland. The first sound was the oddest, seagulls again or still. Did they follow the ship the whole way across the Atlantic? Surely it wasn't possible to have slept through the whole voyage, that would be a feat of narcolepsy beyond even me. But seagulls – there was no doubt about it. They had to be investigated. I tumbled out of the pink sheets, put on a jersey and trousers and deck shoes and clattered up the stairs, feeling like a hand reluctantly taking up his watch.

The most peculiar thing. Thick mist wet against my cheek. Half an hour or so after dawn. But there was no sign of the sun, only the great swathes of fog rolling around the fuchsia funnel and the radio masts. Even so, I could see that the ship was nosing its way up some kind of channel with grey-green banks on either side and not so far away. The river or estuary if that was what it was seemed hardly wide enough to contain the great liner which was moving with the utmost caution. Out of the gloom loomed a tower on a low cliff. Or was it an island or an outcrop of rock in the water? A lighthouse perhaps, but it was not lit, and as we came closer, I could see that it was a tower and the top of it was ruined. The scene was so deadly quiet, the mist so deceiving, that I felt deranged and wondered whether this might be a late add-on to my dream. Or had we lost our way and were just about to go aground on some rocky inlet, in Brittany perhaps? Yet our course seemed deliberate and there was no sign of panic.

For another half-hour or so, I stood leaning over the rail shivering a little, feeling my skin tremble against rough wool. Then the engines shut down and there was nothing but the silence on the water until it was broken by the rattle and clank of the anchor chain paying out. Silence again when the anchor was down. It seemed we might be there for ever hovering in these misty waters.

Then faintly, from far ahead of us, came the puttering of some engine and, a long time later, so long that it might have been a different engine, a big launch almost the size of a trawler crept out of the mist towards me. As the launch came alongside our lower decks and men rushed forward to make her fast, I could see her varnished upper deck gleaming in the wet dawn. The deck was half-hidden by the huge pile of luggage: great matching leather suitcases shining with the wet on them, then a matching set of fashion luggage in assorted shapes with brocade patterns; several long cases for dresses, two flat gun-cases of bruised apple-green canvas with battered leather corners, clumpy vanity cases, hat boxes, golf bags with the sheen of young calves and long floppy bags in light canvas concealing who knew what implements of pleasure – polo sticks, skis, surfboards?

Men in pink jerseys, more Heavensent livery, began to haul these exquisite impedimenta on to a conveyor belt slung across to D deck. I had just heard the purring of the belt as it started up, when I became aware that I was not the only spectator. Standing to one side of the mound of luggage in the launch, and bracing himself against its slopping from side to side was a huge man in a great overcoat which must have demanded the skins of a whole herd of some shaggy Alpine creature. He was joined after a couple of minutes by a woman, much slighter but wearing a coat taken from some other luckless mammals. Her hair was done in a brindled queue, much the same colour as her coat.

Even in that uncertain dawn there was no mistaking the Wilmots. Where had they come from? How and why had they made this rendezvous with the *Zephyr?* Where the hell, in any case, were we? The initial diagnosis, that my trembling body was in reality still asleep and that this strange detour of the *Zephyr* was a figment of the last eye-flickers of that profound slumber, that diagnosis seemed to have a lot to be said for it.

Even in a dream, though, you can wave, in fact dreamers do a good deal of waving as well as drowning, so I leant over the rail and waved with some zest at the goat-coated duo. But I was high above them and the mist was thick and in any case I must have been less easy to identify than they were, so Dodo Wilmot looking up gave me only a perfunctory unrecognising flop of his great paw and Tucker who was busy counting her suitcases as they burbled along the conveyor belt didn't look up at all.

After the cases were all gone into our boat, the two of them stood for a moment or two, like worshippers not wishing to show irreverent haste at the end of the service, then moved out of sight towards the gangway at the back of the launch. I too lingered at my look-out post watching the mist clear from this strange channel, before going to look for the Wilmots or breakfast whichever came first.

It was not until I was coming out of the dining-room that I saw them standing by the rail. He was pointing something out to her and she was smoothing her hair with one hand. The sun was out now behind them so that it was from their outline rather than their faces that I recognised them and only when they came towards the door into the passage where I was standing that I saw that it was not his wife Tucker that he had with him but Jane Stilwell.

'Well, hi and hallo, isn't this great,' Dodo said.

All Jane said was 'You' and clapped her hand to her mouth as violently as though her teeth would have fallen out if she hadn't. She probably meant to show astonishment or delight or both but the effect was more like unashamed panic and when she skipped over the brass threshold to embrace me she collapsed into my arms like a shot bird.

'Well, well,' Dodo said. 'You come aboard at Southampton?'

'Yes,' I said, through a mouthful of mussed-up copper hair.

'We were going to catch the plane at Shannon but I thought to myself, what the hell's the point of owning a boat if you can't holler for her. Besides, the *Queens* always used to drop by here, so I thought why not my little cockleshell? This is one hell of a fun place, you know that. If you're looking for a place to honeymoon, this is it. We had a couple of days in Kildare with John and Ricki Huston, then we came on down to Ballybunion. I played that Sahara hole every which way, never did no better than a bogey.'

'Honeymoon?'

'We got married at Caxton Hall on the way through. Didn't Jane tell you? She's the next best thing to the Voice of America, I was sure you'd be tuned in.'

Jane gave a wry moue of, what, irony? Regret? In fact, she looked so happy in a distracted way that the expression seemed to have trouble sticking to her face.

'Gus here was one of the last of us to see John alive.'

'I know that, dear.'

'Course you do. And he was at the mission, too, with Helen. We were all there.'

'Yes, I know that.'

'The way it was, Gus, first thing I did after the funeral which was a very lovely occasion at Coopers Ferry, the old Stilwell place, first thing I did was to invite Mrs Stilwell down to the farm for a change of scene and –'

'Dodo, perhaps we could talk about this all another time?'

'Sure, anything you say, we've got a hell of a lot to talk about. Say, wasn't that coal strike something? We had 50,000 tons sitting over at Rotterdam, just as a first instalment you understand, but those goddamn dockers wouldn't shift a single sack. Why, look at that sun, it's going to be a great day. You had your breakfast? Well, excuse us, I'm in a mood to run right through the menu this morning, they know I'm coming and if they can't do it right for me then God help the rest of the passengers.'

Cackling with satisfaction, he brushed aside the swing doors and sailed through into the dining-room. Jane paused as though to stay behind and bring me up to date but then thought better of it and gave me one of her quick, nervous smiles that really did come from her heart and pierced mine. It was, I suppose, her most typical and touching way of reaching out, though it was not entirely easy to interpret. Perhaps its ambiguity was part of its charm. How fond we would be of each other if life were easier and we had more time: that was one way of decoding it. But then there was another not quite conflicting interpretation, which implied that the fault was not life's but hers, viz, we are in such sympathy and I am so fond of you, so very fond, but I am also a hopeless person and everything I attempt in the line of love (or perhaps in any line) comes to grief.

The thought came to me soon enough, to be precise about five seconds after she had thrown me her signature smile and followed her – well, it had to be said – her husband through the swing doors. Presumably, the thought went, she had thrown Dodo several of these hopeless smiles while he was showing her his glossy hunters in his honeysuckle-twined paddocks. And in such circumstances – her tragic widowhood, Dodo's last hours with John, their long association – the smiles would count double, being sodden with Destiny. Meanwhile, Tucker – what about Tucker? The first Mrs Wilmot, the brindled *doppelgänger*, seemed to have been erased from the story with clinical, almost Stalinist indifference. Where was she now? Abandoned in Reno or some other place where you could get a quickie divorce, or returned down south to her roots, mournfully sipping too many mint juleps on the verandah of a widowed aunt?

Then another thought: John Stilwell's last days in Africa, his doomed safari (not quite a safari, really, but safari sounded better than investment project reconnaissance), Dodo's long friendship with Jane, his clumsy but tender comforting – none of this might have done the trick without a case of good old mistaken identity. Jane coming in from the garden carrying a bunch of honeysuckle perhaps, with the light behind her, only her outline distinct, the elegant bunching of the Presidential queue unmistakable, or so Dodo had thought and, perhaps a little overcome with the scent of the honeysuckle, had swept her into his arms with a tender yawp of 'Mother' and had held her in a long embrace from which she had, on present evidence, shown no inclination to disentangle herself.

'Come see my ship,' burbled Dodo fed and happy at my ear, the aromas of bacon and fries and eggs benedict streaming around me in the fresh light breeze. We were going about now in the narrow channel, very slow and gingerly – like a goddamn elephant in a boudoir, Dodo chuckled. The prow of the boat seemed almost to nuzzle the tip of the island with the ruined tower, its lichened stones a silvery grey-green against the richer green of the low pastures behind it.

'Hey this is the life, if the *Zeph* don't cure you, I don't know nothing on God's earth that will.'

Mm, I assented, drawing as deep a lungful of air as I could manage and then puffing it out over the rail.

'You asthmatic, or emph, or general bronchial?'

'Asthmatic, well, used to be but not any more.' I stared at him in some surprise and he stared back.

'So what the hell you doing on mah boat?' His new persona as shipping magnate seemed to bring on a touch of the South in his voice.

Puzzled by his question, I tried to recall whether Bobs had somehow defrauded the shipping line, then recollected that it was I who was defrauding the British government by snaffling the money they had given me for the airfare.

I told Dodo that a friend had given me his firm's complimentary ticket.

'Well, good for him, the more folks we can get acquainted with the *Zephyr* experience, the more of 'em will come back again. And to tell you the truth, a shipload of sick folks gets kinda depressing now and then, though, mind you, plenty of them bring their loved ones along for the ride.'

'Sick folks?' I mumbled, trying to keep up with his booming stride along the deck.

'You mean your friend didn't tell you? This is the only floating clinic for respiratory diseases you ever likely to see. Who wants to be stuck in some crummy hotel with their face stuck in an oxygen mask when they could be inhaling God's own oxygen and getting the world's best treatment just down the passage? I'll have you meet Dr Guderian, he's the tops.'

As we went on round the deck, the sun finally drew clear of the mist and the first passengers began to emerge and reserve the teak steamer chairs with their rugs and books. One or two still wore pyjamas and dressing-gowns with scarves wound round their necks, as though they intended only to catch a quick breath before going back down again. But others were fully dressed and came muffled for a longer outing, sometimes taking two trips to assemble their equipment. Towards the stern, we passed Mrs Fitch. She was reading Volume Three of Runciman's *History of the Crusades* and gave me a big smile and a thumbs-up sign.

'It's a great project. You can charge 10, 20 per cent above the standard cruise rates and the medical bills cost you less than half of that and I'm talking about top-quality medical care here. I'm talking Alfred H. Guderian MD and a string of other letters after his name. Matter of fact, he's a cousin of Guderian the inventor of the German armoured corps. I was a tank guy myself, so that created a bond between us. Second cousin, I think he said. You see anything of Helen now?'

'Yes, actually she saw me off yesterday.'

'Did she now? I don't mind telling you I've still got a lot of time for that little lady.'

'Still?'

'Well, she's kinda gone off me, I fear I may have alienated her somewhat.'

He gave a mysterious cackle, or at any rate a cackle intended to provoke me to ask him why.

'The answer's kinda confidential.'

'That's more or less what she said.'

'She's a good girl, and I respect her for respecting my confidence. A lot of broads would have used the opportunity to take a little revenge.'

'How? What sort of revenge?'

'You ask too many questions, my friend.'

He chuckled again and patted me on the back.

'I've been lucky with my women, luckier'n I had a right to be, that's for sure.'

He sighed and blinked at the sun, much moved by the thought of his good fortune.

'Tucker now, you remember Tucker, you couldn't not remember Tucker. She's a great girl, a really great girl and I don't want any misunderstanding about that.'

'She is.'

'And as you might imagine, I haven't treated her right. It wouldn't take any great perspicacity to guess that, would it now? You wouldn't need to have a PhD in personal relations to deduce that the first Mrs Waldo H. Wilmot has had a raw deal out of life. All right, so she went off with the tennis pro, that's her privilege, in her position I'd be sorely tempted to go off with the tennis pro – even if he did happen to be a two-bit guinea who serves like a girl.'

Something like displeasure spread across his mild bulbous features. We walked on, passing Mrs Fitch again, now snuggled down in her steamer chair but not too swaddled to give me another thumbs-up. The sight of the chairs filling up restored Dodo's humour and he began bestowing benevolent smiles on his tenantry.

'You'll find Dr Guderian in the therapy lounge,' the girl in Heavensent fuchsia at Clinic Reception told us with a breathless gulp as though to suggest a treat in store. We went through what looked like a consulting-room into a sort of cramped gym where a row of half a dozen elderly persons were sitting facing us. They were engaged in what looked suspiciously like the breathing exercises I had been forced to practise twice a day in my teens and which, according to a pushy doctor I had recently met on holiday, were now regarded as useless. The passengers/patients were being led through the ritual by a short nurse with frizzy ginger hair and a listless adenoidal voice.

But it was the onlooker standing with his back to us who drew my attention. He was clearly part of the team, wearing a tunic and trousers in the Heavensent livery, both garments piped along the seams in navy blue, and fuchsia-pink deck shoes with navy-blue rims.

Surely no, it couldn't be, but the set of that massive head on those broad shoulders, the posture brooding and inquisitorial . . . And as he swung round to greet us, that saturnine profile, simultaneously fleshy and hawklike conveying its unlikely combination of willpower and melancholy. Though we had not met for a decade, no, quite a bit more, and I had long ago concurred in my father's premature diagnosis that I had grown out of it and was as cured as ever anyone could hope to be, I could not repress a shudder on once again encountering Dr Maintenon-Smith, the self-styled Napoleon of Asthma.

'Nicky, my dear boy. What a pleasure. No one told me that you were sailing with us.'

'Gus,' I said, 'actually.'

'Gus, of course. You still look so like Nicky, I always mixed you two up.'

There had been no Nicky at the clinic, but I had no room to ponder that, being unable to stop goggling at the little white plastic name-tag attached to his left lapel. The tunic was double-breasted, broad-lapelled with pink satin revers, adding to the Napoleonic feeling. He might have shrugged it on to sit for Ingres. What the name-tag said was Dr Alfred H. Guderian MD FRCP.

'You two good people have met before?' Dodo Wilmot's earlier displeasure peeped out again at the thought of any connection he had no part in supervising.

'We have indeed,' said Dr Guderian (it seems simpler to use his alias). 'He was a patient of mine the other side of the water. I never forget anyone who has been under my care.'

'Bet he gave you one hell of a lot of trouble.'

'On the contrary, he was a model patient, but medically a difficult case. His father, I believe it was, chose to remove him at an unfortunate moment, and I cannot say I am entirely surprised to find him on this voyage.'

It occurred to me, for the first time, that my father might have taken me away from the clinic not because he thought I was cured but because he could no longer afford to pay the fees, perhaps indeed had not paid the fees for the previous term either. The glittering menace in Dr Guderian's eye suggested that this might well be so and that this was one thing he had not forgotten.

Dodo Wilmot began to laugh.

'No, no, for once you've got the wrong diagnosis, Doc. This fellow's sound as a bell. He's just come along for the ride. I went all over Africa with him, never wheezed once.'

'I am delighted to hear it. Sometimes I am surprised by the success of my own methods. Medicine is a humbling art. One never knows how little one knows, or how much, until Nature chooses to enlighten one. Gus, we must chew over old times, we have much to talk about.'

'Well, I'll leave you two guys together, I need to go make a few calls. Thought he was a patient, I must tell Jane, she'll just love it.'

He disappeared chuckling.

Dr Guderian took my arm, cradling my elbow as though it were bruised and needed careful handling, and led me out on deck.

'It is a remarkable coincidence our meeting again and in such circumstances. I often think back to our high jinks at the clinic. It will not have escaped you that I am somewhat changed since those carefree days.'

He raised his profile to the gentle morning breeze, inviting me to inspect it for decay, of which there was little sign – the jet-black hair a little sparser perhaps but if anything rather blacker, the eye still commanding as ever.

'You look very well,' I said.

'You know that was not what I meant.'

He tapped his name-tag.

'There,' he said, 'that is what you have been goggling at since the moment you set eyes on me again.'

'Well, I was a little puzzled.'

'You are right to be puzzled. At one moment you see me the respected Dr Maintenon-Smith, director of the foremost clinic of its sort in the South of England, on dining terms with the Chief Constable, and now here you see me Dr Guderian, a mere ship's doctor. What is there going on? Is this an imposture, some bizarre type of conspiracy? Do I read your thoughts correctly, I am sure I do.'

'Umm –'

'Well, I will tell you the truth. As so often in this life, the truth is quite innocent but a little sad. Not tragic perhaps but sad. You remember my wife?'

'Yes, of course.'

Madame Maintenon-Smith was a low-spirited unobtrusive figure who ran the Medical Stores at the clinic. She did not seem to care for the work and spoke little, and then mostly of her two grown-up sons, both working in Clermont-Ferrand.

'Well, she died.'

He threw out a hand over the rail, as though casting her ashes out over the sea. Then he paused.

'I was a broken man, my life seemed finished, purposeless. I did not react well, I lost control. I who was dedicated to self-control – you may recall me saying in the old days that in love self-control is the most exquisite of all perversions – I became intemperate. I drank.'

His voice resounded over the calm milky ocean. The Irish coast was now only a grey-green streak along the horizon. Dr Guderian had not lost Dr Maintenon-Smith's manly baritone, at the same time hypnotic and stagy, so that he sounded as though he were repeating someone else's words, now and then possibly with ironic intent.

'My wife had always done the clinic accounts. Without her, I was as helpless as a baby. Mistakes were made. I hired a jackanapes from Worthing, he turned out to be a good-for-nothing. The Inland Revenue took a pettifogging view. It was an unpleasant period.'

He shuddered at the recollection.

'So the clinic –'

'Is no more. I believe the creditors are hoping to reopen it as an hotel. The matter is of no interest to me. It is a dead chapter. I resolved to begin afresh.'

'Under a new name.'

'Under my real name.'

He snorted with pleasure at my surprise.

'Yes, I was born Alfred Guderian in a small Prussian town a few miles from my cousin Heine, the tank guy as your friend Mr Wilmot insists on calling him.'

'But Maintenon-Smith?'

'My wife was *née* Maintenon, a descendant, I believe, of the great Madame de Maintenon, the mistress and later wife of Louis Quatorze. How strange it was that the King who could have enjoyed every woman in France should have chosen to marry my wife's ancestor, a very devout, very sensible woman, but a widow of a certain age. Just as Madame Bovary found in adultery all the platitudes of marriage, so *Le Roi Soleil* found in marriage with a bourgeoise all the excitements of adultery.'

How often had I heard Dr Maintenon-Smith spout these *mots*, pacing up and down the stone floors of our dormitory or the squeaky parquet of the classroom (the place was a school as well as a clinic for teenage wheezers). The only difference was that, in those days, he had claimed Madame de Maintenon as his own ancestor, an equally improbable boast, since I later discovered that Madame de Maintenon had no children and her family name was different in any case, Maintenon being merely the town she took her title from and only visited a couple of times in her life.

'We met on the Isle of Man.'

'The Isle of Man?'

'I was interned there, as an enemy alien. I had been doing post-graduate work at Manchester when the war broke out. How it rained, in Manchester first and then on the Island. I had never seen such rain. Sometimes in my dreams I hear the gurgle of those boggy streams and the creak of the great water-wheel at Laxey. My wife was one of the camp interpreters, she was a linguist of some distinction.'

His eyes filled with tears which he brushed aside with a curious motion of disdain, managing to convey at the same time his impatience with this moment of weakness and also a satisfaction in demonstrating that a large-souled man was not incapable of tears. My father would have approved. He had no time for a man who could not weep.

'She was half-English?'

'No, wholly French.'

'But the Smith?'

'Ah the wretched Smith.'

He looked at me with sardonic condescension as though it was I who had somehow foisted the Smith on him.

'That was a little *jeu d'esprit*, surely pardonable in those grey times. Towards the end of the war I was allowed to do a little doctoring and we made friends among the local gentry. We had noticed, my wife and I, how they prided themselves upon their double-barrelled surnames which were, after all, very ordinary names. Why should we too not have two barrels? *Et voilà*, Maintenon-Smith. We were received everywhere with the greatest respect. I do not think that, after the war, Dr Guderian would have had so many patients.'

He paused at the end of the recital, then looked at me with sudden recognition, almost as if we had just bumped into each other.

'Yes, yes, you were the tipster. When I came to see you in bed you would give me horses for courses. And in the staffroom they would ask what does Nicky say for the Guineas.'

'Gus.'

'Gus. And when they went down to the Spread Eagle at lunchtime, they would all have their bets.'

I was touched by his remembering. On those mornings when I was too ill to go down to breakfast, the nurse would bring up the *Sporting Life* for me and I would run through the form, to be ready for Dr Maintenon-Smith plumping his bulk on top of my feet and his Dettol breath swamping me as he leant forward to look at the runners and riders with me.

'I hadn't realised I had so many customers.'

'You were keeping us all afloat. *Ah les beaux jours.*'

The wistful look he cast across the sea touched me too. It had not occurred to me that life in the clinic, with its draughty, carbolic-scented corridors, the dismal breathing exercises, the rough rituals of the dormitory, not to mention the starchy, watery food, could be anyone's *beaux jours.*

'But enough of these backward glances, we must look to new horizons. You will excuse me, I have a passenger with advanced emphysema to see, a retired metal-broker. We share an interest in Mahler.'

He went on his way, impervious once more, with hands clasped behind his back, *l'Empereur* stalking the deck of the *Bellerophon*, caged but not tamed.

His departure left me feeling frail in mind and weak at the knees. He had shown me his vulnerable side, if only to explain the name-change. Even he had spent half his life clinging on by his fingernails, it seemed. How could the rest of us hope to cope? And yet he was still clinging to his little *mensonges* about the descent from Madame de Maintenon, probably other things too.

Then it came to me properly for the first time that I was stuck on this boat for the next five days with Jane, about the same length of time in fact that my affair with her, or call it what you like, had lasted. Then, I had longed to see her bright eager face peering through the glass door into the dark sitting-room. Once or perhaps twice, when we had been uncertain whether Brainerd might weary of arranging his Orangina cans or Mr Stilwell (even now that he was dead I found it hard to think of him as John) might come in from golf, which would give us a minute or two to rearrange ourselves because there would be a clatter as he put his golf clubs in the hall stand, once or twice we would huddle in the angle under the stairs where there was a long low stool out of sight of either of the doors. There was room to touch and fondle on the ridged green velvet of the stool but no room for our heads except bent low over one another's shoulders, so that if I opened my eyes I was staring into the dark greasy varnish of the stairboards. In these intense hunched grapplings, we must have looked like wrestlers in one of those specialised codes in which the two contestants scarcely seem to move, although every muscle in their bodies is braced. How white her skin was in that dark corner as we broke away gasping, as white as she had said my teeth looked in that first peculiar overture of hers.

Now it would be a question of finding on this boat a similar dark corner but this time one for me to be alone in. In my cabin I would be a sitting duck. Even if I feigned illness – but she had already seen me, probably the healthiest passenger in this boatload of invalids – even that would offer a pretext for a sympathetic visit. But then perhaps these speculations were all futile self-flattery. She would surely be wrapped up in her new husband, would not wish to be reminded of a stupid interlude which had ended with her wading out to sea. If I lay low and got through *Anna Karenina* as I intended (I had given up on *Moby-Dick*), I might survive the voyage with only a little harmless general chat with her at mealtimes.

Too much to hope for. Within half an hour the little white telephone with its fuchsia frill jangled pertly with a summons from Dodo Wilmot to come and help them get rid of a shakerful of Bloody Marys.

'We're in Mistral on A Deck, it's the one after Sirocco.'

The steamer chairs were mostly taken now. One or two of the patients looked so frail I wondered how they had managed to come up on deck at all, their hollow cheeks trembling with each feeble breath. The scudding sea and the level hum of the engine drowned out their gasps, which must have been one of the reliefs, for the sound of your own laboured breathing I remembered was the most dismal sound in the world and an embarrassment you couldn't extricate yourself from, like being condemnded to tell a tedious anecdote you knew had no ending. So perhaps they were as happy as could be expected with their mufflers frothed up around their stringy gullets and their pale eyes staring at the dark swelling sea.

Dodo and Jane looked like beings from a different race: she stretched out yawning in a pink candy-striped boudoir chair, her long legs brown and surprisingly muscular seeing she was so thin, he massive in a sailor's shirt and white yachting slacks brandishing a bulbous silver shaker as though he was in a steel band.

'Well, how do you like her?'

'Her? Oh, you mean the boat. She's great. Well, to be honest, I haven't had a chance to see her properly yet. I've been more struck, I suppose, by the patients.'

'They're a great crowd, aren't they? Eighty-five per cent occupancy and no discounts, plus a few freeloaders like you. Not bad for off-peak.'

'A lot of them seem awfully ill, I'm surprised some could make it at all.'

'You got it, that's our pitch. If it's the last breath you take, why not take it on the good ship *Zephyr* with the sea breeze in your hair and the sun sinking over an exotic Caribbean island?'

'See Nassau and die,' Jane offered.

'Yeah, but of course we don't say it that crudely. We just reassure them that the medical care is first-rate and we're fully prepared for any emergency.'

'Including the final one.'

'Temperature-controlled mortuary down on D deck, but in case anyone asks, burial at sea is strictly O.U.T.'

'Why?' asked Jane. 'I rather like the sound of burial at sea.'

'Discourages the other passengers, to adapt what Monsieur Voltaire said about them hanging Admiral Byng.'

'It wouldn't discourage me.'

'You're different, honey. Doesn't she look great?'

He bussed her lightly on the lips as he refilled her chunky crystal glass. She did look different now, different from my memory of her at any rate. Her movements seemed slower, almost languid, and the quick look in her eye seemed to have switched off. Perhaps that was what money did for you, removed the urgency, although come to think of it John Stilwell had been rich, perhaps very rich, but then he was also anxious in a buttoned-up way. Or perhaps it wasn't Dodo's easy, spread-it-around style that had calmed her as much as his adoring her so visibly. As he passed to refill my glass, he slid his great paw alongside the inside of her knee up to the edge of her crisp Bermudas.

Suddenly I was so choke-full of resentment that I could not help flushing up.

'Too hot for you in here, is it, Gus?' inquired Dodo with that always startling alertness. 'We Yanks are hothouse plants, ain't a damn thing we can do about it.'

What was there to resent? Obviously I had no moral rights on her, no immoral rights even, never had had. My adolescent fling was a long time ago and an embarrassing fumbling affair best forgotten. That at any rate was what I tried to think, to help recall the colour from my cheeks and look like a normal human being.

Then for some reason I started thinking of Anna Karenina and how dull Anna and Vronsky become after they have run off together and how the betrayed husband Karenin who is the only really interesting character in the book becomes more interesting still, probably more interesting than the author intended or realised. And I thought how interesting it would have been to know John Stilwell's innermost thoughts about his wife, and hers about him and how – this wasn't to be thought but I thought it all the same – how exciting it would have been to come upon them making love, what an awkward yet delicate way he might have had, a delicacy which would have remained pristine, protected rather than blunted by his non-committal public persona and his talk of train timetables. And in comparison how dull and blatant were all Dodo's uninhibited pawings and her languorous responses. That was it, Dodo had made her boring, that was what I resented, he had ironed out her little mysteries.

It was a relief to escape their remorseless healthiness and to seek out the company of the sick. Mrs Fitch had made a friend, another widow whose husband had been in the Gulf too but at another time and for another company, perhaps in another state – I couldn't quite catch every word of their talk over the noise of the *Zephyr* cutting through the glassy sea.

'Woterrooeding?'

'What? Oh? *Anna Karenina.*'

'Silly girl' – this from Mrs Fitch's friend, who spoke tartly as though of someone she used to know, not in that distanced way people normally spoke of characters in books. 'Read a lot out East, odd books, whatever they had in the library, kept you out of mischief, though a lot of the hanky-panky was only pretend. We weren't all Happy Valley types, you know.'

She snorted, amused at the thought of herself as someone with a flighty past, then more reflectively said: 'Though there was a chap in Skinner's Horse who made passes at every girl, simply threw them to the ground.'

'Was that in India then?'

'Not just in India, wherever he was stationed. Simply threw them to the ground.'

She was a big woman, her face swollen under the powder, perhaps by drugs, but even so I could see how lively and cherry-ripe she must have looked.

'Big strong chap was he?' Mrs Fitch asked, smiling. The thought of the man in Skinner's Horse seemed to have cured her speech difficulty for the moment.

'No, he was only a little man, but they often are aren't they, the handfuls? I'm Cynthia Perse.'

She held out her hand, which was swollen too with the flesh half-hiding the rings on her fingers. A certain contentment stole over me as their conversation wandered around various outposts of empire and the afternoon sun crept round to our side of the deck.

Then a shadow fell across it.

'Well hi, there you are, you certainly have picked yourself the perfect spot, haven't you? Good afternoon ladies, do you mind if I borrow this young man for a minute?'

Jane Stilwell – Wilmot, as I supposed I must now think of her – held out a lightly tanned arm with the gawky grace of a gazelle but an irresistible air of command. It was like being back in her employ when she would say, Gus dear, would you be a darling and go fetch the bread from Madame Henri.

'It's kind of you, I know,' she said, putting the gazelle arm firmly through mine and marching me down the deck. 'And I'm sure those old biddies much appreciate you sitting with them, but don't you think at your age you ought to be doing something a little more active?'

'Active?'

'There's the pool, that's where all the other able-bodied passengers spend most of the day, and the gym of course, and the deck tennis and the badminton though it's a bit too windy today, or even the pingpong for Christ's sake. You don't have to just vegetate.'

'Don't I?'

'If you want my opinion, I think you're getting to be too broody. Nobody wants a broody person around. But that wasn't what I wanted to say. Dodo's talking to his broker, so I thought I'd just scoot along and get a few things straight. Now don't get me wrong, Gus, it's great to see you, it was just a lovely surprise, but there mustn't be any misunderstandings between us.'

'I didn't know there were any.'

'You know I'm just incredibly fond of you and what happened between us was wonderful and I'll always keep the memory of it very dear, but it's over and –'

'Of course it is,' I broke in crossly, 'I know that perfectly well, I'm not a complete idiot. It was years and years ago.'

'Well then, you mustn't goggle at me like that, it was a terrible embarrassment, even Dodo noticed, in fact he had to say something and then afterwards when you'd gone he said I think that little guy still has the hots for you.'

'Still?'

'Oh it's been a joke between us, you know, that I was in love with the tutor, which I was of course so it's an easy one to play along with. He has no idea, really.'

'I wasn't goggling at you at all, in fact I was thinking of something quite different.'

'Well, it's sweet of you to pretend but at my age I think I'm a pretty good judge of when a man's making eyes at me.'

'I wasn't.'

'Have it any way you please. I just don't want you to do it again, whatever it was you were doing. Anyway, haven't you still got that dear little blonde person, you know, the chemist?'

'She was never a girlfriend, not properly.'

'Not properly? You carry on with her all summer so shamelessly I try to kill myself and now you tell me ten years later you didn't manage to do it properly. Jesus, you English.'

'We were only friends, it wasn't anything to do with her that you –'

'No it wasn't, was it? It was another of your bizarre escapades. I'll say that for you, you packed a helluva lot into one summer.'

'It wasn't an escapade at all. It was simply mistaken identity, I thought I'd explained it. Tucker just –'

'Are you trying to kill me again or something? How can you dare to talk to me about Tucker in the present situation? That woman is dearer to me than you'll ever know and I'm not going to have her name brought into this whole sordid thing.'

Her slender arm was jammed so hard against mine that it felt like an iron bar.

'Look, Jane, it wasn't sordid, I wasn't goggling at you and even if you still think I was I promise I won't do it again.'

'If you only knew.' She looked at me in a way which she may have meant to seem bitter – that was what I expected anyway – but only came out expressionless, dulled by her brown skin and the shades perched on her brindled hair.

'If you only knew,' she repeated. 'Well, I guess you will know soon enough and then you'll be, no, sorry I don't think, sorry isn't in your nature, but you may understand just a little more of what we women go through. Now you run along back to your senior citizens, at least you can't do them much harm.'

She unhooked her arm, I felt the bone of her forearm sear mine, it was like being unshackled from a chain gang.

'A fine-looking woman, your friend,' Mrs Perse said. 'You knew her before, I suppose?'

'Yes, I tutored her children years ago.'

'Children of the first marriage?'

'Yes.'

'Who are now grown up.'

'Yes, I suppose they must be.'

'Older than she looks then.'

Mrs Perse gazed out to sea, with the quiet satisfaction of the old-fashioned amateur detective who can unravel the whole mystery without stirring from her armchair.

'You will sit with us at dinner, I hope, and feed us a few crumbs from the captain's table. It is so nice to have a friend on the inside.'

Mrs Fitch was taking a puff at her inhaler while Mrs Perse was issuing this invitation, but she seconded it with a vigorous nod. I accepted with unfeigned pleasure. Their company was both restful and bracing, just as a cruise ought to be. Besides, seated between them I would be protected from the Wilmots.

'I hope I may see you at morning service tomorrow.'

Dr Guderian whispered this hope into my ear as we were trooping into the cavernous dining-room.

'Oh I didn't −'

'It is Trinity Sunday. I shall be conducting the service myself.'

'No, I mean −'

'I became a communicating member of the Church of England when I was on the Isle of Man. It was intended that I should become a lay reader, but circumstances forbade it.'

'Doesn't the Captain usually take the service?'

'Captain Bosinney prefers to preside over the bingo.'

Guderian passed on his way, bowing this way and that, dispensing his ingratiating menace in that remote way of his, as though he was rehearsing this courtly progress to an empty room or perhaps not in an empty room but in front of a group of judges who would be expected to award him marks at the end but for the time being had to act as extras for him to bow to.

'He gives me the creeps,' Mrs Perse said. 'I expect you think I say that because he's foreign, but doctors always give me the creeps.'

'You must have seen a lot of creeps recently, dear.' Mrs Fitch's cheeks, so pale and furry when we had met in the train, now shone with pleasure, or perhaps she had caught the sun. The cruise seemed to be doing her nothing but good. You would scarcely know she had any trouble with her speech. Perhaps it was partly a nervous thing.

'That's the worst thing about ill-health, having to be polite to doctors. Still, I always like to see their faces when I tell them I've never smoked in my life and it must be the gin.'

'Oh Cynthia.'

'Call this asparagus. It looks like something they've just caught in the propellers. Great thing about cancer is you don't have to finish everything on your plate.'

'Ladies an' gentlemen ...'

At the far end of the long dining-room with its rococo swags of cherubs and roses roistering along the walls, Dodo heaved into view, massive in his white dinner jacket like some huge creature of the deep long suspected to be extinct but now and then washed up on some far shore to be surrounded by chattering islanders.

'Lemme introduce myself to you good people. I'm Waldo Wilmot and I have the privilege to be the chairman of your line, so I'm where the buck stops. You might say I'm the end of the line. I don't want to keep you from your gourmet dinner here tonight but I know you'd want me to say a big thank-you to Jacques and his team down in the galley for the magnificent work they do. This is a great company because it's a great people company. And I'd like to take this opportunity to introduce to you some of the wonderful people who'll be taking care of you on this trip. On my right here is Captain Philip R. Bosinney, now Phil –'

'It was never like this on the old Cunard ships. If you wanted to talk to the purser, you went to the purser's office.'

'Oh you are out of date, dear. Everyone has to tell you who they are nowadays.'

'*And* their bust size *and* why they don't get on with their daughter-in-law *and* what's wrong with them down there.'

'... and Dr Alfred H. Guderian, one of the finest physicians it has been my good fortune to claim as a friend. Many of you will have met him already. By the end of this trip, I guarantee you'll want to have him on your medical team till hell freezes over. Great to have you aboard, Alfred.'

Dr Guderian rose from his seat at the captain's table under the clock in the shape of a golden sunburst. For a moment he remained motionless, then his imperial eye swept the room before he swooped into a bow, which was both deep and stiff and expressive of the deepest reverence.

It was hard to say whether he had intended this to be all but Dodo wanted more.

'Alfred, may I persuade you to share just a little of your philosophy with us tonight, I know it would be much appreciated and to many of us it would be a great comfort.'

Dr Guderian mimed being startled, embarrassed, at a loss, utterly ambushed by this request. He bowed again, just his head this time, to show that he was striving to overcome this *éblouissement* and to collect his thoughts.

'Waldo, you are too kind and I am not at all sure that these wonderful people, our shipmates' – he flung his arms wide with wrists oddly bent, giving the impression rather of an angler indicating the size of his catch than of the warm embracing motion he must have intended – 'I am not by any means confident that they will thank you for it. But you are my commanding officer, my captain, and I must obey orders.'

Again he cast his sloe-dark eyes around the great low room, from the wan and grizzled heads of the passengers to the rudely pink cherubs chasing each other in and out of the lime-green swags along the walls. The clatter of cutlery was hushed, the asparagus lay limp in its puddle of yellow mayonnaise.

'Many years ago in France when the Palace of Versailles was at its glittering zenith,' was how he began, 'the King had a personal physician, a man of the greatest eminence. His position was glorious, but it was also precarious, for if he failed to cure the King of whatever ailed him, there were many other eminent physicians who would be happy to take his place. Now the King we are speaking of, Louis Quinze, was in general a healthy, easygoing fellow. He was happy with the Queen, he was happy with his mistress, the good Madame de Pompadour. But as the years went by, the King encountered a problem. It was a common problem, one shared no doubt by many of his subjects. He found that he could no longer pursue the pleasures of love with the same ardour that he had taken for granted since the age of fifteen. Indeed, on many a night, he found himself incapable of pursuing them at all. This was an embarrassment, an indignity not to be tolerated. He sent for the Doctor, who told His Majesty that it was nothing, a mere indisposition that would soon be righted. Meanwhile, he prescribed a mild infusion of mandrake root, a modest draught of ginger and fig-water. Nothing worked, matters went from bad to worse. The Queen was affronted, Madame de Pompadour was distraught. The doctor prescribed a little salad of oysters and saffron. There was no response. In his despair, the King's eye alighted upon a young Irish girl, a certain Mademoiselle O'Murphy. Inquiries were made. The girl was agreeable, the mother was delighted. Mamzelle O'Murphy was smuggled in by the usual back door. And in the morning, the King was beside himself with joy. I am cured, the King is himself again, but tell me, Doctor, which was it wrought the miracle? Was it the oysters or the mandrake root? Neither, Sire, replied the honest doctor, it was your new *petite amie*, it was Mamzelle O'Murphy you have to thank, for change, sire, is the greatest aphrodisiac of them all. And with the greatest respect, ladies and gentlemen, that is the lesson I venture to offer you this evening. But I do not need to teach it you, for you have already learnt it yourselves. A change is as good as a rest, you say in England, and on the good ship *Zephyr* a change *is* a rest. And to you who know how much wisdom resides in that simple phrase, I give you a little toast to finish with: To a change of air!'

He raised his glass with the solemnity of a priest elevating the Host and sank it with a toss of his head so passionate that he seemed on the verge of throwing the empty glass over his shoulder Cossack-style. There was a rather ragged response from the passengers, though not from me. The story of the King's impotence had been a favourite of Dr Maintenon-Smith's. I was glad to hear it again after so long an interval, though not sure whether it was entirely suitable for the present audience. Mrs Perse agreed.

'Hit quite the wrong note. We don't want to be reminded of that sort of thing at our age. Anyway, he's talking nonsense. It's a question of the blood supply. My husband had the same trouble as soon as his blood pressure went up. I suppose he thinks it's all in the mind. He wouldn't if he saw my X-rays.'

'Cynthia,' Mrs Fitch interjected, 'I think he was just trying to cheer us up a bit. Anyway, there is a nervous factor in some of these complaints, isn't there?'

'Claptrap,' Mrs Perse said and returned to poking at her asparagus before pushing it away in a final gesture of rejection.

Was it fancy, or had Dr Guderian's toast sent a fretful unease skittering throughout the dining-room? I noticed several plates being pushed away like Mrs Perse's and the sound of the talk seemed to ricochet off the low ceiling in a jerky intermittent way, like a radio with a fading battery. How odd that a Napoleonic figure who put so much into the effect he made should be such a poor judge of his audience, but then Napoleonic figures were always like that, trembling on the edge of embarrassment and bad taste. Perhaps it was just that awkward edge to their discourse which touched some vulnerable part of their audience's souls, and so seduced not only those people who you would have guessed would be suckers for a demagogue, but also those who regarded themselves as cool and fastidious but who succumbed all the same, muttering how vulgar it all was even as they succumbed. Perhaps what was wrong with Dr Guderian was that he wasn't quite embarrassing enough.

'Thank you, Alfred, for those fine words: they will be an inspiration to us in the days ahead, and now it only remains for me to announce the winner of today's Gone-with-the-Wind competition. Remember, you have to estimate the distance travelled by the *Zephyr* in nautical miles only.'

I could tell that Dodo shared the general unease generated by the Doctor's toast.

'There's something sinister about that man,' Mrs Perse hissed at me.

'You mean he's even creepier than other doctors?'

'No, not the doctor, your friend Mr Wilmot. He's not what he seems.'

'What do you think he seems?'

'Well, he wants to seem a genial, friendly sort of American, but he isn't. He's a phoney.'

The next day was foggy. Out on the upper deck, the fog was so thick I couldn't see the radio mast. It was thick and wet in the throat, a change of air all right and one that penetrated to the lower decks, so that as I padded along the soft carpeting of C Deck, the aisle was full of noises, quick hacking coughs, low keening moans, heavy wheezings which seemed to gather themselves into a huge hoarse gulp and then dwindle into shorter spasms. Sometimes the spasms strung themselves together into what sounded like a snatch of conversation until they separated again into the long strangulated uh-hurrrs of a morning asthma attack.

In fact, there was little or no talk to be heard, most of the passengers having more urgent things to do with their lungs.

Even inside my cabin, the same dismal sounds came vibrating through the thin walls, so that I could not help thinking of the rows of fellow-inmates rolling themselves up in their bedclothes or sitting straight up in armchairs with rugs over their knees.

The following morning the fog was thicker still but I could not stand any more of *Anna Karenina* or of the stertorous coughing and spluttering around me and I went up on deck quite early. The place was deserted and quiet as a funeral. Even the scud of the waves and the hum of the engines were muffled by the fog. Now and then there was a strange noise, half-way between a squeak and a sob, repeated, convulsive. Hard to tell whether it was a bird or a human being or some wire scraping against something. Then at the far end, coming out of the door leading to the staterooms, I saw a large man who seemed to be dragging a smaller figure, probably a woman, half-supporting her as the two of them stumbled along the deck. I was almost sure it was Dodo and Jane, but why was she leaning on him so heavily? Had she sprained her ankle? As they turned the corner, I caught sight of the shape of the brindled queue, though not its colour which was muted by the grey-green-white fog, and I saw the massive back of his head, but there seemed something private about them – perhaps it was just that they were wrapped in the fog. It would have felt wrong, intrusive to pursue them and loom out of the mist at them like a spectre.

Then behind them coming out of the same door, I saw a third figure scurrying after them, another woman holding something flapping, a wrap perhaps, or was it her scurrying run that made the bundle seem to flap? She was trying to catch them up, give them something they had forgotten. This time there was no mistake. The lollopy run like a foal's, with the legs like sticks thrown out as though to flick mud off them, this, no doubt about it, was Jane running as she had run down to misplace her bet on the race that had been fixed. She too disappeared round the corner, leaving me alone on the deck, bewildered. Who then was the other woman? Couldn't be, yet how could it not be? Had they actually *brought Tucker with them* on this, well, if it was not a honeymoon cruise it was as close as made no difference?

It was hard to say how long I stood there with my hand resting on the cold polished wood of the railing, but I began to shiver under my muffler and light dimpled raincoat, the sort Harold Wilson had worn, and it occurred to me that it was time to move before they came round the lifeboat-davit on the other side. But I had left it too late and there they were, the three of them, now moving, swaying really, along the deck towards me with the smaller wrynecked limping one between the other two, held up by their linked arms.

I could not see her face which was enveloped in a voluminous grey scarf and in any case her head was nuzzled down into Dodo's chest. He passed by unseeing, without a word, which seemed odd until I noticed how much in the shadow of the lifeboat I was standing and remembered how thick the fog was. But as they went on down the deck, Jane cast a backward glance, twisting her head abruptly like someone trying to catch a child trying to creep up on her in a game of Grandmother's Footsteps. And it was clear she had seen me. I am not sure how I knew, perhaps an extra jerk of the head, or did her mouth fall open for an instant as if she was about to call out to me but had thought better of it? Then, in only an instant or two, they were gone into the fog again and I went below.

It was the last day of the voyage and in the afternoon the shore birds began to mew in the rigging and passengers gathered along the railing to see if they could catch the first glimpse of Long Island, but the fog was too thick.

I lay low in my cabin hoping that somehow Dodo and Jane would leave me alone until I could get off this terrible boat and leave them to their ghastly saga. But that was too much to hope for and the little knock at the door, an uncertain but repeated rat-tat, not a steward's knock, came with a dreadful inevitability shortly after five o'clock.

'There you are,' Jane said, as though it was a brilliant piece of detection to track me down to my cabin. 'What's all that cottonwool for?'

'I'm making a beard, for the fancy-dress tonight. I'm going as Neptune.'

'Oh isn't that just like you, you just carry on regardless. It's the British thing to do, isn't it?'

'What do you mean?'

'You don't need to talk to me like that. I rather think, don't you, that it's you who owe me an explanation.'

'Is it? What am I supposed to be explaining?'

'Why you were spying on us this morning?'

'I wasn't.'

'There's no point in pretending you weren't. I saw you when I came out on deck and I thought you might have the decency to disappear by the time we came back round. But there you were, skulking under that lifeboat like a private eye.'

'Is that what you've come here to tell me?'

'No, of course it isn't. But it would have been much better if you hadn't –'

'What are you doing, what is all this?' I burst out, suddenly distraught and angry after brooding by myself for so long.

'You see, you wouldn't have needed to know anyway, nor would anyone, not for a long time until she was much better and could look after herself. We just wanted to get her back home, you know, quietly.'

Jane was sitting there on the little pink chair leaning forward making eager emphatic gestures with her hands as though she was conducting an orchestra of dwarfs in front of her. I was still half-lolling on my bed with the fringe of cottonwool now firmly stuck to my chin.

'So now,' she sighed, 'I'll just have to tell you the story, but you must promise, really promise to keep it to yourself. We have been friends so long that I think that I can ask you that much, don't you. Please.'

I nodded, but so minimally that she said please again and I said yes all right, but wishing I was several light years away.

'Well, you know how Dodo and I ... came together. He asked me over to Turkey Creek after John died to tell me about how it happened and talk over old times, and Tucker was down in Corpus Christi with her aunt and anyway she was having this thing with the tennis coach already, I know she was, so one thing led to another, ha' – she gave a little short laugh to acknowledge the cliché – 'and there we were and we knew it wasn't just a passing thing, I don't know how but we just knew. So I went back to New York to see Brainerd and Timmy who was just off to Cornell and Tucker came back from Corpus and I don't know how she found out but she did – Dodo's not very smart really – and then he said what about the tennis coach and they had a bit of a spat but after that she was really very empathetic and said yes, well, perhaps they had come to the end of the road, and she went off to Reno with him like a lamb and they even spent a couple of days together in Vegas in memory of old times, then when they got home to sort out stuff and he went off to look at the horses she went off to his sporting room and found the old blunderbuss that he uses for shooting dove, and boom – but she didn't put it to her forehead firmly enough and she didn't do the job, only blasted part of the frontal lobe, just there.'

She raised her hand to her forehead to show the area, and the likeness between the two of them seemed to have some grim significance in the telling of the story, as though she had been chosen to re-enact the disaster because of her similarity to the victim.

'She's coming through quite well, her walking's not good – well, you saw that – and she can't see at all and she weeps the whole time, can't bear for to meet anybody, that's why we take her for walks when there's nobody else about. It's so sad.'

Her voice had lost its eagerness, and at the end she sounded as if she was speaking of some distant misfortune that had happened to someone she knew only slightly.

'But why are you dragging her round the world with you? Wouldn't she be better off at home resting?'

'Oh there's a great plastic surgeon in Harley Street she just had to see and we thought too the trip would do her good. And the Hustons found us a very peaceful home run by nuns outside Mullingar. Besides, there are a lot of other folks on board who are in the same boat, ha' – she laughed again. Then she looked at me, quite challengingly.

'So what do you say to that? One helluva mess, huh?'

I nodded.

'Is that all you can do, just nod? Is that – oh the hell with it. All I ask is just keep it to yourself. Am I wrong or do you owe me for something or other? Don't tell her anyway, that little Goldilocks of yours, *that* I could not tolerate.'

She rose shooting me a glance dripping with dislike and left the room.

The gum had begun to tighten the skin around my chin and the cottonwool was tickling my nostrils. The green blanket I had borrowed from one of the clinic nurses was much too heavy to wear all evening. It would be crazy to go to the fancy-dress party. There would be half a dozen Neptunes there already.

Much more tempting to lie in bed and think about suicide. Or attempted suicide which was the really unnerving thought. The successful suicide – *successful*, what an odd word to use, but was there a better one, so keen are we to congratulate ourselves on bringing off anything, that we instinctively leave a little tingle of approval around the adjective, however misguided the thing we are attempting – the successful suicide, not being that common, had a certain grandeur. The ripples of pain it left behind would go on widening for a lifetime, perhaps longer, a stone cruelly chucked in the gene pool. Suicide in its awful way was an achievement. Martin Hardress would be remembered for years like someone who has scored a goal in some complicated variant of football where the rules make it almost impossible. But all around there were unsuccessful entrants, some barely getting beyond the half-way line, like Jane herself stumbling through the shallows or Black trying to throw himself off the edge of the quarry but too drunk to find the right ledge; some only a pill or an inch away from success, like Bobs or now Tucker, saved, if saved was the word, by incompetence or perhaps some tiny vestigial survival instinct. But all lapped in misery, so that if you were to look at the world properly suicide was not some extraordinary sight, like a spectacular waterfall, but simply the seventh wave in the daily ebb and flow of unhappiness, the one that happened to crash on the rocks.

I had packed my luggage early in a childlike hurry to be among the first to get off the boat, and went off to the dining-room for a gross breakfast to celebrate the end of this horror voyage: grapefruit and prune compote, eggs, bacon, mushroom and black pudding, cinnamon toast and honey – at least the *Zephyr*'s chef lived up to his billing, in five days I must have put on ten pounds. I was even humming in a breezy, tuneless fashion as I ambled along the corridor to my cabin and found my luggage gone. For a moment, I wondered whether I had wandered into the wrong cabin, but no, this was G16 all right.

'Oh your luggage has already been collected, sir. Mr Wilmot's orders.'

The steward was impressed and smiling, his smile becoming broader when in my agitation I gave him a larger tip than I had intended.

Up on the deck – where Sirocco, Mistral and the rest of the super suites were – there was a special carpeted gangway to the shore being assembled.

'Could you tell me where I could find Mr Wilmot's luggage?'

'Mr Wilmot's luggage? That would be priority baggage, already taken ashore, sir.'

'Well then, can I go ashore?'

'Not yet, not till Mr, oh here he is now.'

'They ready for us, Charles?'

Dodo approached the gangway which settled down into place, the canopy being drawn tight by the two seamen and the metal struts clinking into their slots, all as though to his command. In his great belted Alpine-mammal overcoat, he was as huge again as when Jane had first introduced me to the darling Wilmots. Behind him wheeled by Charles the chauffeur in his peaked cap was the other darling, scarcely visible behind the Campbell tartan rug tucked around her and the gauzy black veil turned round her head and neck with a pair of dark glasses poking out. Jane too was wearing dark glasses and gave no sign of recognition.

'You missed a swell party last night. We drank the boat dry.'

'Can you tell me what's happened to my luggage?'

'Your luggage? I guess that went on with our stuff. You don't want to get held up by the hoi polloi, correction, by hoi polloi, hoi being the definite article, so saying the hoi polloi is like saying the the people. Did you know that, Mother?'

No reaction from behind either pair of shades.

'Where is my luggage actually now?'

'It's on the launch taking it over to Sting's boat. You'll come with us, won't you, on a little cruise round the harbour. It's a great introduction to New York, and you'll just love Sting.'

'Sting? Who's Sting?'

The pink carpet had been clipped down into place and the pink rope across the gangway untied, and the petty officer or whoever he was saluted, as the Chairman of the Line led his party ashore.

'Sting Ray Rawston,' Dodo flung back as he padded along the

gangway which creaked and groaned to the tread of his huge feet. 'You never heard of him? It's a fantastic story – ragman's son from the Lower East Side, got himself to Brooklyn Law School, then squeezed on to Joe McCarthy's team as third gofer, never looked back. Now he's one of the two or three biggest corporate lawyers in Washington. He's an amazing guy.'

'But shouldn't the luggage go through Customs?'

'Oh we had the bags cleared on board, Tommy Valenti looked after it. We've been buddies since way back, long before he became Commissioner, wasn't it, Mother?'

Charles was just tipping the wheels of Tucker's chair to minimise the shock of hitting American soil when to my amazement from behind the dark veil in a low but clear voice came the words, 'No, when.'

'No when what?'

'When he became Commissioner. You didn't know him before that.'

'Oh is that the truth? Memory like an elephant, that woman has. Now Tucker will be leaving us here, she's done enough sailing for a girl who's still sick, so Charles will take her off upstate to the Mount Ararat which in my opinion is just about the best convalescent home on the East coast and we'll go see Sting.'

He bent down to give Tucker a kiss, making as though to pull aside the veil without actually doing so, his lips in fact bussing the hinge of her dark glasses. Jane did much the same, and Charles took over again, pushing the wheelchair across the quayside to the limo, over the sodden litter and squashy fruit, through the crowd of yelling porters, dockers and friends and relations of the passengers. I had been so intent on trying to catch Dodo's words that only now did the peculiar impact of this disorderly throng hit me, so unlike the quiet still crowd on an English quayside. To my senses, which were scarcely less disordered, it seemed as though their yells and the rattle of their trolleys and the baying of their hooters were part of some protest against us, or against Dodo's behaviour. It took a minute or two to see that this was a cheerful sort of disorder, cruel if at all only because it was heedless.

Meanwhile, there I was, chained to them if I wanted to see my luggage again. And it was not that hard to deduce that this was not just a kindly gesture, a wish to show me the finest views of New York, although the genial side of Dodo might well have wanted that too, but a calculated device to keep an eye on me.

And then there it was, speeding away in some slinky launch to god knew where, my luggage, suddenly so dear to me: the big sky-blue Samsonite case with its shiny metal edges bought especially for this voyage, and inside the familiar old clothes never thought of with affection till now, the heather mixture sports jacket, the elephant-grey trousers, the suit from E. M. Whaley outfitters of Salisbury bought in a farewell outing with my father before he left the country for good and took to London and went downhill, folded as my father had taught me, sleeves back on themselves and the shoulders together lining outwards before the whole jacket was folded in half (method never questioned, however crumpled the suit was when unpacked), and beside the big suitcase, my only other piece, the bulky black briefcase, weathered now, the leather crackled along the top, and buffed tawny at the seams, the EIIR below the lock already faded after less than a decade's wear, the civil servant's standard model you got from a little shop in Victoria near Westminster Cathedral when you joined the service (although if you were a high-flier, you would soon swap it for a square-edged businessman's case in tan or oxblood to show you weren't a dim bureaucrat, but I liked the dimness).

We had only a moment to wait before another limo, seemingly as long as the liner we had just left, rumbled along the quay and Dodo was calling out, in a mock-cross Italian voice: 'Eh, Giorgio, what-a keep-a you so long?' Numb and seething if it is possible to be both at the same time, I hopped in after Jane and we glided along the quayside.

'Pier 97a, Giorgio, the far end, Mr Rawston's boat, *Sting Ray.*'

Inside the cavernous limo, there was easily room for the three of us in the back seat so that our thighs slopped against each other. Dodo was in the middle and he had hardly settled down on the soft squabs before his great paws were patting Jane's thigh and mine too and he was murmuring, 'Well, isn't this great,' but a shade mechanically as though it was expected of him, even with a hint of anxiety. Perhaps despite appearances, the Tucker business had got to him after all.

At the far end the berths were narrower and the private yachts in them clanked at their moorings in some tranquillity, with only the odd crewman pottering about the deck or slung alongside in a cradle painting and scraping. *Sting Ray V, Puerto Rico*, was twice the size of her neighbours. Her great creamy bow knifed into the hazy sky. Under a canopy on the deck high above us, I could see men in white moving about.

'Sting, I want you to meet a very good friend of ours, Gus Cotton from England. Gus is over here for the British government in a top-secret mission. Leastways he hasn't told me yet.'

'Then he's got more sense than most of them pointyheads down in Washington DC.'

Ray Rawston looked me up and down with eyes of the most brilliant blue, the blue of a hot summer sky, yet not at all piercing, in fact they seemed somehow opaque, as if they were a new type of miniature sunglasses to protect his real eyes from the world's glare. Like the other men standing or sitting under the canopy, playing backgammon or fixing drinks, he was dressed in white from yachting cap down to deck shoes. He was not as much tanned as yellowish and lightly pockmarked. He seemed intensely alert, and his smile was brief as though to let it go too far might cause him to miss a trick.

'Geez Sting, I heard your boat was something, but this beats all.'

'Won it in a poker game, no, matter of fact, it used to be Edgar Schulz's. When Edgar went belly up, the bank was looking for a quick sale so I took it off their hands for three point two. Had it valued the other day at seven and a half, so I reckon I'm saving money instead of you know the old thing –'

'Tearing up hundred dollar bills in the shower?'

'Right. You'll have a daiquiri, Mrs Wilmot?'

'Do you have a Manhattan? Isn't that the way to celebrate coming into New York on a morning like this?'

'It surely is. You're so right.'

One of the young men in white ducks sorted out the drinks and we settled ourselves round the long table with its gleaming blonde and chestnut veneer and looked down over the pier sheds to the towers shimmering along the riverside.

'Gonna be hot today. That mist'll clear soon. You'll have a Manhattan too, Gus. As the lady says, this is the way to say hi to this city.'

The drink dispersed a cool calm through my system and I found myself nestling back in the cushions with a feeling of detachment, as though I wasn't really there at all.

'It was when we were in there for the contract for the South-West highway, you know, the El Paso thing, and there was Muller and a couple of the other big guys in there, and our point man was George P. O'Donnell. You remember Georgie, he was a pallbearer at Joe's funeral, well he was the man we had to have because he had access to the two or three congressmen who mattered on the Transportation Committee but he wasn't any too reliable and he would come in with a sly expression on his face saying I don't know Ray but Consolidated Texas Highways are pitching a pretty good game, which means how about another hundred thousand on my consultancy fee and he was really pissing us around. Gus, you must be well acquainted with fellows like that in government work, guys who just won't stay bought and think the Good Lord brought you into this world to keep filling up their pail, isn't that right?'

'Right,' I said vaguely, the second Manhattan just beginning to keep the passages cool.

He paused to take a flicker at his daiquiri and Jane rose from the depths of her white upholstered deck chair in that abrupt gawky way of hers and said:

'Would you excuse me, I think I'll just take a walk along the deck, I didn't realise how homesick I was for old New York.'

'Go right ahead, Jane, great to have you aboard,' Rawston said before carrying on:

'So I said to our guys, man does not live by bread alone, it's time to bring on Billy. You remember Billy McVea, face like a choirboy, personal habits of a sewer rat. We sent Billy into the washroom on the executive floor, he had accreditation being a Senate page, and he had Georgie on his knees begging for it before the end of the lunch break. We had no trouble after that, didn't even need a camera. Poor Billy, you heard about that?'

'Yup, it was suicide was it, because I heard –'

'Sure it was. The guy had a load of debts and a cocaine habit that you or I would have had trouble financing.'

The blue eyes looked more opaque than ever.

'He was a friend of that friend of yours, Lonzo something or other, the one who was killed in that air crash with the other guys.'

'Was he? I didn't know that.'

Dodo Wilmot shifted fractionally in his chair as though he had just discovered something digging into him.

'You didn't know he was that way? Lonzo?'

'No, I did not.'

'Oh yes, there was a club they all hung out in, the Chameleon.'

'Is that so?'

'That was a bad business, that crash, for you, I mean.'

'Well, of course, it was a very great personal sadness. They were all good friends of mine, but businesswise it didn't make a dime's worth of difference, because they were all corporately committed before the trip.'

'Really? I heard they came over to decide whether to commit for the second tranche.'

'That was a technicality,' Dodo returned a touch coldly. 'Matter of fact, there were a couple of penalty clauses in there that would have kicked in if they'd decided to pull out. Anyway, some of the Reagan people wanted a piece so I had plenty of other options.'

'So it's a done deal?'

'Just tying up the loose ends as of now, Sting.'

'Tying up the loose ends,' Rawston echoed in a tone of gentle wonder. 'I heard there was some politics in there, export licences, things like that. You know anything about that, Gus? Country still belongs to you, don't it?'

'Well, it's part of the Commonwealth, but it's independent now. I don't know if you need an export licence for emeralds.'

'Emeralds,' Rawston repeated, gazing up at the canopy flapping in the breeze. 'A beautiful stone. But it's a funny thing, Dodo, I never heard of any emeralds worth shit coming out of that part of the world. You must have found one hell of a mother lode for all those important investors to fly down there.'

Wilmot chuckled, a heavy, satisfied chuckle as if he himself had just cracked a joke which had surprised him by its excellence.

'It didn't actually state emeralds on the prospectus. Precious stones and other minerals is what it says.'

'Other minerals. I bet those folks over by the East River would like to take a peek at those other minerals.'

'We took legal opinion, Sting. You tell me where it says sanctions cover the kind of business we had in mind.'

As Dodo was speaking, the engines started up and the boat glided away from the pier and began a shallow arc across the Hudson easing over toward the Jersey shore where a faint mist still hung over the sandy cliffs. In a couple of minutes we were far enough off for the whole steepling throng of the Midtown skyscrapers to stand out clear and breath-taking against the sky.

With a third Manhattan on its way down me I found it hard to concentrate on anything but the view sliding past under the dappling canopy.

'... there was a certain little lady who would not have liked it if she'd known.'

'She must have been pretty goddamn dumb if she couldn't work it out. What the hell she think those boxes were full of?'

'Rock samples, Sting. Rock samples going down to Jo'burg for analysis.'

'You lost a coupla crates in the crash, I heard.'

'You hear a lot, Sting. Yeah, there were a couple burst open.'

'And she didn't dig even then?'

'Well, you were there, Gus. Helen ever say anything about those boxes?'

'Not to me. She was very upset about the crash, of course.'

'As we all were, Gus, as we all were.'

'But the girl, the blonde, she was a chemist wasn't she?'

'How'd you know that?'

'You told me, five minutes ago.'

'I knew your Manhattans were strong, but I didn't know they were that strong. Yeah, she was a chemist all right and a little bit more than a chemist if you get me. A great piece of ass, but out of this world.'

'Well, they do say blondes have more fun.' Rawston seemed not much interested in this side of things. 'But wouldn't a chemist recognise raw beryllium when she saw it?'

'Oh now there you've spoilt our little secret,' said Dodo in a mock-sad baby voice.

'Which route you send it through, Beira and up the Gulf?'

'Sting, you are too persistent, you don't leave a fellow no privacy.'

'Big new reactor project starting up in Iraq, they tell me.'

'Let's talk about emeralds, I don't know a thing about the other stuff.'

So at last it trickled through to me, as it must have trickled through to Helen after the boxes burst open on the hillside and she saw the powdered beryllium, not the rock samples she had been told they contained. Perhaps she had more or less known before but had not liked to admit it even to herself.

'You need to get in quick there, Dodo. They tell me some other stuff's coming along, half the price, no supply problems, alloys better too.'

'Don't you worry, I'll be in and out quicker than a rattler up your pants.'

As they were laughing, a man in white ducks came past and peered in under the canopy. He was carrying my big blue case. The sight of it sent a throb of affection and panic coursing through my fuddled nervous system.

'Where you want this one, Mr Rawston?'

'You put it in *Marlin*, Danny, – no, *Crawfish*.'

'No,' I said trying to suppress the hysteria in my voice, 'I'm sorry but I really have to get to my hotel because I have to –'

'You won't come cruising with us? That's terrible. OK, then you just take a raincheck and we'll do this again, Gus. I know there's a lot we have to talk about, both of us working for the government an' all. I'll call you, and that's a promise. We'll let you off at 42nd Street. It's been a pleasure to have you aboard.'

'I'm so happy I could bring you folks together. A trip to the States wouldn't be complete without meeting with the one and only Sting Ray Rawston.'

'Geez, Dodo, you'll make me blush,' said the one and only, without the faintest hint of embarrassment, grabbing a black microphone on a flexible metal stalk above his head and snapping into it like a man talking to a cabdriver. 'Luca, will you drop our guest off at 42nd Street?'

'I'm sorry to take you out of your way,' I said as the boat curved back on its track and nosed across the river towards the throng of Midtown towers.

'No sweat, we're not going any place, just cruising, aren't we boys?'

'That's right, Mr Rawston,' said the couple of young men in white ducks freshening the drinks and laughing as they freshened them.

'Tara – Mrs Rawston – will be sorry to have missed you. She's still down in Key West, waiting for the next hurricane,' Rawston said. He was still laughing as he shook my hand and repeated his promise to call me.

It was small comfort that he hadn't got my number.

As I walked along the deck behind the boy with my case, which suddenly looked cheap and shoddy, a hand gripped my elbow and Jane came out from behind the bridgehouse.

'You're so right, to get off the boat now.'

'Well, I have to – '

'These are bad men, you don't want to have anything to do with them.'

'No, I – '

'Goodbye. Friends after all?'

And before I could say friends back, she reached up and gave me an awkward firm kiss, which reminded me of the times in France just as her warning reminded me of the warning she had given me against my father's old racing friends. The advice wasn't much use then, even less use now.

They threw out the gangplank to the pier (only a few hundred yards from the pier we had set out from) and I stumbled down it with the black briefcase under my arm and the big blue case knocking against my calves. When I reached the quay, I put the case down to catch my breath and looked back up at the *Sting Ray* towering above me. Leaning over the side I could see a sallow figure in a yachting cap. As the boat reversed engines and began to slide out of the berth, the sallow figure raised his hand in one of those casual US Navy salutes and I waved back.

This was a bad beginning. My first hours in New York had been spent on a cruise round the harbour with a known associate of the late Senator McCarthy on the associate's yacht, no doubt bought with drug money, discussing a scheme to evade UN sanctions, a scheme which moreover I had been (to say the least) in contact with in another continent, where a mysterious plane crash ... all this would look bad enough for a private citizen, but for a government official on a mission to burnish his country's image it was a disaster.

Then it also came to me, but not until I was safe in my comfortable old room at the Hotel Roosevelt with its huge gold taps and 1930s furniture, that Wilmot had his own reasons for welcoming me into his unsavoury circle. The more he entangled me, the less inclined I might be to discuss with others his strange treatment of his first wife, if she was his first wife and if indeed I knew the half of it. There was only Jane's word for it that Tucker had shot herself and scarcely a disinterested word at that. They might not have thought the whole calculation through, Dodo seemed to operate by instinct half the time, but instinct would surely tell him that he didn't want me running around letting off my mouth about his affairs, business or personal. Then, besides, they were such friendly people that it would come so naturally to them to keep in touch that they would not need to think of it as keeping tabs. But I knew they would not leave me alone.

All the same, it was hard to brood too much as I walked up Fifth and stretched my neck to look at the steepling cliffs of the Rockefeller Center and the massive renaissance palazzos of the Ivy League clubs and the Avenue stretching away to the Plaza and the Pierre and the beginning of Central Park and that feeling not to be repeated anywhere else that life was bursting with a promise you couldn't exactly define – the vagueness being part of the promise, perhaps the best part because if you had known what the promise was you could also see how it could be broken. I found a permanent room in an apartment hotel over on the West Side just behind the Mayflower, on a street where old ladies from Central Europe sat on the benches looking exhausted to be still alive after enduring so much, and secretaries staggered home with big brown bags of groceries from Zabar's, and there was always the smell of coffee brewing. Somebody had said that you could become an American in a day. Well, you could become a New Yorker after a cup of coffee.

That instant immersion in the city gave me a false sense of security and a false sense of time too, so that Dodo seemed to have left an interval which I might call almost decent before contacting me, and it came as quite a shock when a message from the office of Waldo R. Wilmot, President, turned up in the middle of a pile of otherwise useless memos, briefing papers and invitations to launches, celebrations and symposia organised by people trying to burnish the image of their own nations, corporations and institutes. It came somewhat curiously in the form of a letter to the British Consul, my boss. They had set up down in Virginia, Dodo wrote, a small group of leading industrialists who met regularly to discuss world economic prospects and developments, and who would be particularly eager to have an update on the UK from his old friend Gus Cotton whom he understood to be a recent recruit to the team.

'This is just the sort of thing we are after,' the Consul said. 'Well done.'

The Consul was a mild man with a sudden smile which creased his whole face but left me feeling somehow sad and depleted. His upper lip had that naked quivering look which demanded a moustache but I could see he was not the kind of man who would grow one.

'Well done,' he said again. 'Some of us have been trying for years to make that sort of contact. Hilary spake sooth when he commended you to us.'

It took me some time to work out why Dodo had written to the Consul and not directly to me. Then I saw that by writing to the Consul he would make it impossible for me to refuse and at the same time he could claim he was giving my career a leg-up.

'You'll be our house-guest at Turkey Creek,' he boomed over the phone. 'I'll send the Gulfstream up Friday. You happy with Laguardia? It'll be great, just a downhome family kinda thing.'

There were only a dozen or so seats spaced out around the cabin of Dodo's Grumman Gulfstream. At first it seemed I was going to be the only passenger, and the soothing peach and eau-de-nil colour scheme failed to keep down a swelling sense of embarrassment as Barbara, the hostess, pulled out the side-tables attached to my seat and dotted salvers of pistachios and olives and pretzels around them, not to mention a whisky sour which she insisted I must have because Mr

Wilmot said she made them better than any bartend on the Eastern seaboard.

Just as the pilot began to rev the engines, a gawky young man in black spectacles with floppy black hair ducked in through the open door.

'Brainerd, you don't know what you do to my blood pressure, cutting it so fine every time.'

'Sorry Barbie doll.'

'If you call me that again, the bar stays closed.'

'Who cares? I'm on the wagon anyway, so just fix me a tomato juice, will you?'

His banter sounded a little grudging as though he had been pressed into playing the part of the unreliable son of the house who could always get round the old retainer, but Barbara seemed pleased to see him and the smile fixed on her big mouth seemed to relax.

'Remember me, the tutor from the Ville?' I leant across and he took my extended hand.

'Gus, hi, I heard you were coming.'

He was not unfriendly but he didn't put a lot into it. We might have met on the same flight a week ago instead of not having seen each other for fifteen years.

'You been to Turkey Creek before?'

'No.'

'It's pretty, very pretty. Mom likes it.'

'And you?'

'Oh they leave me alone. I try to get some work done.'

'What is your work?'

'Oh analysis, trends, it's hard to explain. You won't mind if I –' He gestured at the squashy shoulder-bag beside him which had papers spilling out through the open zip.

'Of course not.'

He pulled out a handful of papers and spread them across his lap, not bothering to extract the table from the arm-rest. He was too far across the aisle for me to see what sort of papers they were. But he seemed to be murmuring to them as though they were pets he was stroking rather than studying them with the close attention he had implied was involved. It was an abstractedness that seemed close to day-dreaming, not unlike the way he had played with his tin can collection as a child. Perhaps both occupations were simply a polite escape route from unwelcome company, not so polite though in the adult version. He took out a pocket calculator and pressed a few buttons, then smiled to himself.

Barbara offered me another whisky sour and I resigned myself to getting pickled. Every now and then, I nipped a glance across at Brainerd. He was now hardly focusing on the papers at all and the smile had lodged on his face almost as though he had gone to sleep in mid-smile, but he was not asleep. He began to unnerve me and I could see he was unnerving Barbara who was not holding back from her own whisky sours.

'Mr Wilmot says if you can't drink on duty when can you drink,' she said when she saw me looking at her glass.

'That apply to the pilot too?'

'No sir,' she said, 'he's as sober as a judge, though if you look at some of the judges in Terence County, that don't count for much.'

As the plane droned on through the night, a feeling somewhere between impatience and anxiety took hold of me. It began to seem important to rouse Brainerd.

'How's Timmy?'

'Timmy, my little brother? Oh he'll be there. You'll see him.'

'What's he up to these days?'

'Up to? You mean, like work?'

'Yes.'

'Oh I don't know really.'

'Timmy's going to law school in the fall,' Barbara broke in, she was sitting sideways in the seat in front of us with her brown legs swinging over the arm of the chair.

'That's right, I guess, law school.'

'You don't know what your own brother's doing? You're weird, Brainerd.'

'Do you think so? Do you like weird people?'

For the first time, he seemed interested in what someone had said to him.

'You were quite weird as a little boy, weird but nice,' I said.

'Weird but nice. That's neat, I like that.'

Now you could see the connecting line between the infant Brainerd and the present version. Although his teeth had been fixed and the front centrals no longer hung over his lower lip, I recognised that vacant, self-absorbed look.

'You used to collect tin cans, set them out like an art exhibition.'

'Tin cans, that is *weird.*'

Turkey Creek

Barbara opened the door and let in a blast of night air, hot and scented heavily.

'Don't you just love that honeysuckle fragrance? Ah only have to open the door to know Ah'm home.'

As I was hefting my bag towards the exit, I looked at Brainerd. My ex-charge had not moved, and had not wiped the smile off his face either. That mild rictus suggested he might have been drugged or knocked out by some undetectable poison gas.

'Brainerd, you're ho-ome,' Barbara trilled.

A minute or two later, slowly enough to make it clear that it was not her wake-up call he was responding to, Brainerd shrugged, swept the papers off his knees into his bag and slung it over his shoulder without bothering to fasten the zip.

'Bye Barbie,' he murmured, scarcely troubling his lip muscles, and shambled out ahead of me into the warm southern night. He submitted to the greetings of Charles the chauffeur in the same underpowered style before flopping down beside me in the back seat as though he had just run a marathon.

'You see Mr Wilmot bought the new Lincoln after all.'

'Yeah, I see,' Brainerd said, gazing indifferently at the roof.

'How're you keeping, sir? It seems a long time since those days at the Ville. Mr Wilmot don't go there any more, keeps his horses down here now, says France is too expensive, but I reckon there's too many memories over there. And Miss Helen, you see anything of her? I like that girl. She had a good word for everyone.'

Brainerd came suddenly to life with a cackle.

'That's not what my Mom thinks. She hates Helen, says she's a two-faced bitch and if she didn't have that blonde hair everyone would see her for what she was.'

'That right?' crooned Charles, delighted by this response. 'And Mr Wilmot, what'd he think about her?'

'Charles, don't play dumb. You *know* what he thinks about her.'

I could see Charles was giggling by the way the umber rolls of fat above his collar trembled.

The big car rumbled along a gravel drive that circled the low farmhouse at about fifty yards' range. Across the lawn, I saw three figures sitting in rocking chairs on the creeper-clad verandah. They were lit from above like people on a stage. A dance band was playing 1940s dance music, could be Tommy Dorsey.

'You go say hallo,' Charles said, 'I'll take the bags round the back.'

Brainerd and I walked across the lawn, my town shoes sinking in the crab grass. Suddenly, with a peculiar sound half-way between a roar and a sigh, jets of water began to drench us from all angles. We dashed the last few yards through a fusillade of sprinklers.

'Oh Dodo, you shouldn't have.'

'Five seconds they said, from hitting the switch. I reckon that was just about on the button. How ya doing, Gus? How'd ya like our good old southern welcome?'

'You're soaking. Oh Dodo.' Jane embraced me with anxious vigour as though the tighter she squeezed the more of the water she could wring off me. I felt her tremble.

Dodo Wilmot was up and pouring drinks. The third figure remained in a wicker chair, almost without moving. For a terrible moment, I thought it was John Stilwell come back to life to haunt his wife: the dark neat figure, the odd pursed lips, that air of containment which made him seem prissy rather than good-looking. It *was* John Stilwell, eerily so, but with a couple of differences which dawned on me slowly one after the other: this man was twenty years younger than the John Stilwell I had known, and he was stonkingly drunk. Then Jane reminded him who I was and he waved a hand in a friendly way and had a shot at saying 'Remember me? Little Timmy?' with only mediocre success.

We sat down, those of us who were standing up, and at the same time Timmy made an effort to sit up, perhaps with getting to his feet as a long-term project, but had no luck here either. As he sank back into the wicker rocker, he jabbed a finger at me vaguely, if you can jab vaguely, which is what he could do, and said with a pleasurable, almost sensual, effort of recollection: 'You gave me the ice-lolly, right?'

'Ice-lolly?'

'The ice-lolly she wouldn't let me have when Brainerd broke his ankle.'

'Oh yes, so I did.'

'I hail thee, amigo,' he said with a huge goofy grin, 'Sorry I can't get up. Too many ice-lollies.'

'Timmy's going to law school in the fall,' Jane said.

'So I heard. That's great.'

'Isn't that great,' Dodo intervened as though insisting on rights to his signature tune. 'A lawyer, and a stock market analyst. Great kids.'

Brainerd had taken off his jacket and his shoes and socks and was ambling off through the french windows.

'Honey, not through the sitting-room, go round the back, please.'

He paid no attention and walked on through the lighted sitting-room behind us, at the pace of a visitor come to admire the pictures.

'Don't worry, baby, the Aubusson can take it.'

The sprinklers were still sighing on the lawn, tracing tremulous arcs against the old trees beyond, which seemed floodlit too.

'You better go change, Gus, you'll catch cold else.'

It came to me now that when we had embraced it had been me trembling, not Jane.

'Would you mind,' I said haltingly, 'I suddenly feel rather trembly. I think I'll –'

'You go upstairs and turn in. I'll send Charles up with a hot drink. We want you bright-eyed and bushy-tailed for tomorrow.'

'Oh tomorrow,' I said weakly, not wanting to think about the fifty leading industrialists assembling to hear my remarks on the British Economic Recovery.

'Hey sorry to wake you up like this.'

The dimity blue curtains were still drawn in the little attic bedroom (surprising how small it was) but the light was coming in strongly, and through my rheumy eyes – there was no doubt about it, I had a cold, not helped by Dodo's sprinklers – it was easy enough to make out my visitor, a hefty girl in jeans and grubby T-shirt with writing on it. She was bending over the chest of drawers and tossing out clothes into a big open hold-all.

'Hi, I'm Dodona,' she said, twisting her neck to look at me and shaking the hair out of her eyes at the same time.

'Dodona?'

'Yeah, a chip off the old block or my little acorn, as my father likes to say.'

'Acorn?'

'You don't get it? You are the boys' old tutor, aren't you, for Chrissake? Dodona, sacred oak, biggest oracle in ancient Greece. Dodo, Dodona. Oh forget it, you look pretty rough. Bad flight?'

'I came down with Brainerd.'

'That *is* a bad trip. They're weird, my step-brothers, don't you think?'

'Brainerd seemed to like the idea of being weird.'

'That's how weird he is.'

Now that I focused on her more, it was easy to see the likeness, not as eerie as the likeness between Timmy and his father but unhappier because Dodo's bulbous features were never meant to be planted on a woman, or on a man, come to that. She was friendly but somehow ill at ease. At any rate, she made me uneasy, not least because she seemed to be stashing away all the moveables in the room, including a set of silver-backed hairbrushes and matching hand-mirror and two small rustic water-colours.

'You're moving out then?'

'Yup, clearing out my stuff and Mom's. I got the U-haul round the back.'

'Where are you taking it?'

'Down South. Whose side are you on anyway?'

'Nobody's. I'm just visiting.'

'Well, I won't burden you with my little secret then. Jesus, I better get moving. The idea was to be out of here before Big Daddy surfaced. With a bit of luck, he'll still be enjoying the incestuous pleasure of his bed. You dig the literary allusion? I was majoring in English Literature before I dropped out of Tulane.'

'Not incestuous exactly, is it?'

'It is too. We called her Aunt Jane when we were kids. What brings you to this hellhole?'

'I'm giving a lecture.'

'Oh yeah, I heard. On the British recovery or something. What a laugh.'

'I couldn't agree more.'

'No, I didn't mean your lecture, I meant the audience. Lecture – they couldn't even spell the word, certainly not after the happy hour. Sorry I shan't be there. You couldn't give me a hand with one of these bags, could you? Just down the stairs.'

My bare feet slithered on the thick pile of the stair-carpet and the fresh morning air frolicked through my pyjama bottoms, as I followed her down to what looked like the back door.

'Doh, what the hell do you mean by this? This is ... it's an outrage. You're a goddamn thief.'

From the back door, I could see Dodo Wilmot standing behind the open doors of a big removal van and wearing, no, yes, riding-breeches of a peculiar saffron colour. In his hand he had a riding crop which he was swooshing to and fro in his anger, more like a conductor whipping up a sluggish orchestra than a man preparing to hit someone.

'I'm just taking what's Mom's and mine.'

'Thief, thief. That *bonheur-du-jour* ...'

'It's Mom's.'

'No, it fucking isn't. I bought it at Partridges, in London.'

'I don't care which bunch of vultures you bought it from. It's hers, it's always been in her boudoir, and it's hers.'

'Look, your mother doesn't need a goddamn *bonheur-du-jour* any more.'

'No, and whose fault is that?'

Having slung the last bag in the van, Dodona shut the doors. From my barefoot viewpoint it wasn't possible to see how much she had piled up in there, but to judge by Dodo's vibrations it must have been quite a haul. As she passed by him, I thought he was sure to hit her, but he didn't. In a curious way, having the riding crop in his hand seemed to deter him. You felt with his hands free he would have shaken her at least. In fact, her decisiveness seemed to deflate him.

'Look, Doh, you can't just strip the house like this. Besides, you haven't any place to store all the stuff. You can't take it to Mount Ararat.'

'That's my problem.'

'You've no right to half of it, you know that. I could have the lawyers repossess it, just like that.'

'That would look great, wouldn't it? Waldo R. Wilmot reduced to putting the bailiffs in on his daughter. Must be down to his last nickel, better sell the stock before everyone else does.'

'Oh come on, Doh, it's not like that. Just leave that stuff and come eat breakfast.'

'I don't eat breakfast, because I don't want to look any more like you than God made me, which was a dirty trick in the first place. Besides, I've got a date.'

She jumped into the truck and scorched off down the gravel sweep.

Her father stood in the yard, the rage drained out of him, disconsolate yet not so absorbed in his misery that he failed to spot me standing in my pyjamas at the back door.

'Hey you better get some clothes on. You look pretty rough.'

'That's what your daughter said.'

'We're so goddamn alike. That's the trouble. Headstrong, wilful, you pick the word for it, but it boils down to we don't like to be crossed. Hey, you sound like you caught cold last night. I'm hells sorry about that, it was just irresistible, you know, when you've got that little titty by your chair to press it. I know I shouldn't, but when those sprinklers start up and you guys start running, it's just a terrific sight.'

The thought of our soaking had gone quite a way to restoring his humour but not mine, because it was suddenly plain to me that the jape was not a whim of the moment but needed some planning, viz, instructing Charles to make us get out of the car and walk across no man's land.

'Now let me fill you in a piece about the Trumbull Club. We named it for Gideon H. Trumbull, First Secretary of the Treasury in the Commonwealth of Virginia, great feller, lost an eye in the revolutionary wars, made a fortune in military supply, first-rate economist, first-rate drinker and fornicator, our kinda guy. Elbow said his treatise on the circulation of money was the best thing to come out of the States before Harry Johnson or maybe Milton Friedman.'

'Elbow?' I gasped. Wilmot seemed to have forgotten I was only in pyjamas and was leading me by the arm across the lawn still sloshy from the sprinklers towards a vine-clad barn at the far end of the grass. Beyond were blue hills. The sun was silvering the dewdrops.

'George Elbow, only goddamn economist worth a cent, born Georg von Ellbogen in Vienna, Austria, has a chair in Chicago now, you could say he was the Trumbull of our day, they said he had the biggest cock in Vienna. Well here we are, the Captain's cabin, how do you like it?'

The barn was panelled inside and hung with pictures of naval engagements. Thirty or forty little gold chairs were drawn up expectantly facing a lectern with a screen behind it. I was filled with a terrible foreboding.

'They'll be coming for an informal brunch-type thing, eleven-thirty. Don't worry, they're a fun crowd.'

It was on the dot of eleven-thirty that a red-faced man driving a spruce little gig pulled by a high-stepping pony with a foamy mane came up the drive, removing his cap to Jane and the rest of us.

'Everton Billings, Billings Lifts, number two to Otis in the South but rising to all floors.'

Billings tossed back the first cocktail he was offered in a single gulp, then picking up a few lumps of sugar from the coffee table in his yellow-gloved hand tossed them to the pony who caught them with a swirl of its mane. He greeted me with enthusiasm and enquired whether I had been to Badminton lately.

'And this is Frank Freed – Freed, Torpor & Sloth, slowest lawyers in the States.'

'Tarpion & Sloan,' corrected the tall lugubrious man in the cream linen safari jacket and jade foulard.

'Abbey Headlamp from Golgotha Cement.' A stately woman with dollops of blonde hair piled above her smiling pudgy face.

Already I was not sure how much of these names I was mishearing, how much was Dodo's embroidery.

'Bing Busby, Northern State Insurance, Eddy Barkovitz from

Bluehills, how ya doing Ed, Bluehills is the biggest manufacturer of prosthetics in the East, that right Eddy, you lose an arm or a leg, you go to Eddy and that's what he'll cost you.'

'Heard that one before some place, Dodo.'

'The old ones are the best, you know that. Well, look who's here. I want you to meet a very dear friend of ours, Senator Hamilton Sandfish.'

This was an impossibly tall man in a grey suit which fitted him as well as his fine weathered face in which even the liver spots of old age seemed to be put there deliberately. I don't think I had ever seen a person of such distinction and the smile which slowly crinkled across his face like a crumbling sandcastle left me so weak at the knees that I could hardly take in the few courteous words he burbled down to me. As he moved on to greet Jane, I could feel how proud Dodo was to have landed such a specimen. Over his shoulder I caught a glimpse of a yellow glove tossing another cocktail to its owner's lips. It was hot on the verandah and the Trumbullites were shouting as hard as they were drinking, spilling out on to the lawn as their numbers grew, the creamy linens and flashing silks – silver, petunia-pink and a delicate shimmering shade of magnolia – looking brave against the dark green of the sodden pelouse. Back on the verandah, Charles and the rest of the staff were wheeling in silver trays: eggs benedict, Virginia muffins, soft-shelled crabs, and a dozen other dishes pretending to be less substantial than lunch. A few of the younger Trumbullites wheeled back from the lawn like a flock of startled pigeons to scoop up these delicacies, but the older magnates held their ground waiting for refills as two black maids moved among them with cocktail shakers glinting in the sun.

'Well isn't this the most enormous fun? How nice to see you again,' said an English voice.

I half-turned to see a face I didn't immediately recognise but then pinned down as Pettifer, Pettigrew or whoever – the man famous for charm whom I had met the evening of the disastrous re-encounter with Jane.

'What, er, brings you here?'

'To hear your lecture of course.'

'No, seriously.'

'I'm looking forward to it immensely. It's a piece of luck that I happened to be over here following up a little bit of business with our friend Dodo. They're wonderful, our cousins, aren't they?'

'Cousins?'

'Americans, so resilient. There's poor Tucker, you know about Tucker? Yes, well, it's only a month, certainly no more than two since her accident and here they are putting on such a fine show. Absolutely first-class,' he added reflectively after a little pause, as though considering other examples of such resilience before deciding in which class to place this one. 'Dodo's an amazing chap, you know,' he went on.

'Yes.'

'Basically, he's a romantic. That surprises you, but that's the way I look at it and I've been knocking around with him for more years than I care to tell. He falls in love just like that – he sees a girl, doesn't matter who she is or what she's doing, could be serving in a shop, could be a princess, and he just has to have her. Don't know if you ever came across a blonde who worked for him? A geologist I think she was, a bit too serious for me and you wouldn't have thought his type at all. But he fell for her, head over heels, wouldn't let her out of his sight.'

I soared out over the lawn, and the bright silks of the crowd, and fixed my eyes on the low blue hills beyond and thought how clean the air would be up there.

'Must be a peculiar experience, for a girl like that, I mean she was from nowhere, and suddenly she had Dodo bearing down on her like a rogue elephant. The funny thing was, he was a bit scared of her, didn't want her to think badly of him, so he wouldn't tell her about the beryllium thing, kept her thinking up to the last minute he was digging for emeralds. And that was the end of that. Next thing you know, he falls hopelessly in love with Jane who he's known for years, wife's best friend and all that. I don't know how he does it. They're so sweet together, like a couple of teenagers, don't you think?'

He paused, in that way he had of seeming to listen to his words die away as though savouring the last echoes of his own charm.

'Have you met the Senator? He'll be introducing you.'

'Senator Sandfish?'

'Yes, the dear old Ham Sandwich. I don't know how he gets away with it.'

'Gets away with what?'

'You go along to his office and there's always half a dozen fellers waiting with envelopes stuffed full of hundred-dollar bills – oil, construction, you name it. Dodo's had him on a retainer for as long as I can remember. Not a lot upstairs, but he's still awfully decorative, ah there's old Billings. I must just tip my hat to him.'

Pettifer/Pettigrew drifted off into the crowd. Watching him go, I saw to my surprise Dodona coming towards me. Surprising, not just that she had come back, but that she had tugged on a cotton frock of a colour that could only be described as beige.

'You said you weren't coming.'

'Couldn't miss it. I changed in the truck,' she said. 'Wore it in my junior year, depressing isn't it? You seen the boys yet?'

'Brainerd and Timmy?'

'Your kids, yeah. You ought to look after them better, they're stinkaroo.'

'Already?'

'We work fast in these parts. Look at this distinguished assemblee, not a sober man among them.'

'Well, I'm doing all right myself.'

'Yeah, you look smashed enough to pass unnoticed. You got any slides? Well, I'll look after them for you. You need a steady hand on the projector.'

Just then a microphone crackled into life somewhere and I saw Senator Sandfish standing on a bench, amid the roses that fringed the lawn.

'Ladies and gentlemen, it is my pleasant duty to call you to order at this convocation and to invite you to drink the health of our founder, the Honourable Gideon H. Trumbull, coupled with the great Commonwealth of Virginia.'

Glasses held high in the hot sun, solemn chanting of the toast, blue hills shimmering in the haze. Party then shuffled across the lawn to the place of execution.

Cool, measured, not without a touch of irony – that was to be the tone of the lecture, so that its message would steal up on the audience and take them off guard. My text would begin by guiding them through the derelict industrial landscape of *Britain Before* – the bombsites overgrown with ragwort and buddleia, the grimy winding gear in the Welsh Valleys, the silent shipyards on the Tyne – before swinging into the *After*, the gleaming new strip mills, the swooping motorways, the soaring tower blocks, a little Manhattan in every British city.

This strategy was a mistake. The audience in its hyped-up state was too easily moved by the first images that Dodona clicked up on to the screen.

'Geez, isn't that awful?'

'Even Pittsburgh was never that bad.'

'We went to Stratford last year, and Oxford, but we never saw anything like *that.*'

These expressions of horror seemed to release them from any obligation to be quiet, and a steady muttering, occasionally breaking out into chuckles and even open guffaws, set in for the rest of the lecture. This should have stirred me to talk louder over them, but in fact a kind of drowsy indifference drifted over me. I sensed the beginnings of that disembodied feeling which often comes with being medium drunk, a sensation of hovering a few feet below the ceiling and watching, not unkindly, your *alter ego* continuing to perform down below. Now and then, one of my statistical slides seemed to quieten the audience for the time it took them to read the figures, the one showing the recent rise in Britain's share of the European semi-finished steel products market being particularly effective, but then the background chatter resumed and my own attention continued to wander, pausing for an instant or two on stray unfocused thoughts – about the nature of human lust, why Dodona had come back, whether I was going to be sick – before returning to the text I was reading out, with a renewed sense of how dull it was and consequently a growing sympathy with the audience who clearly felt much the same. Now and then, tips about the art of lecturing wandered into my head – don't gabble, speak deliberately – which would have been good advice if I had not already been speaking at something like dictation speed. Also: don't be ashamed of your notes, in fact brandish them, Churchill used to. Good advice, too, except that in brandishing them I chanced to swat the mike lightly to and fro, producing a quick succession of rhythmic squawks, such as might be obtained by applying a mute or baffle to some brass instrument. At which point I remembered that the technique for recovering from any hitch of this sort was to look up at your audience and by frank and warm eye contact re-establish sympathy. As my gaze ranged to the far end of the barn so that not even the backmost rows should be spared, I saw through the big back window two faces peering in with hideous grimaces. At first this gurning, not to mention the steam of their breath on the glass, made it hard to identify them, but then their features relaxed into something approaching normality and I saw that it was Timmy and Brainerd. Their faces disappeared for a minute or two before something large and white moved slowly across the window, which turned out to be a naked bottom apparently propped up on some other person's equally naked shoulders. The bottom disappeared, to be followed by one of the heads again, with the other person clambering up on top of him in order to manoeuvre his crotch into view but falling off again before managing it. Derailed by this sight, my speech had slowed to a crawl and, when I reached the bottom of the page, to a halt. At my side, Senator Sandfish, sensing the opportunity presented by this impasse, rose with marvellous briskness to lead the applause, leaning over to me at the same time to burble inaudible felicitations into my ear. He was followed by a flock of Trumbull clubbers. Billings clasped my hands with *empressement*, Abbey Headlamp stroked my forearm and said 'So clever' as she might to a cat. She had been chatting to her neighbour from about three minutes in and couldn't have heard a word. This tide of insincere congratulations ebbed soon enough, and it can only have been a couple of minutes before I was alone sitting on my gold chair on the little platform. As I got up to shamble out after the audience, I felt a little pinch at the back of my upper thigh and turned round to see Dodona looking up at me with an expression of such cheerfulness as I had not yet seen on her.

'That was one lousy lecture. What a turkey. Come on, you need a break.'

She flipped back a green velvet curtain behind the miniature stage to reveal a little back door which she unlocked and beckoned me through. We were immediately in a low-growing wood of scrub oaks and some hazy-leafed trees which the sun could only just flicker through. Here and there the sun caught a patch of stagnant water, almost overgrown with moss and water-lilies. Our feet were flip-flopping along a narrow boardwalk with planks broken in places and a lichened railing, some of that broken too. There were crickets zinging and now and then the croak of a frog and dragonflies pulsing low over the green pools. Ahead of us a bright scarlet bird jinked through the trees.

'The enchanted wood.'

'Yeah, that's right. How did you know we called it that? No one comes here any more. It was Mom who loved it, so it's going back to nature now.'

The boardwalk zigzagged through the wood for what seemed like a mile but was probably only half that and then finished at a broken-down gate on to a sandy dirt road. The U-haul van was parked across the road in the entrance to a field full of sweetcorn waving its rusty tassels in the steamy breeze.

'Come on in, it'll be cooler inside.'

She hopped up into the back of the van and cleared a space on a small sofa covered in a sheeny chintz patterned with blowsy pink roses.

'No it isn't, it's hotter,' she corrected herself and as she spoke tugged the beige dress over her head and, it seemed in almost the same motion, began to kiss me.

'I came for the lecturer,' she laughed, 'and his projector,' and laughed again. 'Did you know I was voted the wittiest girl in my class in Tulane? Isn't this a neat sofa? Mom had it resprung last fall,' and then she began to cry but told me not to worry, she always cried afterwards just like Lucretius said, but if she was happy, she cried before too.

'Lucretius?'

'*Post coitum omne animal triste*, you must know that. Especially *triste* when your father's pretty near murdered your mother. Don't mind if I try a little s-and-m on you, it's the best way to get it out of the system.' And she dug her fingers into my back and ground herself against me, which I said, truthfully, was lovely and not s-or-m at all, because her nails were short and her body was so deliciously cool.

'I *am* cool,' she said, lazily falling away from me so that the honeybrown curve of her hip was outlined against the intricate marquetry of a small desk which looked French.

'The *bonheur-du-jour,*' she said, 'such a pretty name for a crummy little desk, but I like it because it was Mom's. Don't worry, I'm not going to cry again, when I'm really happy, I only cry before.'

All the same, neither of us spoke for a while. It was as though we had agreed to listen to the creaking of the sofa under us.

'It's the blonde you're in love with, isn't it?'

'The blonde?'

'Don't play dumb, Dad's blonde, everyone's blonde, what's her name, the one who's so shocked about Dad selling the stuff to make bombs with. That clear enough for you?'

'How do you know all that if you don't know her name?'

'Because that creepy Englishman told me – not you, the other creepy Englishman. Don't try to weasel out of it. Are you or aren't you?'

'Well, in a way, I suppose.'

'In a way,' she mimicked. 'That's the kind of phony complicated stuff that sort of person always dumps on you. Nothing like a straight screw involved. She has to be all mysterious and subtle.'

'I don't think that's true at all. She's really rather straightforward, very down-to-earth in fact.'

'Yeah, but she ties men up in knots, just because her hair looks like a bunch of hay. If her follicles had a different juice in them, you wouldn't think twice about her.'

'Well, why do you go on about her when you haven't even met her, have you?'

'Because she causes a helluva lot of trouble, that's why, because she was the one who was responsible for screwing up my mother's life and I expect she'll screw up your life too if you don't look after yourself.'

'Don't be stupid. You can't blame anyone but Dodo.'

'I've got a whole load of blame to attach to dear old Dodo, but there's plenty left over.'

She was smiling now, though lying on her back with her legs hooked over the arm of the sofa and her arms drawing me back to her.

It was that moment of sinking back on to her that I remember best, her face with that open look which was beyond being beautiful or not beautiful but simply said here she was and this was not a time for fussing over miseries and betrayals but for just going ahead. And a bit later I couldn't help thinking about all my old hesitations and fumblings and wondering how I could have been so perplexed because it was all really quite simple when you came at it from the right angle. That was the beauty of it in fact and you only spoilt it by wondering whether you were doing the right thing. Some kind of breeze found its way in through the slats in the sliding door of the U-haul, cooling our damp bodies, and I could hear the corn-tassels outside shifting in the breeze. It came to me with a little after-tremor that I wasn't really a complicated sort of person at all.

When I think of America, it is Dodona in the U-haul who comes up most often. There are other memories too – the lights going on across the well in the apartment block on hot summer nights and the men in vests leaning out to catch the breeze from the air conditioners, the smell of doughnuts and coffee from Horn & Hardart's on 34th Street, the rattle of the yellow cabs on the Triboro Bridge – but for me Dodona was really the spirit of America. She had one front tooth larger than the other, and a little mole at one corner of her mouth and her father's beryl eyes, and she was large with long strong arms and legs and she was wholly lovable, which makes it all the odder that we only saw each other a few more times when she came to New York, but she didn't stay more than a couple of days and when I wrote to her in New Orleans (she had gone back to Tulane), she wrote only a jolly letter back with no hint of intimacy, as though she feared the letter might be censored. So she was open and fearless in the obvious physical way, I suppose, but distrustful in the other, which was probably the right thing to be in dealing with me but seemed to rule out something in life which was worth having and she didn't pretend it wasn't. So perhaps in that too she was the spirit of America with its enormous longings and its wonderful going on regardless of them.

I wondered what she had done with the *bonheur-du-jour.*

St Col's

'You'll be glad to be getting back,' the Consul said.

'Not particularly,' I said, suddenly candid because I didn't expect to see him again.

'No, I never am,' he said, reflectively, 'it's only setting out that seems worthwhile.' Perhaps he was just as candid because he didn't expect to see me again either.

I was strangely numb and drained for the first few weeks back in London, as though I had completed some heroic mission. Time seemed to rumble past like buses that won't stop in the rain, so it is hard to estimate at all precisely when I received a curious call from Helen's mother – a month, perhaps even two. Helen herself I hadn't seen, didn't want to see snuggled up with Bobs in married bliss or married anything – well, I would need to be feeling a good deal more confident than I was to go looking for such an experience. But Mrs Hardress sounded anguished and I had liked her and so I went.

For the third time – was it only the third time, the journey seemed so familiar – the little green train hissed and zinged its way along the river. Coming close at each bend it offered the same quick glimpse of the wallowing silver water and the oarsmen moving over the surface with that leggy water-beetle's motion. Then we ducked back again behind the red-brick Dutch-style houses past scruffy back gardens with broken-down loungers and unkempt apple trees, clunking to a halt in the little station with its frilly cream roofs just downstream of the island, which still had the dank chill of winter on it with the first leaftips only just beginning to uncurl and the reed-spears hardly showing above the mud of the slack tide.

Hadn't Helen told me her mother was going to sell, had already sold perhaps? Yes, yes, that was what everyone had told her to do, but she thought what was the hurry, she had the rest of her life in which to move and anyway the market had come down 30 per cent after the oil went up. Besides, it was a small house, it was only because they were all so small that they had fitted in to it. She was thinking about selling the field telephones, though, when the market picked up. A man had come from Christie's and said America was full of strange men collecting these things.

'Well, he was strange too, my husband,' she laughed, 'there's no denying that. Perhaps we all are, though it's awful when someone tells you we're all mad here, as though it was something to boast about, don't you think?'

She was not at all as I remembered her. I don't mean that I wouldn't have recognised her, but her soft, anxious manner had gone. She spoke in a drier, harder way, looked handsome in the way her daughter looked handsome when you were looking at her as a person not as someone you might fall in love with. It was difficult to imagine that Helen used to call her Clutchpaws. Perhaps all her nervous mannerisms had simply been reflections of her husband's own nervous intensity. Perhaps widowhood was the making of her. As though she could read my thoughts, she quickly said that a day didn't go by when she didn't miss him, quite violently sometimes, but she did have to admit that life was less of a strain without him.

'But that only leaves me more time to worry about Helen. Naturally you always worry about an only daughter, but she was always so self-sufficient.'

'But now she isn't?'

'No, I don't think she is.'

'Were you worried about her being on the picket line? That was almost the last time I saw her, before I went to America.'

'Oh that. No, not at all. We're Lancashire. My father was a colliery overseer, Martin's father went down the pit before the WEA rescued him and he became a teacher. No, I like her standing up for the miners. You should have loyalties, even if that Scargill is a nasty piece of work.

Anyway, with all the policemen there, you're probably safer on a picket line than crossing the road.'

This robust reaction took me aback. Would she have said half of it if her husband had been around?

'No it wasn't the strike, though it must have been funny seeing you there, being on the other side. Like, I don't know, Romeo and Juliet – except not quite.'

She added the last phrase, laughing a slightly merciless laugh.

'Truth is,' she went on, 'she could join the Trots for all I cared. But the drinking, that *is* a worry.'

'The drinking?'

Mrs Hardress suddenly looked at me with a severe disbelieving stare.

'You must have noticed. I mean, she probably doesn't drink as much as you men, but it's too much for her, much too much. She's bleary a lot of the time – bleary, that's what we used to call it in our family. And she starts too early in the day. When she's here, she goes to that pub behind the station as soon as it opens which you wouldn't go to in your right mind at any time except to get drunk.'

I couldn't think of anything to say which wouldn't make me seem even more crass.

'How long,' I said hesitantly, 'do you think she's been like this?'

'You really haven't noticed, have you? She was bad before she went away, but since she came back she's much worse. Another way you can tell, I don't mean to sound snobby, but she hasn't got any discrimination. She'll go out with any man who'll buy her a drink. That d'Amico person – remember him? – she brought him here once when they were both pickled and he was all smarmy but you could see he was no good from a mile off. Of course, these East End villains know how to charm a girl. A bit of rough, isn't that what they call it, but it always ends in tears. Then there's that other one, Robert something or other. Little squirt if you ask me. She wouldn't have taken up with him if she was seeing straight. You can see he did all that Support the Miners stuff just because it was the trendy thing to do. Doesn't know any more about politics than he knows about nuclear physics. You must know him, father's a vicar.'

'Oh yes, Bobs.'

'He's a complete waste of space, that little man.'

She was standing up now, for no particular reason I could see, except to ease her rage. And for the first time her little fists began to clench and unclench in the way her daughter mocked. 'It's not good enough. She's got such a good brain, she could do equations when she was seven, I mean, she's not a genius but it's a really useful sort of brain, it's a shame to let it go to waste skivvying in that travel agency of his.'

'You mean the place Bobs works in?'

'It belongs to him now. He came into some money, from an aunt, I think, and bought the man out. Isn't that a peculiar phrase, "came into some money", as though you were just walking along and came upon a sixpence lying on the pavement. I suppose that's what it's like for some people. But could you speak to her, she'll listen to you, well, she won't listen to me, and perhaps someone her own age –'

Her voice trailed away in the way I remembered it when her husband was alive, as though she herself knew her hopes of my being able to help were futile. To come out to Minnow Island in the first place had amounted to acceptance of whatever it was she wanted of me, so there was nothing else to do but mumble that of course I would go and see Helen which I had been meaning to do anyway. This was only half-true. Even the thought of her had become a little daunting. I had never really known what she wanted out of life and not having seen her for so long thought she would be more mysterious still. I couldn't understand why Mrs Hardress spoke of Bobs as of an unsatisfactory, perhaps discarded, boyfriend. They had been engaged years ago, before I went to America. By now they must have been married for ages, or if not married surely the bust-up would have been too bitter for them to go on working side by side. It was odd, I admit, that I didn't ask Mrs Hardress what the situation was but then she was odd too, as she had said herself, odd and a little frightening. Anyway I was in no hurry to have my fears confirmed, and it was nice to be able to play a little longer with the thought that Helen might still be – but that was not a sentence I dared complete, even in my head.

The little shop had been repainted, cream and blue, and there was a fresh sign, Moonman Travel, with a smirky blue-and-cream man-in-the-moon in the middle of the window. I couldn't see Bobs through the window, because he was now in the inner office previously occupied by the large man with hair *en brosse*. Bobs himself seemed larger and rose from his chair to greet me in a fair simulation of that boss's greeting which says you're lucky really to get in to see me but I make a point of being accessible. The office had been painted up inside, but it had a peculiar smell, not paint.

'Well,' he said, 'well, what do you think of it?'

'Very smart,' I said limply, not saying that it looked like it did before, only repainted.

'The relaunch has had quite an impact, especially the specialising in Eastern Europe. We've got some great contacts with the Czechs and the Hungarians. Zoltan's an absolute winner.'

He waved back through the glass window in the door to his old desk where a skinny young man with a yellow face was talking on the phone. Gherkins, that was the smell, authentic certainly, perhaps good for business.

'Helen's out this morning with a client. I'm meeting her for spag bol at the old Salerno. It would be great if you came along.'

Why couldn't he just say lunch? There was something irritating about his habit of specifying the dish that he was going to have – let's grab a vindaloo at the Shalimar was another favourite line – as if these restaurants didn't have huge menus, though to be fair half of the items at the Shalimar were usually off.

The Salerno was crowded. Bobs stared across the room, his gaze suddenly troubled by the possibility of her not being there, and I was stabbed by envy. Another stab when I saw her at a table squashed in the corner half-buried by the coats bosoming out from the coat-stand. She was reading, her face in profile, a pair of horn-rims perched unconvincingly on her nose as on a film star pretending to be a librarian in a romantic comedy, but her face pale and intent, not like a film star's. Her golden hair was longer than I had remembered, reaching to the collar of her grey-blue shirt but a little tangled as though it needed cutting. She seemed unmoved by the people around her fishing for their coats or the new arrivals groping for a hook. Even as it occurred to me how much I still loved her, it also occurred to me that it was ridiculous to love someone for their yellow hair.

Coming out of a warm embrace which sent my spirits soaring, I spotted that the book she was reading was called *Principles of Social Work.*

'No, I don't believe it.'

'Don't believe what?'

'You're not reading it for pleasure?'

'Of course not. So I'm going to be a social worker. What's wrong with that?'

'Nothing.'

'Isn't that what you always imagined I was underneath?'

'I thought you were a scientist.'

'As I've told you a million times, I was never nearly good enough to be a pure scientist. And as for the applied bit, it's a pile of shit.'

'I expect you're right.'

She looked at me with some irritation.

'So you saw Dodo in America.'

'Yes, I did. How do you know?'

'Wake up. Because you sent me a postcard telling me.'

'Oh yes, I did.'

'And he told you all about the beryllium.'

'I didn't put that on the postcard.'

'You didn't have to. You're so pathetically easy to read. People who are secretive just have no idea how much their faces are giving away. What a dirty trick that was, I knew he was a prick but I didn't know how big a prick till then. Bobs, will you order me another orange juice and a saltimbocca?'

She spoke to him distantly, mechanically, not unkindly, as to a servant who might be a little slow in the uptake. Bobs ordered a carafe of house wine for us two and then seemed to make quite a business of the orange juice order, as though it was a drink which demanded careful preparation and some particular ingredient which might be hard to get hold of. Perhaps it had been a struggle to persuade her to go for the soft drink, though his approach seemed as always likely to have the perverse effect, of provoking her to cancel it and demand a double scotch instead. But she didn't seem to notice and started talking about her new career.

'You'd love to watch me going into college with the rest of them, it would confirm all your worst prejudices, anoraks and pimples as far as the eye can see. You'd like to see all social workers strangled at birth, wouldn't you?'

'No, I wouldn't, that's your prejudice imagining that I –'

But I could scarcely complete the sentence because my eye was arrested, manacled if you like, to the fourth finger of her left hand which carried a glittering chunky ring.

'It's real,' she said ruefully, 'Bobs insisted.'

'So you really are married?'

My lips could scarcely get round the word, which had the effect of making the enquiry sound roguish, verging on the obscene.

'Of course we are. Didn't Bobs say anything? You didn't really expect us to stay engaged until you got back to give us your blessing?'

'Oh,' I said, 'well done.'

'You make it sound like coming third in an egg-and-spoon race.'

'No, no, congratulations, really, it's just that I didn't know when you were going to do it.'

'Do it, what a sad phrase.'

'And, it's a funny thing, but your mother didn't mention it when I went to see her.'

'You went to see my mother? Why?'

While we were speaking, my gaze had drifted away from her to Bobs who had just finished talking to the waiter. He seemed intensely agitated, his squashed face almost trembling with emotions that you would have expected to be easy enough to read but weren't. He looked proud and happy but somehow insecure, as though he himself had only just heard that they were married and, while wanting it to be true, suspected it might be some kind of misunderstanding or, worse still, an elaborate joke. He gazed at her adoringly, his eyes oddly screwed up at the corners. In fact, his look was so peculiar and unsettling that I had scarcely thought about what I was saying. Mrs Hardress hadn't quite told me not to tell Helen that I had been down to Minnow Island, but on the whole if someone's mother summons you to say how worried she is about her daughter's drinking, the subject of such a visit should be introduced delicately, if at all.

'Yes,' I said lamely, 'it was nice to see her. She was looking very well, I thought.'

'I know how she is looking. That wasn't what I asked. Do you normally go down to see your friends' mothers to check how they are looking?'

'Not often.'

'She wanted you to spy on me, I suppose. She's become all confident like that since Dad died. It's peculiar.'

'No, no, of course she didn't. I mean mothers are always anxious but –'

'You know why she didn't mention us being married?'

'Because she doesn't approve?'

'Of course she doesn't.'

'So she didn't come to the wedding?'

'She didn't. But that's not unusual in our family. Her parents didn't come to their wedding, nor did Dad's. The tradition probably goes back generations on both sides. Bobs's Dad came to ours in spite of it not being in a church, and brother Gerald came because it wasn't in a church. Gerald's rather an amazing person, don't you think? But Mum carries the tradition one stage further. She pretends it hasn't happened at all and some charming surgeon or barrister is going to scoop me up any moment.'

'How do you mean, pretends it hasn't happened?'

'Treats Bobs as if he were just some casual acquaintance. "Do bring that Bobs person down if you want to" when she's in a good mood, or "Can't you think of anyone else to bring?", when she isn't. That's what I mean by weird. She's totally in denial. This orange juice is disgusting, Bobs, tastes of drains.'

The anxiety on Bobs's face now seemed less mysterious. Repeated incredulity from Mrs Hardress might well wear down his own confidence in the reality of their being married. Keeping her on the orange juice must be an extra worry.

'Peculiar,' I murmured in feeble assent.

After a couple of glasses of wine it seemed possible to tolerate the thought of them being married, tolerate it as a melancholy illustration of the cockeyed course of events, not as a good idea. When Bobs had finished his cannelloni, he interlaced his fubsy little fingers with hers, the chunky ring still showing above them, and he talked of how they were going to redecorate Padders.

With the other hand, she was starting in on a goblet of assorted ices, demolishing it with strong swift scoops. How fast she ate and what a lot, but without an extra pound on her, her pale boat-shaped face just the same as when she had loomed up through the mist on the beach fifteen years earlier. If you were her mother, you certainly wouldn't want her marrying Bobs, but then you wouldn't if you were almost anyone's mother. Still, what was marriage? No big deal, in fact a very modest deal, one scarcely worth thinking about, not a fit subject for agony or debate any more. If you did happen to go through with it, you made embarrassed excuses: we've just been posted to Poland or Saudi Arabia and it would be difficult if we weren't, or she really doesn't want to upset her parents. If you felt strongly, you wouldn't do it even so, on principle. It was one of those compromises you could never quite recover from.

'You'll come and see us, won't you?' she said, placing her hand on mine but lightly, no entrelacement.

'Yes of course,' I said, the strong bitter coffee bump-starting my heart, a little flushed anyway from the volcanic Sicilian wine and the mixed emotions.

'You'll have to anyway, to keep up your reports to my mother. The spy who loved me,' she added carelessly.

Her annoyance about my visit to Minnow Island seemed to have melted. She never bore much malice. Perhaps she was really not very complicated either. A decent saltimbocca and a few scoops of ice-cream and she would forgive anyone.

'The spy who lost me,' I corrected with mock melancholy or melancholy masquerading as mock.

'Double oh six and a half,' Bobs added. Marriage had not done much for his wit. In any case, I suspected he had read the joke somewhere or heard it on a sitcom.

It was time for me to go back to the office and I managed to say goodbye in a practised way almost as though they were old friends who had been married for years, so long in fact that we had begun to lose touch and we needed to protest that it had been much too long and we must not leave it so long next time. I was half-way down the street before I remembered my raincoat on the bulging coat-stand. They never noticed me coming back, were talking easily not intently to one another, already insulated from me by being married. Perhaps they were talking about me: how dull or stiff I had become, or how fat. One last look at them as I half-turned to pull the swing door towards me. No, not Beauty and the Beast. From this distance, his chubby fair face belonged to the same race as hers, he could have been her younger brother, a squatter, duller version but not wholly alien. That might make a subtler version of the fairy-tale: the Beast would be plain to look at but not unbearably ugly, only when he opened his mouth or perhaps not even then, only when he interlaced his fingers with hers would a shudder run through the audience, and the audience wouldn't quite know why they shuddered. A hard trick for the director to bring off, though.

They were gloomy days after lunch at the Salerno, days which lingered on into weeks. Gloomy is not the right word, that suggests a slow-paced melancholy which you might learn to enjoy. This gloom came in sharp pangs, a sudden stabbing awareness of missed opportunity, the kind of awareness that spreads from its original cause – my failure to see how much I wanted her – to a wider sensation that missing opportunities was my speciality.

'Hallo. Isn't it wonderful news? They are both thrilled and, well, for me it's the only good thing that's happened since Martin.'

'Oh, hallo, how nice to hear from you,' I said, recognising Mrs Hardress's voice quickly enough, though she was so excited she hadn't said who was calling.

'You haven't heard? I can tell you haven't. How odd they didn't tell you. Helen's going to have a baby in April.'

'Wonderful, absolutely wonderful,' I said, thinking of Tolly and wondering how Bobs had done it.

'She said she'd seen you. I'm surprised she didn't tell you,' said Mrs Hardress unable to keep the triumph out of her voice.

'Perhaps she wasn't quite sure then,' I said, suddenly realising that I had completely misunderstood the orange juice.

Bobs was now to be freely spoken of, it seemed, as an accredited or at least tolerated partner. True, Mrs Hardress had not yet graduated to using his name, referring to him as 'he', as in 'He's hoping to get that flat redecorated before the baby'.

'Beryl. We're going to call her Beryl. It's going to be a her, I'm sure of it. I couldn't possibly have a boy.'

'You can't call her Beryl.'

'Yes we can. Why? Don't you like it? Too common for you, I expect.'

'Well, why do you like it?'

'Don't you remember?' She giggled. 'That lovely pale greeny colour.'

'Oh,' I said. 'You haven't told Bobs *that?*'

'Certainly not. I'm talking about the stone.'

'I should have thought stones were rather a painful memory.'

'Nothing Dodo could do would affect how beautiful the stone was, could it?'

'No,' I said, but thinking how strange she was wanting to refer back, even indirectly, to something so humiliating for her, even if she hadn't heard the way Dodo had talked about her on *Sting Ray.* Then again, even if she had, she might still call her daughter Beryl, just to show that mere human villainy could not corrupt the scientific reality. The little stains we left on the earth would fade away soon enough.

'You haven't come to see the baby.'

'I sent a telegram, didn't you get it?'

'Yes of course I did and thanks, but a telegram's not the same. Anyway, it doesn't matter, because you'll see her at the christening.'

'*Christening?*'

'Yes, you'll be a godfather, won't you, that's why I'm calling, you believe in all that sort of thing.'

'But you –'

'Bobs's Dad would be hurt if we didn't and anyway I'm sure you'll renounce the devil and all his works very nicely. I looked it all up, it's weird, but you'll love Beryl, she's so funny.'

It must have been five years, perhaps more since I had been to St Columba's (not quite two years of the intervening period in the States). But the memory of it already seemed distant, as though it was in childhood that I had first seen the mottled green spire and the battered creamy finials climbing out of the dirty brick buttresses and the litter blown against the laurel hedge and inside the chocolate and blue tiles and the glowing stained glass telling how the faith first came to Iona.

We stood in a sparse little circle in the corner of the church squeezed up against a table piled high with SPCK leaflets which looked as though they had been there for a while.

Helen stood by the font holding the baby. Both seemed indifferent to their surroundings. Bobs was fussing about, unable to decide where to put a brass vase of flowers that had been on the font. Next to Helen was Sue, her friend from work. They were both qualified social workers now, she told me. Sue was looking round eagerly as though this might be her last chance to gather the details of such an interesting folk ritual. Helen had made no concessions to the occasion, but Sue was smartly dressed in a royal-blue coat and skirt and a blue beret. Behind her Bobs's brother Gerald stood utterly still, his face upturned at that misleadingly beatific angle affected by his father, who was telling us about the purpose of the service.

'Now you godparents, Sue, and Gus, how nice to see you again, Gus, and Mrs Hardress who is kindly standing proxy for my niece Everilda who is in Botswana and is unable to be here, you're here to speak up for Beryl. You're her sureties, like a surety in a court of law who stands up to guarantee that his friend won't skip bail. On her behalf you have to renounce the devil and all his works, and the vain pomp and glory of the world. That's quite a lot to be going on with, isn't it?'

He cast his eye mildly round our little circle as though offering an opportunity for anyone feeling unequal to these challenges to opt out now. A powerful odour of mothballs came from somewhere very close to me, probably Gerald's long black coat. I wondered whether his father's sermon was making him boil with rage, but his beatific ceilingward gaze gave nothing away.

Not for the first time in Mr Moonman's sermons my mind began to stray to his old-fashioned diction, dwelling for quite a long time on its precise consonants and liquid vowels and his occasional 'haugh', which seemed to be a sort of shift-key marking the end of a passage, and while I wasn't bored I didn't take in much either. Odd words came to me, perhaps because he gave them that extra French-sounding accentuation. Now he was saying something about Christian belief, separating the two syllables of 'belief' in an un-English way, and I remembered

Scrannel's homily about how 'belief' really only meant 'be lovable' and how the words we now used to describe the impersonal physical reality of the world were once the language of our affections. In the old days 'truth' had meant simply loyalty to a lord or lover, or to a god or God. A 'fact' was some deed you had done, whether glorious or monstrous, not some dreary verifiable proposition. Nothing, Scrannel went on, betrayed more nakedly the irreversible and appalling shift in the nature of our world, from a world created for us, one in which what really mattered were the promises we made and the loyalties we bound ourselves to, a human-centred world, to the universe we now occupied, one of which we were merely an insignificant part, a chance conglomeration of atoms. The more we learnt of nature, the more power we acquired over nature, the more insignificant we became. That was the hideous irony. When we were weak, the world was strange and beautiful and our dealings with it shone with a heroic gleam. But now we were strong, and nothing we said or did mattered in the slightest. At the time, these remarks of Scrannel's had seemed to me rather melodramatic. But now standing in the cold dusty light of St Col's with Mr Moonman dismissing us with a blessing and in the same breath beckoning us to refreshments at the vicarage, I could see what he meant. These pledges and beliefs that we had muttered out together were hollow, not only because we lacked the sort of faith we were supposed to have but because the whole language was alien to us. We didn't believe in our promises even when we kept them. That wasn't the way we talked. How did we talk instead – but before I had got around to thinking of the answer, Gerald Moonman turned to me, or perhaps to Helen who was coming up behind me with the baby, and said: 'Well, we got through that mumbo-jumbo all right.'

Beryl, who had not cried once throughout the ceremony, squawked and splayed her rosy little fingers at him.

'She didn't seem to mind,' Helen said, cocking her head to peer round the fleecy folds of the shawl at her daughter's face which crinkled and then stretched into a yawny smile.

'She seems to like church. I'm afraid she may have a vocation,' he said.

'It's wind.'

It felt hot outside. At first I thought only by contrast with the mildewed coolth of St Col's. But the sun was really blazing fiercely for May and Helen put her hand out to shade Beryl's face, although she had a white bonnet on. We walked in straggly file past the litter-blown laurels a little way down the hill to the vicarage which was also a confused building of grimy brick and crumbly cornices and mullions of creamy stone. The house was shabby and dark inside. All I took in at first was the sour cabbagey smell, less sickly than Mr Moonman's own smell but no better. In a square bare room at the back with a green-slimed window into what looked like a conservatory there was a table with sandwiches and a large jug of some pale brown liquid which turned out to be cider. Sue poured it out for us. It started by tasting quite refreshing and then revealed a deep rotten aftertaste. The room had a lincrusta wallpaper in a ridged pattern of brownish roses. The only picture was a large framed engraving, also brownish, which despite being over the fireplace so undulated with damp that it was hard to identify the precise subject, though it looked rural. Today, it was hot and stuffy in the room and Mr Moonman sat down and mopped his brow.

'I must say this cider is even better than last year. I make it myself you know, from the trees out there. Do go out in the garden, it's the best time of year to go out in the garden, don't you think?'

With difficulty Bobs shoved open the glass-panelled door and led us out past the conservatory which we could now see had fallen in on itself, most of the glass lying shattered amid the invading brambles. Beyond was tall grass tangled with cow-parsley and lanky buttercups and a few twisted apple trees with the last of the blossom still on them. The ground fell away beyond the tumbledown brick wall at the end, so that the view beyond was mostly sky.

'It's got fantastic potential, this place,' Bobs said.

Helen stood under an apple tree rocking Beryl, perhaps singing to her or perhaps just cooing. Even under the trees it was hot and I felt the sweat between my shoulder-blades. Gerald Moonman had disappeared. Then looking back at the house I saw a dark figure moving across the upper windows. After a minute or two, one of the windows was flung open and Moonman poked his head out and then thrust out his hand holding a silver candlestick which glinted in the sun.

Helen laughed and nodded back at her brother-in-law, but Bobs frowned and turned away.

'Gerald said he'd come mostly to make sure his father hadn't flogged all his mother's silver,' she explained.

Just then Sue came out through the glass door with a look of panic on her face.

'Quickly,' she said, 'it's Mr Moonman, he –'

We hurried inside. The vicar was still sitting on the same chair with his mug of cider almost empty in front of him. His head had fallen on to his shoulder and at first he seemed lifeless, but when we ourselves had quietened down, we could hear his low, stertorous breathing.

'I know this one,' said Gerald, who had just come downstairs, 'let's take him out.'

The brothers each took one side of the chair and carried him out, chair and all, and set him under an apple tree. Sue took his pulse, which she said was faint and fluttery but still there.

'Leave him alone for a bit,' said Gerald, 'he'll surface.'

So we moved away and talked furtively among ourselves, leaving the bent figure in the chair to breathe for himself. And after a few minutes his head rose and with a few mild moans, scarcely more than a clearing of the throat, he began to look about him.

'It's lovely at this time of the year, the orchard, is it not?' he said to nobody in particular.

'How did you know he'd be all right?'

'It's just hardening of the arteries. He gets these little black-outs. Nothing to worry about or rather nothing to be done about it.'

Gerald Moonman resumed his beatific upward gaze.

'It is curious,' his father said, 'do you not think, that when people lose their faith they usually take up sexual intercourse instead. Or perhaps it is the other way around?'

'Dad, I should rest if I were you,' Bobs said, 'you've had a little turn, you know. You ought to go upstairs and lie down.'

'I don't think I will. I don't want to miss the fun.'

The brothers brought some more rickety upright wooden chairs out of the back room and placed them in two groups at either side of the garden with their father by himself under the tree in the middle. It was a strange arrangement which they came to quite naturally without any bickering. Bobs and Gerald sat down together, and Bobs gave a skittish little wave at the rest of us. We might have been waiting for some ritual to begin or some spell to be lifted which would release us from our positions. Sue and Helen started talking about a case conference.

'If they're not going to prosecute, I don't see why we have to wait.'

'Apparently the police told Jackie they were only not prosecuting on condition we had all their notes because otherwise he'd just pull the wool over our eyes again.'

'The mother still says he never laid a finger on the child.'

'It's amazing how they go on saying that when you can see the bruises.'

They were speaking in a low professional tone. I let my drowsy gaze wander past the stray fair fronds of Helen's hair to the tangled cow-parsley and the Reverend James Moonman sitting on his chair under the unkempt apple tree, or rather not sitting in it any more, because he had slowly slid off it, so slowly that at first I thought he might be bending over to pick a flower. But there he was on the ground, his black cassock twisted around and the chair tumbled away from him and this time he didn't move and it wasn't hard to see that Beryl's had been his last baptism.

'Suddenly in the orchard,' Gerald said.

'Is that a quote?' Bobs asked.

'Who cares whether it's a quote,' Helen said furiously, 'can't you try his chest, Sue?'

Sue obediently hunkered down over the figure in the twisted cassock and pumped away with the flat of her hands. Bobs fussed around his father's head, smoothing away the pale stalks of cow-parsley and buttercup and then smoothing down the lank white hair. Our running towards the fallen figure had woken Beryl and she began to whimper and Helen took her away, rocking her as she went. Moonman stood motionless and very close so that Sue's sleeve brushed against him as she went up and down. He might have already been standing at his father's funeral.

Eventually Sue admitted defeat and stood up again brushing the white cow-parsley blossom from her bright blue skirt. The brothers knelt down side by side and Moonman slid his hands under his father's knees and Bobs did the same under his shoulders. Awkwardly they staggered to their feet and carried him indoors. I had seen dead people before – my father in the hospital, a French peasant lying in the road – but I had never before seen a dead person being carried and that shook me more than the sight of him lying in the grass.

They put him upstairs in the bedroom. The rest of us waited in the room with the sandwiches in it.

'They'll only go to waste.'

'I don't quite –'

'You would at a funeral.'

'All right.'

We sat munching lettuce-and-marmite wedges until Bobs came in with a suitcase.

'No-o, I don't think anything in here,' he said with a questing gaze, 'I've rung the undertaker, he'll be round in two shakes, he said.'

'What are you doing with that suitcase?'

'You have to move quickly before the vultures descend.'

'Vultures?'

'Empty house bound to be burgled. Stuff's much safer at Padders.'

'What stuff?'

'Well, the candlesticks, my mother's vanity set, some of the cutlery's worth a bit. Gerald's happy, so –'

'But isn't it –'

'Then there's probate. Probate's a bugger. Must put it all in the boot before the undertaker arrives. Some of these chaps are in league with the Revenue, you know.'

And he strutted out like a man about to catch a train.

Moonman may have been happy about Bobs's precautions, but he was not at all happy about the Will when that later came to light in one of the few drawers Bobs had not been through that afternoon. Sparsely furnished the vicarage might have been but to everyone's surprise it emerged that it did in fact belong to the deceased. He had bought it off the parish with the money his wife had left him – it seemed she hadn't lost all her money and he had never intended to go back to Norfolk, thus turning out to be as unreliable in what he said as Bobs – and he now left it to the younger but more beloved of his sons, the one who seemed to get left things.

'And what's wrong with that?' Helen said rather sharply as though I was about to contradict her. 'They never got on at all. Gerald never came to see him at the end, hated God, and thought his father a silly old fart.'

'Well, they used to be very fond of each other, didn't they, before they quarrelled, and anyway you hate God too.'

'There's no such person to hate.'

She looked lovely that summer, really lovely, lovelier in fact than when I had first met her. She was still just a little plumper from having Beryl. A certain tenseness that had been growing on her now melted away. They had moved straight into St Col's and were both too busy to do much about the house or garden. Later on, there were to be pattern-books from Sandersons and Habitat and John Oliver the paint people lying about the house and a new teak bench from the Highgate Garden Centre under the apple trees but just now there were only the three of them moving about the dingy three-quarters-empty rooms or lying on a moth-eaten old rug flattening the high grasses. Bobs found an old hook under the rotting shelf of the greenhouse and sharpened it with a chunk of carborundum he also found there and began to hack a clearing in the grass. He went brown quickly in the long sunny spell which lasted most of June, so that he was almost good-looking.

How odd and difficult Helen's life had been, partly of her own making, mostly not and this little clearing Bobs had made in the long grass where they could sit on the grubby old blanket without the long stalks poking through was something of a clearing in her life too, very nearly an idyll, though how anyone could have an idyll with Bobs still beat me. Yet that was her gift, that she could have an idyll with anyone if he loved her.

When she was feeding Beryl, Bobs sat gaping for hours, his normal fussing stilled by the sight of Beryl so eagerly going at her swollen milky breast. I, the awkward visitor, the old friend, would turn half-away and chat about other things, but the quiet, insistent sound of the feeding and Helen shifting in her chair to allow the baby to switch to the other side and settling her when Beryl showed signs of flagging – all these things unnerved me so that I would sometimes forget what I had been saying.

Even when Beryl was finally weaned (later than any other baby she knew, Helen said, because they both enjoyed it so much), Helen still looked different. 'I think I've lost the bloom of childbirth if I ever had it,' she laughed, but she had not, to my eye anyway, and going up to St Col's, sometimes just for a drink in the evening after work, was like a dip in some refreshing spring which had a miracle-working legend vaguely attached to it. I should have been jealous of Bobs but somehow I wasn't. Quite often he wasn't there, kept late at the office – it was the time when things were beginning to happen in Eastern Europe and Moonman Travel was one of the few ways of getting there if you wanted to catch a bit of the action. But one evening towards the end of a drizzly week in May – a year or so later I think – he was there and looking rather pleased with himself.

'You ever been to a *Frag* lunch?'

'Once, or perhaps twice. Ages ago.'

'It's amazing isn't it? You go into that funny old toyshop, well it's not really a toyshop any more, though he has still got toys at the back.'

'Get on with it, Bobs.'

'And then this pretty girl comes down, Fiona, they call them all Fiona, you know, whatever their real name is, and takes you up to the place where they have lunch and there's absolutely everyone you can think of, that man who produces the late-night satire, and the MP who everyone says is a spy but Moonman says isn't really but only pretends to be, and an Australian economist who turned out to be working for Ziegler though Moonman hates Ziegler but he wanted to pump this man, and Bella Barone who used to sing at the Establishment when it first opened. I thought she was great then and she was actually very friendly but she smelled rather peculiar. Oh and Willie Sturgis who was going on about how the government was selling arms to Iran in spite of the embargo. I think it was Iran, there isn't an embargo on Iraq, is there?'

'Sounds very interesting,' Helen said. It was odd that even having known her so long, I still couldn't tell how ironic she was being, if at all. 'Pick up her elephant, could you? I can't reach. You didn't tell me you were going. Moonman doesn't usually ask you.'

'Big Brother only rang me up yesterday, at the office. He didn't tell me then, you know how he keeps his cards close to his chest, but he wanted to have a chat, a private family sort of thing.'

'Not a very good place for that, was it, a *Frag* lunch with the spy who wasn't and smelly Bella and the rest of them.'

'No, no, afterwards. We went into this office, you know that place with all the funny postcards and the dartboard with Nixon's face on it.'

'I don't know,' Helen said patiently, 'I've never been there.'

'Anyway he took me up there and told me he was leaving Mile, his wife.'

'I know Mile's his wife.'

'Yes, but I thought Gus might not.'

'I'm sure he does, get on with it.'

'So he said he's leaving her and I said why and he gave that weird laugh and said in a funny voice as though it was being read out on the news, "It's an amicable trial separation, Mr Moonman is currently in intensive care with multiple stab wounds." So I said, but seriously. And he said, seriously she's gone off with somebody in the BBC, in Current Affairs, which I thought was quite ironic but Brother didn't see the joke.'

'I can't say I blame Mile,' Helen said, 'I'm sorry for him, but he is creepy, even though he is your brother. I mean, you've more or less said so yourself. I couldn't live with him.'

'Well, that's a pity,' Bobs said, 'because he's coming to live with us.'

'What do you mean?'

'He needs somewhere for a few weeks, because it's her house really and she wants the Current Affairs man to move in because he's just come back from, yes, it must be Iran because that's where – anyway he doesn't want to stay in the house a moment longer, which you can understand.'

'So *you* said he could stay *here*?'

'Well, it is partly his house in a way, I know he and Dad didn't get on too well towards the end, but he does need somewhere.'

'Without asking *me*?'

'Well I was rather on the spot. I couldn't say, yes, it's all right by me but just hang on a minute while I ring the wife. That wouldn't have been very fraternal.'

'Your brother is just about the least fraternal person I've ever met.'

'What do you reckon, Gus? Would you have Moonman to stay?'

'Well, he's not my brother.'

'He means no,' Helen said.

The next time I went up to St Col's, there was a bicycle in the hall, a sturdy black battered bicycle, not rusty but giving off, quite aggressively, the feeling of an age when machines were made to last. It had peculiar triangles of black cloth stretched over its mudguards as though the machine was in permanent mourning like Queen Victoria. This was Moonman's legendary bicycle. I had seen it often before with him on it, but never indoors where it made an even more formidable impression. The bicycle accompanied him in his quest for Anglo-Saxon churches all over England and was the cause of many rows with British Rail staff on trains which were not permitted to carry bikes. Moonman might be an implacable enemy of organised religion, but he hunted down these churches because he had an obsession with the Anglo-Saxon era, believing that democracy, truth and a good many other desirable things had disappeared from England after the Norman blitzkrieg. He covered a lot of ground in London too, in search of old woodworking tools which he would carry home in the bike's wicker basket, which had a peculiar high rounded shape suggesting that perhaps it had originally been made not as a bike basket but as an eeltrap by some ancient craftsman in the fens who still kept allegiance to Hereward the Wake. I would quite often see him pedalling along the streets of Notting Hill or Highgate with his milky eyes set at the familiar heavenward angle, so that he might well have been a blind cyclist for whom there was no point in keeping his eyes on the road and who managed to navigate by some arcane combination of his other senses.

'He just turned up on his bike?'

'Well, he had Bobs behind him with the van and all his clobber. There's an awful lot of it.'

She took me into the back room with the brown walls where we had eaten the sandwiches. This room, then so stark and empty, was now piled high with books, mostly dusty folio-sized volumes stacked on top of each other. Moonman either had no access to cardboard boxes or tea-chests or didn't hold with them. In among the books were some of the old tools – adzes, chisels, lathes, I don't know what else. An old-fashioned brass picture rail ran round the room high above our heads and there were now jackets and overcoats dangling unsteadily on coat-hangers from it, all in standard Moonman black. These grim garments shifted in the draught from the window like hanged men at a gibbet complex.

'The obvious thing is to take them up to the attics, but then –'

'They'll never go.'

'Yes, and nor will he. He's sleeping there at the moment.' She pointed to a mattress made up with clean sheets and blankets in the corner of the room protected by a rampart of books which was why I hadn't noticed it till then.

'And if you make up a proper bedroom for him, he'll take that as an invitation to become a permanent part of the household.'

'He will.'

I tried to think of something to cheer her up.

'You used to think he was rather amazing, didn't you? I mean, you admired *Frag* and the way he didn't care who he went for and the jokes.'

'Oh yes, but –' This only seemed to make her more distressed and she found it hard to answer. 'I think he's almost too funny, too funny to have about the house. I mean, I'm not sure you want someone being brilliantly amusing all the time, do you? It's sort of icky, when people are too clever.'

'You're all right with Bobs then?'

'Gus, don't be horrid.' Suddenly there was something odd, unlike her, about the way she was talking. Not only the words were little-girlish, the voice was little-girlish too. Her level serious tone had deserted her. Perhaps some alien had invaded her body, or perhaps she and the baby had changed places and if I went upstairs I would find Beryl discussing the parameters of case work.

Helen began piling books into something more like order. I gazed without much interest at the pile next to me, which was a run of some pre-war annual for boys about mechanics, then I looked out through the grimy windows which Bobs had not yet got around to cleaning. There was a bumble bee bobbing against the window-pane in a low-key way.

'Who's been peeking in mah bedroom? Didn't Ah tell you, Momma, nobody was to go in mah room without mah permission?'

There had been no sound of Moonman coming into the room. All the *Frag* crowd did funny voices, but they sounded different, disembodied almost, coming from Moonman because he was silent so much of the time. And when he did a Baby Doll or a Harold Wilson, it appeared to come from nowhere, not because he didn't move his lips, though he scarcely did, but because you weren't expecting him to say anything. His silences were legendary, almost as legendary as the bike, and nervous guests would sometimes stumble out of a *Frag* lunch reflecting with wonder that he had not said a single word except to complain that there was no custard with the apple pie.

This didn't mean he didn't like talking. Sometimes I had heard him discourse for a quarter of an hour or more, fending off attempted interruptions – even if the interrupter only wanted to say how much he agreed – repeating himself, sliding off at a tangent, making a joke that one of the others had already made as if his making it created a fresh occasion for laughing, which it sometimes did and when it didn't people still laughed again because they had laughed the first time and anyway it was his lunch. Besides, his long pauses often infected others at the table, so that they too were cowed into silence and were happy in a nervous way to hear noise of any sort resume, because they had expected the lunch to be an uproarious affair, which it could be when they were all talking at once, complaining that Clapp, the Caliban who served them and kept a sort of toyshop downstairs, had undercooked the cabbage or failed to provide any gravy in some doomed attempt to raise the standard of cuisine against their wishes.

Until the break-up with Mile none of us, even those who had known him for years, had much idea about Moonman's home life. He was known to live in North London, with a wife who never went out, either because she was a hopeless drunk or because she was an anaesthetist or a gynaecologist whose hours were too unsocial. Some people, mostly men, doubted whether Mile even existed, and preferred to attribute to Moonman deviant sexual habits or no habits at all. Women either found him attractive in a way they didn't normally find men attractive, or unattractive though they suspected that under the Lytton Strachey beard he was probably rather handsome. Perhaps these two views amounted to the same thing. Anyway women all agreed that there could be no question of his being gay. By now we were creeping into the 1980s and I suppose Moonman must have been well into his forties, being so much older than Bobs, but he was ageless – or rather, had been so precociously aged that he had nowhere to go but younger.

Bobs had confirmed at least that the wife, Mile, existed and that she was reclusive or at any rate never asked Bobs to the house but there was nothing weird about her, she was just a hard-working teacher without much of a sense of humour, never laughed at his jokes or Moonman's. Of course not asking Bobs to your house didn't make you a recluse. Yet the evidence suggested he might be right all the same. By now Moonman had made so many enemies in every known walk of life that going out to any social occasion would be perilous. Victims might be too badly winged to confront Moonman himself but would not hesitate to denounce him to his wife. And as for the jokes, if he was anything like the same at home as he was in the office, a certain glazed indifference might be the best survival tactic.

'Momma, yew didn't tell me you had a gentleman caller. Yew know Ah don't like you to entertain gentlemen.'

The voice, while remaining somewhere in the deep South, slid from a squeaky eight-year-old to a middle-aged retard frustrated in love.

'Mile rang when you were out.'

'What did she want? I told her to get the lawyers to talk.'

'She said they needed to turn the water off, something to do with a leak.'

'She knows about that sort of thing, I don't.'

His own ordinary voice was rather mellow even when, as now, it had a petulant edge to it.

'Well, she said to ring.'

'She can fucking well get Current Affairs to sort it out. He's supposed to be good with his hands. Oh, Trevor, I do love the way you touch me.'

'Is he really called Trevor?'

'Current Affairs doesn't have a name. He's just a telly person.'

'So you're not going to ring her. Is that what you want me to say?'

He seemed not displeased at the sharpness in Helen's tone and replied mildly:

'You want me to have to listen to what a shit I am and how nobody in their right mind would have put up with me all this time and how Current Affairs at least talks to her and even listens?'

'I don't see why you shouldn't.'

'Because I've heard it about fifteen million times already, my dear Helen, and because if you've wasted twenty years living with the most boring, stupid bitch in North London, you don't want to waste another precious second listening to her silly whining voice. Is that clear, men? We scramble at 0600 hours. Good hunting.'

He half-turned as if to go with a little half-salute, more Hitler than Douglas Bader, but Helen persisted, seeming not to notice.

'She's obviously right, isn't she?'

'Is she? Right about what exactly?'

'About you not listening, and not talking to people. I mean, you do talk, but you talk at them not to them.'

'Why thank you, ma'am, I do appreciate those kind words, you sure know how to make a feller feel mighty proud of himself.'

'Sorry,' she said.

'Sorry, is that all you can say, when I've given you the best years of my life? I married you when you were nobody, my mother said I'd regret it, no good ever came from marrying out of your class' – I could not quite identify the voice even when it rose to a shrilling sob, some 1940s movie, I suppose, might have been Greer Garson.

'Oh fuck,' he said suddenly, quietening. 'It's such a fucking mess.'

And this time he was gone, stumbling over the books and half-bumping into the edge of the door as he went.

'Where's he –'

'Oh upstairs, I expect one of the attics. I'd have shown you if he hadn't come in. He's making a doll's house for Beryl, you know, with all those old tools. No, he's gone out,' she added as the door slammed. 'Wait five minutes and I'll show you. He's like that when he's in a state.'

'How do you mean?'

'The funny voices.'

'I've heard him do them before.'

'Not all together like that, in a flood as if he couldn't control them.'

'Like the gift of tongues at Pentecost, but you wouldn't –'

'I know what Pentecost is.'

She led me up the stairs. At the half-landings, the sun shone through the long window upon her golden hair, and I had a sudden blissful illusion that she was taking me upstairs to – but no of course she wasn't and as soon as I realised this, which was in the same instant, my head ached as though I had hit it glancingly on a low doorway.

'Oh you're there,' she said.

I peered over her shoulder through the open door to the long attic room with a ceiling so low you couldn't stand up in it. Moonman was on his knees by the window, planing the edges from a triangular piece of wood. He had taken off his long black shirt and had only a white singlet on his top. The whiteness was shocking and so was the menacing swell and dip of his biceps as he moved the plane up and down. His heavy black clothes usually discouraged any thought of his body and this display of rippling physique in the low stuffy room was disconcerting. He turned to look at us and gave a maniacal laugh: 'So thee've come to spy on poor old blind Moonman, hast thee, well fine folks may do as they please, but thee shan't have her, she's mine, I tell'ee, she's mine.'

He rose to a hunchback's crouch and began limping towards the window cradling the piece of wood in his bare arms.

'Sorry, we thought you'd gone out.'

'Out, out? Where should old Moonman go on a night like this, this bain't no night for lost souls to go a-walkin in.'

Behind him, you could see the bare rudiments of the doll's house, the outer walls already stuck together with the roofbeams in place. The edges were heavily stained as though they had taken a good deal of gluing to hold together. Wood-shavings and discarded pieces of wood were scattered about the floor, also suggesting that work had not gone smoothly.

'I didn't know you actually used your old tools,' I said.

'Bless you sir, old Moonman be using his old tool this many a long year. He ain't much of a hand at book-learning, but he can tell one end of a chisel from the other right enough.'

He let his jaw go slack in a village idiot's grin. That effect was rather wolfish and menacing.

'Do you want supper, Moonman?' Helen asked.

'That would be nice, very nice,' he said, in his ordinary mellow voice.

I looked out of the window at the untidy fruit trees and the ground falling away and beyond the houses a sprawling wooded hillside which must be the Heath.

'Great view,' I said.

'Do you like attics?' he asked in a severe tone as though I had failed to complete some necessary formalities before venturing this opinion.

'Yes,' I said unable to think of anything better to say. It wasn't a subject I had an opinion on, or even thought there were opinions to be had on.

'I like attics very much, they are my favourite room.'

The force of personality which resonated through this pronouncement seemed itself to fill the room, so that there was no space left in it. When he said things like this, it was usually to break a silence he had himself imposed upon the company and there was often an awkwardness about his phrasing, as though he was out of practice at talking or perhaps not even a native English speaker.

Helen stepped over the tangle of wood and tools and gluepot to stand by me looking out of the window. As she passed Moonman, still in his forced crouch, he put up a hand to caress her hair, spreading his fingers into a slow combing motion.

'Ah missee, that be angels' hair. No good never came of such hair for we poor mortals.'

'Oh shove off Moonman,' she said, removing his hand, quite gently, and shaking her head with a shivery flounce, as though to erase the memory of his touch, but again gently.

I had an overwhelming desire to get downstairs and out of the house.

But somehow this became difficult. Helen began to ask me about my work which for the first time interested her because in the puckish fashion of the Civil Service I had now been transferred from industrial policy, which I had almost begun to learn something about, to the Social Services Inspectorate which, being new, apparently required handpicked ignoramuses to get it up and running.

Then Moonman asked me what I knew about Stoyt-Smith. He was seated cross-legged now like a craftsman in an Oriental bazaar, still planing the triangular piece of wood in a jerky fashion which looked uncomfortable.

'Stoyt-Smith?'

'Beyond what there's already been in the public prints.'

'I'm afraid I missed it.'

'Come off it, Gus, he was mentioned in court last week.'

'Is he the one who was a Tory MP, or wants to be one?'

Moonman sighed.

'He was official visitor to a boys' home.'

'You see, even Helen knows.'

'Well, it's sort of my subject now,' she said.

Now they mentioned it, some vague echo of the story had reached me, but only at the furthest edge of consciousness. There had been a trickle of such stories, but this one had been little more than a stray phrase in the course of a report about something else.

'If it's so important, why hasn't there been more in the papers?'

'Because all they can print at the moment is that one of the boys has named him in a case against the man who runs the home but only named him as someone who took an interest in him not as one of the people who assaulted him.'

'Well then?'

'The boy's being leant on not to tell the whole story.'

I could have told them how little such things interested me, and how I didn't even feel guilty about this lack of interest because there was nothing to be gained by paddling in that kind of human squalor. But the first priority was to escape from that stuffy attic and its overpowering fishy aroma of glue and things being amiss.

It had occurred to me at this moment that Moonman might have deliberately slammed the front door shut while staying inside the house, in order to lure us up to the attic so that he could catch us snooping on him.

But there was never much chance of seeing exactly what he was up to, even if this didn't stop you trying. In fact, it pricked me on – the silences, the cascade of funny voices, the sudden savagery, the occasional mellow even courteous aside, as though he wanted me to know that he had been hoping to talk to me all along, had several things to say which he thought might interest me but had been distracted. I found myself scrutinising the latest issue of *Frag* for some clue to his state of mind, but of course there was nothing there – only the usual pastiches of celebrity idiocy and stories of skulduggery in high places. Then one of the Fionas rang up and asked me to one of their lunches – this was quite a long time later, another couple of years at least – and at first I said no, but then this seemed feeble and I called back and said yes after all.

The old unease came upon me, redoubled this time, as I ducked down the alley off the Tottenham Court Road between the audio and video shops. Clapp's green shopfront with the flyblown plastic grapes and sacks of pulses had recently undergone a makeover. It now said 'CLAPP, FROMAGIER' on the window with a display of huge round ridged cheeses, like a convention of millstones. Upstairs, beyond the clacking typewriters of the Fionas (*Frag* still stuck to the old technology, to save money, which it already probably didn't), the old gang were already in session – Moonman, Willie Sturgis the left-wing rabblerouser in his tomato and yellow jersey, Tazzy Smith the Australian monetarist who looked like a marmoset – the whole court in fact with the latest guests waiting like puzzled sheep to be fleeced of their inside information: a beetle-browed Labour MP who kept carrier pigeons, a gossip columnist with cheeks as purple as a bishop's vest, and an overripe agony aunt covered in clunky gold jewellery. It was only when I sat down that it came to me that for some reason I had hoped to see Helen and that her not being there made the occasion seem lacking, even desolate, not that there had not been desolate moments in this company before. But this time, well, this time was worse.

'Seemed quite a nice bloke, for a Tory, that is,' the pigeon-fancying Labour MP said.

'Stoyt-Smith a nice bloke!' Willie Sturgis spluttered gleefully into his hot-pot.

'Straight as a die,' embroidered Dr Tasman Smith, giving his bow tie a tweak as he tended to when he joined in the fun.

'Sort of chap you could go tiger-shooting with.'

'Ken, I don't think you've met Alan Timmis,' Moonman was indicating a young man with a green face and a pleasant rabbity look. 'Alan was in one of the homes which had the honour of being regularly visited by the said Stoyt-Smith.'

'He seemed really friendly to start with, well he was friendly, not stuck-up like he looked, and he'd ask Sears if he could have a little chat with one or two of us, on our own like, so we could tell him how we were getting on without Sears and the others breathing down our neck. So he gave us fags and that and we had a chat and it was really nice and it wasn't until the third or fourth time ...'

The boy's voice trailed away as he became aware of the whole table waiting. The woman with the chunky jewellery must have thought, like me, that he was on the edge of tears and she patted his arm, but he managed to say quite calmly: 'No, I don't think, not at lunch, but you know what I mean.'

'We'll talk afterwards, Alan,' Moonman said, seeming not at all disappointed at the young man's sudden withholding, rather the opposite, in fact, as if the thought of the details yet to come was juicier than the details themselves could hope to be. Round the rest of the table, though, you could hear the tiny gasps of disappointment.

'Little bugger won't sing for his supper,' the gossip columnist growled, 'wonder what he thinks he's been asked for, certainly not his pretty face.'

Moonman sat at the end of the table as always, with the window to his right so that the light shone in on him showering him with a dusty radiance, and it was this and his spiritual heavenward gaze that, I fancy, must have inspired the bright spark who had said when asked what a *Frag* lunch was like, Oh it's like the Last Supper only with twelve Judases instead of one.

In the silence that followed, broken only by the clatter and scrape of cutlery on plate, you certainly could feel Moonman's power. Perhaps I felt it more intensely than I had before, now I knew how firm and muscular he was beneath his dark clothes, as if the physique reinforced the moral authority, although moral authority was a strange phrase to use. But then perhaps that was the only kind of authority that survived, the inquisitor's power. We all knew so well the shabby methods which propped up the other sorts of power, the PR tricks, the trumpery rhetoric, the adulation which nobody sincerely felt. You had to be very young or very stupid to revere even those few political leaders and film stars who were supposed to possess charisma. The only power that could seriously chill you was the kind that was veiled from the public eye, the gang boss whose name nobody was quite sure of, the *éminence grise* who fed the politicians their lines, the scientist who was about to crack the secret of the universe (after he had cracked it, he was of no more interest than anyone else, just as the eminence wasn't as soon as he stood for Parliament). And so Moonman had it, too, had it more than any of them because he was inexhaustible. As long as there were secrets to be teased out into the daylight, he would go on sitting there in the shadows, or rather, not quite in the shadows, because the limelight couldn't help washing over him now and then, which he wasn't averse to, so that you were always uncomfortably aware of his presence.

At two forty-five I went down the stairs and out into the street vowing never to go again.

Bobs a few weeks later took a different view.

'Went to the *Frag* lunch again this week. It was fantastic. You'll never guess who was there, apart from the usual crowd I mean.'

'Who?'

'Stoyt-Smith. My eyes nearly popped out of my head. He had obviously decided to come and face them down. I rather admired him for that, though he was a bit pompous. Said he would sue anybody who made any allegations of wrongdoing and that includes all of you, my good friends.'

'So what did they all do?'

'Just roared with laughter and told a lot of rude jokes about queers which he joined in with, looking a bit bewildered. But Moonman was bloody funny, I must say. He's in great shape since he came to St Col's. Gets on fantastically well with Helen. To my surprise.'

'And what about the anaesthetist?'

'What anaesthetist?'

'Your sister-in-law, or ex-sister-in-law, Mile.'

'She's not an anaesthetist, she's a teacher, I told you. She's OK as far as we know. Moonman doesn't talk about her.'

The doll's house was to be ready for Beryl's fifth birthday. She had apparently taken part in the later stages of its building, climbing all over Moonman as he lay on the attic floor gluing the tiny banisters to the staircase, and throwing out impulsive instructions while riding on his back only to contradict them the next day, at first demanding a red front door then a blue one, like a spoilt rich bitch in Bishops Avenue, as Helen said. But at last both Beryl and Moonman agreed that it was finished and a formal opening was arranged but it had to be before her friends arrived for the tea party, so as not to make them feel jealous. So there were just Beryl, me and the three Moonmans, as I suppose we must call them, after lunch standing round the huge shape rather untidily wrapped in silver paper – Beryl had insisted on the wrapping. She was jumping up and down on the spot in a high state of excitement, clutching her mother's hand.

'What's it going to be like, Mummy? Will it have a toilet?'

'Don't be silly, Beryl. You know what it's like.'

'It might have an enormous swimming-pool in the kitchen,' Moonman suggested, 'or a tree in the bathroom.'

'No-oh,' squealed Beryl, 'don't be silly.'

Bobs counted to three and then Beryl tore at the wrapping paper, tangling herself in the sticky tape. Finally she staggered away from the doll's house, now engulfed in the silver paper but leaving the doll's house standing naked, and naked was somehow the word for it. I had not seen it since its early stages and had expected, I don't know why, something like St Col's in warm red brick with complicated gables, but this was a bleak terrace house in a grubby shade of cream with crude green windows and a smeary blue front door which had BERYL'S HOUSE written on it in large red letters, hopelessly out of scale and unevenly painted, so that it looked more like a hastily scrawled mark of the plague. You could take the roof off and peer down into the bedroom and bathroom or unhook the front of the house and look into the sitting-room and kitchen. The four rooms were all sparsely furnished and papered in oppressive floral wallpapers so that internally the effect was not unlike St Col's.

'It's lovely,' Beryl squealed.

'I think the place must be haunted,' Bobs said.

'It's lovely, lovely,' Beryl squealed again.

'Wouldn't care to call after dark.'

For once, Bobs was right. It did have a sinister quality.

'Don't be horrid, you're not my daddy any more. Moonman's my new daddy.'

'I'm Moonman too.'

'No, you're not proper Moonman. This is my real daddy.' Beryl grasped Moonman's hand and swung herself round behind him so that she disappeared for a moment before peeping round his leg to see how the audience was taking it.

'Sorry, Beriberi, I can't magic that trick. You're stuck with old Bobs, I'm afraid.'

'I'm not, I'm not. I hate old Bobs. You're my daddy.'

'Stop showing off, Beryl, and say thank you to Moonman.'

'Thank you, thank you, Moonman Daddy.'

He stood smiling while she swung to and fro clinging to his hand.

That was the last time I saw the four of them together. A month later, perhaps a little more, Bobs telephoned me and told me that Helen had gone off with Moonman to a cottage somewhere by the sea, taking Beryl of course but this could be sorted out. That was as far as he got before breaking down. When he recovered himself a little, he promised he wouldn't do anything stupid, not like last time which he took this opportunity to apologise for, but now he had something to live for, he had Beryl and he wasn't going to let her down.

It must have been an awful shock, I ventured lamely, not wanting to put the telephone down and also wanting to express my own astonishment.

'Shock, no, why should it be?' he said with a kind of vagueness which sounded inappropriate.

'Well,' I said, 'I had never thought Helen would do anything like that.'

'Going off, you mean?'

'Not the actual going off, but –'

'Oh you mean, having an affair. That's been going on for months.'

'Ah.'

'I assumed you must have known. In fact, I thought of discussing it with you, but then I thought you might have had a basinful of us lot. In fact, I rather hoped you might have been thinking how sophisticated of Bobs to turn a blind eye. Well, I didn't really, what I really thought you must be thinking was how pathetic. Then I wondered whether you weren't having it off with her too, for old times' sake.'

'God, no.'

'Don't take offence. Probably everyone else has, so I don't see why you shouldn't. But I didn't want her to go, I really didn't.'

He began crying again.

Fairness

'Would anyone in their right mind have built a holiday resort here,' Francie Fincher exploded on his first sight of it, but then we found out they built the power station when the resort was already long past its heyday. Now it was dead. We agreed we had never seen a deader place, not even on this desolate coast with its low crumbly cliffs, though it was kind to call them that, when they were only eight or ten feet high, with the coal showing through the sand so that even on the sunniest day they looked dirty. We hadn't had any sunny days yet. Francie had told me to bring golf clubs but we hadn't had any time off either.

A flood of depositions had come in just after we had arrived and there were endless conferences with the police and the lawyers about how the evidence ought to be taken: should we hear the children, or should we confine ourselves to the adults – but then when did children start being adults and might it not be better to hear those whose memories were fresh – which meant some of the youngest – and not rely solely on reheated recollections from those who were now seventeen or eighteen? So it was decreed that Dr Brightwell, the child psychiatrist on the team, should talk privately to the children so as not to frighten them by putting them before another tribunal, and Francie and I would listen to her tapes.

'I think I've had enough of this for today,' Francie whispered to me, 'let's go down there. I always believe in walking the course.'

So Mr Justice Fincher drove me in his old dark-green Jaguar down to Pleasure Beach from the draughty little red-brick schoolhouse built to mark Queen Victoria's Diamond Jubilee. There was an east wind blowing, which rattled the flaps of the ice-cream hut and swished the sodden leaves into the rickety verandah of the Pier Theatre. The theatre wasn't much more than a large hut. The face of a laughing clown painted on its pediment was only a piece of flimsy hardboard. Beyond the theatre there was a round bandstand with rusty metal pillars, at least we thought it was a bandstand, until Francie pointed to the grimy machinery in the roof and the places where the horses had been bolted on to the pillars.

'Not merry, not going round,' Francie muttered, 'that just about sums the place up.'

Mr Garforth, the trim muscular-looking man who used to manage the theatre and still looked after the place – 'Call me Mr G,' he said, 'everyone does' – let us in and showed us round. There was not much to see: a minuscule stage with a backdrop left over from the pantomime, a little door at the side of the stage with steps leading down to the auditorium – forty or fifty tip-up chairs all covered in dust.

'The council wants to knock the whole lot down,' Mr Garforth said gloomily, 'don't blame them, but they haven't got the money to build the leisure centre. Still with all this trouble, they may knock it down anyway.'

There were a few derelict booths either side of the crumbling asphalt, with doors and windows smashed or covered with graffiti, and then a high chain-link fence supported by concrete posts with floodlights mounted on them at intervals. Beyond, overshadowing the entire funfair, was the power station, its dull grey walls lowering over us so close that I couldn't even see the gigantic chimney which otherwise was visible for miles.

Francie Fincher took in every feature with a quick dart of his lean head, his spare body thrusting forward as though he was making a sharp point to a jury. He was at the same time curiously awkward, almost lumpish in his movements. This lack of co-ordination showed up in his riding which was said to be reckless but also graceless. He just flung himself on a horse any old how, as though this carelessness was part of being on holiday from his meticulous courtesy in court and his unrelenting forethought out of it. I'm a bogman from Fermanagh, he would say, that's why I'm such a grasping sort of bugger. His parents had scraped to send him to some Catholic public school in

England – Beaumont? Douai? – and that had knocked the Irish out of his voice. Fifty-eight years old now, he had been famous when he was just a jobbing barrister for never buying a round at the Garrick or the Old Cock, and much loved for his stinginess – but he was always the last to leave the bar, without the drink showing on him, except perhaps to exaggerate the precision of his speech. He smiled little and laughed not at all, so that his wit, of which he had a fair amount, was mostly deadpan. This I found offputting on first acquaintance, because I had to listen carefully to gather whether the point he was moving on to was serious or ironic. I suppose that is partly what people mean by lawyers being dry, but it was unnerving because he was at the same time so sympathetic, which you couldn't help being aware of the moment you met him. He had spent his early years breaking his collar bone once a month out hunting or in some disastrous point-to-point. He was a generation younger than my father and his friends, but he knew their names and had once ridden a horse at Larkhill that Froggie O'Neill had a leg of, a terrible animal. And when he said that he always liked to walk the course, the phrase brought back those stumbles across the damp downland with my father, him plunging in a stick near the rails or on the take-off side of the fence to find the firmest ground, with the wet smell of the laid brushwood fences and the morning mist still hanging in the thorn bushes and the dull gleam of the sun trying to get through.

Francie was a criminal Silk, not a family lawyer, though he admitted to having sat a couple of times in chambers on custody cases, but he was a family man and devout, dragging a cross-section of his large brood to the Oratory every Sunday, and he seemed to be a popular choice for this job which he said was because being a Papist everyone assumed he must be an expert on devil worship, though he never remembered any of those kind of things back in Ballyturbet, a little bestiality now and then but nothing serious. His assessor, Joan Brightwell, the consultant child shrink from Birmingham, didn't much care for that line of talk, but Francie was as quick as anything to woo her back by showing an exhaustive knowledge of the material we had already been sent and consulting her opinion every five minutes on the finer points of social work, and in any case she wasn't without a glint in her sensible eye. I was the secretary to the inquiry, ignorant, sceptical, apprehensive about the whole business, which had been dumped on me so that the new Social Services Inspectorate should be seen to be 'getting its hands dirty', in Hilary Puttock's ill-chosen phrase.

'We really must not rush our fences,' Francie said. 'We have to go very carefully and not jump to anything that looks like a pleasing conclusion as soon as it presents itself. We shall no doubt hear a great deal of nonsense, but some of it may be true. Joan, this is all a memo to myself and to our learned secretary, you don't need telling a word of it, I'm sure.'

She smiled and took the flattery nicely, like someone accepting a small piece of jewellery.

'I have a problem,' I said. 'An old friend of mine will be giving evidence, Helen Moonman, she's a social worker, Cases J and K. Should I step down or go for a walk or something when she's here?'

'No, no need at all, she's not on trial. We can slip the fact into the questioning to forestall any possible embarrassment.'

'I didn't realise she was mixed up in this when I was asked to –'

'Don't worry.'

It sounds odd not to have thought that Helen might be mixed up in this business, or not to have found out whether she was, but my appointment had happened in something of a rush and her name had not come up in any of the newspaper reports. Anyway I knew that she and Moonman were living miles away, the other side of the county, because I had been to visit them. It was only when I saw her name on the list of potential witnesses that I discovered that the children referred to as J and K, or rather their parents, had moved over to Helen's area a year or so after the alleged incidents and had told their stories to her.

That is a reasonably convincing explanation, at least I hope it is, but it isn't the whole truth. The reality, part of the reality anyway, is that I had not the slightest wish to get in touch with Helen ever again. Some betrayals shock you for a while, they are even exciting to hear about, give you a creepy thrill spiced with a little tremble of guilt. Then they disappear from view, under the heap of other betrayals. But Helen's leaving Bobs was different, because after everything I still thought she was different. There had been something about her that made her incapable of deliberately harming another human being. There might be a little collateral damage when she took up with someone new, which was inevitable if she was trying to be helpful to everyone. But then helpfulness has nothing to do with love. In fact, they were opposites, and that was why men ran after Helen in such a puzzled, frantic way (that and the golden hair, of course). They wanted to stop her being helpful, to make her lose control, surrender to passion. And Moonman seemed to have cracked it.

The side-effect was to change my attitude to Bobs. To see him suddenly bereft of wife and daughter, knocked off his perch, reduced to the ranks, was to become aware of his basic superiority to other characters in the drama, of his eager human softness, his noble nature – noble really was the word. Which didn't stop him driving me crazy. He would telephone me at strange hours, not tragic three a.m. calls but in the middle of office hours, like eleven forty-five in the morning.

'This maintenance thingy, what do you reckon?'

'What do you mean, what do I reckon?'

'Well if I start making out a banker's order, won't that be sort of accepting the situation?'

'Don't then, let her stew. Unless you *want* to accept the situation. Anyway, Moonman must be coining it.'

'It's not that. But if I don't support Beryl, then Helen can accuse me of neglect. She's missing her dancing lessons,' he added mournfully.

'Beryl? There must be dancing teachers in wherever it is. Do you really think Helen would be in a position to accuse you of neglecting Beryl? It's not you who's run off.'

'You don't understand what it's like, nobody understands what it's like till it happens. She's so angry when she speaks to me, so it's like it was me who'd done a runner.'

He looked at me – I was sitting in the guest's chair in his sanctum at Moonman Travel – and his little squashed face was illuminated with a sad kind of what can only be called wisdom – not a word I ever thought I would use within a hundred miles of him. Perhaps you needed to pack in a lifetime's practice as a butt in order to learn things like how angry people could be when they themselves were behaving badly.

'And another thing,' he said, 'I don't like the sound of that cottage.

Beryl said on the phone she was all shivery and Big Bro doesn't care about comfort at all. It's probably filthy damp.'

'What about Helen though?'

Again he looked at me with this new sad-wisdom face.

'Haven't you noticed how she doesn't care about that sort of thing either? She was always forgetting to turn on the heating and change the sheets. Mind on higher things. You didn't notice any of that?'

'No,' I said uneasily, 'I didn't.'

'She's odd, you know,' Bobs said. 'Really quite odd. Not like normal people.'

'I know what odd means,' I said irritably.

'You probably don't really. It's probably only very ordinary people like me who can see when people are a bit peculiar.'

'Well, if you're so worried, why don't you go down and see them?'

'She doesn't want me to. I rang and she said not to come till we'd talked to the lawyers. But I don't want any of that because I still want her back, Beryl and her, I want them both.'

He was going to start crying again, so I tried to focus his mind on practical steps, which was a mistake because the first practical step he suggested was that I should go down there and see how the land lay.

'Just call in by accident, say you were passing and wanted to drop off the doll's house which Beryl has been pining for.'

'I can't just accidentally be carrying someone else's doll's house in the back of my car.'

'All right then, forget the doll's house. Just drop in.'

'I can't.'

'Why not?'

'Just can't face it. Anyway, they'd know I was spying for you, because otherwise how would I know the address?'

'Look, it's not your marriage that's broken up and it's not your daughter that you haven't seen for months and you –'

'All right, what's the number? I'd prefer to telephone her first.'

Hard to say what exactly I had expected from her – a certain awkwardness perhaps, even surprise at hearing my voice after so long, then possibly an unenthusiastic invitation or more likely the brush-off. Not a bit of it. She said how lovely it was to hear from me, and how I must come down immediately while the weather was still nice, and how eager Moonman would be to see me, as he was so fond of me and thought of me as one of his oldest friends. None of which sounded like Moonman at all, and not very much like her. As for the doll's house, she said off her own bat that Beryl was missing it and would I mind very much picking it up from St Col's – the word Bobs was not mentioned – and was my car big enough, perhaps if I laid it sideways.

The cottage was in the middle of a huge wired-off plantation of firs which seemed to go on for miles either side of the single-track road. Cottage was the correct name for it in terms of size, but the word suggested thatch and plaster, and so I didn't stop the first time as I passed the square red-brick modern dwelling sitting in the middle of the firs. But there was a notice in front of it saying Firs Cottage, so I reversed almost into the onrushing figure of Helen who, I saw in the rear view mirror, had her arms outstretched which recalled, in one of those high-speed recollections your mind is sometimes jogged into, our other meetings on the beach at the Ville, at the D.O.'s house, on the picket line at Woden Heath, and how cool and serious she had been, not unfriendly but cool. And now here she was jumping up and kissing me like a puppy and jabbering nineteen to the dozen.

'Isn't it absolutely hideous? Moonman says it must have been designed for prison warders and somehow got transferred to the Forestry Commission, there are supposed to be red squirrels in the trees but we haven't seen any, though there is a badger sett up at the end and when there's a moon you can see them playing.'

So this was what it was like, the real thing. Never too late to experience it, probably more potent than ever when you were coming up for forty. Her eyes were shining – difficult not to say they were dancing – her hair was blowing all over the place, although there was no wind. Yellow was the word for how her hair looked that day, like in the Yeats poem, not dreamy golden because there was nothing dreamy about her, not now. She tugged me out of the car while I was still whimpering about parking it properly.

'Come on, Moonman's longing to see you, he's chopping wood.'

She whirled me through the house, so I caught only a blur of plain furniture and swirly wallpaper. Moonman was kneeling at a chopping-block in the small patch of rough grass that was all there was in the way of garden before the firs started again, splitting logs into kindling with a small axe, fiercely, not with that easy absence of force I remembered my father had when doing the same thing, but when he turned wiping his brow, he said, 'Ah Gus nice to see you' in the gentlest way imaginable.

'How about a cup of tea, lovey?' he added in the same gentle tone.

'Coming right up, honey,' she said in a raunchy Southern-waitress drawl.

She seemed to do the funny voices now, while he spoke in a quiet, serious voice which was almost unnervingly natural, asking me about the drive down and whether it had been an awful bore to bring the doll's house. They seemed to have exchanged roles. Yet I didn't feel that their being together had merely led them to imitate one another. Rather it was somehow that their adventure had freed both of them to display a side which had been kept firmly under control before. Helen had never given the slightest sign of wishing to imitate anyone else's voice or even a stock type of voice. When she reported what someone else had said, she reported in her own plain, serious voice, so much so that the effect could sometimes be comic or shocking as when she had told me what Farid Farhadi had said he wanted to do to her.

'Let's take the doll's house out now, otherwise we'll forget and you'll drive back to London with it.'

We eased the doll's house out of the back of the car. There was a wooden platform by the side of the road, for milk churns or logs, and we lifted it on to the platform, while I fished out the cardboard boxes containing the doll's-house furniture. Bobs had carefully wrapped each piece in tissue paper, much of it no doubt drenched with tears (my pity for him came and went because of the irritation factor).

'It's an evil-looking thing, isn't it?' Moonman said, staring at his creation through his droopy Lytton-Strachey specs.

With the fir forest behind it, the doll's house had an even more brooding, sinister aspect. The 'BERYL'S HOUSE' on the front door looked as if it had been scrawled in blood.

'Terrible things have gone on in that house,' he continued. 'By the way, did you know they are going to nab Stoyt-Smith? He thought he'd squared them, but the police got a statement from one of the girls.'

'Girls? I thought it was boys he went for.'

'Oh he'll screw anything that isn't nailed down. I don't think even the shrinks have got a word for him. This time he was wearing a white dress with roses on it, in a funfair.'

'A funfair?'

'A place called Fairness. Sort of clapped-out theatre. He was conducting auditions.'

Moonman gave one of his old cackles followed by his beatific skyward look which seemed to be addressing some higher authority, either to offer congratulations or to share in Moonman's incredulity at what His creatures could get up to.

That was the first time I had heard the word Fairness – it was several months before the full furore was to break out – and I listened to the rest of the story with only mild interest as we carried the doll's house up the narrow stairs.

Beryl was drawing at a little child's table and scarcely looked up as we came in to her room. She seemed thinner, more like a schoolgirl than when I had last seen her. She received the doll's house politely and when prompted said hallo with no great enthusiasm to the person she was instructed to call Uncle Gus. Her manner was so serious in fact that for the first time she reminded me strongly of her mother, or of her mother when I first met her, which now seemed to have happened in another life. Beryl opened up the doll's house and inspected it silently like a householder checking the inventory in the presence of the departing tenants. When we brought up the cardboard boxes with the furniture, she unpacked them and started putting the things back in the house, again with scarcely a word.

'Doesn't it look great, Beriberi?'

'Yes,' she said, 'thank you, you can go away now.'

Which we did. 'Well, I suppose we couldn't expect her not to mind,' Moonman said as we went downstairs, 'but it has been more difficult than we expected. I think perhaps she should spend some time with Bobs, but Helen thinks that might make her worse. What do you think?'

'Hard to say,' I said, adding, 'He does miss her.'

'You're a sort of health visitor.'

'What do you mean?'

'Sent to check on us. Not by the council, though. I expect we'll have that too. But Bobs sent you, didn't he?'

'Yes.'

'Don't blame him. Well, here we are. House is warm and dry you can tell him, that's the sort of thing he minds about, and there are no infectious diseases around so far.'

'All right.'

'You think I wanted this to happen?'

'No I hadn't —'

'It's the last thing I wanted.'

He didn't say any more, and the awkwardness was swallowed up in the clatter of tea-things in the living-room. Helen began talking about the job she had just landed, with the social work team in the local overspill town, which was already a fearful dump although it was only about twenty years old, and how difficult it was not to start blaming the families for their environment, rather than the other way round. There were a couple of families who had just moved in, you simply wouldn't believe their carry-on. But it was time to summon Beryl for fish fingers and jaffa cakes, and so then we talked about old times, how we had both been nannies at the seaside in France and then together again digging up emeralds in Africa. Beryl responded adequately to these topics pointing out that boys couldn't be nannies and asking if we had got any emeralds to keep, but her heart was not in it. She took part in the talk with the mechanical politeness of a dinner guest who wishes she hadn't come.

Her face was so sad I didn't want to look at her, while Helen was describing the past we had shared, and my eye happened to fall upon Moonman instead, who by contrast was intensely interested and seemed suffused by some emotion which, hesitantly at first and then more surely, I identified to my surprise as jealousy. It would have been a relief to dispel any such feeling by saying that there had never been anything between us (with one strange fleeting exception, which was best forgotten), but I couldn't see how. Perhaps in other circumstances Beryl might have fed me the opportunity by asking if we had ever been boyfriend and girlfriend, but this was one subject which her grim little face proclaimed was utterly forbidden, and so I said nothing and counted the minutes till I could leave.

That was the last time I saw Helen before the Fairness Inquiry which must have started a year later, more like two years in fact, because first there was the removal of the children into care under Place of Safety Orders, then there was the press hullabaloo, and the release of the children, and then the inquiry, which wasn't nearly such a big affair as some of the others, just as Francie Fincher was really not the cream of high court judges.

Francie kept the headteacher's room at the back for himself to store his papers in and for a place to have a quiet smoke when it was raining and we could not go out and walk round the tarmac playground behind the school. The larger schoolroom we used for public hearings and the smaller was the interview room, although Joan Brightwell usually went to the children's own homes to talk to the children or the council homes for the ones still in care. During that first week we sat mostly in the little interview room listening to crackly tapes several hours a day before Francie broke for a cigarette. Sometimes I sat and chatted with him while he smoked, sometimes I went for a walk along the seashore, once or twice with Joan who couldn't bear the smell of tobacco but was otherwise amiable. She collected jet jewellery which you could buy from a couple of shops in Fairness and fretted about her Jack Russell which didn't like being boarded out with her sister.

'Mr G took us down to the Clown Theatre to show our dance.'
   'You mean the Pier Theatre?'
   'Yes, only we call it the Clown theatre, because it's got a clown on the front. He said a very important person wanted to see us dance. And when we got in there, there was the Mister like in the photo.'
   'You mean Mr Stoyt-Smith?'
   'Yeah, that's him, only he was wearing a costume, like Mum wears.'
   'A dress you mean?'
   'Yeah, a dress, it was white, with roses on it. And he told us to dance round him in a ring and then he made a white circle on the floor with a long stick and then he pulled out his willy and told K

to show him her fanny and then he made us sing a song which he said was a magic song.'

There was more, much more of this, the notorious 'White Dress' tape, which had started the whole business off. Patricia the stenographer spent most of the day transcribing it, tapping away in Francie's room. It was at the transcript stage that the letters were substituted for the real names of the children, which made the interviews even weirder to read, as though they were part of some highbrow Kafka narrative. Nobody was quite sure how news of the White Dress tape had leaked out. Francie thought that it must have been one of the police officers connected with the interview who was sceptical about what J was saying and had been outvoted at the case conference which had decreed that J, the little girl being interviewed, should be taken into care, along with her sister who had also made allegations of sexual abuse at the theatre, though, unlike J, she had described neither the white dress nor the ritual.

At least we did not have to see the children face to face. Francie was right about that. We would have scared them stiff, and in my case vice versa. Seeing the parents was bad enough. They were defiant, of course, but also furtive in a way that made me ashamed to be badgering them. Few of them had the gumption to dress smartly to make a good impression. One or two wore the shiny shell-suits that were just coming in then, the fathers often hadn't shaved. You wouldn't in a million years mistake one of them for one of the social workers, though the social workers were defiant and furtive too. After all, they were just as much on trial as the parents, Joan Brightwell said. Not just as much, Francie corrected, the social workers are unlikely to go to jail, whatever we may say about them.

But the tapes were the worst. They were horrible, those hours in the dusty schoolroom, listening to the jerky, painfully slow dialogues, with their restless background hum that made the pauses – which were frequent – weigh all the heavier. Occasionally a policewoman's reassuring voice gave the time and place of the interview and the names of those present. But then a child's voice began speaking, sometimes in a zombie drone, now and then quickening into an eager rushing speech which sometimes went off into a noise somewhere between a gulp and a giggle. And we were carried into a world which was just as sinister and frightening as the newspapers said, but was also somehow null, affectless, beyond everything.

'It's mesmerising isn't it?' said Francie, looking a good deal less mesmerised than the rest of us, Patricia, the duty sergeant, myself, even Joan. 'But except for the allegations against P, who is after all the father of three of the other girls, there's no corroboration. The medical evidence is inconclusive, and I think we had better accept that it's likely to stay inconclusive, isn't that right, Joan?'

'In these three cases certainly; not in cases where there are unmistakable internal tears or bruising.'

'I wasn't talking about those. Gus?'

'Well, there's nothing any of the girls says which actually contradicts any of the others. Some just add more details.'

'But that's just the trouble. The details J adds are precisely the most colourful ones, Stoyt-Smith in his white dress with the roses, the sort of details a child couldn't possibly forget.'

'Even if that child were scared out of its wits?'

'J doesn't sound scared out of her wits exactly. She sounds disturbed, and from her behaviour at school and in talking to the social worker there is reason to think she is disturbed.'

'The literature on satanic abuse suggests wide variations in the rituals,' Joan put in.

'But Joan, even if J is telling the truth, is this really a ritual?' Francie said. 'Or is it just a trick to get the girls to do what he wants?'

'Is there a difference?' Joan retorted, nettled by his putdown.

'The fact that social workers all over the country apply for a Place of Safety Order the moment they hear this kind of story doesn't mean it's true or that there's a nationwide outbreak of satanic abuse. I'm surprised that you should believe it all so unquestioningly. After all, it's me who's supposed to be the poor credulous Papist.'

'I certainly didn't say I believed it *all*. I was only pointing out that there are a large number of comparable reports on the file. The fact that the children come out with memories that are not identical might be – I only say might be – evidence that there *is* something in them.'

'Or might not.'

'Or might not. I'm no more credulous than you are.'

'No, of course you aren't, my dear. Listening to this stuff the whole day makes us all edgy. Look, I must go up to London to see Stoyt-Smith, I'm not going to give the hacks the satisfaction of dragging him down here. He's the only thing keeping them here anyway. As soon as it's merely a case of poor kids complaining of being buggered in an amusement arcade, they'll buzz off. I'll be back in time for your Mrs Moonman on Thursday.'

So we suspended the inquiry for a couple of days – judge called away on another case – and I mooched around Fairness, picking up a bag of fish and chips from the only place open and taking it down to a sheltered nook in the crumbly low bank above the beach. As I sat looking out at the dark broth of the North Sea, it came to me that after nearly three weeks of the inquiry I hadn't a clue. The unnerving tapes, the social workers all convinced that the nation was being swamped by an unprecedented wave of sexual or satanic abuse or both, my own natural scepticism, not to mention prudery – how could people want to do such things? – there was no sign of anything that would give a decisive nudge in any direction, just an endless swamp of squalor and uncertainty.

Francie must have got up at dawn to arrive in time for a nine-thirty start, almost deadheating in the car-park with Helen who hopped out of her little Peugeot 205, looking brisk with a slim brown briefcase under her arm.

'Good of you to come all this way, Mrs Moonman, I'm Francie Fincher and this is Dr Joan Brightwell, Sergeant Thursby of the regional Child Protection Unit and Mr Cotton, our learned secretary, whom I gather needs no introduction to you and I hope will look after you if we get too rough with you.'

She took this in the intended spirit and gave me a confident little smile or hallo Gus, perhaps both. Curiously, although she was one of the more junior people to be interviewed, her presence gave me a certain confidence that this dismal tangle could somehow be disentangled in the end.

Francie took her in his usual painstaking way through her training as a social worker and her experience in this particular field (part of his brief was to make recommendations on these matters). She had got her CQSW six years ago, had been on a course on child protection, had attended a residential conference on ritual abuse set up by an American organisation.

'Rather a brief experience for a person burdened with your present responsibilities, wouldn't you say?'

'I think my qualifications are about average for the post.'

'Like a lot of your colleagues, you seem to have come to social work relatively late in life.'

'Is that such a bad thing, to have some outside experience?'

'You don't think you've suddenly developed an urge to set the world to rights because your own life hasn't turned out so well?'

'I'm separated from my husband, if that's what you mean.'

'That seems to be a common misfortune in your line of work.'

'I'm not sure I see the relevance.'

'You may be more inclined to take a dark view of human behaviour, especially if I may say so, of male behaviour. You might be inclined to imagine or exaggerate wrong-doing where there is insufficient evidence for it.'

'Perhaps if you asked me some questions which were more closely relevant to the case, you might find out whether your presumption is true.'

'Very well. What did you think of the conference on ritual abuse?'

'I wasn't impressed. I thought they were exaggerating the dangers.'

'Why would they do that?'

'They had their own agenda, a religious agenda.'

'And you think that's a bad agenda to have?'

'Since you ask me, yes. But that's just my personal opinion. Professionally, I don't think you should have any agenda, you should look at the evidence.'

'I couldn't agree more,' Francie said. I thought at first he was taking against her, but almost immediately I saw that he wasn't and that in fact he liked the way she spoke up for herself. 'So what do you think of the evidence that you have gathered yourself? We have the transcript of your interview with J after her release from care, you don't mind me using this alphabet soup, do you, we've got used to it here.'

'Well, J's obviously very disturbed. She's had some sort of extremely unpleasant experience and she's been exposed to sexual ideas which are inappropriate for her age group, but that's common enough in her environment. But as compared with the original interview, the first interview before she was taken into care, well, there's lots J left out. All the colourful detail about the magician's wand and the white dress, she didn't tell me any of that.'

'And those are the colourful parts no one would forget?'

'Exactly.'

'And K?'

'Poor little thing. She said exactly the same to me as she had said to Mrs Hunter before she was taken into care, almost word for word.'

'How her stepfather Mr P took her into the shed and so on?'

'Yes.'

'There was no change at all in her story? Not after Mr P admitted the offence and was sent to jail?'

'Not really. She was relieved to be out of care of course, but she wished her family hadn't moved down to our area because she missed her friends. Otherwise she had nothing more to say.'

'Do you deduce from the fact that one child has consistently told the same story and the other hasn't that K is telling the truth and J isn't?'

'Yes, I do. J is older, more imaginative, more highly strung. Both children have been damaged, but K is not clever enough to say anything except what happened. J can make up a story out of nothing.'

'Why do you think so many of your colleagues have taken a different view? Why did they attach such importance to J's testimony and hasten to see to it that other children were taken into care on the strength of her testimony? In some cases, on her testimony alone?'

'I can't say for sure.'

'Not for sure perhaps, but would you care to hazard a guess?'

'I think they were over-influenced by the conferences they attended. They latched on to anything that sounded like satanic abuse.'

'Even though they were not necessarily Christians themselves?'

'Yes.'

'You think people in a secular age still have a need to believe in such things?'

'Or to believe that other people still believe in them.'

'Thank you, Mrs Moonman. It was extremely kind of you to come all this way. Your testimony has been most enlightening.'

'Well that's it, I think I've cracked it,' he said as Patricia brought our ham salads into the headteacher's room.

'Cracked it?' said Joan.

'Solved the riddle.'

'I know what "cracked it" means. I just can't see how you can be so sure, indeed we don't even know what it is you're sure of.'

'No, of course you don't. You haven't had my advantages, particularly my interview with Mr Stoyt-Smith. And you must forgive me if for the next twenty-four hours I still keep you in the dark. This is partly because I wish to play the great detective, partly because I would value your opinion of my whole scenario when I have tied up the loose ends. Starting from cold as it were, you'll have a more detached view.'

'So the butler will call us all into the library after breakfast?'

'He will, Gus, I promise you,' and Francie gave one of his dry frosty smiles which none of us could resist. 'Meanwhile, Joan will buy a few more jet baubles, and you and I will hack our way round the links.'

'But I thought you were tying up loose ends.'

'Sergeant Thursby and Constable Dykes will be checking out a couple of facts and conducting two brief interviews. They don't need me.'

The light was already poor and the rain was coming in off the North Sea as we hit off from the exposed first tee, a midget plateau half-lost in the high grass of the dunes: Francie played with his legs wide-splayed and his torso lowering over the ball before he gave it a slash, leaning out seawards to counteract what would otherwise have been a slice in the general direction of Norway. He stumped over the dimples and hummocks of the darkening fairways – more often the rough – with a blithe ferocity. I felt that if he had been a better player he would have found the game too dull to bother with. He wouldn't talk shop, said he wanted a break, but then half-way round, when we were playing the short hole at the end of the course, by the lighthouse, he turned to me after chipping out of the tussocks with the rain plastering his grey hair to his scalp, and said: 'I don't know why we expect these people to tell the truth. We make them take an oath which doesn't mean a thing to them. We threaten them with all sorts of hideous punishments if they lie, punishments which we have no intention of carrying out, otherwise the courts would be jammed solid with perjury cases.'

'So you can't expect them to have any allegiance to the truth?'

'No they don't, though that sounds like a rather Irish way of putting it.'

For a long time, I had not thought about Scrannel and his homily on truth. Curious that it should not have occurred to me sooner, but then ever since we had come to Fairness, I had not thought about anything much except what we had come for.

When we got back to the hotel for the usual tea and fruit-cake, with a drop of whisky in the tea, Dykes and Thursby were already there, and Francie went off to hear their reports.

'On second thoughts,' he said, when he came bustling back rubbing his hands, 'I think we might do better to go down to the Pier now, that'll give us a head-start in the morning. Will you raise Joan?'

There were four of us in the Jag, the police car following with the two officers.

Mr G in a long mac with the rain dripping off it was waiting for us beneath the crumpled hardboard clown to open up and turn the lights on. To my surprise, Francie asked him to turn the stage lights on but leave the house in darkness. Francie then led us through the side door on to the tiny stage and sat us down on half a dozen of the folding chairs which were already set out facing the audience. We stared into the dusty darkness, shivering in the unbearable damp chill. The place probably hadn't been opened up since our initial tour of inspection.

'Let me start by saying,' Francie began, standing in front of us at the edge of the stage, 'that I have not the slightest criticism of the police in this particular matter. It was their task to establish whether Mr Iain Stoyt-Smith was or was not mixed up in this whole business, nothing more, nothing less. And what they established beyond peradventure was that he paid one, and only one, visit to Fairness, in his capacity as chairman of the Regional Federation of Boys' Clubs. Throughout his visit, which lasted some five and a half hours, he was accompanied by the Chief Education Officer and for different overlapping parts of it by the chairman of the Education Committee and the Regional Arts Officer. He was never out of the sight of at least two of them. This corroboration was so strong, unlike most of the evidence that has been presented to us, that the police felt able to eliminate him from their inquiries. There was no further need to interview him or his friends.'

Francie paused. He was enjoying himself like anyone with a good story to tell, but there was also on his face an expression of relief, and it suddenly came to me that with all his experience he had been as perplexed and distressed as I had been, distressed not only by the horrors he had been forced to listen to but at the seeming impossibility of making any sense of it all. Now he was in full flow.

'But we are not in the position of the police. Our task is to range wider and not least to gain some idea of the atmosphere in which these things are alleged to have occurred and any possible motive for them, to make an informal guess as to why people should do such things or, if the children are inventing some part of it, why they should so invent, and how. Thus it seemed to me that we needed to strive to build up some picture in our mind of the more crucial events in the business. And no event is more crucial to our enquiry than the dance display by the Fairness Primary School on the 7th of May in this place. And not just the dance display. You will recall that it was mentioned in passing, by the Headmaster, I think, that the display had been preceded by a gymnastic display given by the boys from the secondary school. Now you may wonder how a display of that sort could possibly be given on a stage as tiny as this, barely twelve foot wide. Come to that, even the dance display must have been exceedingly cramped.

'The answer is, of course, that neither display was given on the stage at all. As Mr Stoyt-Smith explained to me, both displays were given in the auditorium – on the floor of the theatre – which, as you will observe, is suitable for the purpose, being dead flat, not raked at all. Indeed, to hold such displays there was anything but a novelty, since the theatre had been used as a temporary gym while the school's own gym was being refurbished. Thus the distinguished visitors, with Mr Stoyt-Smith as the Louis Quatorze of the afternoon, were seated here on the stage as we are, and they watched the two performances down on the floor.

'Mr Stoyt-Smith told me quite frankly he preferred the gymnastics, he was not much of a one for the ballet. He also told me equally frankly that he was homosexual by inclination, there was no point in hiding the fact, and that this might have originally led him to take an interest in boys' clubs, but he vehemently denied any wrongdoing in that capacity, and with even greater vehemence he denied having the slightest sexual interest in girls of any age.'

'So if we can forget Stoyt-Smith,' I said, 'then J is making it all up, or a lot of it. But why?'

'I would rather ask *how*. But if you would allow me to continue. What Stoyt-Smith did say, however, and he struck me as a credible witness despite having once been a Conservative Member of Parliament, is that he thought the little girls did look rather sweet sitting round the edge during the gymnastics. The boys left before the dancing, but the girls saw the gymnastics.'

'So –'

'I must admit I can't quite see the relevance.' Joan, like me, was beginning to resent this Hercule Poirot monologue.

'Would you be so kind as to turn on the house lights, Mr G?'

Somewhere behind the stage, there was a click from the invisible Garforth and the lights went on. We blinked into the little auditorium, bare now with the folding seats piled neatly along the sides.

'You will observe that the floor has been swept, as it was not at the time of our earlier visit, and of course it was then obscured by the chairs. But now –'

Our eyes followed his triumphant index finger. The floor had been marked out in thick white paint for a basketball court. The bank of house lights fell directly on the centre circle.

'And now, if you wouldn't mind turning your chairs round and facing the back of the stage for a minute.'

'Oh really, this pantomime –'

But even Joan turned round so that we were all facing the painted backdrop, a country scene in bright colours with a mansion rather like Buckingham Palace in the middle distance and the words of some song on a scroll, all rather faded.

'And now, Mr Garforth, would you mind stepping out for us as we agreed?'

There was the sound of footsteps trotting down the side-steps leading from backstage.

On further instructions from Francie, we turned round to look again into the auditorium.

Mr Garforth had removed his mac and was standing in the centre of the basketball circle. He was wearing a white tracksuit with a large embroidered rose and was pointing to the edge of the circle with a billiard cue.

'Perhaps, Mr Garforth, you would tell my colleagues what you told Sergeant Thursby?'

'Well, sir, nobody thought to ask me at the time, but I qualified as a PE instructor when I was in the army. Then when I came out, I managed the theatre for a time until it closed, but I kept up the PE work at the school, and we like to hold a display every year, gives the kids something to work towards, and Mr Stoyt-Smith said he was most impressed.'

'He was indeed and he remembered the details of the display most accurately down to the tracksuit you are wearing, which is –'

'Regimental rugby squad, sir.'

'And the billiard cue –'

'The principal boy uses it for pointing to the words in the panto song up there when we open up at Christmas. And I use it for commands during the gym. Gives more of a dramatic effect than a whistle.'

'So there you are: the circle, the white dress, the rose, the magic wand. All perfectly innocent. The sources of invention usually lie close at hand. Even for novelists, I dare say.'

Francie's smugness was olympian, cosmic, insufferable.

Joan attacked first. 'J said a white *dress*. A tracksuit isn't a dress.'

'It wasn't J who first used the word dress. She herself couldn't immediately think of the word, there is a slight pause on the tape before she says "costume", then another pause, "like Mum wears". When the interviewer suggests "dress", J takes up the word dress, perhaps thinking, quite rightly in my view, that a man in a dress makes a more dramatic and hence more convincing detail. Constable Dykes has checked that J's mother does wear a tracksuit, in fact she was wearing one when Constable Dykes called, and she does refer to it, I know not why, as a costume, which may have occasioned J's hesitation because at school such a garment is obviously called a tracksuit and she was caught between the two different words.'

'But why cast Stoyt-Smith as the villain?' I put in. 'After all, J can't have had a clue who he was, she'd only seen him that one time.'

'Very good reasons for making him the villain. She knew he was tremendously important. Bringing him in would grab the grown-ups' attention, as indeed it has ever since, and as she was never going to see him again, pointing the finger at him didn't present any danger to her. Or so she thought. Thank you very much indeed, Mr Garforth, I'm sorry to drag you out on such a ghastly night, you can turn the house lights down now.'

As we were talking, Garforth was holding the cue with hands stretched wide apart and flexing his arms so that his whole body tensed. It was the tensing – and the white suit – that suddenly reminded me of Monsieur's trim white figure, all sinew, looming out of the beach-mist. Then the lights went out, and we stood up, stretched and shrugged on our coats, with that awkward, deflated feeling that occurs when the curtain comes down.

That night Francie got pickled. That was his word. He apologised to Joan who said she didn't mind at all, one needed some kind of release. All of us shared an end-of-term feeling, although there was a mountain of evidence still to be taken before we could even think about writing the report. But the knot had been unravelled. At the heart of the mystery was no mystery, or only a sad little girl with a novelist's imagination – or perhaps imagination is too grand a description – with a novelist's knack of seizing on the material that came to hand and remixing it into something fresh.

'It was your friend Helen who woke me up,' Francie said, slurring his words now. 'She made me see that J wasn't making it up out of nothing.'

'But if I remember rightly, that was just what Helen said J did.'

'Exactly. It takes somebody saying something unimaginative to make you think,' he said heavily. 'Tell me, does your friend Helen ever make up stories herself?'

'No,' I said after thinking a bit and remembering her struggling to make up a bedtime story for Beryl, 'No, I don't think she can.'

'Exactly,' he said again. 'She doesn't know how you do it. None of these people know how you do it, because they never do it themselves. But I know. I hear people do it every day in court.'

'But a child –' Joan attempted.

'It's just the same process. In fact it's a child's game, making things up. Dangerous game. Your friend's not a child, though, is she? Helen's not a child, is she? Sweet Helen, make me immortal with a kiss, her lips suck forth my soul, see where it flies.'

'No, she's not a child. She never was,' I said.

'I think it's bedtime, we've got a long day tomorrow,' Joan said firmly, rising with a chinking of her jet baubles.

But Francie wasn't finished. He was relentless when he had had a few, and after Joan had gone upstairs he didn't hold back on the drink or anything else.

'When I was a young barrister out on circuit, it used to be shagging sheep. Fields behind here used to be full of sheep, they'd graze them on the golf-course in the winter, only place there was no frost. Sheep all gone now, so this. Not so new anyway, I suppose. There was a man came up before me in Lincoln once, had told the police his father had always "broken in" his daughters as he put it so he didn't see why he shouldn't carry on the family tradition.'

'But you can't –'

'Of course I don't justify it, I'm just telling you what people get up to. You read about that place in New York where respectable couples – lawyers, civil servants, people like you and me – go and roger complete strangers, then go out for a nice dinner in a nice restaurant?'

'Yes, but they're all adults.'

'So they are adults. It's only adult entertainment. Quite a different matter.'

He peered deep into the silly balloon glass as though he was going to try it for size as a helmet, then sat back emitting a long low noise, somewhere between a sigh and a groan.

'Are you all right?'

'Never better, apart from being rat-arsed. It gets you down, this stuff, looking at them all trailing in, all of them, and knowing that it's doing none of them any good, including the innocent ones. Perhaps they're all innocent, even the social workers. Perhaps they're all doing their best.'

'Well it may –'

'No, no, don't listen to me. I don't mean a thing. The important point is, we are doing our best. That's the point.'

'I think perhaps –'

'You're right. It's bedtime. Dame Joan is right. Everyone is right, and it's all all right.'

At nine a.m., Constable Dykes reported a call from Mrs Garforth who said she knew her husband had gone down to meet us at the theatre last night and she hadn't seen him since.

'Three to one they find him before the week's out.'

'Dead or alive?' I was catching on to this hard-boiled style.

'Dead of course. I'll give you five to one against finding him alive.'

Francie would have won both bets if anyone had taken them. The car was found on Saturday parked up a deserted lane twenty miles away, with a length of heavy-duty hose attached to the exhaust and running back through the front window, the necessary chink being expertly filled with a flexible draught-excluder which Mrs Garforth hadn't missed at the time.

Mr G was wearing a dark suit for the occasion.

'Extraordinary that the first casualty should be somebody who really *is* known by an initial.'

'That's not funny,' Joan said.

'None of it's funny,' Francie said.

'Had you any suspicion?'

'It would be pleasing to reveal that I had staged the whole scene to frighten Mr G into thinking that we were on to him in the hope that he would then confess, which would be the only way of getting a conviction because we didn't have any evidence. But I have to admit that I thought it was all in a little girl's imagination. I had not the least suspicion in the world and of course if I had had, I would be feeling even more remorseful about my vain and stupid exhibition than I already am. So it wouldn't be pleasing at all. What remains an interesting question is what were J's motives in telling her story the way she did.'

'Well, she must have been frightened of Garforth and thought it was safer to put the blame on Stoyt-Smith, as you said?'

'Yes, I was half-right about that. But why tell the story at all? Did she hope that we would be clever enough to follow the trail that would lead us to the real villain?'

'That's excessively ingenious surely for a girl of her age and –'

'Education, Joan? Perhaps you're right, though you might need native cunning rather than O-levels. In any case, if that was her intention, we failed her. Or – no, this is more fantastical still – perhaps she intended to frighten G. But that would be an even more dangerous game. Well, as they say, we shall never know. Perhaps J doesn't know herself. Should we go to his funeral? No, I think not, it'd be a mawkish gesture, though these days it's hard to be too mawkish.'

Mr Garforth had been a late entrant but he had boosted the success rate among people I knew to two out of six and added a new method to those already logged, viz, drowning, hanging, overdose, jumping off a cliff and shooting yourself. Even so, with all these methods available, it was odd that people brought it off so rarely, or did I happen to know people who were below average in practical matters? The idea of doing yourself in might tend to attract the wrong sort, people who weren't much good with their hands. It was noticeable that the two who had managed it – Mr Garforth and Martin Hardress – had both seemed formidably competent. I didn't know either of them well enough to tell whether they had anything else in common (being out of work wasn't at all like fearing imminent exposure and arrest as a paedophile). Perhaps they had shared a bleak view of the world, had both thought that life's being unfair wasn't just like travelling on a bumpy road but rather loomed up at you like a dizzying view of the abyss. Better to get it over with under your own steam and not hang about pretending it wasn't going to happen to you.

'You've gone white as a sheet,' Joan said. 'Why don't you sit down?'

It took another week to finish off collecting the evidence. Then we settled down to write the report. We had given up our quarters in the school, because term was just starting, and we worked in the hotel, in a little first-floor conference room, not much more than a sitting-room, looking out towards the links and the sea. It was a reassuring time. Setting out the narrative, describing the principal scenes and characters, and the procedures involved – the workings of a case conference, the criteria required for a Place of Safety Order, the current medical debate about the reliability of the physical evidence – all these tasks restored us to a world of calm and logic. The pity was only, as Francie remarked, that this catharsis was not available to most of those involved. He wrote with a beautiful lucid fluency – I am speaking of his handwriting as well as of his thought. The rest of us had scarcely anything to do but check the occasional fact or correct his memory of some minor point in the evidence, but most of this huge body of material he already had stored in his spare bony skull. In the evenings, he drank only mineral water and he made none of his earlier sardonic remarks. By contrast, being largely a spectator, I had time for a huge sadness to sweep over me. Perhaps Joan, and Patricia too, shared something of that feeling. They both seemed subdued.

When Francie got to the end of each chapter, he handed us copies to read through. 'It's like skating,' he said, 'I want marks for artistic impression as well as technical merit.' The evening he gave us the chapter on the social workers to read, I thought I would cheer myself up by ringing Helen.

'I'm not supposed to tell you this, but the report, anyway the draft so far, says you were the pick of the bunch, an admirable witness.'

'I expect you'll get that bit removed, but thanks for letting me know.'

'Are you all right? You sound – I don't know.'

'I didn't mean to let it show.'

'Let what show?'

'Moonman's gone. Why did I say that, sounds as if he's dead, almost wish he was, I don't want to say left me, I suppose, because it sounds so pathetic.'

'How awful.'

'Do you really think so? Don't you really think, serve her right? I expect you'll be pleased to hear that he's gone back to his wife.'

'Of course I'm not pleased. I've never even met her.'

'Does that matter? Aren't you pleased to hear of a sinner repenting?'

'No.'

'I thought you people believed in marriage being indissoluble, those whom God hath joined and all that.'

'I don't believe in anything much any more,' I said, surprising myself a little by saying something that I hadn't really thought till then. The dragging misery in her voice must have squeezed it out of me.

'Oh I'm so miserable, will you come and see me, I don't know what to do, I can't think.'

Tidying up the report had been quite a business after all, and the light was going by the time I reached the single-track road between the dark fir plantations, so much so that I overshot the cottage again and had to reverse. This time there was no welcome party and there was scarcely a glimmer of light from the squat little house. I had to ring the bell twice before I heard footsteps slopping along the passage.

She flopped into my arms as though she had tripped and when she stood away from me she was glassy-eyed. Her cheeks were flushed and swollen with crying.

'You look like you've been in a fight,' I said.

'Do I? There isn't anyone here to fight with, except Beryl and she just buries herself in her homework, just like I would if my mother had gone mad. You need a drink, I do anyway.'

There wasn't much left in the bottle and, after we had finished it, she scrabbled around in the cupboard over the sink. All she could find was a bottle of cooking marsala and so we finished that, and I felt sick as well as drunk.

'That's it for me, you know.'

'What is?'

'I really loved him, you probably didn't think so, you probably thought, well, at least he's not quite such a dead loss as Bobs, who was an obvious mistake, so she's just cutting her losses or whatever.'

'No, I didn't think that. I could see that this was, I suppose the real thing is the word.'

'You could see that, could you? Oh Gus, you aren't quite as thick as I thought.' And she got up from the other side of the kitchen table and gave me a kiss which was slobbery but touching all the same. 'Anyway that's it, there won't be anything else like that for me, it's all over, that sort of thing. I've just got to look after Beryl. You haven't seen Beryl yet, have you? She's longing to see you, I'll get her.'

'Please don't —'

But she was already bumping into the chunky kitchen chairs that Moonman had knocked together as she headed towards the stairs calling up at Beryl, who didn't answer. So Helen climbed the stairs, calling again as she went and still getting no answer. There was only a brief bickering above before she came back down with her daughter now almost as tall as she was, which was not saying much, a serious, slight figure as Helen had been and now wasn't, not this evening. But Beryl's hair wasn't like her mother's. It was a dull brown, scraped back and tied in a ponytail, so she looked only severe and nothing more. She didn't have that quality that had caused us all so much trouble, not yet anyway. She greeted me just politely enough not to annoy her mother and then said she had to finish her French homework.

'What's the point of it all?' Helen said after Beryl had gone upstairs again, 'homework, more bloody homework and then you end up like this ditched by a sod like Moonman who doesn't even leave any drink behind. You know he's found God, so you've got a little friend.'

'I told you I'd stopped all that.'

'Lost one, found one, so He's all square. At least Moonman hasn't given his father the satisfaction of crawling back to the C of E.'

'His father's dead.'

'Makes no difference if you're Moonman. Doesn't like the thought of him chortling wherever he is. Anyway becoming a Catholic means his father can't be anywhere better than Purgatory or have I got that bit muddled?'

'Haven't a clue.'

'Tell me, was it awful losing your faith? Did you just wake up one day and discover you'd lost it, like finding you've lost a tooth?'

It was hard to tell whether she was being derisive or trying to be sympathetic, or both at once. In any case, I was annoyed with myself for having referred to the subject at all. If there was one spectacle more dismal than a grown-up person dabbling in that area, it was the same grown-up confessing that he no longer found any of it at all interesting, that the whole idea of belief had suddenly become repellent. Luckily her interest evaporated even faster.

'So,' she said, 'what shall I do? I can't stay here. It's horrible, everything reminds me of him, these ghastly chairs he made, the vegetable patch he dug which only produced these leggy cauliflowers one of which I'm about to inflict on you, the whole self-sufficiency bit.'

'And the doll's house?'

'The doll's house is all right. I mean, it's not all right, it's sinister, but it's properly Beryl's and anyway he made it before.'

'Will you go back to London?'

'Bobs has offered us St Col's. Well, as you'd expect, he's offered himself too. One thing the Moonman brothers have in common, they don't understand that you can't go back, you can't love or even half-love the same person twice. So when I said no to that, he said he'd get a place near by so he could come and see Beryl. I don't much like the sound of that either, but Beryl will like it. There must be something else to drink apart from this horrible stuff.'

She rummaged in the brown cupboard behind me and dragged out a small aluminium step-ladder. Even standing on the top step she could only just reach the upper cupboard. I looked at her slim legs and her heels arching up out of her slippers and imagined her as I had first seen her, so delicate and severe and in control of the world.

'Ah,' she gurgled, 'I never knew these were here. The last people must have left them behind.'

She came down clasping two bottles of red wine.

'Bulgarian,' she said, as if it was the most beautiful word there was.

So we drank them and ate the cauliflower with a watery cheese sauce and then had some more cheese to finish up the wine with and then she said I could fuck her if I liked, which was probably all I had come for because it was all anyone ever came for. So I said it was a bit too late for that in every sense of late and in any case hadn't she said that the whole point was that you couldn't go back, you couldn't love or even half-love the same person twice? To which she said that I was just trying to catch her out, and this was what I really liked doing, which was why I didn't understand, couldn't begin to understand what people who were capable of loving other people went through, what they had to endure. So I said that was probably true.

After I had dossed down on the sofa, she came and lay down quietly beside me for an hour or so and said she was going to be all right.

Afters

The light was shimmery and also somehow pink, not the pink of dawn or even dusk, but rather of some everlasting afternoon, a light for lotus-eaters. The elderly figures on the long benches seemed stunned, suspended in time, as though they had been carefully placed in their haphazard attitudes, some lolling sideways almost recumbent, others lying back with their heads over the top of the bench so their adam's apples throbbed at the ceiling, some hunched forward with their heads almost between their knees as though about to be sick, but all with this frozen interrupted look, suggesting they had been ordered by the director to simulate the after-effects of a nuclear explosion, or stage a modern-dress re-creation of the last days of Pompeii, so that I felt that at any moment the director might blow a whistle and they would break up and shuffle off to location catering for a cup of tea. Perhaps all this was something to do with the light which flooded down from the high windows in great pinkish-gold shafts flecked with glittering particles of dust, so dense it seemed to be made of some quite other substance, gauze perhaps or jelly, a substance that enveloped, even preserved, the stunned figures stretched out in front of me.

'I love this place,' breathed Hilary Puttock as he settled himself down beside me, his broad beam forcing me to edge into the corner where gothic protuberances pressed into my kidneys. 'I think we can just squeeze in the Ambassador.'

'Ambassador?'

'The Strangers Gallery was full. But I squared it with the L.C.'s office. Ah, here he is.'

A burly bronzed figure, almost as burly and full to bursting with *bienséance* as Hilary himself, opened the little half-door into the gallery and edged himself along the bench towards us in an eager, buttock-thrusting crouch.

'You know the Ambassador?'

And, as he turned to flash me a brilliant impatient smile, I did know him. Farid Farhadi seemed hardly changed from the day I had first seen him standing on the steps of the Casino bursting out of his dinner jacket, his restlessness no more contained now than then.

'Of course I remember you perfectly. The nanny. How wonderful,' he said but only after I had explained who I was. He reached across Hilary and patted my thigh.

'Nanny?' queried Hilary with a touch of pique, as though suspecting some code he had not been properly briefed on.

'It is all so long ago. What fun we all had,' Farid sighed.

'Gus has not a little to do with my presence here this afternoon,' Hilary said. 'It was he who recommended a certain Mrs Moonman to me. I in turn had the opportunity to introduce her to the Minister responsible for such matters and he was as impressed as I was, bowled over in fact. He complimented her on her evidence to Fincher and said we must on no account omit her from the working party.'

'Party? What party?' Farid asked.

'On the future of social work.'

'Social work? What fun, what fun.' Farid was only half-listening, being already occupied in trying to catch someone's attention with a little finger-fluttering wave.

'From there it was all stations go as you might say. My wife had died some eighteen months earlier and I found solitude not to my taste. At first our contacts were professional as I say but then – well, you know how charming Helen is.'

'Enchanting, enchanting.'

Farid's attention had wandered again and I wondered if he remembered what he had whispered into Helen's ear that evening at the Casino.

'At our age, there was little to be said for delay.'

'Nothing, nothing.'

'It was simply a matter of waiting for the divorce to come through.

Bobs, I must say, was most remarkably helpful, particularly since he had his own troubles at the time.'

'What troubles?' I put in, both because I was curious and because I couldn't bear any further rerun of Hilary's courtship.

'You didn't know? I thought you were a good friend of his. His travel business went into voluntary liquidation just before Easter.'

'But surely with the Wall coming down, isn't everyone going to Eastern Europe now?'

'Indeed they are, but they no longer require the services of a specialist travel agent who possesses the expertise that was once necessary in visa matters, hotel vouchers and the other impedimenta that are now, I am happy to say, a thing of the past. Well, well, there he is. He remains devoted to her, you know.'

And there leaning over a frail ironwork balcony above us, bathed in a shower of gauzy light, was Bobs, looking paler – that might be the light – but otherwise not much different from when he had first hopped out of the MG outside St Col's. Perhaps that was the new irony, our peculiar modern destiny, that we didn't age externally at the same rate as people used to. All the damage was internal now, like fighters who exchange body blows to the point of collapse but with still scarcely a mark on their gleaming skins. Even so, only Bobs could go bust in Eastern Europe in 1989.

As though answering my thoughts, Farid said: 'There are wonderful opportunities out there, you know. My friend Dodo Wilmot, you remember Dodo of course you do, he has a lease on half a million square miles of Siberia, gold, diamonds, the kitchen sink. He is having a ball now that he has got rid of those tiresome wives, you know, the women one could never tell apart.'

'Got rid of?'

'Dead, divorced, who knows, both perhaps. Look, your friend is waving to you.'

Bobs had caught sight of us and was making one of those pointing gestures that American politicians make when they are pretending to recognise someone in the crowd.

'I must say I wonder how many old boyfriends of Helen's are going to pop out of the woodwork this afternoon,' Hilary said. 'Still, one must be prepared for such things when one marries a beauty.'

'Married? You are married to my darling?' Farid seemed only now to catch on and in the same instant that he asked the question thrust one hand into Hilary's and wrapped the other arm round his broad shoulders.

'Yes, yes, of course we are married,' Hilary answered rather crossly. 'We did the deed at Caxton Hall five weeks ago though we have not as yet managed to synchronise our schedules sufficiently to arrange a honeymoon.'

'But that is marvellous. I thought that you were just embarking on a little *affaire du coeur.*'

'Well, that too indeed,' Hilary managed. 'But we decided that we wanted to put the affair on a more permanent basis.'

'Members desirous of taking their seat,' chanted a voice from somewhere and a dignitary led in a little procession through the double doors: two tall stooping men in scarlet robes trimmed with white fur and between them a tiny figure with fair hair in the same robes.

'Desirous,' murmured Farid leaning forward to drink in the scene with his arms spilling over the knobs of our pew-front, 'I think I am desirous. Doesn't she look wonderful, your wife. A mere child still.'

And so she was, or not a real child but like a child drawn by an artist, perhaps a medieval artist who had just progressed beyond drawing children as midget adults. She looked much as she had looked the first time we met, when she came through the shimmery mist with Farid's little boy (who must now be an overfed playboy like his father if someone hadn't had the sense to shoot him). You would never have guessed that anyone could make her go to pieces, certainly not a man, which hadn't prevented men from trying, though only Moonman had succeeded. In fact, it was little more than a year, certainly less than two, since she had fallen into my arms at Firs Cottage, swollen-eyed and sozzled.

Then it came to me – an awful thought – that it was *Hilary* who had got her off the booze, in fact put her back together again. And this was more shocking than that Moonman should have been the love of her life. All the same, her looking so well again made me feel something which on examination could only be described as happiness. Perhaps that wasn't so surprising. Noticing signs of misery or decay in anyone you once loved was a nasty little injection of death, and conversely seeing Helen as fair as she had first been, even in this geriatric reserve, even married to Hilary, was an inkling of youth, a false inkling of course but you couldn't have everything.

'Isn't her hair wonderful?' Hilary whispered. 'She doesn't dye it at all, doesn't need to.'

'Wonderful,' I said.

'She's done so much you know, makes me feel awfully unadventurous.'

The ill-assorted threesome bowed, the two ungainly men low and slow, Helen giving a brisk nod a little out of time with them, the sort of nod you give a colleague who has just come back from a slightly extended lunch break. They moved forward a couple of yards and bowed again, then moved forward once more and bowed a third time.

'Tell me,' Farid said, 'your wife, you invited her to this party and then, boom, here she is. Is that how one does it? But of course one must be beautiful.'

'Normally, a considerable record of public service is necessary before any such elevation could be considered, but these days the party is eager to advance one or two younger men and women who may be expected to earn their spurs in the saddle, so to speak. I am speaking here of the political party naturally, not the working party of which I spoke earlier.'

'Parties, parties,' murmured Farid.

'Then it so happened that we bumped into the Leader at a New Year's party. He was most impressed by Helen, not just the way she performed on Fincher but her whole background – food science, mining – she's just the sort of person they will be needing, apart from being a woman of course.'

'And the miners' strike,' I said, 'what about her part in that?'

'Old unhappy far-off things, Gus, they're drawing a line under that one as you know.'

The threesome had now handed over a scroll to a rather stouter elderly man in black robes who was seated on a huge pouffe which could have accommodated three or four other persons. The stout elderly man then read out something, possibly from the scroll, but his voice was so indistinct that the only words I caught – perhaps because he called them out louder so that you could hear how languid his voice was – were Baroness Hardress of Minnow Island. Then I think he mentioned the county, which I was keen to hear because I could not remember whether Minnow Island was in Middlesex or Surrey, but Farid was chattering again and the words were lost to me. At that moment there was a murmuration of yer, yers from the Pompeii victims on the red benches, one especially harsh, prolonged and sonorous – Yer, yer, YERRH – which seemed tinged with mockery of the proceedings, perhaps of all human proceedings. The threesome then began their retreat, bowing or nodding again, this time more in unison. They were too far away for me to see whether Helen's expression gave any hint of what she thought of this ancient mummery. Probably she didn't care. She might have been right. All the same, it did seem a funny place for a serious person to end up in. But then as often as not, the golden city on the horizon turned out to be a ghost town when you reached it. Arrival was usually a let-down, the journey was the thing.

On the way out, I ran into Bobs coming down the stairs from the gallery.

'I'm not staying for the drinkies, she asked me, but I thought I'd cramp her style.'

'Where's Beryl? I didn't see her.'

'She's not coming, she doesn't approve. We've all tried to explain that Helen's not doing it for herself, they need her because of her special expertise. But Beryl's not an easy one to budge, like her mum in that way of course. Anyway she doesn't go a bomb on old Hilary.'

'You look pale,' I said, not meaning to, but struck by the fact that it wasn't the light that had taken the bounce off him.

'Oh I've got this cancer thingy. Luckily I'm on to this ace chap who says I've got absolutely the best sort to get, if you're going to get it at all of course. Look, you must buzz on in. I'll catch you later.'

And in an instant he was gone bounding on past me down the next flight of stairs. He seemed to know his way round this warren, but then it was possible that he didn't and I would run into him five minutes later charging back in the other direction.

For my own part, I needed to ask several people the way to the tea-room and even so made a couple of wrong turns before finally catching sight of a familiar figure, strange how familiar she was since I had seen her only a handful of times, none of them recently. She was a little bent, but still fine-looking in that way that always reminded me she was actually more beautiful than her daughter.

'I'm glad you've come,' she said. 'It's only going to be a small party. Beryl's not coming. She doesn't approve.'

'So I hear.'

'Who told you? Bobs, I suppose. That little man, he's still a total waste of space. I was not pleased to see him in the gallery. At least he's had the decency to stay away from the party. Hilary's being extremely good to him. I expect you think Hilary's rather pompous. You probably laugh at him in the office. But he keeps going, he's got stamina. That's what I like in a man. Martin didn't have it, you know, my late husband. He thought he was a serious person, but he didn't really understand that you can't be serious unless you keep on at things. I thought Helen was going to turn out like him, but I'm glad to see she hasn't.'

'So you approve of all this?'

'Of course I do. You need a few people with a bit of sense in this place before they do away with it.'

'Come on, Mum.' Helen took her by the hand. 'Hilary wants you to sit next to him.'

She had removed her robes and was wearing a neat magenta coat and skirt which showed off how slender she was. She was glowing with health and efficiency – somehow the phrase floated into my mind from the old airbrushed nudist magazines we used to hide under the mattress – and I thought of her diving off the rock in Africa and how she hadn't been at all airbrushed and an ache of pointless longing overcame me as she passed me a plate of mixed sandwiches.

'You look wonderful,' I said.

'I go to the gym, it's quite easy once you get in the habit of it.'

When the hairs on his nape stood up, he knew that Kathleen had come into the kitchen.

Gideon felt her gaze and straightened his shoulders, resisting the urge to peer back at her. He dated women all the time, but none of them had caught his attention the way she had.

Deep down he sensed a connection, as if she knew what it was to be hurt deeply and had held herself back from others because of that. Like him. Was that why he got the bright idea to bring dinner to her tonight?

No, it was her sons. They reminded Gideon of himself and his younger brother growing up.

He pivoted toward her, transfixed by the soft blue of her eyes. *Run.* The word set off an alarm bell in his mind. His chest constricted.

In the distance he heard her son Kip speaking to him, but Gideon couldn't tear his eyes from Kathleen, her delicate features forming a beautiful picture that could haunt him if he allowed her to get too close. But he wouldn't do that.

Books by Margaret Daley

Love Inspired

*Gold in the Fire
*A Mother for Cindy
*Light in the Storm
The Cinderella Plan
*When Dreams Come True
Hearts on the Line
*Tidings of Joy
Heart of the Amazon
**Once Upon a Family
**Heart of the Family
**Family Ever After
A Texas Thanksgiving
**Second Chance Family
**Together for the Holidays
†Love Lessons
†Heart of a Cowboy
†A Daughter for Christmas
§His Holiday Family

Love Inspired Suspense

So Dark the Night
Vanished
Buried Secrets
Don't Look Back
Forsaken Canyon
What Sarah Saw
Poisoned Secrets
Cowboy Protector
Christmas Peril
  "Merry Mayhem"
††Christmas Bodyguard
Trail of Lies
††Protecting Her Own
††Hidden in the Everglades

*The Ladies of Sweetwater Lake
**Fostered by Love
†Helping Hands Homeschooling
§A Town Called Hope
††Guardians, Inc.

MARGARET DALEY

feels she has been blessed. She has been married more than thirty years to her husband, Mike, whom she met in college. He is a terrific support and her best friend. They have one son, Shaun. Margaret has been writing for many years and loves to tell a story. When she was a little girl, she would play with her dolls and make up stories about their lives. Now she writes these stories down. She especially enjoys weaving stories about families and how faith in God can sustain a person when things get tough. When she isn't writing, she is fortunate to be a teacher for students with special needs. Margaret has taught for more than twenty years and loves working with her students. She has also been a Special Olympics coach and has participated in many sports with her students.

His Holiday Family
Margaret Daley

Love Inspired

Recycling programs
for this product may
not exist in your area.

 LOVE INSPIRED BOOKS

ISBN-13: 978-0-373-08215-5

HIS HOLIDAY FAMILY

Copyright © 2011 by Margaret Daley

www.LoveInspiredBooks.com

Printed in U.S.A.

Therefore my heart is glad, and my glory
rejoiceth: my flesh also shall rest in hope.
—*Psalms* 16:9

To Joe, thank you for your support

Chapter One

Gideon O'Brien hopped down from Engine Two and assessed the chaos in front of him. Strapping on his air pack, he started toward his captain. A hand gripped his arm and stopped his forward progress. He turned toward the blonde woman who held him, her large blue eyes glistening with tears. She looked familiar, but he couldn't place where he knew her from. His neighbor's daughter, perhaps?

"My two sons and my cousin—their babysitter—must still be inside. I don't see them outside with the other tenants." Her voice quivered. She tightened her hand

on his arm and scanned the crowd. "I'm
Kathleen Hart. My sons are Jared and Kip.
I tried Sally's cell but she didn't answer.
Please get them out." A tear slipped down
her cheek.

"Where are they?" Gideon moved
toward his captain, his palm at the small
of her back, guiding her in the direction he
wanted her to go. Yes, he realized, she was
his neighbor Ruth Coleman's daughter.

"Sally's second-floor apartment is on
the east side, the fourth one down on your
right. Number 212. Hurry." Her round eyes
fastened on the fire consuming the three-
story apartment building on Magnolia
Street.

Gideon paused in front of Captain Fox.
"Mrs. Hart says her sons and babysitter are
still inside. Pete and I can go in and get
them." He looked toward the west end of
the large structure where the men of Engine
One were fighting the flames eating their
way through the top level. "There's still
time."

"Okay." His captain surveyed the east

end. "But hurry. It won't be long before this whole building goes up."

The scent of smoke hung heavy in the air. The hissing sound of water hitting Magnolia Street Apartments vied with the roar of the blaze. Gideon turned toward the mother of the two boys. "We'll find them." He gave her a smile then searched the firefighters for Pete.

When Gideon found him a few feet away, he covered the distance quickly. "Let's go. There are three people trapped on the second floor. East end."

At the main entrance into the building Gideon fixed his mask in place, glancing back at the blonde woman standing near his captain. He had seen that same look of fear and worry many times over his career as a firefighter. He wouldn't let anything happen to her sons and Sally.

Gideon switched on his voice amplifier and headed into the furnace with Pete following close behind him. Through the thick cloud suspended from the ceiling in the foyer, the stairs to the second floor loomed. Crouching, he scrambled up the steps. The higher he went, the hotter it became.

On the landing, he peered to the right, a wall of steely smoke obscuring his view. To the left, the way he needed to go, the gunmetal gray fog hovered in the hallway, denser at the top.

Gideon dropped to his hands and knees and crawled toward Sally's apartment. Sweat coated his body from the adrenaline pumping through him and the soaring temperature. The building groaned. Visibility only three feet in front of him, he hugged the wall, his heart pounding. He sucked air into his lungs, conscious of the limited amount of oxygen in his tank.

Calm down. Not much time. In and out.

Mindful of every inhalation, he counted the doors they passed in the corridor. One. Two. Three. The next apartment was Sally's. His breathing evened out as he neared his goal.

At number 212's door, Gideon tried the handle. Locked. He rose and swung his ax into the wooden obstruction, the sound of it striking its target reverberating in the smoke-filled air.

When a big enough hole appeared, Pete reached inside and opened the door. A pearly haze, not as heavy as in the corridor, engulfed the room. His partner rushed into the apartment, Gideon right behind him. In the small foyer, he noticed a large television on in the living room but didn't see anyone in there.

"I'll take the left. You the right," Gideon said, making his way down the short hallway to the first bedroom. "Fire department, is anyone here?" His gaze riveted to a double bed. He quickly searched everywhere two young boys might hide. Nothing.

For a few seconds a memory intruded into his mind, taking his focus off what needed to be done. He shoved it away, went back in the hall and crossed to the other bedroom. After checking it, he came back out into the corridor and opened the last door to a bathroom. Empty.

He pictured his neighbor's daughter next to his captain, waiting for them to bring her sons out safely. The thought that he might not be able to quickened his breathing for a moment.

When he met up with Pete in the small entryway, his partner said, "All clear in the kitchen as well as the living and dining rooms."

"The same in the bedrooms."

"Gideon, Pete, get out. Mrs. Hart sees her children and their babysitter. They just arrived and are safe," his captain's deep gravelly voice came over the radio.

"We're on our way." Relieved the two boys and Sally were all right, Gideon and Pete made their way back into the main hallway.

The smoke had grown thicker, darker. The crackling and popping sounds of the fire overrode the rumbling noise from the water continually bombarding the structure. A warning went off, signaling Pete only had five minutes of air left in his tank.

Our time is running out.

As those words flashed into Gideon's thoughts, his breathing sped up for a few seconds before he reined it in. He'd been in similar situations. They would make it.

Gideon gestured to his friend to go first. Every second counted. Pete came out of the apartment and got down on all fours, hurriedly heading for the stairs. Gideon crept along a body length behind his partner. As he crawled past the second apartment, his low-pressure air alarm alerted him to the need to move even faster.

But the nearer he came to the stairs, the soupier his surroundings were. He barely made out the back of Pete only a foot in front of him.

Gideon's shoulder brushed against the door frame of the apartment nearest to the steps. Almost there. His inhalations slowed even more to conserve as much oxygen as possible. But heat warmed the inside of his protective suit, and sweat rolled down his face. Its salty drops stung his eyes. He blinked, his vision blurring for a few seconds.

Then suddenly from above, wood and debris came tumbling down. Gideon lost sight of Pete in the dense smoke and dust. The crashing sound of a beam boomed through the air.

Lord, help.

Rolling onto his back, Gideon reached for his radio when another metallic moan cut through the noise of the fire. A piece of timber landed across his chest, knocking his radio from his hand. A sharp pain lanced a path through his upper torso. Then a second slab of lumber fell on top of the first. Gideon stared up as the rest of the ceiling plummeted. Air rushed out of his lungs, and blackness swirled before his eyes.

Holding her two sons' hands, Kathleen Hart watched them carry a firefighter out of the burning building. Fear bombarded her from all sides. He could die because she'd mistakenly thought her children and Sally were inside. She relived the few seconds when she'd seen Jared and Kip racing toward her with Sally Nance right behind them. The elation they weren't trapped took hold. Then the knowledge she had unnecessarily sent two men into a blaze to find the trio swept away the joy. Now one of them was injured. Because of her.

She turned to Sally. "Please keep the boys with you. I need to see how the firefighter is doing."

"Sure. I'm so sorry you didn't realize I took Jared and Kip to the park. When the weather's good, we've been doing that. With the storm coming, I didn't know when we would get another chance anytime soon. I never in a thousand years thought my apartment building would catch fire and…" Her cousin gulped back the rest of her words and stared at the man on the stretcher being attended to by the paramedics.

"I know, Sally." Kathleen looked down at her sons, whose eyes were round and huge in their pale faces. "We'll talk later." She squeezed their hands gently, drawing their attention. "Stay with Sally. I'm going to check on the firefighter."

Tears shone in Kip's eyes. "Tell him we're sorry."

She stooped and grasped her nine-year-old's upper arms. "Honey, it isn't your fault."

And it isn't my fault, either. It was an unfortunate accident. If only she could believe that.

Even knowing that in her mind didn't make her feel any better as she rose and headed toward the ambulance into which the paramedics were loading the firefighter.

One of the paramedics hopped into the back of the emergency vehicle while the other shut the doors and started toward the front of the truck. She knew the paramedic because she worked as a nurse at Hope Memorial Hospital. Kathleen hurried her steps and caught up with the driver before he climbed into the cab.

"How is he, Samuel?"

"O'Brien may have some internal injuries." Samuel gave her a once-over. "Did you just come from the hospital?"

Still dressed in her scrubs, Kathleen nodded. "Will he make it?"

"He should, barring any complications." The paramedic jumped up into the ambulance.

Kathleen backed away from the vehicle and watched it leave the scene. She squeezed her eyes closed, still seeing the flashing lights in her mind. She couldn't shake the tragedy of the situation—one she'd had a part in. Just like another one, not long ago.

She tried to clear her mind of the memory. When would this go away?

Someone tugged on her arm. She looked down at Jared, her seven-year-old son, with worry in his expression. "Sally said he went in searching for us. Is that true?"

"Yes. When I didn't see you outside with the other tenants, I thought you all were still inside."

"Is he going to be okay?" Kip asked as

he approached her. Sally followed right behind her son.

"The paramedic thinks so." She hoped Samuel was right.

"Mom, he's got to be." Kip's lower lip quivered. "I begged Sally to take us to the park."

"Honey, you didn't know what might happen." She needed to listen to her own words, but that wasn't as easy as it sounded. "Let's get you two to Nana's, and then I'll go back to the hospital and check on him after the doctor has had time to see him in the E.R." Kathleen shifted toward her twenty-three-year-old cousin. "I'm so sorry about this, Sally. Do you want to go to Mom's?" She threw a glance toward the blaze. "It doesn't look like much will be left. You'll need a place to stay. You're welcome to stay with me and the boys."

"I appreciate the offer, but I can go to my mom's. I need to stay and talk with some of my neighbors. See what happened. Then I'll give Mom a call and have her come pick me up. She should be home. With Hurricane Naomi bearing down on us, I would have stayed at Mom's anyway." Sally looked south toward the water only a few blocks from the apartment building.

Kathleen couldn't think of that. The storm in the Gulf was still several days away from Hope, Mississippi, a quaint town of twenty thousand between Mobile and New Orleans. Her hometown of stately antebellum homes along the water thrived on tourism and the fishing industry. But anything could happen between now and the date the National Weather Service projected Naomi would come ashore in the vicinity of Hope.

"I called your cell earlier when I arrived. All I could do was leave a message."

Sally dug into her jean pocket and withdrew her phone. She winced. "Sorry. I had the sound off." Her cousin peered off to Kathleen's side. "Will Kip and Jared be okay?"

Kathleen followed the direction of Sally's attention. Both of her sons' gazes were glued to the commotion taking place at the Magnolia Street Apartments. Kip chewed his lower lip while her younger son took several feet forward. "I'd better get them away before Jared is in the middle of the chaos. I'll talk to you later. If you need any help, please call." She hugged her cousin, then made her way to her children, who were entranced by the plume of smoke bellowing into the sky being chased by yellow-orange flames.

Her mother would watch them while she went to check on the firefighter. She owed him that much for what he did for her. Kathleen clasped first Jared's hand, then Kip's. "We need to go to Nana's."

"But, Mom, I want to see what happens." He had told her on a number of occasions he wanted to be a firefighter.

"No. They don't need any more people here watching." Kathleen scanned the crowd that had gathered across the street from the apartments. "Besides, if Nana hears about this, she'll get worried."

"Will she even be back from Biloxi yet?"

Kip trudged toward her car parked several buildings away.

"I hope so." Because she needed to go to the hospital. The firefighter had to be all right.

Will he make it?

The question plagued Kathleen the whole way into the E.R. thirty minutes later after she'd left her mother's house. Luckily her mother had returned from her weekly visit to her friend in a nursing home in Biloxi. Activity and tension met Kathleen as she came through the double doors. Ashley, an E.R. nurse who had befriended her when she'd begun working at Hope Memorial six weeks ago, hurried from behind the counter, saw her and came toward her.

"Thank the Lord you are here. We need a hand. One of the nurses got sick and had to go home. Can you help me with a patient? I have two that need attention." Ashley held up several vials of medicines and an IV bag.

"Is one of them the firefighter from the

fire on Magnolia Street?" She rushed behind the counter and disposed of her purse in a drawer.

"Yes, he's in room two."

"I'll take him. I just came from the fire. My cousin lives in those apartments. I wanted to check to see how he is."

"I think he'll be all right. I haven't had much time with him yet. Besides him, there was a wreck on Interstate 10. Three injuries. It's been hopping around here. I don't want to even think about how it will be if Naomi hits here."

Neither did Kathleen. As a child, she had gone through two minor hurricanes that had gotten her out of school for a couple of days but, other than that, hadn't changed her life much at all. But Naomi was gathering speed and her winds were increasing.

Ashley thrust an IV bag into her hands. "He needs this."

Her breath caught in her throat, Kathleen took it and started for the second door on the left. "What are his injuries?"

Ashley slanted a look at Kathleen and said, "I think several broken or cracked ribs, possible internal bleeding and smoke inhalation," then entered E.R. unit number four.

When Kathleen went into room two, she stared at the firefighter lying on the bed. His damp black hair was plastered against his head, and there were dark smudges on his tan face. His steely gray eyes locked on her and seized her full attention.

"Pete. What about Pete? Did my partner get out okay?" His raspy voice weakened with each word he uttered.

"Yes, there were no other injuries at the fire." Guilt swamped her at seeing the man she'd sent into the fire hurting, pain reflected in his gaze. The feeling was familiar. Hadn't her husband, Derek, blamed her for causing his stress that led to his heart attack? Shaking away the memory, Kathleen hung an IV drip on the pole and hooked up his line.

"I'll be fine." The firefighter struggled to

sit up. His eyes clouded, his face twisting into a frown.

Kathleen rushed forward to restrain the patient's movements. "You need to lie down."

"You're the lady with the boys. Ruth's daughter." He swung one leg to the floor.

"Yes." Kathleen touched his left arm to stop him.

He flinched but proceeded with putting his other leg on the tiles, pushing himself upright. With a moan, he sank to the floor. Kathleen caught him as he went down and lessened his impact with the tiles. Kneeling next to him, she supported his back with her arm.

His head rested against the bottom of the bed. He fixed his weary gaze on her, pain dominating it. "I guess I'm not all right."

"Let's get you back in bed. The doctor will be here soon."

"Yeah, sure." His eyes fluttered and closed.

With her attention fastened on his face,

Kathleen settled him on the floor and pressed the emergency call button.

"I thought you left here a couple of hours ago," Mildred Wyman, the floor supervisor, said as Kathleen exited the elevator and walked toward the nurses' station.

"I did, but there was a fire at the Magnolia Street Apartments where my cousin lives." She filled her in on the details. "When I came back to the hospital, Ashley recruited me to help until another nurse was able to come in. She just arrived so I wanted to see if Gideon O'Brien was settled into his room before I go home for sure this time."

"He's in room 345. He was asleep a little while ago."

"I'll peek in. See if he's up. If he needs anything."

Kathleen strolled toward the last room on the west wing's third floor. The memory of the look on Gideon O'Brien's face wouldn't leave her thoughts. Clearly he'd been in pain but he tried to deny the seriousness of his injuries. If only she had known that Sally had taken the boys to the park, Gideon O'Brien wouldn't be hurt.

She rapped on the door. When she didn't hear anything, she inched it open to see if he was still asleep. The dimly lit room beckoned her. She stepped inside and found him, lying on his bed, his head lolled to the side, his eyes closed.

With the black smudges cleaned from his face, his features fit together into a pleasing picture. High cheekbones, the beginnings of a dark stubble, strong jaw. His features drew her forward until she stood by his side, watching him sleep. She could remember seeing him a couple of times jogging past her mother's house when she had visited. When she'd told her mother who the injured firefighter was, her mom had said Gideon O'Brien had moved in down the street several years before.

"He sure is a handsome lad. Single, too." Her mother's words came back to taunt Kathleen. Before she'd had time to say goodbye to her sons so she could return to the hospital, her mother had ushered her

out the door without further questions—
which was unusual for her mom. Kathleen
knew what was going through her mother's
mind. A nice young man would solve all of
Kathleen's problems. She would discourage her mother of that thought when she
went back to pick up her sons.

Her glance ran down Gideon's length,
categorizing his injuries. Two cracked ribs,
wrapped but very painful, a broken arm
above his left wrist, which would be set tomorrow, and an assortment of bruises. The
doctor was still concerned about internal
bleeding and wanted to keep a close eye on
him overnight.

When her survey returned to his face,
it connected with his gaze. Molten silver,
framed by long, thick black eyelashes. Cap-
tivating. Powerful. Those thoughts sent
warmth to her cheeks that she was sure rivaled the fire he'd fought.

Kathleen looked away. "I didn't mean to
wake you up."

"You didn't," Gideon said in a scratchy

voice. "You were at the fire. In the E.R. Ruth's daughter."

She nodded. "I'm so sorry you and Pete went into the building after my children." She reconnected with him visually. "They were supposed to be there. I had come to pick them up. I didn't know Sally had taken them to the park and was running late getting them back to her apartment."

He shifted, gritting his teeth. "I'm glad they're safe."

"But—"

"So why are you up here?"

She wanted to say so much more to him, but a closed expression descended over his pain-filled features. "I wanted to make sure you were all right before I left."

"Define all right." One corner of his mouth lifted for a second then fell back into a neutral line. He tried to reach for the plastic cup of water on his nightstand and winced.

"Let me get it for you." Kathleen picked up the cup and held it to his lips so he could take a few sips. The scent of smoke clung to his dark hair. "Is your pain manageable?"

"I've had worse."

"You have?" She'd heard from other patients in the past how much broken or cracked ribs could hurt.

"Afraid so." Creases in his forehead deepened. Gideon gulped in a breath of air and started coughing. Agony contorted his features, his eyes shiny. "That hurt."

"Let me see if you can have more pain meds." Anything to help make him feel better. Then maybe she wouldn't feel so guilty.

He coughed again. His pale face urged her to hurry. She left his room and hastened to the nurses' station. "Mildred, can Gideon O'Brien have any more of his pain medication?"

"I'll check and take care of it. I was just coming to get you. Your mother called and said you need to get home right away. Something about Jared falling off the side of the house."

"Is he okay?"

"She didn't say. But she sounded shook up."

Kathleen rushed to the elevator, punching the down button. Seconds ticked by so slowly she started for the stairs when the doors swished open. This day was quickly going from bad to worse.

Two minutes later, after retrieving her purse in the E.R., she hastened out to the parking lot while digging for her cell. She slipped behind the steering wheel of her eight-year-old Dodge and punched in her mom's number.

"How's Jared?" In the background Kathleen heard her son crying, and her grip tightened on the phone.

"I don't know. He's holding his arm. He might have broken it."

"I'll be there soon." She flipped her cell closed and pulled out of the parking space.

Ten minutes later Kathleen turned onto Oceanview Drive. Her seven-year-old son was too adventurous for his own good. She guessed he was going from climbing trees to houses now. Next he'd want to try flying off the roof. The thought sent panic through her as she drove into the driveway and parked.

The front door banged open, and Kip came racing out of the two-story stone house. "Mom, Jared climbed up there." He pointed toward the second floor. "You should have seen him. I can't believe he did it."

"Did you dare him?" Kathleen charged up the steps to the porch. At the door Kip's silence prompted her to glance back at him. "You did."

"Aw, Mom. I didn't think he would really do it."

"We'll talk later." Kathleen entered her childhood home and headed toward the kitchen where the crying was coming from.

Kathleen's mother stood over her son, her face leached of color. "I'm so glad you're here." Relief flooded her features. "If you need me, I'll be—"

"Mom, I'll take care of this. Don't worry." Her mom never did well when someone was hurt or even sick. She usually fell apart. She certainly hadn't gotten her desire to be a nurse from her mother.

Jared sat cross-legged on the tile floor, cradling his left arm to his chest, tears streaking down his face. His look whisked away any anger she had at him attempting something dangerous.

Kathleen stooped down, putting her hand on his shoulder. "Honey, where does it hurt?"

He sniffled. "Here." He lifted his arm and pointed at his wrist. "Nana thinks I broke it."

When Kathleen gently probed his injury, Jared yelped and tried to pull away.

"Let's take you to the doctor. You'll need an X-ray."

"Am I gonna get a shot?" Jared's brown eyes grew round and large.

"I don't know."

"I am! I don't want to go." Jared scooted back from her. "I can tough it out."

"If it's broken, it needs to be fixed. It'll hurt a lot more than a shot if you don't get it taken care of."

"Don't be a baby," Kip said behind Kathleen.

She threw a warning look over her shoulder. "I'm sure you have homework. Go do it. Have Nana help you if you need it."

Jared stopped moving away from her. He peered down at his wrist, sniffed and then locked gazes with her. "I'm not a baby." He pushed to his feet, tears swimming in his eyes. Blinking, he ran his right hand across his face, scrubbing away the evidence of his crying. "I'm ready," he announced as if he were being led away to some horrible fate.

While Jared trudged toward the front door, Kathleen spied Kip sitting on the stairs. Before her older son could open his mouth, she followed Jared into the foyer. Jared went outside on the porch, sticking his tongue out at his brother as he left.

Kathleen swept around, her hand resting on her waist. "Don't forget you and I need to have a talk. This fighting between you two has got to stop."

"We don't fight."

She arched her eyebrow. "Oh, since when?"

"We're playing."

Gesturing toward the den, she said, "Homework. I want to see it finished by the time I get back to Nana's to pick you up."

Kip leaped to his feet and stomped toward the den, making enough racket to wake up anyone who was within a several house radius.

As Kathleen covered the distance to the den to tell her mother what she was going to do, her mom said, "Glory be. This is great news."

Kathleen stepped through the entrance into the room. "What is?" she asked, swinging her attention to The Weather Channel on TV. She could certainly use some good news.

Her mom muted the announcer. "Hurricane Naomi has changed course. I think we're going to miss most of it. Maybe get a touch of the western tip, but not like they had predicted."

"We don't have to board up our house

now?" Kip sat down at the gaming table with his book bag.

"It's not looking like we do." Her mom peered at her. "I know it's not good news for someone else, but maybe it will peter out before it reaches Florida."

Kathleen doubted it from the information she had heard. "Mom, I'm taking Jared to the minor emergency clinic. I don't know when I'll be back to pick up Kip."

"Fine. Kip and I will put away all the supplies I bought for the hurricane, especially all those boxes of tape I got for the windows, which I really don't need. Don't know why I bought them."

"I'll take a box, Nana," Kip announced while digging into his bag for his homework.

"Sure. Just don't tape up Jared with it." Her mother rose and moved toward Kip. "Kathleen, when you get back we'll order something for dinner. We're celebrating tonight. No Naomi."

Kathleen left her mom's, not feeling the least bit in the mood to celebrate anything—even the fact the town would avoid Naomi. Her cousin's apartment burned today. She could have lost Sally and her sons. A firefighter went into a burning building because of her insistence her family was still inside.

Her life continued to come apart at the seams, starting with the last year of her marriage to Derek. She had wanted coming home to be a new start but hadn't counted on her sons' rebellion against moving to Hope. There was no going back to Denver, however. She couldn't afford to live there, financially or emotionally.

Chapter Two

The crashing sounds of the falling timbers and the crackling of the fire haunted Gideon when he tried to sleep at the hospital. He remembered being put into the ambulance and glancing at the Magnolia Street Apartments as the structure caved in on itself, flames shooting upward as the blaze rampaged through it.

The noises around him amplified in volume. The antiseptic smell of the hospital overwhelmed him. Sweat popped out on his forehead. His breathing became shallow, his throat raw.

Finally, Gideon inhaled a deeper breath

and regretted it the second he did. A sharp pain pierced through his chest. He clenched his jaw and rode the wave until it subsided to a throbbing ache. In spite of how he felt, restlessness churned through him. Scanning the hospital room, he resisted the impulse to walk away. The doctor should be here within a few hours to give him the okay to leave. But as he stared at the clock on the wall across from his bed, the second hand seemed to be moving in slow motion.

The sound of the door opening lured his attention away from watching time inch forward. Kathleen Hart—last night he'd finally remembered she'd told him her name at the fire—entered his room. Her long blond hair pulled back in a ponytail emphasized her delicate features—large, blue eyes like the Gulf off the shores of Hope, lips with a rosy tint that wasn't from lipstick, and two dimples in her cheeks as she smiled at him.

Dressed in blue scrubs, she approached his bed carrying a little plastic cup with his meds. "How are you doing today?"

"Well enough to go home." He held out his right palm for his pills.

"Dr. Adams should be here soon. He does rounds after lunch." Dark shadows under her eyes attested to not enough rest.

He recalled her apology and hoped what had happened at the fire hadn't caused her a sleepless night. "Where did you go yesterday? Nurse Ratched brought me my meds. She wouldn't tell me what happened to you."

"I won't tell Mildred you called her that."

He grinned. "She's definitely a no-nonsense nurse. I'm glad you came back today."

"I work on this floor. I had to."

"Ouch. I think my ego was just wounded."

"Only think?" A twinkle danced briefly in her tired eyes.

The shadow in her gaze tugged at him. He wanted to prolong the light tone of the conversation, but he needed her to understand how he felt. His injuries weren't her fault. "You were upset yesterday. Are you all right today?"

"The more important question is, are you?"

"I will be in time."

"You shouldn't be here right now. If only I had waited a little…" Her voice faded into silence, and she glanced away, swallowing hard.

"I would rather err on the side of caution than have someone trapped in a burning building. What I did yesterday is part of my job. Occasionally we go into a fire looking for a person who isn't there. It happens. You are *not* to blame." He would never forget the firefighters who had rescued him and his younger brother from a fire when he was eight. If they hadn't come into his burning house, he and Zach wouldn't be alive today. "No more guilt over yesterday. I'm glad your sons are safe."

With her gaze still averted, she nodded.

He wasn't totally convinced she wasn't blaming herself anymore, not if the furrowed forehead and the darkening of the blue in her eyes were any indication. "I've been hurt before. I won't let a few cracked ribs and a broken arm get me down."

She swiveled her attention back to him, her expression evening out, but the dark circles under her eyes were still there. "Tell that to my son. He broke a bone in his wrist yesterday after I took him to his grandmother's while I came to the hospital. That's where I had to go. He told me at the doctor's office that he wanted to see the hurricane coming in the Gulf. He thought the view would be better from the roof."

"I heard it turned toward Florida. We might get some high tides and rain, but hopefully that will be all." He shifted in the bed and caused another shaft of pain to constrict his breath, but he tried to keep from flinching. He didn't succeed.

"Are you all right?" The wrinkled forehead returned with a slight tensing.

"Just a twinge. Nothing that won't go away with time. So how did he get to the roof? Ladder?"

"That would have been safer. But he climbed the side of the house on a dare from his older brother. He didn't make it. He fell while trying to hoist himself onto the roof."

Gideon whistled. "You've got a daredevil on your hands. What did your husband say about it?" The second he asked the question he wanted to snatch it back. He didn't see a wedding ring on her left hand, but there was paler skin where one would have been. He couldn't remember Ruth saying anything to him about her son-in-law, but then he and Ruth were only passing acquaintances on Oceanview Drive.

"Derek died last year."

"I'm so sorry. I…" He didn't know what else to say.

"Is there anything I can do for you before I leave?" A professional facade fell into place as she checked his IV drip.

He could respect that she wanted to shut down the subject of her husband. Losing a loved one was difficult. Although he had never been married, he'd lost too many people in his life not to feel a kinship with her.

He grinned, wanting to see the light back in her eyes. "Other than get me out of here, no."

"Sorry, but Dr. Adams might take exception to that. Just as soon as he signs your discharge papers, you can escape."

"A hospital isn't my favorite place." Again he was reminded of his parents' deaths. His father had died in the fire, but his mother with third degree burns had lingered for a day in the hospital. He had only been able to say goodbye to her at the end when she was unconscious. He would never forget that last time he saw her.

"It usually isn't for most people." Her smile reappeared on her face, a sparkle shining in her eyes—making him forget where he was for a moment. "If you need anything, use your call button."

He watched her saunter out of his room. Occasionally he and Ruth would talk when they saw each other on the street, but with his crazy schedule, it wasn't often. She had mentioned she had only one child, and then this August she had talked about her daughter returning home in September to live in Hope. Other than Ruth being excited her two grandsons would be close, she hadn't gone into details about the move.

From his and Kathleen's few exchanges, he had sensed a deep hurt and now that he knew about her husband dying, he figured that must be why. One more reason he didn't get too involved in people's lives. He found after being shuffled between one foster family and another that it was safer to stay emotionally apart from others. Much safer.

After passing out the medication to her patients, Kathleen came back to the nurses' station to write in their charts. Dr. Adams nodded to her as he headed down the hall toward Gideon's room. She smiled, thinking about how the man would finally be able to leave. Even with his injuries, he had exuded restlessness. When he had told her about a hospital not being one of his favorite places, she'd heard pain behind the words though he'd no doubt tried to hide it.

Although he had reassured her she wasn't at fault for his being hurt, she had been married to a man who had blamed her for all his woes. Even with some of his last words to her right before he slipped away after having a massive heart attack at the age of thirty-five, he'd blamed her for the stress he'd lived under. No matter how much she told herself that she hadn't wanted him to take all the money out of their savings for Kip and Jared's college fund to invest in the stock market in risky companies, it didn't ease the guilt. In fact, she hadn't even known about it until after his death. The stocks hadn't done what her husband had dreamed they would. In fact, when he'd had his heart attack, she had discovered Derek had put the family thirty thousand dollars into debt and just that day had gotten notification the bank was foreclosing on their house if the mortgage wasn't paid. She'd tried to do that, but it hadn't been enough.

She shook the past from her mind. Coming to Hope was a fresh start, even if she still had twenty-eight thousand dollars to pay back. When she had lived here, she had flourished in the small-town feel and kindness of others. She desperately needed that now.

An orderly went by her desk and entered Gideon's room. Not long after that she saw Gideon appear in the hallway, dressed to leave, sitting in a wheelchair.

At the nurses' station he had the orderly stop. "Thank everyone for me for their excellent but *brief* care," he told her with a smile.

"I see Nate is helping break you out of here."

"Yep. I was getting ready to walk out of the hospital when he showed up."

"Oh, we cannot have that. Against Hope Memorial's policy," she said in dead seriousness, but the second the words came out she chuckled. "You aren't the first who has threatened that."

He motioned her to bend down closer to him, then he whispered, "Now my only complaint is that I would have liked a prettier escort. Too bad you're busy." Gideon winked and flashed her a grin before the orderly wheeled him toward the elevator.

Kathleen touched her cheek. It felt hot beneath her fingertips. She hadn't blushed in years and this was the second time since meeting Gideon. The injured firefighter was charming, but that was all he was. She didn't have the emotional energy to get involved with anyone, even if she felt guilty for his injuries. Raising her sons and slowly paying off the mountain of bills her husband had left her were enough to deal with.

Her mother kept telling her to turn it over to the Lord. She used to, but in the past two years she hadn't seen any evidence of the Lord in her life. Her prayers for help had gone unanswered. She was still in debt. Her sons desperately needed a man's influence. They hated being in Hope. They fought all the time. Then to top it all off, she felt responsible for Gideon's injuries, no matter what he said.

Which means I'll make sure he's comfortable while he's recuperating at home.

That's the least I can do. Then maybe I won't feel so bad when I see him in a cast and wincing from pain.

Kathleen came into the house by the back door, thankful that her car had made it at least to her mom's, although she'd had doubts several blocks away when it died on her yet again. After the third time cranking the engine, it turned over and started.

Her mother told her to use her kitchen to make Gideon something to eat, then she could just walk down a few houses and give it to him. This was something Kathleen could do for him. She'd grown up with neighbors helping neighbors. That was part of Hope's charm. With one arm in the cast it would be hard for Gideon at first learning to do things one-handed. He didn't need to worry about making something to eat.

Kathleen set the bag of food she'd gotten to make her Mexican chicken dish on the counter. After emptying the sack, she placed the pieces of chicken in water to cook. Then she went in search of her sons to see what kind of homework they had. When her mother didn't go see her friend in Biloxi, she watched Jared and Kip after school until Kathleen got off work and could pick them up. And when her mother couldn't watch her sons, Sally would fill in, no charge. That was a huge help to her because she couldn't afford to pay child-care along with everything else to raise two growing boys.

"Mom, do you know where Jared and Kip are?" Kathleen asked when she entered the den where her mother was watching The Weather Channel.

She peered toward Kathleen. "I didn't hear you come in. Been glued to the T.V. I'm charting the progress of Naomi even if it is going to miss us."

Kathleen wasn't surprised by that fact. Her mom had done that for years. She had a stack of charts of past hurricanes that had come into the Gulf. "I'm going to fix some Mexican chicken for us and take some to Gideon O'Brien down the street like I mentioned to you."

"I'm sure he'll enjoy that. He seems quite lonely to me."

Before her mother had her fixed up on a date with Gideon, Kathleen asked, "Where are the boys? They need to get their homework done. After dinner they are useless. I can't get much out of them then as far as schoolwork."

"They said something about riding those old bikes I had in the garage. I told them they could but not to go farther than this block and not to ride in the streets."

Kathleen glimpsed the time on the clock above the mantel. "It's getting late. I'd better round them up and see where they stand with their homework."

"We'll need to pray for the people in Panama City." Her mother listened to the reporter on the T.V. give the latest coordinates of the hurricane and jotted them down. "I'm sure you'll see the boys if you go outside and look."

That was assuming her sons obeyed their grandmother when she babysat them. Lately there was no guarantee they would.

Kathleen made her way toward the front door. Outside on the lawn she looked to the left and saw no one. Then she peered toward the right and thought she saw a bike that was like the one she'd ridden as a child lying on the sidewalk three houses down where Gideon lived.

She remembered Kip's questions the night before about the firefighter who had been hurt in the Magnolia Street Apartments fire. He had wanted to know if he would be all right. Who was he? Could he and Jared make get-well cards for him? She'd kissed her boys good-night and told them she would talk to them today when she got home from work.

She charged down the street. Knowing them, they had taken matters into their own hands without waiting to discuss it with her.

At Gideon's one-story white house with a neat yard, she skirted around both of her mom's old bikes and headed straight for the front door. After ringing the bell, she waited, trying to temper her anger that Kip and Jared would disturb a man recovering from some painful injuries.

Her older son opened the door. "Hey, Mom. Come in."

"No, I think you all have stayed long enough. You and Jared need to come back to Nana's. You're both supposed to have your homework finished by dinner." *Haven't we done enough to disrupt this man's life?*

"Aw, Mom, Gideon was telling us about some of the rescues he's done."

"Why are you answering his door?" She swung open the screen, the one standing between her and Kip.

"Gideon doesn't move too fast. I told him I'd get it."

Kathleen glanced over her son's shoulder at the slow-moving firefighter making his way toward them with a small white dog with a curly tail. His stiff movements coupled with the sight of his cast only reinforced why the man was in the pain he was.

"Hello, Kathleen. Your sons came over to

give me their get-well cards. I asked them to stay if it was okay with you. They assured me it was." Gideon's gaze swept from Kip to Jared, who had joined them in the foyer.

Her younger son poked his head around Gideon. "He has a cast just like me. Isn't that neat? We're twins."

"And that is Butch. He's so sweet," Kip added, pointing to the dog near Gideon.

"It's time for you two to come back to Nana's and get your homework done."

"Mooomm, can't we stay for a while longer?" Kip's mouth formed his classic pout that he had stood in front of the mirror one day to perfect.

"Another time, guys. This is a school night, and you've got work to do." Gideon tousled Jared's, then Kip's hair.

Jared giggled then scooted out the front door.

But Kip remained where he was standing. "Will you tell us some more stories about being a firefighter?"

"Well, sure, anytime it's all right with

your mother." Gideon flashed her a grin that melted any irritation she had toward her sons for bothering the man.

"Great. Call if you need us to do anything for you. After school we stay with Nana until Mom comes to pick us up." Kip raced past Kathleen and stamped down the porch steps.

While her sons grabbed their bikes and rode them toward her mother's house, Kathleen faced Gideon. "I know how tired you must be. Your body has gone through a trauma and needs rest, not my sons bothering you. I'm sorry—"

He held up his palm to still her words. "I enjoyed their visit. I was resting on the couch, getting more bored by the second when they came and rescued me from my boredom. I hope you'll let them come again."

She completely surrendered to the kindness in his eyes. Her legs grew weak, and she clutched the door frame to steady herself. "Only as long as they don't pester you." The pale cast to his skin spoke of the strain of standing. "Let me help you back to that couch."

He shook his head. "As much as I'd like a pretty lady to hold me, I can make my own way there."

"Are you sure?"

"Yes. Do you need to watch to make sure I don't falter halfway there?"

She grinned. "I'll take your word for it. Besides, I need to get home and make you a dinner, which I plan to bring you if that's okay with you."

"Normally I would jump at the chance to have someone fix me dinner, but you should see my refrigerator. There is nothing like good ole Southern hospitality. I don't think I'll be able to eat half the dishes stuffed in it. The ladies at my church decided they would stock it for me, so I wouldn't have to worry about what to eat for the next week. Well, more like several."

"Then I'll wait until later when you've run out of their dishes. I know it takes a while for ribs to heal, and they can be painful."

"Like I said, I don't usually turn down a

home-cooked meal, so you'll get no argument from me. When it's my time to cook at the fire station, I've actually heard some groans from the other firefighters."

She chuckled. "If you need anything, I only live two blocks away. Down the hill and around the corner."

"On Bayview Avenue?"

"Yeah, the yellow cottage. One of Mom's rentals. Good night." Which was the main reason she could save a little money to pay off her debt. Her mother didn't charge her rent, but Kathleen had insisted on paying all the utilities and other bills connected to the house.

He stood in his doorway with his dog next to him as she descended the porch steps. She felt his gaze on her the whole way down his sidewalk. Heat flared into her cheeks. She couldn't resist glancing over her shoulder, only to find him staring at her, as she thought. He nodded, then swung his door closed.

Kathleen hurried to the foyer to answer the door. When she opened it, her breath caught for a few seconds. Although she'd found herself thinking about Gideon several times since she'd seen him yesterday, she hadn't thought she would see him this soon. "This is a surprise. What brings you by here?"

He lifted two large pizza boxes. "I came bearing dinner. I couldn't stand staying in my home another moment. I immediately thought of you and your sons. You were kind to want to fix me dinner. I thought I would beat you to the punch. I called earlier to see if y'all would be home and Kip said yes. I asked him if you had started dinner. He said you had to run next door and were behind schedule." He handed her the boxes. "He was supposed to tell you I was bringing dinner."

"A minor detail he forgot. I wondered why he kept coming up with things I had to do before starting dinner. You didn't have to bring pizza. I owe you a dinner, not the other way around. Remember?"

"I'm not used to inactivity. It was a spurof-the-moment decision. I figured the boys would like pizza."

She smiled. "Pizza and just about every other junk food there is." Stepping to the side, Kathleen opened the door wider. "Come on in."

As Gideon entered the house, one corner of his mouth hiked up. "I was hoping you wouldn't send me home with all this pizza."

"You may change your mind after being here a while." She started for the kitchen at the back of the house. "I should warn you. My sons have been fighting most of the day. At the moment they are in time-out. And we've only been home an hour."

"Sounds like a few boys I have in my youth group at church."

"Youth group?"

"I help out when I can with the group for eight- to twelve-year-olds. When I'm not working, we sometimes play a game or two of basketball in the evening at the park near the Hope Community Church. There are several courts there. By the time they go home, they're too exhausted to fight each other. A couple of the dads have joined our little games, too."

"Is that Broussard Park on the Point?"

"Yeah. I like to run there sometimes."

Memories intruded into her mind. Memories of happier times before her father had been killed in an accident at the shipyard. "When I was a child, my family used to go to the Point to watch the sun set and have a picnic dinner."

"Since I came here, I've seen some beautiful sunsets on the Point."

Kathleen went into the kitchen with Gideon following close behind her. After placing the boxes on the table, she peered over her shoulder at him. "Where are you from?"

"New Orleans, originally. I've been here for five years."

"How long have you been a firefighter?"

"Fifteen years."

"Why did you decide to become one?"

He opened his mouth but a few seconds later snapped it closed. A nerve in his jaw twitched. Clasping his hands so tightly his knuckles whitened, he stared straight ahead at a spot over her shoulder. "Someone needs to fight fires."

Behind what he'd said there was a wealth of words left unspoken, but his stiff posture and steely expression told her the subject was off-limits. What was really behind him being a firefighter? On the surface he seemed open and friendly, but deep down she felt his need for privacy as though he were used to being alone and liked it that way. She could respect his need for that.

She'd felt the same way when she'd discovered the extent of Derek's debt and betrayal after he died. Leaving her to deal with the aftermath. Alone. So yes, she was used to dealing with her problems alone.

For a long moment an uncomfortable silence vibrated in the air between them.

Gideon cleared his throat. "I've filled in as a paramedic when they've needed me. I'm surprised I haven't met you before at the hospital."

Covering the distance to the refrigerator, she took out a carton of milk and a pitcher of iced tea. "That's because I started working at Hope Memorial Hospital a little over six weeks ago. Knowing your aversion to a hospital, I doubt you hung around once you delivered your patients to the E.R."

"Ah, you know me too well. Where did you move from?"

"Denver, Colorado." Kathleen poured milk into two large glasses.

"Can I help you set the table or something?"

"No, I've got this. You brought the dinner. That's enough, and my sons will be ecstatic they aren't having what I planned tonight—tuna casserole."

"I ran into your mother as I was leaving my house. She asked me where I was going when I should be resting. I told her I was feeling better and decided to take dinner to you and the boys. She gave her stamp of approval."

I'm sure she did. Her mother was a romantic at heart and had encouraged Kathleen to start dating almost immediately after returning home. "She goes out every Thursday night with Mildred."

"Not Nurse Ratched?"

"The one and the same."

Gideon rubbed the back of his neck, his forehead creased. "She's a friend of the family?"

"Yes."

"That will teach me to keep my mouth shut."

"She comes across tough and no-nonsense, but she really has a very loving heart. That is, once you get to know her." Kathleen pressed her lips together to keep from smiling at the sheepish look on his face. "I tell you what. You can get the plates down from that cabinet and napkins from that drawer—" she pointed to the locations "—and I'll go get the boys before this pizza gets cold."

As she strolled from the kitchen, the sensation that he was staring at her sent a tingling wave through her. Goose bumps rose on her arms. She quickened her pace down the hallway to Jared and Kip's room. She'd had her younger son go into the bedroom the boys shared while Kip was in hers. Time-out in the same room only escalated their skirmishes, which had been growing worse since they'd moved to Hope.

When she opened the door to the boys' bedroom, Jared sat on his twin bed, chunking paper wads into the trashcan. A whole notebook, almost gone, littered the floor.

"Jared!"

He glanced at her, grinned and said, "Watch me, Mom." He tore the last sheet from the pad and scrunched it up into a ball, then tossed it toward the basket. It bounced off the rim and dropped into the pile of other missed shots. He frowned. "Maybe I should move it closer."

"No, maybe you should clean this mess up and then come to dinner. We're having pizza."

"Not tuna? Yay!" He scooted off the bed, taking half the covers with him. "The only reason I didn't make many baskets was cause I can't use both arms."

"Then I would refrain from climbing houses."

He bent over and picked up the first wad, frowning at his cast on his left arm. "This is gonna take forever."

"You should have thought about that before you decided to make the mess." She turned away before he saw her smile. Natural consequences were great teachers, but her son could have broken something much worse than his wrist.

Across the hall, she found Kip at the door listening to her and Jared. She peeked into her room to make sure he hadn't left a similar mess.

He looked up at her with those big brown eyes and long eyelashes and said sweetly, "I'm sorry I fought with Jared, but he was bugging me. I had to do something to shut him up."

"Getting into a wrestling match isn't an option. Dinner is ready."

"I heard the doorbell. Did Gideon come with pizzas?"

"Yes."

"Sweet." Kip hurried ahead of her toward the kitchen.

"Next time, young man, warn me when someone is coming over, especially with dinner."

Jared came out of his room and followed behind Kathleen. "Why did he bring pizza?"

Kathleen waited for Jared, cradling his cast to his chest. "To see you all."

"Really? Us?"

"I think he enjoyed your visit yesterday. He thought you and Kip might enjoy pizza."

"Kip talked his ear off. I hardly got to say anything. He was constantly asking him about what a firefighter did."

When she and Jared entered the kitchen, Kip was already seated at his place with three pieces of pizza with all the toppings on it. "I'm starved, Mom."

"We're coming." Her gaze latched on to Gideon standing by the counter. She crossed to the table and took a seat. Gideon moved behind her and helped her scoot her chair forward before he sat. She couldn't remember the last time a man had done that for her.

After Jared plopped down in the last place between Gideon and Kip, Gideon looked at each boy. "I remember Kip mentioning how much he loved pizza yesterday. Earlier that sounded good to me, so I thought I would share some with y'all."

"Pizza is okay." Jared dug into the box nearest him and pulled out four pieces, piling them on his plate.

"Hold it. You never eat that many." Kathleen clasped her hands into fists in her lap. "Take one at a time."

"Kip has three pieces," Jared whined.

"The same goes for him, too." Kathleen pinned her older son with a stare that told him to behave.

"Sorry." Kip began to put his slices back.

"Leave them. You've already put them on your plate, but next time one piece at a time. I expect you two to eat every last bite of what you have on your plate." *Lord, give me patience.* "Remember your manners. We have a guest tonight."

Both of her sons hung their heads but exchanged narrow-eyed glances.

"Jared, it's your turn to say the blessing." Kathleen uncurled her hands.

"Bless this food. Amen." Jared jerked up his head, grabbed his first piece and took a big bite.

When Gideon reached for a slice of Canadian Bacon, her favorite, Jared's gaze fixed on his cast on his left arm that came down to his wrist but allowed him the use of his hand.

"No one has signed your cast," he said with a full mouth of food. Kathleen gave him *the look,* and Jared immediately chewed his pizza and swallowed before adding, "I've got most of my friends to sign mine at school. Annie wanted to, but I wouldn't let her." He held up his arm as though he had a trophy in his grasp.

"Why not?" Gideon poured some iced tea into his glass.

"A girl? No way. I would never hear the

end of it." Jared's mouth pinched together, and he tilted his head in a thoughtful look. "Can you work with that cast? I'm having trouble doing things with mine."

A fleeting frown flitted across Gideon's features. "Not where I want to be. I'll be stuck behind a desk at headquarters until this comes off."

"I have to wear mine for six weeks. How about you?"

"Seven or eight weeks."

"Bummer," Kip said, pulling Gideon's attention to him. "That sounds boring."

"Yep. But I'm not much use to the team with only one arm fully functioning. That's why it's important to be as careful as you can, so you don't end up in a situation like this." Gideon tapped his cast. "Not fun."

"Can I sign your cast? I want to be the first." Kip jumped up and headed for the desk to retrieve a red marker.

"Sure. I noticed it was a little bare after seeing yours, Jared."

"Can I sign yours, too? I'll let you do mine."

Kathleen relaxed back against the chair while the boys wrote their names on Gideon's cast. As he searched Jared's cast for a blank space to put his signature, her throat tightened. Lately her two sons hadn't done anything together without launching into a fight. When Kip finally spotted a place for Gideon to scribble his name, Kathleen lowered her head and blinked away the moisture in her eyes. How could she let something as simple as this get to her?

Chapter Three

Later that evening, with darkness beyond the porch light, Kathleen drew in a deep breath of the cool air with a salty tang to it. The Gulf of Mexico was one block away. She could almost hear the waves crashing against the shore. When she got a chance, she loved to run on the beach early in the morning before the town woke up. It had become her haven since she'd come back to Hope.

Still in her scrubs from work, she rubbed her hands up and down her arms. "It's starting to finally feel like fall some. I'd gotten used to having four seasons in Colorado."

Gideon came up behind her and leaned back on the railing. "I'm going to hate seeing October end next week. It's one of my favorite months. In the middle of football season. Not as oppressively hot as in the summer. But I'll take that over cold weather any day. I'm a New Orleans native—hot and muggy is what I'm used to."

"Jared and Kip won't like the fact it rarely snows here. When I was growing up in Hope, it only did once. An inch. Shut down the whole town for a day until it melted."

"Do they know that?"

"I'm not telling them."

The sound of his chuckle filled the space between them, warming Kathleen. His gaze roamed over her features and for a few seconds wiped all thoughts from her mind, except the man who had shared a dinner with them and entertained her sons with stories about his job. Kip had hung on every word Gideon had said. Even Jared had listened until he couldn't sit still any longer. He'd lasted fifteen minutes, five minutes longer than usual.

"Thanks for bringing the pizzas over. You're a big hit with my sons."

"They're good kids."

She opened her mouth to agree with him when she heard a scream then, "Mom!"

She rushed into the house and hurried down the hallway, Gideon right behind her. Past calamities caused by her sons zipped through her thoughts. Jared ran out of his bedroom with Kip on his heels. Her older son tackled his brother to the floor.

"You're dead meat. How many times do I have to tell you not to touch my stuff?" Kip sat on Jared's chest, pinning his brother's arms to the carpet with his knees. He raised his hands and balled them.

"Kip, get off Jared."

Kip flashed her a scowl, his fists still hovering over Jared's face. "He tore up my notebook. I had my homework in it for school tomorrow."

Kathleen settled her hand on Kip's shoulder. "I'll take it from here."

"But, Mom, I've got to do my homework over. It's all torn up. It was hard. I hate math, and now I've got to figure it all out again."

Gideon stepped into Kip's line of vision. "You know I'm pretty good with math. I'll help you while your mom and Jared have a talk."

Kip's eyes grew round. "You will?"

Gideon nodded.

"I'll get my book. There's paper in the desk in the kitchen." Kip bounced once on his brother's stomach, which produced a grunt from Jared, then stood.

Scrambling to his feet, Jared grimaced, holding his middle. "Mom, did you see him? He hurt me. On purpose."

Kathleen waited to answer him until Kip and Gideon disappeared down the hallway, then she whirled to face Jared. "You used your brother's school notebook to make paper wads?"

He suddenly found a spot on the floor by his feet extremely interesting. Scuffing his tennis shoe against the carpet, he murmured, "He hadn't finished his homework. He only had four problems done. He'd told Nana he had done more than he had after school."

"That's not the point. You have to respect your brother's things."

Jared lifted his head. "I want my own room like I had in Colorado. I hate sharing with him. He's always bothering my stuff. He always has to be first. He always has to have the last word."

"That isn't going to happen anytime soon."

"Why did we move here? I hate this place. I miss my friends." Tears glistening in his eyes, he curled his fingers into tight balls, his face screwed up into a frown.

"I had to sell our house in Colorado. We needed a place to live. I grew up here, and I thought you all would enjoy it like I did."

The frown deepened into a scowl. "You're a girl. All my friends are back home. Not here."

"You've got friends. How about Charlie

down the street? How about the kids who signed your cast?"

A teardrop shone on his eyelash then rolled down his cheek. He knuckled it away. "It's not the same." He spun on his heel and raced into his room, throwing himself on his bed and burying his face in his pillow.

After entering, Kathleen sat next to her son and laid her hand on his arm. "Honey, I know this house is small, but it's all I can afford. One day we'll get to move to a bigger place."

Jared popped back up, his eyes flaring wide in hope. "Back home?"

"No. We're staying in Hope. I need my family around me."

"They can come visit. I'll even let Nana have my room when she does and share with Kip."

"Honey, that's not possible."

Jared turned his back on her and hugged his pillow to his chest. "You don't care about what I want. We were fine where we were."

Coming to Hope hadn't been an easy decision. She'd hated asking for help, but she'd had no choice. She'd needed a support system and a means to save money to pay off the debts. "I'll always care, but we had to move. The cost of living was too high in Colorado."

Still facing away from her, he murmured, "Cost of living?"

"How much it takes to pay for things you need."

"I don't have to have ice cream, and you can forget I want a new bike for Christmas. The one at Nana's is just fine, even if it's a girl's." He twisted toward her. "And I can wear Kip's clothes when he can't anymore. Can we move back?"

"As much as I appreciate your offers, we still can't move back to Denver. This is our home now."

The frown returned, and he faced away from her. "You never listen to me. Only Kip."

"One day you'll understand there are some things that can't be changed no matter how much you want otherwise." Something she had learned painfully the past couple of years. She sat for a few more minutes, but when Jared didn't say anything else, she pushed to her feet. "You need to apologize to your brother. If you bother his things anymore, you'll be grounded next time. Understand?"

"Yeah, you love him more than me."

She leaned over and kissed the side of his head. "I love you both the same. Don't forget to tell your brother you're sorry."

Jared scrubbed her kiss away and put his pillow over his head.

Kathleen walked from the bedroom, releasing a long sigh. *Lord, I need help.*

With his tongue sticking out the side of his mouth, Kip wrote down the answer and waited to see if Gideon said it was right. When he did, Kip beamed. "Thanks, Gideon, I think I get this long division now."

"I'm glad. I used to struggle with math until one year I had this teacher who I connected with. I finally understood what I was supposed to do. After that, math has come easy to me."

"I've only got one more problem. I've never done my homework this fast."

Gideon watched him finish his math sheet. When the hairs on his nape stood up, he knew that Kathleen had come into the kitchen. He felt her gaze on him and straightened his shoulders, resisting the urge to peer back at her. He dated women all the time, but none of them had caught his attention like she had.

Deep down he sensed a connection as if she knew what it was to be hurt deeply and had held herself back from others because of that. Like him. Was that why he'd gotten the bright idea to bring dinner to her tonight?

No, it was her sons. When he'd talked to them there was something that reminded him of his younger brother and him growing up in foster homes—until one day a family had adopted Zach, leaving Gideon alone. It was obvious she needed help with her sons, and for the next seven weeks or so, he would have more time on his hands than usual while he recovered from his injuries and finally could return to full duty.

He pivoted toward her, transfixed by the soft blue of her eyes. *Run.* The one word set off an alarm bell in his mind. His chest constricted.

"Is this right, Gideon?"

In the distance he heard Kip speaking to him, but Gideon couldn't tear his eyes from Kathleen, her delicate features forming a beautiful picture that could haunt him if he allowed her to get too close. But he wouldn't do that.

Run. Now.

He wrenched his gaze away and glanced down at the last problem. "Sure. You did great. I'd better be going. I imagine you need to go to bed early with school tomorrow, and I have a lot to do in the morning. I…" He clamped his jaws closed before he made a fool of himself with his ramblings.

"I'm going to show Gideon out, Kip. You

stay in here. Do not go to your bedroom until I get back."

"Can I have some ice cream? I finished my homework, and it's all correct. Gideon said so."

"One small bowl."

As Kip jumped up and went to the refrigerator, Kathleen swung around and exited the kitchen.

"See you soon, sport. I'll see about that tour of the station." Gideon left and found Kathleen in the foyer, waiting for him. "I told Kip I'll arrange a tour of Station Two for him—for all of you. But only if you say it's okay."

"He wants to be a firefighter or a doctor. He hasn't made up his mind."

"I'd say he has a few years to do that. How about Jared?"

She shrugged. "He hasn't said anything. But the way he's going, I could see him being a test pilot or some other kind of job that is daring. Danger means nothing to him while I'm getting gray hairs at the young age of thirty-two."

"How about professional mountain climber?"

"Please don't mention that. Sides of houses are enough for me," she said with a laugh.

He liked seeing her two dimples appear in her cheeks when she laughed. Her eyes lit with a bright gleam that transformed her. "I enjoyed tonight. Of course, I'm not sure what I'm going to do until they allow me to work behind the desk at headquarters."

"Read a good book."

"I'm more an action kind of guy. Reading is too sedate for me. I tried today to circumvent procedures by reporting for desk duty and was told by the chief in no uncertain terms to stay away until I get the go-ahead from the doc. That should be in three days."

"Does that mean your ribs aren't hurting? That's quick."

"I didn't say that." As he stood in the foyer, his cracked ribs were protesting all the activity he'd done that day, but he wasn't going to let that stop him.

She shook her head. "Men. You and Jared are too much alike. I wouldn't be surprised if he tried climbing the house again with his cast on."

He crossed to the door and opened it. "I wouldn't be surprised, either."

"I was hoping you would disagree with me." Kathleen came out onto the porch. "Now every time the phone rings, I'll wonder what else he has gotten himself into."

"My little brother used to be the same way. I had to get him out of a lot of scrapes."

"Does he live here? New Orleans?"

This was the reason he didn't like to talk about himself. So often it led to questions he didn't want to answer. "I haven't seen him since he was four."

The front door swung open and Kip, with his eyes huge, thrust the phone into Kathleen's hands. "It's Nana. She says Hurricane Naomi has made an almost one-hundred-eighty-degree turn and picked up speed—lots of speed—and is heading straight for Hope. It should be here by tomorrow night."

Chapter Four

Kathleen clutched the phone with a trembling hand, hoping somehow Kip hadn't heard her mother right. "Mom, what's going on?"

"Exactly what Kip told you. The hurricane is coming right for us. It has picked up speed. This time I don't think we're going to dodge the bullet."

Kathleen's eyes closed, and she drew in a deep, fortifying breath. "He said tomorrow night—early or late?"

"It will start by early evening, and the eye should be going over us right after midnight if it continues to move at the same speed it is now."

"I guess you don't have to put up those supplies after all. We'll take care of this house and come over to help you after that."

Kathleen hung up and passed the phone to Kip. "You and your brother need to go to bed. First thing tomorrow, we'll have to board and tape up this house then help Nana."

Kip's eyes widened. "How bad will it be?"

Gideon stepped forward. "A lot of wind and rain."

"Like a bad thunderstorm?" Her son gripped the phone tighter.

Gideon settled his hand on Kip's shoulder. "Yeah. You'll be okay."

"Does this mean we don't have school tomorrow?"

"Yes. We'll be busy getting ready as will everyone else." Kathleen opened the screen door.

"Cool. Wait till Jared hears this."

"I don't want any more fighting between

you and Jared. We have other things to deal with right now. Okay?"

Kip spun around and charged back into the house, saying, "Yes."

Turning to face Gideon, she let the screen door bang closed. "The last time I was in a hurricane was over twenty years ago. I've forgotten what to do. I remember Mom filling the bathtub and other containers with water. Getting candles, lanterns, batteries for a radio and flashlights..." With memories racing through her mind, it went blank.

"Stock up on food you don't have to refrigerate. We will most likely lose our electricity. Bring indoors everything that can be picked up by high winds. Since this house doesn't have hurricane shutters, tape or board the windows. Then pray. Are you going to stay here?"

"I don't know. I might go to Mom's."

"I think that would be better. If there is a big storm surge, this house could be flooded. It's nearer the beach than your mom's."

"Then that's where we'll be."

Gideon stared down at his cast. "If it wasn't for this, I'd be at the fire station." Frustration edged his voice.

"I'm on the B team at the hospital. I work post-hurricane. I'll contact work tomorrow morning and see when they want me to come in. There's so much to be done. This house isn't prepared."

He took her hand. "Get a good night's sleep, and I'll come over and help tomorrow morning first thing."

"Only if you'll let me help you."

"I have hurricane shutters, which will cut down on what I have to do. Let's get your house and your mom's prepared first. There shouldn't be too much to do with mine."

"I'll have breakfast ready at 6:30. At least let me feed you before you work."

He squeezed her hand then dropped it and turned toward the steps. "You've got yourself a date. See you at 6:30."

Kathleen stood on her porch and watched him stroll down her sidewalk, hop into his Jeep and leave. As his taillights disappeared down the street, she peered up at the sky. Roiling clouds obscured the moon. It had begun.

The next morning, using the electric screwdriver that Gideon brought, Kathleen secured a large board over the picture window in the living room while Gideon held it in place for her. When she finished with the last screw, she descended the ladder and stepped back. "I hope that will hold."

"You've done what you can." He hoisted the ladder with his good arm and moved toward the detached garage behind the house.

Kathleen followed Gideon toward the backyard where Jared and Kip were hauling the patio items to the garage to store them. She passed several smaller windows she and Gideon had taped in the past hour since they had eaten breakfast.

"You haven't done your share of the work. I've been carrying all the heavy stuff," Kip yelled from the backyard.

Rounding the side of the house, Kathleen found Jared and Kip playing tug-of-war with a seat cushion. She slowed and shook her head. "I guess I should be thankful this hasn't happened before this. Kip still hasn't forgiven Jared for the homework last night."

"I seem to remember Zach and I fighting over nothing at times," Gideon said with a chuckle. "He used to love to bug me."

"I got this first. You take the table." Jared jerked the cushion toward him.

Kip let go of it. "Fine. Take it."

Jared staggered back and fell on his bottom into a puddle of water left by the rain during the night.

Stomping to the table, Kip lifted it and headed for the garage. When he saw Kathleen, his mouth pressed together in a thin line.

"Mom, did you see him?" Jared scampered to his feet and turned his back to her, showing her his jeans soaking wet with muddy water. "Look at this."

Kathleen inspected the dark clouds surg-

ing over them. "Jared, go in and change.
Kip, you can help us finish clearing the
patio."

"Jared doesn't have to work?" Kip disappeared into the garage.

"I'm counting to ten before I answer that
one," Kathleen said to Gideon then trailed
her son into the garage. She covered the
space between them and blocked his path.
"This is not a time for fighting. We have
to get this house, Nana's and then Gideon's
ready for the hurricane that will be here
soon. If you two don't want to be grounded
for the rest of your life, you'll work together
and be civil with each other."

Tears welled into Kip's eyes. "I'm scared.
I've listened to what they've said about hurricanes. I don't want to be here. Why did
we move here?"

Kathleen knelt in front of her son and
clasped his arms. "Honey, you'll be all
right. We are preparing for it. This town
has gone through hurricanes before, and
it is fine. It has been here for almost two

hundred years. It will be here for another two hundred."

"Don't be a scaredy-cat," Jared said from the doorway into the garage.

"Come here, Jared." Kathleen waved her hand toward him. When he approached warily, she took his hand. "We are a family, and we stick together, especially through trying times like this. I told Kip and now I'll tell you, Jared. We can't fight a hurricane and each other. I depend on you two for your help and cooperation."

Jared squared his shoulders and thrust out his chin. "I'll protect you. I'm not scared, Mom."

Kip yanked free from Kathleen and stormed toward the exit. "I'm not, either."

Jared opened his mouth to reply to his brother. Kathleen put two fingers over his lips. "Shh. Not a word. This may seem like an adventure to you, but it's a serious situation that could be dangerous. Like climbing up to the roof. Look what happened when you did that."

"It's starting to rain again." Gideon came

into the garage, hauling part of a wooden lounge chair while Kip had the other end. "This is the last of the furniture. Let's get to your mom's and see what needs to be done there."

Kathleen rose. "That's a good idea. I want to get there before Nana decides to climb the ladder and close her hurricane shutters on the second floor."

"I can do that." Eagerness lit Jared's face.

Suddenly, Kathleen pictured her young son with a cast on each arm. "No more climbing for you for a while."

Kip stepped forward, his chest thrust out. "I'll do it."

"No. I'm going to." Kathleen headed into the house to get her purse. "You two go and get into the car."

Gideon followed her inside. "I'll meet you at your mom's."

She snatched her handbag from the kitchen counter and started out to the garage. Gideon touched her arm, the feel of his fingers momentarily grazing her skin, stopping her.

"Everything will be all right. We had a storm the first year I was here. A lot of wind and rain, but the town came through it."

"I hope so. I'm on the team that reports to the hospital right after the storm passes. I hate leaving my boys even then, but at least they'll be with Mom."

"I hate that I can't be out there helping, but my captain told me in no uncertain terms when I called him this morning not to come. Then he went on to give me his brief lecture on being injured. But it's hard standing on the sidelines watching others do what you feel you should."

"If you don't take care of yourself, you'll hurt yourself even more. Cracked ribs and a broken arm take time to heal."

He smiled. "I've never been a good patient."

"I'm used to that."

He strode toward the door. "We'd better go before it really starts raining. The few showers we've had are nothing compared to what will be coming soon."

"I'll follow you to Mom's."

In the car, Kathleen switched on the engine and backed out onto the street as Gideon climbed into his Jeep. Sprinkles fell onto the windshield. Silence ruled in the car. Glares were exchanged between her sons in the backseat. She clasped the steering wheel in such a tight grip, her knuckles whitened. The day had only begun. Before it ended, they would be drenched in water and hammered with wind.

"Mom, please get down from there. I can do that." Kathleen raced toward her mother, who was on the ladder against the house.

Ruth perched on one of the top rungs, wrestling with the wind to close the shutter. After finally shutting it, she swung around to stare down at her daughter. "What took y'all so long? I've got to go to the filling station and get gas. I only have a fourth of a tank. I should know better with a hurricane out in the Gulf. I always keep it topped off.

But the storm fooled me when it turned toward Florida."

Ruth took a step down, lost her footing and began to fall. When she clutched the ladder, it teetered. Gideon hurried past Kathleen and grabbed it with one hand and steadied it against the house. Ruth sagged against the rungs.

Slowly she made her way down to the ground and collapsed back against the ladder, her hands shaking. "My word, I had visions of me landing in the same spot as Jared, but I can tell you I would not be able to bounce to my feet like he did. And a broken arm would be the least of my worries."

"Exactly, Mom. I told you I would do it."

"I'm gladly turning the job over to you— on one condition." Her mother swept around toward Gideon. "You need to hold the ladder for her. The rungs are a little slippery and the wind is picking up. I'll take the boys to the filling station with me."

"I've got a better idea. Take Jared. Kip

will stay and help us." Kathleen picked up the ladder and moved it to the next window.

As the boys slowly walked across the front lawn, their heads down, their arms hanging listlessly at their sides, her mother leaned close to Kathleen and said, "Do you really want to do that? They will fight because one got to go with me."

"Yes. I have a project for Kip."

"Okay, I've warned you. I'll send him over here." She sauntered to the boys, spoke to them and then Jared cheered while Kip trudged toward Kathleen with his shoulders slumped even more.

"I need you to go next door and tell Miss Alice we'll be over to her house to help her just as soon as we get through here. Then stay and make sure everything outside is put in for her." Kathleen ascended the first rung.

"Aw, Mom, do I have to? She's mean. She yelled at Jared and me when we came into her yard to get a soccer ball last week."

Clinging to the ladder, Kathleen shifted around so she could peer down at Kip.

"Yes, you have to. We help our neighbors, especially in times of need."

"But, Mom, she isn't our neighbor."

"Go. I've got to get these shutters closed." She waved her hand at Kip in the direction of Miss Alice's house.

When Kip stomped off, splashing water in the soggy grass as he went, Gideon used his lower limbs to anchor the ladder. "You are asking a lot of Kip."

"Tell you a secret. When I was a little girl, she scared me, too. But she is eighty-six and not getting around like she used to. She'll need help through this hurricane."

"I already have it taken care of. Pete is coming over to help me with a couple of the older residents' houses."

"Doesn't he have to work at the fire station?"

"Like the hospital they have two shifts. No one can do a good job if they are dead tired. He's on the second shift after the hurricane passes."

Kathleen proceeded up the ladder and fought to close the shutter, then she descended and started all over with the next one. Three windows later, Kip ran back across the yard.

"Mom. Mom!"

Kathleen jumped down several rungs to the ground and hastened toward her son. "What's wrong?"

"It's Old Lady Beggs. I knocked and knocked, but she didn't come to the door. I peeked through the window. She's sitting in a chair, her eyes closed, her head to the side." Kip stood in the middle of the yard, chewing on his fingernail. "I really banged loud on the door. She didn't move at all. I think she's dead."

"Honey, you stay here. I'll go check." Kathleen started across the lawn.

"I'm coming, too. Kip, when my friend, Pete, comes, tell him where we are."

"Can't I come?"

Both Kathleen and Gideon halted and whirled around. "No."

Kathleen glanced at Gideon and then continued her trek toward Miss Alice's house. On the woman's porch, Gideon pounded on the door while Kathleen checked through the open draperies into the living room. Just as Kip said, she lounged in a chair with her feet propped up and her head lolled to the side, one arm dangling toward the floor.

"Kip might be right. She isn't moving. We need to break in and get her some help."

Gideon came to Kathleen's side. "If she is alive, she isn't gonna like it."

"Do you think she has a spare key somewhere?"

Gideon looked under the welcome mat. When he rose, he shook his head. "This door is pretty sturdy. I don't think I can break it down without an ax, which I left at work. I'll go around and check the windows and back door. Maybe something is unlocked, and I can get in that way."

"Hurry. She might have lost consciousness. I'm calling 911 to be on the safe side."

Gideon started for the back, checking the windows as he went while Kathleen called 911 on her cell. The operator was dispatching an ambulance immediately.

Two minutes later, as Kathleen watched

the old lady in the recliner for any signs of life, her white cat came charging into the living room from the kitchen, leaped and landed in the woman's lap. Miss Alice shot straight up at the same time Gideon barged into the room. Miss Alice let out a rip-roaring scream.

Gideon skidded to a stop, his eyes round, his face pale. He said something to Miss Alice, but Kathleen couldn't hear over the yelling. The woman wasn't even looking at Gideon. She stared right at Kathleen, who stood at her window peering inside.

Gideon moved toward her and bent down toward the woman. Miss Alice blinked, clutching her cat to her chest and glaring at Gideon as if he were a total stranger breaking into her house. He backed toward the front door and opened it.

"Kathleen, come in, please." The stress on the word *please* quickened her pace into the house.

As she passed the mirror in the hallway, Kathleen caught sight of herself and paused. From the occasional rain, her wet hair lay plastered against her head and her mascara ran down her face in a couple of places. And Gideon hadn't said a word to her. She scrubbed the black streaks from her cheeks and kept going into the living room.

"What did you say, young man?"

"We thought you were ill. We knocked on the door." His voice rose with each word he said.

Miss Alice shook her head and held up her hand. "Wait a minute." She fiddled with something in her ear then said, "My batteries must be going in my hearing aid. Help me up, young man."

Gideon did as instructed, and Miss Alice shuffled toward the kitchen, yelling, "I'll be right back."

When she left, Kathleen came to Gideon. "Why didn't you tell me I looked like a drenched raccoon?"

He looked away, a sheepish expression taking over his face. "I know better than to tell a woman that. I thought Kip would say something and get me off the hook."

"I scared the poor woman."

"I didn't think anything scared her. I thought she scared others. At least that's what the boys in my youth group have said when they found out I lived down the street from Alice Beggs." He put his finger into his ear and wiggled it. "I think my hearing is damaged. There is nothing wrong with her lungs."

"I heard that, young man." The woman appeared in the entrance to the dining room. "I should call the police. You broke into my house."

"Oh, no. I've got to call 911 back." Kathleen dug into her pocket for her cell.

Miss Alice's wrinkled forehead wrinkled even more. "You've already called 911 on him?"

Kathleen put the numbers into the phone. "No. For an ambulance. For you."

While she told the 911 operator that Alice Beggs was all right, the older lady shuffled her feet toward her recliner, shaking her head. "I was taking a nap. Can't a woman do that without everyone thinking she's dying? I need more beauty rest than when I was younger." She held out her hand toward Gideon. "Be useful. Help me into this chair, young man."

As Gideon took Miss Alice's arm to assist her into her recliner, Kathleen hung up. "We're sorry to disturb you, but my son thought something might be wrong with you. We knocked a long time on the door, but you didn't move."

"That's because I finally got to sleep after being up most of the night. Why in the world was your son over here trying to wake me up?"

"To see if you needed any help." Kathleen stuffed her cell back into her pocket.

"Yeah, help sleeping. No thanks to y'all."

Kathleen sighed, drawing on her patience she had stored up for dealing with her sons. "I thought we could get your house ready for the hurricane."

"What hurricane? Didn't you hear it's going to hit Florida?"

"No, Miss Alice, it's heading for Hope."

"Where's your mother? She told me yesterday morning we were safe, that it's going the other way."

"It changed its course."

"Why in the world can't it make up its mind? Reminds me of some women I know. No wonder men don't understand us. We don't understand ourselves." Miss Alice leaned back in the chair, fumbling at the side to lift the leg rest.

Gideon stooped and did it for her. "You're perfectly right."

Miss Alice swiveled her attention toward him. "You live down the street, don't you, young man?"

"Two houses away."

"Ah, yes. I've admired you when you've gone jogging."

Gideon's face reddened.

"Miss Alice, your windows need to be covered and—"

The older lady swung her gaze toward the picture window, jerked back and screamed.

Kathleen and Gideon pivoted to see Kip's face pressed against the pane.

Kathleen relaxed and waved him toward

the front door. "Sorry, that's my son who was worried something was wrong with you." The one who didn't follow instructions to stay put.

She strode toward the front door to tell him to go back to Nana's, but the second she opened it, Miss Alice shouted, "Have him come in here."

Kip heard the words and shook his head, whispering, "No way, Mom. She's gonna yell at me."

Kathleen took Kip's hand. "I'll be with you."

He took baby steps toward the living room, hanging back from Kathleen. "My friends say she hates kids."

"What did you say, young'n?"

Kip's eyes widened, and he stopped dead in his tracks.

Miss Alice tried to turn her body to glimpse Kip, but she couldn't all the way. "C'mon in. I can't see you from there."

Kip moved forward a few more paces but dropped his head and stared at his feet as he dragged them across the floor.

"So you are Ruth's grandson. I've seen you a couple of times with another little boy. Who is he?"

"That's my other son, Jared."

Miss Alice ignored Kathleen and said to Kip, "What's the matter? Cat got your tongue?"

Kip kept his eyes on the floor.

"Can't you speak for yourself?" Miss Alice's lips thinned and almost disappeared completely. "Where are your manners? I'm here, not on the floor. Look at me when I talk to you."

Slowly Kip lifted his head, but his gaze focused on her chin, the lower part.

"That's better. I'm perfectly fine, but thank you for caring enough to go get help when you thought something was wrong." She flipped her hand toward the door. "Now you can git."

Kip didn't wait for another word. He whirled and ran out the front door and off the porch.

Miss Alice chuckled. "He's braver than

most. But that's no surprise since he's Ruth's grandson. Where is your mother?"

"Getting gas because of the hurricane."

Gideon glanced outside, then back at the woman. "Miss Alice, can we board up your windows for you?"

"Don't have any boards. Haven't had a hurricane in years that amounted to much. Not like back in sixty-nine."

"Then we can tape most of them, and I can see if I can get a piece of plywood for your picture window." Gideon turned to Kathleen. "Unless your mom has a tape measure, I'll need to get mine."

Miss Alice twisted her mouth into a thoughtful look. "Who's going to remove all that after the hurricane? I certainly can't."

"I will," Gideon answered before Kathleen could reply. "We'd better leave and get your mom's house done, so we can come over here."

"When is this hurricane coming?" Miss Alice pushed the lever down so her footrest dropped, then she scooted to the chair's edge. "I haven't got all my supplies. I'm not prepared at all."

"Kip knows where the tape measure is. Go have him get it for you," Kathleen said to Gideon, then she put her hand under Miss Alice's arm. "Let's go look at what you have. We'll make a list of what you need, and I'll go get it for you."

"Bless you, child. Hurricane Naomi kept dancing around out in the Gulf, playing with us, that I just forgot about her after a while. Same thing happened a couple of years ago and nothing occurred. Thought that was what would happen this time. Don't keep up with things like I used to."

As Gideon left, Kathleen escorted her mom's neighbor toward the kitchen. The thought of the shutters on the second floor windows in the back of her mother's house still needing to be closed lent a certain urgency to her steps until she realized Miss Alice only moved in slow motion. Contrary to what she'd heard, Hurricane Naomi was finally doing in the Gulf.

Chapter Five

"This will teach me to keep my gas tank filled when there's a hurricane out in the Gulf." Kathleen's mother stood up after scrubbing the bathtub out and making sure the stopper was secured before turning on the water. "There, that is the last one. Both tubs will have water in them."

Kathleen took the cleaning supplies and put them back under the bathroom sink. "I wasn't able to fill Miss Alice's order totally, but I think she'll have enough batteries for her flashlights and radio."

"At least you didn't sit in line at the gas station for three hours only to be told I get five gallons and that is it. Of course, it seemed like half the people in Hope were in that line."

"I didn't have to stand in line because there was little left on the shelves at the store. The other half of the town must have struck the grocery stores."

"Nope. They're on the road evacuating. Are you sure you don't want to take the boys and go to Aunt Cora's?"

"I can't. I have to go to the hospital right after it passes. You could take the boys."

"No, she only lives about fifty miles north of here. This house sits up on a hill and has never gotten any water. The wind wouldn't be much less than here. But I can go if you want. I'll probably have enough gas to get to my sister's."

"If you don't get caught up in traffic. I can't take the chance of you running out of gas, and I wouldn't trust my car on the road the way it's acting up." All morning Kathleen had wrestled with whether to send her children away with her mother to Aunt Cora's. Jared had flat out told her that he wanted to stay and see the hurricane while Kip told her he wouldn't leave her.

Her mother left the bathroom. "You need to take my car to the hospital when you have to report to work after the hurricane. I'm certainly not going to be going any-where."

Kathleen headed back to the kitchen where the boys were helping Gideon fill jugs and other containers with water. "Mom, will you ask Miss Alice to come here to stay this evening? I hate her being by herself, but she wouldn't come when Gideon and I tried to get her to."

"I'll try. But she is a stubborn old lady."

Kathleen clamped her teeth down to keep from replying, "Kinda like you." She went into the kitchen to find the water containers all over the counter.

While her mother shrugged into her rain gear and rubber boots, Kip and Jared faced Kathleen with big grins. "We did this," Kip said, gesturing toward the jugs. "Gideon supervised. We did the work. Three gallons of water for each person a day. Isn't that right, Gideon?"

"You've got it. I think y'all are set."

"Did you get yours done when you went home a while ago?"

"Yep. My house is battened down and as secure as it can be. I have my supplies and enough water for a couple of weeks."

Kathleen scanned the kitchen. "The same here."

"Are we staying at Nana's tonight?" Kip started carrying the jugs of water to the pantry on an inside wall.

"We don't want Nana to be alone," Jared added while lugging his share across the room.

"Yeah, we're staying." Kathleen helped her sons store the containers.

"How about Miss Alice?" Kip asked when he came out of the walk-in pantry.

"I'm going right now to see if I can convince her to come over here." Her mother put on her rain hat and tied it down.

"Can I go, too?" Kip crossed the kitchen to his grandmother.

"It's okay with me if your mom says okay."

Kip spun around and asked her, "Can I?"

"Fine. Wear you raincoat and stay with Nana. It's starting to get windy out there."

Jared came out of the food closet. "You're gonna go see Old Lady Beggs? She yells."

"I didn't say anything the first time I heard that name, but I don't want to hear you two call her that. Either use Miss Alice or Miss Beggs. Understand, Kip?" Kathleen peered at him, then turned to her younger son. "Jared?"

They nodded.

As Kip left with her mother, Jared took another jug to the pantry. "I've got to make sure Bubbles has enough water. Can I go check and fill the bowl up?"

"Sure."

When Jared left, Gideon asked, "Bubbles? I didn't know you had a pet."

"A goldfish. The boys want a dog for Christmas along with a whole list of other things, the top of the list being bikes that are not girl ones like Mom has."

"Christmas? That's two months away."

"Yeah, I know, but they are already thinking about it. Their idea of Christmas is so commercial, and no matter how much I tell them this year that we'll celebrate on a smaller scale, they don't listen."

The door flew open, bringing in rain and wind as Kathleen's mother and Kip entered. "Whew. It's starting to get nasty out there," she said as she untied her rain hat and hung everything on a peg in the mudroom off the kitchen. "We ran back. I've had my exercise for the month today."

"Where's Miss Alice?" Kathleen leaned back against the counter next to Gideon.

"She doesn't like crowds. Told Nana she would be just fine at her house. She planned on turning off her hearing aid and sleeping through the whole thing."

Her mother emerged from the mudroom, fingering her damp hair. "Actually, I don't blame her. It's getting wet out there, and she moves so slowly."

Gideon released a long breath. "I'd better

head home then. Butch doesn't like loud noises."

Kip giggled. "Butch is a funny name for a girly dog."

"Hey, he'll take offense if he hears you say that."

"Yeah, and he might nip my ankle if he did." Kip covered his mouth to keep his laughter inside.

"Why don't you bring Butch and come ride out the hurricane here with us? I personally don't like being alone in a storm." Her mother averted her head, suddenly sliding her gaze away from Gideon.

But Kathleen didn't need to see her expression to know what her mom was up to. Gideon was an available bachelor, and her daughter was available now. Bingo. Why not get them together? As that went through her mind, Kathleen said without really thinking about it, "I agree. You shouldn't be alone. You're injured. I wouldn't want you to do anything to strain your cracked ribs."

"Right, Kathleen has a point."

"Yeah, Gideon, please stay and bring Butch." Kip took his hand and dragged him toward the mudroom where the rain gear was. "I'll come with you and carry your dog."

"I think I'm being bulldozed by all of you."

"If that means we're ganging up on you, yep, we are. I don't want to be the man of the house. I've never been in a hurricane."

Hearing Kip say that twisted Kathleen's heart. Ever since his dad had died last year, he'd tried to be the man of the house because some of their friends in Denver had said that the job was his now that his father was gone. Although he'd only been eight, he'd taken the role seriously to the point of even bossing Jared around right after Derek's death. That was what had started the fighting between them that had escalated when they'd moved to Hope.

Gideon captured Kathleen's gaze and held it for a long moment. For a brief time a connection between her and Gideon sprang up, taking her by surprise in its strength.

They had spent the whole day helping each other and neighbors get ready for the hurricane. Even with his broken arm, he'd managed to participate fully in the preparations and get her sons involved, without any arguing.

"Is it okay if Kip helps me bring Butch?"

Kathleen's throat swelled at the emotions sweeping through her—seeing the eagerness on Kip's face, the compassion on Gideon's as if he knew how much her sons needed a man's influence. "Yes, but hurry."

The clash of thunder boomed as Gideon unlocked his front door. The forty-mile-per-hour wind whipped his poncho about him. Kip huddled close, letting the house block some of it. The second the boy could he charged into the foyer, dripping water all over the tiles.

He glanced down at the puddle forming on the floor. "Sorry."

"If that is all this place gets, I'll be happy. Butch!" Gideon headed toward the back.

His bichon frise yelped, the sound coming from the den. When he entered, he saw the white curly tail sticking out from under the couch. "Butch, come on. We're leaving."

The dog whined, trying to burrow deeper under the sofa.

"What's wrong?" Kip moved toward Butch.

"He's scared. Loud thunderstorms really bother him."

Kip stooped and bent down to look under the couch. "It's okay, Butch. I'm scared, too. We can take care of each other. I won't let anything happen to you."

His coaxing voice held a soothing quality that Gideon's dog responded to. He shifted until his face pressed against Kip's leg. The boy stroked him, continuing to murmur reassurances.

"I'm going to grab a couple of things. I'll be right back." Gideon left the two to bond and went down his hallway to his bedroom.

He retrieved a duffel bag out of the closet and stuck in a high-powered flashlight and then went to the garage for some tools he might need right after the storm. As he gathered his supplies, he thought back to that moment in the kitchen when he and Kathleen had looked at each other. For a moment he saw a future with her. Until he remembered that anyone he had really loved had been taken from him. Usually he could suppress the pain of a loss, but locking gazes with her made him remember the last time he'd seen his baby brother or his parents right before the fire that had taken their lives. His shoulders slumped and his head dropped as the memories washed over him.

"Gideon, Butch is ready to leave," Kip said from the kitchen door to the garage. "I told him I would hold him tight and not let the wind get him."

Gideon sucked in a deep breath, zipped up his duffel bag and rotated toward the boy, forcing a look of reassurance on his face. "First, I need to disconnect some appliances since there's a good chance the electricity will go off."

"That happened in Denver to us during a snowstorm. It got cold in the house. We didn't have electricity for a day." Kip cradled Butch against his chest.

"It might be off longer than that here." Gideon made his way through his house and unplugged various items like his computer and television set. When he was finished, he strode toward the foyer. "Let's get back to your grandma's."

"How long?" Kip stepped out onto the porch, shielding Butch from the wind.

"Could be a week. Could be shorter than that, but it could be longer."

"Longer?" Kip shouted over the howl of the wind and another clap of thunder.

"That's why we have supplies for a couple of weeks. To be prepared." Gideon hurried his pace, crossing Miss Alice's yard and glancing toward her boarded front window. Light leaked out of the slits around the edges of the two-by-fours he found to cover it.

When they reached Ruth's porch, Gideon glanced down at Kip. He chewed his bottom lip and clutched Butch tight against him. Gideon put his bag down and clasped the boy's shoulder. He lifted his gaze to Gideon's.

"It's always wise to prepare for the worst, but that doesn't mean it will happen. Worrying won't change what is to be. We'll deal with whatever happens. The Lord is with us."

"Mom used to say that. She doesn't anymore."

The front door swung open, and Kathleen stood in the entrance. "I was beginning to worry about you two."

Kip entered, saying, "I had to coax Butch out from under the couch. He's scared." He kept going down the hall to the den.

Gideon moved into the house. "Sorry. I also decided to turn off some of my major appliances in case there were electrical surges."

"Is everything all right? Kip was frowning."

"He's concerned about the electricity going out for a long time."

"Then I'd better not tell him I am, too. I try to reassure him as much as possible, but he worries about everything. It has gotten worse since Derek died. Whereas Jared is fearless, Kip is the opposite."

"I went through that as a boy when my parents died. I cried all the time. I didn't understand why they weren't coming back for Zach and me."

"When anything changes, he freaks out."

"I did, too. That's probably why I didn't do well in a lot of my foster care homes. Things changed all the time. When I couldn't control my life, I acted out. It took me growing up and getting to know the Lord to change that reaction. I'm trying to let Him control my life. But it isn't always easy to do."

"I used to feel that way and look what happened. My husband died and left me with a ton of debt to pay off. To top that, my boys are hurting with everything that has happened. To make ends meet, I had to move here, and they weren't happy about that."

"Because it is a change. Kids depend on stability."

"I wouldn't mind it, either."

He stepped closer in the foyer. "Whether we want it or not, chaos is coming in the form of Hurricane Naomi."

Jared came out of the den. "Kip won't let me hold Butch. I should get a turn, too."

"Ah, I wondered when Kip and Jared's truce would end," she whispered to Gideon then walked toward her son.

He'd wanted to ask questions about her situation, but this wasn't the time. There might never be a good time. It wasn't his business, but he cared about her and beneath her words he heard the pain she carried.

Wind and rain slashed at Kathleen's childhood home as though beating its fists against the exterior and demanding entrance. Sitting in a chair that Gideon had brought into the laundry room—the only interior room in the house—she watched her sons play Go Fish in the glow of the flashlight. Seated in the corner, her mother listened to the radio for any news concerning the hurricane raging outside. The howl of the wind continually pulled Kip's attention away from the game, to the frustration of his little brother.

"Why do we have to stay in here? I can't see what's going on." Jared tossed down his cards after losing again to his brother. "I'm bored."

Kathleen gestured toward two pallets on the floor. "Then try and sleep."

Jared shot her a look as if she'd gone crazy. "What if something happens? I've got to be ready."

Butch yelped at the door right before it opened, and Gideon came into the room. "Everything looks okay right now."

Static suddenly filled the air. "Oh, great, the radio station has been knocked off the air," her mother muttered.

His eyes huge, Kip scooped up Butch. "Did the hurricane get it?"

Her mother turned off the static noise. "No, honey. They either lost their backup power or the storm is interfering with their signal. Nothing to be concerned about."

Gideon picked his way through the pillows and blankets littering the floor to Kathleen and sat next to her. "The electricity is off up and down the street. I don't see any evidence of flooding." He turned his head away from the boys and lowered his voice, "But I think one of us should go out and check every fifteen minutes. The wind has picked up, and I see debris everywhere."

"I'll go next."

"Go where, Mom?" Kip asked, holding the dog close to him, laying his cheek against the animal.

"Just to check the house. We don't have windows in here to look out so it's a good thing to do that every once in a while."

"Why don't we camp out in the den? It's more comfortable." Standing against the washing machine, Kip followed Bubbles swimming around in circles.

"It's safer staying away from windows," Kathleen's mother answered, turning the radio on again and finding more static. Frowning, she switched it off.

The steady sound of the rain and wind hung in the silence that had descended. Even Jared bit his lower lip and hunkered down on the pallet.

"Why don't you listen to your music on your MP3 player?" Kathleen wished she had one to take her mind off the hurricane.

"I forgot mine at home when we packed our bags." Kip flinched when the noise increased in intensity.

"I've got mine." Jared reached for his backpack and dug into it. When he found it, he stuck the earplugs in and lay on the pallet.

The relentless sound pounding at the house continued. Kip chewed on his fingernails, looking at the ceiling. Finally he curled up on his blankets, burying Butch and him beneath the covers.

"I hope he goes to sleep, but I don't think that's going to happen," Kathleen whispered to Gideon.

The blanket flipped back and Kip sat up.

"I heard you. I can't sleep. Who can with all this noise?"

"Then why don't you tell me about the snowstorm you had in Denver where you lost your power. How many inches was it?" Gideon leaned forward, clasping his hands, resting his elbows on his thighs.

A crack and boom rent the air. Kip shot to his feet. Butch burrowed deeper into the covers. "What was that?"

"Tell Gideon about the snowstorm. I'll go check." Kathleen schooled her voice and her expression into a calmness she didn't feel. Inside, her heart thundered against her chest, and she squeezed her hands into fists to keep them from trembling. Kip didn't need to see that.

She pushed to her feet and hurried out of the room before her son saw fear on her face. Another sound reverberated through the air. Like a tree crashing into something nearby.

Since most of the windows were shuttered, Kathleen went to the front door and opened it slowly. It was protected from the direction the wind was coming, but she didn't want to take any chances. She knew the folly of going out in the storm, but she needed to discover the source of that noise. The yard had tall pines and live oak in it. She moved a couple of feet out onto the porch with Gideon's powerful flashlight.

When she peered out at the rain and wind lashing the ground at a forty-five-degree angle, she couldn't see anything. Through the early morning light she accounted for all the trees in front. As she started to back away and close the door, she noticed out of the corner of her eye the base of an up-rooted pine in Miss Alice's yard.

Quickly going into the house, Kathleen slammed the door closed and rushed into the garage where there was a taped window that faced Miss Alice's place. Through the strips she spied the pine. Its massive trunk halved the one-story house right where Miss Alice's bedroom was. Rain and wind whipped through the hole in the structure.

Kathleen remembered the older woman had planned to sleep while Hurricane Naomi raged outside.

Chapter Six

That Miss Alice was probably trapped beneath the pine tree gripped Kathleen with immobility for a few seconds as the howling wind vied with the drenching downpour. Then another crack followed by a boom propelled her into action. She whirled around and raced toward the door into the house. When she burst into the laundry room, Jared lay curled on his pallet, asleep finally, while Kip, buried by mounds of covers, stayed hidden with Butch.

Her mother glanced up. "What's wrong?"

In midstretch, Gideon riveted his attention to her.

"Miss Alice's house was struck by a tree right through her bedroom where she was going to be. We've got to help her."

Gideon bolted to his feet. "I'll go."

"No, not alone." Kathleen blocked his exit. "Mom, remain here with the boys. If you can get through to 911, let them know about Miss Alice."

"Hon, I doubt I'll be able to, but I'll try. What if Jared or Kip wakes up?"

"Tell them we went to help Miss Alice, and we'll be right back." Kathleen spun on her heel and moved into the hallway, waiting until Gideon left and closed the door.

"I heard another tree either go down or split, but I didn't see where."

"You should stay here." Gideon began donning his rain gear.

When Kathleen finished snapping her waterproof jacket, she grabbed her heavy-duty flashlight and started for the back door. "I'm a nurse. If something is wrong with Miss Alice, I might be able to help."

Right behind her, he stopped her progress. "I'm a paramedic. Let me handle this. You take care of your family."

She tapped his cast underneath the rain slicker. "With only one arm?"

He scowled. "Let's go. Take hold of me and stay close."

As she stepped out into the wind, its force nearly snatched her flashlight from her. She tightened her grip and lowered her head. She dragged one foot forward, then another, fighting the crosswinds and the driving rain. The beating of her heart battered at her chest as the hurricane battered Hope.

Gideon paused near the downed tree, inspecting what he could, but the downpour and high winds made it hard to see anything. Hugging the side of Alice's house, Kathleen used it to shelter herself from the fierce storm and continued toward the back door. She reached it and tried the handle. Locked. She peered back toward Gideon approaching her.

"It's locked. How do we get in?" Kathleen asked.

"I'll try to climb in through the hole the tree has created. There's a gap. I might fit," he yelled over the din of the hurricane.

"I might be able to better than you. Let me try first."

"But—"

"I have two arms I can use to climb." She started back the way she'd come.

Gideon dogged her steps, and when she arrived at the place where he thought he could get into the house, Kathleen examined it and wondered how she would get through the slit. She grabbed hold of the trunk, the rain pummeling her. Gideon positioned himself next to the tree, and she used him to hike herself up and into the small opening.

The wet bark scraped against her as she wiggled through the hole. Her raincoat snagged on a broken branch, stopping her progress. She yanked on her slicker and freed it, then slithered through the rest of the opening.

With her flashlight she inspected the area where the tree came down. All she could see was the edge of the bed. The pine obscured the rest of it. She stepped closer and peered through the limbs to see if she saw Miss Alice. The storm still hammered at her.

She knelt next to the bed and probed the green foliage for any sign of Miss Alice. She couldn't see anything. "Miss Alice!" she yelled several times over the noise of the storm. Even though her neighbor had intended to turn off her hearing aid, she had to try in case Miss Alice hadn't.

Standing, she hurried into the hallway and closed the bedroom door to keep some of the wind and rain out although part of the corridor's ceiling had caved in as well. She headed toward the kitchen to open the door for Gideon.

After letting him into the house, she pointed toward the dining room and living room. "Let's check the house. I didn't see her in her bedroom. Maybe she used her other one. Or maybe she's on the other side of her bed where I can't get." As she voiced that last fear, she sent a silent prayer to the

Lord that Miss Alice would be safe somewhere else in her house.

"We'll find her."

Kathleen swept her flashlight in a wide arc on half the dining room while Gideon took the other part, making her way toward the living room. *Please let Miss Alice be safe in her recliner as before.*

But when Kathleen entered the room ahead of Gideon and shone her light on the chair, its emptiness mocked her. "Where's Miss Alice's cat? I haven't seen or heard it."

"With her probably. Or hiding."

A slamming sound caused Kathleen to jump, nearly falling back into Gideon. He steadied her with one hand, then skirted her and strode toward the noise. In the hallway he slowed his quick pace. Kathleen spied the bedroom door she'd shut banging against the wall as the wind whipped through.

"Let's finish checking the rest of the house then recheck her bedroom." Gideon covered the distance to Miss Alice's other bedroom.

Kathleen took the closed door across the hall. When she entered the bathroom, she came to a halt, her light illuminating a sleeping Miss Alice on a small, blow-up mattress with her cat curled next to her.

"Gideon, she's in here." Kathleen knelt next to Miss Alice and shook her shoulder.

The woman's eyes popped open. For a few seconds confusion marked her expression until recognition dawned in her gaze. "Why are you here? I'm perfectly fine. I told you I was going to bed and sleep through this."

"Miss Alice, a pine tree fell on your house. On your bedroom. I was afraid you went to sleep in your bed."

The older woman's eyes grew round. "My bedroom? Something told me to set up in here. This is the only room without windows." She struggled to sit up.

Kathleen helped her. "Please come over to Mom's house. We'll help you. You've got a couple of other trees close to your house."

"I'll be all—"

Gideon moved into the bathroom. "Miss

Alice, do you want us to worry about you? Because we will if you don't come with us. There is no way we can leave you here with your house damaged like it is."

"A tree could fall on Ruth's house."

Gideon plowed his hand through his wet hair. "Yep, you're certainly right, but right now one hasn't. At least wind and rain aren't blowing through her place."

"What about my things?"

"You're more important than any of your possessions. I'll help you carry what you think is important."

"I've got to take Cottonballs. I can't leave him here." Miss Alice scooped up her white cat and held it against her chest. "Help me up. My knees don't work like they used to."

Gideon took Miss Alice's left arm while Kathleen clasped her right one, and they hoisted her to her feet.

"I have to have my pocketbook. I don't go anywhere without it."

"Where is it?" Kathleen scooted the air mattress back so Miss Alice could walk unhindered.

"In the bathtub along with some of my most prized possessions. I need them, too."

"I'll get them while Gideon helps you."

"Miss Alice, you'll need to stay close to me. The wind is fierce."

"Don't you worry about me, young man. I've been through some bad storms before. You don't live to be eighty-six and not. I could tell you some stories…" As she and Gideon made their way toward the kitchen, the roar of the wind streaming from the bedroom drowned out her words.

Kathleen turned toward the bathtub and saw Miss Alice's purse along with a sack of other items. Taking the paper bag, she panned the room for something to put her possessions into that wouldn't fall apart the minute she stepped outside. Finally, she dumped the contents of the trash can out on the floor and stuffed the sack down into it, then hurried into the hall.

Her slicker flapped in the wind coming from the bedroom. She didn't want to think of the damage being done to the inside of the house. In the kitchen, before she followed Gideon and Miss Alice and her cat out into the tempest, she drew in a fortifying breath.

Lord, please help us get back to Mom's safely.

A couple of hours later, Gideon opened the front door and stood in the entrance to Ruth's house, surveying the street. The rain still fell, backing up at the drains and flooding the road. He ran his fingers through his now-dry hair then kneaded the tight cords of his neck. Tension gripped him.

Limbs, leaves and debris cluttered the rain-soaked ground. Downed trees crisscrossed his neighbors' yards. A small magnolia in front of Ruth's lay uprooted and blocking the sidewalk. Months of work stretched before the town. It took a day to destroy, but it would take a long time to repair.

"How bad is it?" Kathleen came to his side to peer outside.

"We probably fared better than some

areas nearer the water. The storm surge was supposed to be bad. I think most of those people evacuated. At least I hope they did."

She clicked off her flashlight. Although it was daylight, a steady rain grayed the sky, and the shuttered windows darkened the interior of the house. "I'm afraid of what I'll find at the cottage. It sits at a lower elevation near the beach."

"When do you have to report to work?"

"I should go in as soon as possible. The people who've been at the hospital have been there for over twenty-four hours."

"I want to drive you. You said your car has been giving you problems. I don't want you to get stranded."

"Thankfully, the hospital isn't but a few miles from here. If I have to, I can walk."

He turned toward her, grasping her arm. "No, I will take you. It's going to be dangerous with flooding and downed power lines."

"I hate leaving Mom and the boys, but they need me at the hospital."

"Don't worry about them. I can stay here and help."

"Don't let Miss Alice go home. It isn't safe."

He grinned. "I'll do my best, but she's stubborn. I thought for a moment last night I was going to have to throw her over my shoulder and carry her out of her house."

"That would have been a sight, especially with your cracked ribs and broken arm."

"Yeah, I was doing some heavy-duty praying she'd agree without a fight."

The look in Kathleen's eyes softened. She took hold of his hand. "Thank you for being here. I think your presence helped the boys, especially Kip."

"It's much better to ride out a hurricane with someone than by yourself." Most of his life he had been by himself, but when he said that to Kathleen, he realized he meant every word. He'd felt needed and liked that feeling.

"I'd better get ready," Kathleen said with a deep sigh.

"I'll get my Jeep and be back to take you."

She turned back into the house and crossed to the hallway, using her flashlight to guide her. Gideon shut the front door and went to the kitchen to get into his rain gear, then he headed out the back and cut across Ruth's yard toward Miss Alice's, circling around toward the front. As he strode past her place, he took note of the extensive damage. Another tree had fallen on her porch and crashed through its roof, barely missing the main house.

When he arrived at his home, one of his shutters was ripped off its hinges and the window was broken, allowing rain into his place. He went inside and hurried to the front spare bedroom. Now that the wind wasn't driving the rain at an angle, water was no longer pooling on his hardwood floor. He would take Kathleen then come back to patch the hole the best he could. Maybe he could get Kathleen's sons to help him now that the rain had lessened and the wind had calmed. It would be good to keep them busy, especially Jared.

Ten minutes later he pulled up in front of

Ruth's. Kathleen came out before he could get out of his Jeep. She hurried toward his car and climbed into the passenger's side.

"Jared wanted to come with us. I told him he can't leave the house until it's safe."

"I thought I would see if Kip and Jared would help me repair one of my windows. Other than some rain damage in that bedroom, I think my house weathered the storm okay. I noticed some shingles off the roof and some branches down but nothing like Miss Alice's place."

"I went upstairs and the ceiling in my old bedroom is leaking so I'm sure Mom's roof has some problems, too."

"There's a lot of work to do, but first I need to get you to the hospital."

He came to a stop at the end of the block where a downed tree impeded his progress. Climbing from the Jeep, he started for the medium-size pine to move it. He grasped it and started dragging it, a grimace of pain on his face. Kathleen joined him and took hold of it as he did. Together they managed to drag it off the road enough to allow cars around it.

Back in the Jeep a few minutes later Gideon threw the car into Drive and pulled forward. "That probably won't be the only time we'll be doing that." He steered clear of a power line down on one side of the street and continued toward the hospital.

By the time he reached the front doors of Hope Memorial, his hand ached from gripping the steering wheel so tightly and the tension in his neck had intensified. What little he'd seen of the town left an impression of chaos, as though he'd driven through a war-torn area.

When he parked, he angled toward Kathleen. "When do you want me to pick you up?"

"My shift will end tomorrow morning at this time. We'll rotate teams until things calm down, but from the looks of the town that may be a while."

"This is the worst possible time to be on medical leave."

"But you are for a good reason." She touched his cast.

He captured her hand and laced his fingers through hers. "I know, but it doesn't make it any easier to accept it. Thanks for trying to make me feel better. The department can't curtail my activities around the neighborhood, though. I can focus my energy helping people on my street. There will be a lot to do there."

Smiling, Kathleen shook her head. "Why does that not surprise me? Just remember it has been less than a week since you were injured. Don't overdo it and make your situation worse. Promise me you'll take breaks, at least."

The concern in her expression warmed him. She had a kind heart. From what he'd seen, that made her a good nurse. But she was able to do her job while he wasn't. He had never been an inactive person, and it would be hard to start now, especially with all that had to be done.

He cocked his mouth into a grin. "I promise. I want to get better so I can go back to work."

She leaned across the seat and gave him a quick kiss on the cheek then opened the door and slipped out of his Jeep, leaving him to wonder about that brief touch of her lips on his cheek. He closed his eyes for a few seconds and could imagine the kiss all over again. He could smell her lingering scent of vanilla. The sensations she'd produced in him had nothing to do with friendship. Whoa! This was not good. He had no business being anything other than a friend to Kathleen. Neither of them was looking for anything more.

"Mr. Miller in room 320 is finally settled down. Per the doctor's orders, I increased his pain meds." Kathleen took the chart of the older man who had broken a hip when he fell off a ladder. She made some notes, then placed it back behind the counter at the nurses' station.

"We've been so busy I never got to ask you how Ruth fared in the hurricane." Mildred eased into a chair and massaged her temples. "I don't think I've slept in forty-eight hours."

"Who can sleep through a hurricane?" Kathleen snapped her fingers. "Oh, I forgot. Miss Alice slept through a good part of it until Gideon and I came to rescue her. Then she was up with us in the laundry room, refereeing between her cat and Gideon's dog. Not a pretty sight. The cat kept hissing the whole time. A couple of times his banshee cry rivaled the noise of the storm."

"Ah, poor thing. Alice Beggs can be a handful."

"Mom!"

Kathleen peered toward the stairs and spied Jared and Kip racing toward her. She held up her hand to slow them down, but Jared crashed into a doctor coming out of a patient's room, knocking the distinguished-looking man to the floor while Kip skidded to a halt a foot from him. Not far behind the boys, Gideon came down the hall, a frown on his face.

"Sorry, Kathleen. They got ahead of me racing up the stairs."

The six-foot-five doctor picked himself up from the floor and glared down at her sons. "No running in the hospital. We have injured people here, and I don't want to be one of them."

Jared leaned back and looked up at the man. "Sorry."

"What are you doing here?" Dr. Allen set his hands on his hips. "This isn't a playground."

"Mom works here." Jared pointed toward her, then turned his big eyes on the man, pure innocence in his expression. "I'm really sorry, sir. I won't run again."

And her son believed that until the next time. Kathleen quickly covered the space between Jared and Dr. Allen.

Dr. Allen straightened his white coat, saying, "I'm glad to hear that," then nodded toward her and made his way to another patient's room.

Jared grinned from ear to ear, turning on that little-boy look intended to melt her heart. "I'm sorry, Mom. I was just glad to see you."

"They worked so hard yesterday helping the neighbors and your mom clean up that I couldn't say no to coming with me to pick you up."

Jared spotted the head nurse behind the counter, waved and said in a loud voice that could carry beyond down the hall, "Hi, Miss Mildred. Do you need any help? I've been helping anyone that does."

Kip punched him in the arm. "Shh. This is a hospital. People are sleeping."

"But it's ten in the morning."

"Boys, why don't you go downstairs with Gideon? I'll be right there."

"We're parked in the left lot when you come out the front entrance. The other one is still blocked with a downed oak." Gideon grabbed Jared's hand before he shot for the stairs.

Mildred came up behind Kathleen. "Go home and sleep. Be with your sons. I'll see you in two days."

"Call me on my cell if someone can't

come in. I don't live too far away, and we are in okay shape." With cell reception working some of the time, she'd talked to her mother yesterday evening, and she reconfirmed what Kathleen had thought. Her childhood home didn't have too much damage, especially compared to Miss Alice's house and others she saw on the way to the hospital.

"Knowing Ruth, she has the neighborhood organized with the cleanup."

Kathleen walked into the room behind the counter and pulled her purse out of her locker. "You know my mother well," she said with a laugh. "The trick will be getting some rest before I'm put on a work crew. How about you? When are you going home?"

"I'm camping out here for a few more days. I don't have family and unfortunately my duplex near the beach didn't make it. Thankfully I was here, but one of my neighbors let me know when he went back after evacuating."

"Then you need to come to Mom's. She has the room."

"Aren't you and your sons staying with her? And how about Alice?"

"I hadn't planned on it, but with all that has happened here I haven't had time to check about Mom's rental I was living in. It wasn't as close as you were to the beach so it might be all right. Still, you know Mom will insist. You are like family."

Mildred smiled, a tired gesture because she'd been working for two straight days. "I'll think about it. Now you'd better go before your boys overpower that nice young man and come looking for you."

Kathleen laughed at the image that came to mind. "Don't forget there's a place for you if it doesn't work out at your sister's. The hospital isn't where you should stay. You'll work all the time."

"We're mighty busy, but I could use a break."

Kathleen hugged Mildred then walked toward the stairs. Five minutes later she climbed into the front passenger seat of

Gideon's Jeep while Jared and Kip were sitting still and quiet.

"Okay, what have you done with my sons?" She slid a look toward the backseat.

"We're being good." Jared folded his hands in his lap.

"Yeah, Mom. We want to go to our house, and if we don't act good, Gideon will take us back to Nana's."

"Oh, I see." She straightened forward, slanting a glance toward Gideon. "We're going by the cottage?"

"Your mom wanted me to check on it. We've heard that area was flooded."

"Why didn't someone tell me?" She'd thought about it while working then another emergency had come in and she hadn't had time. That had been her past twenty-four hours—one crisis after another.

"Because your mom didn't want you to worry. We had so much to do in the neighborhood yesterday just to make it safe. We didn't have time for anything else. A couple of people have generators. One is keeping food cold. Another is where people can do their laundry. I brought mine down to your mom's since y'all and Miss Alice are staying there. Between those two generators they're cooking a hot meal for everyone on the street. Your mom has set up headquarters for the hurricane cleanup."

"Headquarters?"

"She has organized all of us. She's very good at getting things done."

"Miss Alice didn't demand to go home?"

"At first, until she saw her house. She may be stubborn, but she's not a fool. She's actually settled in at your mom's quite well. Now, her cat is another thing."

"Is Butch still there?"

He turned onto the street where the rental cottage was. "I fixed my window so there won't be anymore rain damage, and Butch is happily back at his house."

Kathleen scanned the houses where she lived, sucking in a deep breath and holding it. The sight of the destruction churned her stomach. She could see where the water had come up to houses—some over their first story. The smell of rotting vegetation and rancid water saturated the air, causing her stomach to roil even more.

Gideon pulled into the driveway and switched off his engine. The silence from the backseat spoke of the horrific sight where the cottage used to be. All that was left was the foundation with pieces of what could be their place scattered around it, but Kathleen couldn't tell for sure. The neighboring homes were gone too, as if a surge of water had focused its power on this area that dipped down. It probably had formed a river in the middle of the hurricane.

"Mom, where are our things?" Kip finally asked in a choked voice.

"I don't know, honey. Maybe we'll be able to find some out there." She waved her hand toward the litter mixed in with the dead foliage and tree limbs. She thought she saw Kip's skateboard sticking out from under a pile of debris, but wasn't sure.

She heard the back door open and angled around. "Jared, I don't want you getting out."

Tears shone in his eyes. "Why not? We've got to look for our stuff."

"Tell you what. I'll check the area out and make sure it's safe and then you all can come over and go through everything. How about tomorrow?" Gideon started his Jeep.

Jared slammed the door closed. "What if it rains today?"

Kathleen bit her lower lip, her own tears making her vision blurry. "Hon, I don't think that will make a difference. If it's out there, it has survived a hurricane. A little rain won't hurt it. Everything we had can be replaced." Except the pictures and a few treasures, but she didn't want to say anything about them right now. It was hard enough seeing the destruction. "Let's go to Mom's."

Gideon sent her a reassuring smile. "I'll take care of it later today."

"I appreciate that." The sight of what was left of her cottage drained what little energy she had. The past two days had finally crashed down on her. All she wanted to do was sleep.

* * *

Later that afternoon as she awakened from a long nap, the scent of coffee brewing drifted to Kathleen. The aroma lured her to full alertness. She glanced at the battery-operated clock on the nightstand and bolted up in bed. Four o'clock. She hadn't wanted to sleep almost the entire day. Now she wouldn't get to sleep later tonight. That thought broke the dam on her emotions she'd kept reined in ever since she'd seen the destroyed cottage.

Her tears finally streamed down her face, flowing freely. Could things get any worse? Hope was devastated. The house she'd been living in was gone. She was drowning in debt her husband had accrued. Her sons were hurting emotionally. The tears turned to sobs that shook her. She drew her legs up against her chest and clasped them. For so long she'd been desperate to hold it together. Now she couldn't.

A soft knock at the bedroom door startled her. She tried to scrub away the evidence of her sorrow as she asked, "Who is it?" If it had been her sons, they would have burst into the room.

"Gideon."

She glanced down. Having no energy to change when she got home at ten-thirty this morning, she still wore her blue scrubs. As she swung her legs over the side of the bed, she continued to swipe at her tears.

"Are you all right?"

She stood—too fast. The room swirled before her eyes, still swimming with tears. "Yes. Be right there."

Steadying herself, she started for the door but caught sight of herself in the mirror. A gasp escaped her lips as she stared at the hollow look in her gaze staring back at her. Other than holing herself up in the bedroom, there'd be no way he wouldn't know she'd been crying. Inhaling several times, she opened the door.

He peered at her with an intensity that robbed her of the decent breath she'd just taken in. "Can I come in? I went by your house again while you were sleeping."

She stepped to the side and allowed him

into her childhood bedroom, then shut the door. She didn't want her sons to overhear anything concerning the house. They already had enough to deal with.

"I'm glad I did. I found a nest of snakes under a pile of limbs and lots of boards with nails sticking up, but I think I've made the area safe enough for you and your sons. There are a lot of items among the debris that might be yours. It's hard for me to tell."

Kathleen sank down on her bed. "I don't want Jared or Kip going back there right now. I'll go over tomorrow and look around. They've lost so much. I don't want them to see their possessions destroyed. If I find any of their stuff, I'll bring it back."

"You know they won't like that. They've been very quiet today, but when they talk, they discuss what they're going to do when they go back home."

"Home?" The word came out on a shaky breath. Tears clogged her throat. She didn't want to cry in front of Gideon. She'd shed enough tears over the past year since her husband's death but always in private. "I don't know what that is anymore. When I came back to Hope, I felt this would be it. I wanted to make a home for my sons. I had hoped I could save enough money to buy the rental from Mom eventually. It was starting to feel like a home to me. Mom wanted to give me the cottage, but I wanted to make this work on my terms. This hurricane changed everything."

The overwhelming sense of loss suddenly hit her. She could no longer contain the sorrow. It swelled up and spilled down her cheeks.

Gideon put his arm around her and tugged her close to him. "You aren't alone."

Through the sobs, she mumbled, "I know the whole town feels that way right now." She swallowed hard, trying to tamp down her tears. What good did they do?

"No, I mean the Lord is with you through this. He is here to give us what we need."

"I need a home for Jared and Kip even if it is a two-bedroom house and they have to share a room. It was our home. We had one in Denver until it was repossessed and we had to move."

He tilted up her chin so their gazes connected. "Your home isn't a physical place. It's people. I know. I've been searching for one most of my life."

For a few seconds she thought she saw bleakness in his expression, but it vanished so quickly she wasn't sure. But he was hurting, too, and it had nothing to do with Hurricane Naomi. "What happened?"

"I lost my parents to a fire when I was eight. My brother and I were put in foster care and finally he was adopted. I wasn't. I had a lot of anger. Not your easiest child to handle. Zach's family moved away and over the years I've lost touch with him. He was five years younger than me and I couldn't keep us together. I blew it."

"Have you tried to find him?"

"Yes. I connected with him finally online about six months ago. He's serving in the marines and is overseas right now. I don't think he really remembers me. He was only four when he was adopted."

"I'm sorry. Don't give up on him."

"I'm not, but I'm not getting my hopes up that I'll suddenly have my brother back."

She came from a large extended family, many with roots around Hope. She couldn't image her life without them. Sniffing, she took his hand. "I know that my boys fight a lot, but they really love each other. If anyone threatened Jared, Kip would be there defending his brother and the reverse would be true. I've seen it happen right after they were yelling at each other."

"My family now is Station Two. The guys would do anything for each other. If Zach and I ever get together, fine, but I'm not counting on it."

"The people at the hospital are becoming an extended family to me. The way I've seen them coming together during this crisis awes me. Mildred—Nurse Ratched to you—is staying at the hospital. Mostly I think because she wants to let others stay home to help with their families. She doesn't have one. I hear she's always filling in during the major holidays so people can be with family."

He winced. "Okay, let's agree to forget my name for Mildred."

"I don't know. I may not let you live that one down."

"What can I do to change your mind?"

"Hmm. I'll have to think about that."

"When things calm down, I'll give Kip a grand tour of Station Two."

"You were already going to do that."

"A ride in a fire truck."

Kathleen tapped her chin with her forefinger. "Tempting. I'll keep that in mind."

Gideon rose and tugged her up, her body close to his. His masculine scent surrounded her, and the gleam in his eyes warmed her as the feel of his hand on her arm sent shivers down her spine. "I'm just gonna have to persuade you I'm one of the good guys."

He dipped his head toward her. Every nerve became alert, anticipating the meeting of their lips. Wanting it. She leaned toward him.

A knock sounded on the partially open door and her mother stuck her head through the opening. "I can't find Jared and Kip. They told me they were going upstairs to play in their room for a while. I went there to get them to do something for me and they aren't there. I've looked everywhere in the house and even in the yard. They're gone."

Chapter Seven

Kathleen quickly stepped away from Gideon. "Do you think they went to help someone in the neighborhood?"

"They've been helping the Johnsons but they've been good about letting me know and getting my okay." Ruth pushed the door open wide.

"Would they have gone back to the cottage?" Gideon headed for the hallway. "I can go look for them."

"They know never to leave the block without talking to me first or Mom and that is without a hurricane." Kathleen followed Gideon into the corridor.

"Gideon might be right about the cottage. I heard them whispering before they decided to go play in their room. That in itself should have been a red flag, but I've been cooking all afternoon so people on the block can have one hot meal a day. For a while they were helping me."

"Since this house is in the middle of the block, I'll go one way toward the cottage and you go the other," Gideon told Kathleen, then strode toward the front door. "We'll find them."

"Mom, you go on and finish cooking. Don't worry." Kathleen joined Gideon on the porch, the creases on her forehead deepening. "Now if only I could follow my own advice."

"Maybe they thought they could join me while I was over there. One of the neighbors helped and then I went to the fire station to see if there was anything I could do there. The boys wouldn't have known that."

"I'll go this way." Kathleen pointed east.

Gideon made his way to the end of the block and turned the corner, glancing back at Kathleen who'd been stopped by a neighbor. When he started down the street where the cottage was, he spied Kip out in front. He quickened his pace.

Kip looked up from digging through a pile of trash, grinned and waved at him. Hopping up, he yelled to Jared then ran down the middle of the road toward him. The boy's foot caught on a limb on the ground and he went flying forward, hitting the asphalt with a jolt.

Gideon rushed to the child, who had tears rapidly filling his eyes. Kip rolled over and held up his hands. They were bleeding. Gideon knelt next to him, noticing his jeans were torn at one knee. "Are you okay?" Taking Kip's hands, he examined the palms.

"It hurts."

"I know. It needs to be cleansed. Let me help you up."

The boy pushed up to a sitting position but didn't move any more than that. Suddenly he burst out crying and hugged his arms to his chest, rocking back and forth.

For a moment Gideon didn't know what to do.

"Besides your hands, where else does it hurt?"

"Everything is gone. I can't find anything of mine."

Gideon settled his hand on Kip's shoulder. "You might not be able to. I know how hard that can be."

Kip looked up at him, his eyes shiny, tears coursing down his face. "But your house is all right."

"When I was about your age, my home burned down. Everything was destroyed. All I had was the clothes I had on when I escaped from the house."

Kip's gaze widened. "It did? What did you do?"

"Exactly what you did. I got upset. Then I grew very angry at the world. In the long run, that didn't help me at all. I pushed everyone away, even people who were trying to help me. I became so difficult that I ended up being moved from foster home to foster home. I never stayed in one place long. I was the one hurt by that."

"Like Mom moving here?"

"Not exactly. You still have your brother and mother. She will provide a home for you even if that means living with your grandmother. Y'all will be together."

Kip dropped his head and knuckled his eyes.

"I'm not gonna kid you. The next months will be hard. Everyone in Hope will have to pull together to put the town back even better than it was. You and your brother will have to do your part. The more united we are, the faster Hope will recover."

The child lifted his face, squaring his shoulders. "I can do my part."

"C'mon. Let's go get Jared. Your mom is worried about you two. She should be here shortly." Gideon rose and offered Kip his hand.

As the boy struggled to his feet, grimacing as he put weight on his leg with the torn jeans, Gideon saw Kathleen hurrying down the street toward them. A frown carved deep lines into her face.

"Kip, what happened?"

"I tripped, but I'm okay," he said in his tough-boy voice Gideon remembered using even while inside he'd been hurting.

"I found your skateboard," Jared shouted, holding it up.

"My skateboard!" Kip limped toward his little brother and took it from him. He turned and grinned at Gideon and his mother. "I didn't lose everything."

"How am I supposed to get angry at them when I see that?" Kathleen whispered, shifting toward him.

"Kip and I talked. They're scared. Everything familiar to them has been changing lately. They came over here to find anything of theirs they could cling to. I remember when I escaped the fire at my home, I grabbed my baseball card collection my dad and I started. It was my most prized possession."

"Do you still have it?"

Memories washed through him, sharpening the pain of loss. "At one of my foster homes someone stole it from me. I thought I knew who had it and started a fight with him. He didn't have it, but it got me thrown out of the house. It had been the last straw with the couple I lived with."

Kathleen covered her mouth and shook her head. "You never found it?"

"No. But no one can take away the memories I have of my dad and me going to the store, deciding who to buy, putting it in a scrapbook."

Kathleen cleared her throat and turned back toward her children. "Do you mind if we take a little while to look around for the boys? Maybe there is something besides the skateboard."

"I was going to suggest that. At least until we find something of Jared's."

She threw him a grin as she moved toward her sons. "Or it gets dark."

"Good idea. Besides, your mother was determined to fix a big batch of spaghetti for everyone."

Kip heard Gideon. "Spaghetti! This day is getting better and better."

Kathleen stopped next to Jared. "Let's see what we can find of yours."

"Mom, I've looked everywhere. I don't think there is anything. At least I've got Bubbles at Nana's."

Gideon stood back for a few seconds while Kathleen and Jared went to a pile of items he'd stacked up earlier after clearing some debris and limbs away. These past few days had made him think about having a family. Years ago he'd given up on that idea. He'd been determined to go it alone in the world. But being with Kathleen and her sons revived that dream he'd had as a little boy. He'd been by himself for so long he didn't know if it were possible.

Half the neighborhood sat in her mother's living and dining rooms. Kathleen handed the last person to arrive a plate with spaghetti. Someone else had brought a pre-mixed salad and another person had two loaves of French bread. As she scanned the faces of the people on the street, tired expressions met her perusal but each person gave her a smile.

When everyone was served and had a seat, her mother stood in the wide entrance between the two rooms and said, "I'd like to offer a blessing." After several people bowed their heads, she closed her eyes and continued, "Lord, I know You are here with us even if at times it doesn't seem like it. We need You. We need Your help rebuilding Hope. Bless this food we are sharing and the people who are gathered here. Amen."

A few around Kathleen murmured amen, but there were some people who grumbled. At the moment she didn't know what to feel. She fought the urge to shut down physically and mentally, but spiritually she was teetering on a ledge—ready to fall any second.

Gideon leaned toward her. "You okay?"

"Yeah, I'm still trying to sort out all my feelings. I feel like I'm at a boxing match and I'm down for the count. And it looks like most of the people are experiencing that, too."

"There's a lot to do in the coming months."

"Jared informed me earlier today that Christmas isn't too far away."

"The first of November is in a few days. I can't believe it."

"I think Jared wants to start a new rock collection. He was disappointed that he couldn't find it at the house."

"There's still more to go through. It might turn up."

"I'm not telling him that, or he'll get his hopes up. I don't want him to be any more disappointed than he was when we left the cottage this afternoon."

"What was it kept in? That way I'll know what to look for."

"It was in a wooden chest. He'd carved his name into it and about scared me to death. He'd gotten a hold of his dad's pocketknife. I wondered why he was so quiet. When I found him in his room, he had all but the 'd' carved in the box. Kip had helped him. The rocks are some we found on our hikes in Colorado." *When we were a family before the trouble started.* "He had a rock tumbler that polished them and made them shiny."

"And that's gone, too. That doesn't mean we can't collect rocks around here."

"He already has. He found one on the ground by the cottage and put it in his pocket."

"Kids have a way of bouncing back."

Kathleen chuckled. "Probably before us adults." Her gaze found Miss Alice sitting in a chair with a stool because her mother didn't have a recliner like Miss Alice was used to. "I hear she threatened to go home when she discovered there was no recliner here."

Gideon followed the direction of her look. "I fixed that stool for her. She calmed down after that."

"I imagine being here with Kip and Jared is a bit much for her. She never married and had children. I don't think she's been around very many."

Kip approached Miss Alice and said

something to her. Handing Kip her plate, the older lady smiled, a dimple actually appearing in her wrinkled face. He darted away and threaded his way through the crowd as the neighbors finished and began standing.

"Mom told me that he's been trying to help her, whereas Jared is staying as far away from her as he can living in the same house."

Tom Baker, who lived across the street, stopped in front of Gideon. "Some of us are going to help remove the tree and cover the hole in Miss Alice's house tomorrow. The weatherman is saying there could be rain in a few days."

"Great. I want to help. What time?"

"We're thinking eight. It's gonna take a good part of the day. Her house is the worst one hit on the block."

"I'll be there."

Tom nodded at Gideon. "I figured you would say that. Do you have a chainsaw?"

"Yes."

"We'll need it."

"Is there anything I can do?" Kathleen asked.

Tom peered at her. "We could use some people to help haul the branches away."

"I can do that. Does Miss Alice know?"

The man stared down at the floor for a moment, dragging his hand through his hair. "I figured you could tell her. You two have a way with her."

Kathleen pressed her lips together to keep from laughing. Miss Alice's reputation was far worse than the woman really was. "I will."

"Good. We aim to help everyone on this street, even Miss Alice."

When he left, Gideon shifted toward her. "What about your house?"

"It's gone. There isn't much we can do now but look for some of our possessions. If we have time, we'll do it tomorrow afternoon."

"We? You mean Jared and Kip?"

"Yes, today I realized they need to do that. They need some closure. We'll be staying at Mom's for a while. I think it will help them to understand the why of the tragedy by helping others and cleaning up the mess at the cottage."

"Besides, it will keep them out of trouble if they're working."

"Well, that, too. At least until school resumes."

"At the fire station I heard that might not be for a couple of weeks. Some of the schools sustained serious damage. The one on the Point flooded. They're going to have to find another place for the children to go to school—at least for most of the rest of the school year."

"Mom!"

A silence fell over the room at the sound of Jared's yell.

"Mom! Cottonballs is gonna eat Bubbles."

All gazes turned to her. She rose. Miss Alice struggled to sit forward in her chair.

"I'll take care of this, Miss Alice." Kathleen hurried from the room and up the stairs with Gideon following.

Upstairs in the room Kip and Jared

shared at her Mom's, she found Jared holding a dripping wet white cat. Kathleen immediately looked at the goldfish, which was swimming around the bowl as though nothing had happened.

"He's a menace. We need to lock him up until he leaves." Jared's forehead was scrunched, his eyebrows slashing down. He held at arm's length a wiggling Cottonballs with his claws out, waiting to sink into something soft like flesh.

Gideon crossed the room and gingerly took the cat from Jared. The beast kept squirming, determined to get back to his food in the bowl. "I'll take him to Miss Alice."

After Gideon left, she shut the door and turned toward her son. "Let's keep this closed while Cottonballs is staying here."

"Why is he, Mom? Miss Alice is always frowning at me. She doesn't like me."

"Have you tried to talk to her?"

"Well, no. What do I say to her? She isn't like Nana. I've heard her yell at kids in her yard."

"I don't think she is used to kids."

"What do you mean?"

Kathleen sat on the twin bed nearest her. "She isn't around children much."

Jared gave her a confused look.

"Sometimes kids require a certain kind of patience not everyone has."

"I was thinking the same thing about Miss Alice."

"Hon, it won't be too long. Once her house is livable she'll want to leave. Put yourself in her shoes. She has always lived alone. Now all of a sudden she is living with two children and two adults. She knows Nana, but she really doesn't know us well. We're all family. She isn't part of our family and may be lonely. Maybe she feels left out a little. And she can't do much to help everyone with cleanup."

"Why not? She could help Nana fix the meals."

"You're right. I don't think anyone has asked her. But remember, Jared, she's a guest in our home."

"This isn't our home. It's Nana's. We

don't—" His voice caught. "We don't have a home."

"Yes, we do. Home is where we are together even if it is at Nana's. We might not have a house or apartment for a while, but we have a home."

He cocked his head to the side. "Why can't we?"

"Because we were not the only ones who lost their house. There will be a shortage of places to live until people can rebuild. That will take time."

"Like Miss Alice's house?"

"Yeah. Her place will need extensive work to be livable again."

"While Nana's and Gideon's don't?"

"You're right. We only sustained minor damage compared to others." Kathleen shoved to her feet. "Now I need to go help Nana clean up. Are you coming downstairs?"

"No, I need to make sure Bubbles is all right."

Kathleen hugged Jared. "I love you. Everything will be all right in time."

As she left her sons' room and descended the steps to the ground floor, she wondered if everything really would be all right in time. She hoped—prayed—it would be, but she felt buried under a pile of rubble the storm created.

Seeing the house cleared of neighbors now that darkness was settling outside, Kathleen checked in the den where the sleeper sofa was set up for Miss Alice to see if she needed anything. The woman wasn't in the room. Voices coming from the kitchen drew her toward it. When she entered, she found Miss Alice drying the dishes while her mom washed and Gideon put them away in the cabinets.

"This is an efficient team. I guess you all don't need me."

Gideon slanted a look over his shoulder then continued to stack the glasses into the cupboard. "Yeah, we'll have this cleaned up in no time. Miss Alice was telling us about her first job when she was a young girl. She was a dishwasher in a fancy restaurant in New Orleans. I've eaten in the place a couple of times."

"You lived in New Orleans, Miss Alice? I thought you'd lived here all your life."

"Child, I lived all over the world until I was thirty and retired to Hope."

"Retired? At thirty?" Kathleen bridged the distance between them and made herself busy putting away the rest of the food.

"That's what I call it when I stopped traveling and put down roots in one place. I chose Hope for that."

"Why?" Gideon took the dried plate from Miss Alice.

"It was smaller fifty years ago, quaint and hospitable. I didn't want a big city where I didn't know many people. You might not believe this, but at one time I was a mover and shaker here in Hope. I've been through my share of hurricanes. I even organized groups to deal with the aftereffects here in town."

Kathleen shut the pantry door. "What did you do?"

"If people group together, the cleanup can

go faster. A lot like what you've gotten this neighborhood to do, Ruth."

Her mother grinned at Miss Alice. "At your suggestion."

"Like what we're doing right now, cleaning up after dinner. Teamwork." Miss Alice's eyes twinkled as they fell on Gideon. "Like you do as a firefighter."

"It's hard fighting a fire without teamwork." Gideon put away the last dish.

What happened to Miss Alice while she was upstairs? Kathleen wondered. For the past couple of days, the old woman had been depressed and quiet but for now. Kathleen stared at her, trying to figure out the change.

Miss Alice caught her attention and winked. "It was Kip who reminded me I still have a lot to give. That I could still be part of the team."

Kathleen's mouth fell open, feeling as though the woman had read her mind.

"When Gideon brought Cottonballs downstairs a while ago, Kip hurried and took my cat, telling me he would take care of him. He knew I must be tired so I should rest. I suddenly realized that had been the way I had been acting for the past two days. No more. I may be eighty-six years young, but I'm not gone yet. So tomorrow I'll be at my house helping with whatever I can."

"You know what the neighbors are going to do?"

Miss Alice grinned. "Gideon broke the news to me. I may be set in my ways, but not that set, I can't appreciate the help." She folded the dish towel and shuffled toward the door that led into the hallway. "With that in mind, I need to get my sleep so I'll be ready. Good night. Ruth, the dinner was delicious."

When Miss Alice left, Kathleen swung her gaze between Gideon and her mother. "Is that the same lady who we kept over here during the storm and sat in a chair, not speaking or doing a thing for hours?"

"I've heard stories about Miss Alice in her younger days. She's right. She was a regular dynamo. Then about fifteen years ago she stopped going to church, being involved with others and holed herself up in her house. I was never sure why." Kathleen's mother started for the same exit. "I think I'll follow her. Good night."

Kathleen released a slow breath. "It's only eight but I feel like I've been up for the whole day instead of four hours."

"A lot has happened in that time."

"I'm tired but not sleepy."

"Me, too."

"Where did Kip go?"

"To feed Cottonballs and settle him in the laundry room. I guess I probably should also leave. I have some work I want to do at home."

"In the dark? We have your generator."

"I have lanterns like you do."

"Stay." The word came out before Kathleen could censure it, but she didn't want to be alone at the moment.

"I should— Okay, for a little bit."

Out of the corner of her eye, Kathleen saw a flash dart by the doorway. "Why don't we go out on the porch so little boys with big ears don't eavesdrop?"

Gideon glanced toward the entrance and laid his forefinger over his mouth. "Surely you don't mean Jared or Kip?" he asked as he crept out of the kitchen through the dining room.

"Well, they have been known to listen when they shouldn't. You can never tell if…"

A roar erupted in the hallway followed by a yelp from Kip. Two seconds later her older son and Gideon came into the room.

"Look who I found standing by the door. Listening."

"Imagine that. My son with the big ears."

Kip frowned. "I don't have big ears. Jared does, but I don't."

"No, I don't," Jared squeaked from the dining room.

Kathleen made her way to where the sound came from and peeked around the door. "Come out. What were you doing behind there?"

Jared trudged into the kitchen, his eyes downcast. "If Kip can listen, so can I."

"Both of you need to get ready for bed. Now."

"But, Mom, it's only eight-twenty, and we don't even have school tomorrow." Kip's mouth twisted into a frown that he shot at his brother. "See what you made Mom do."

"I did not."

"Jared. Kip. Enough. We have a lot to do tomorrow, and we need to get up early. I don't want two cranky kids. That's why you're going to bed a little early. I understand from Nana you both were up late last night. You've got some sleep to make up."

"I don't need a lot of sleep. Besides, I shouldn't have to go to bed at the same time as Jared. I'm older. Age should have some privileges."

"I agree. And I'm older than both of you. So I get the privilege of you two listening to me then doing exactly what I say."

"But that's not what I meant."

"Go." Kathleen fluttered her hand toward the hallway.

"See you two tomorrow bright and early. I'm going to need two helpers. I can't do all I would like to do because of my cast." Gideon struggled to maintain a serious expression, but the second they disappeared into the hall, he chuckled.

"I heard that," Kip said right before he stomped up the stairs.

Gideon laughed even more. "Finally alone at last," he said to Kathleen.

"You think this will last? You don't know my boys. They'll come up with one excuse after another to come down here just so they can stay up."

He grabbed her hand and tugged her toward the foyer. "Then let's escape onto the porch like you suggested."

"Great minds think alike."

As Kathleen shut the front door, she glimpsed Kip at the top of the stairs staring down at them. When he saw her, he turned around and went into his room.

The cool night air washed over Kathleen. She sat next to Gideon on the top step and surveyed the neighborhood. Dim lights, from candles and lanterns, shone from some of the houses, the only illumination on the street. The darkness hid the piles of debris and torn up landscape. Across from them, Tom Baker had a tarp over part of his roof covering a hole where some of the shingles had blown away. The place next to him had its carport ripped away from the house, pieces of it lying scattered all over the yards along the street.

The scent of salt water drifted to her, reminding her of how far the Gulf came ashore and covered the area near the beaches and swamped the whole peninsula known as the Point in Hope. The sea retreated but had left its mark on the town, the stench of dead fish and rotting vegetation.

Gideon laid his flashlight down beside him. "When I went to the station, I felt so useless. An alarm went off while I was there, and I had to stand by and watch the others leave to fight the fire."

"I'm so sorry. I'm the reason you're in that situation."

"Hold it. That isn't the reason I told you that. You're not to blame for my injury. I thought we were past that. What do I have to do to make you understand that?"

Her husband had always made her feel she was the cause of things that had gone wrong in their marriage. As though she had been the one to get them into debt. She'd begun to wonder if she was the reason. Had Derek thought she'd wanted a new car or a swimming pool? She hadn't, but he'd acted as if she had.

"Old habits die hard." Placing her elbows on the tops of her thighs, she leaned forward and clasped her hands.

"What do you mean?"

"According to my husband, I was the reason everything went wrong." She turned toward him and realized how close he was to her on the step. Their arms brushed against each other. His coffee-laced breath mingled with the night scents. Her heartbeat reacted to his nearness by speeding up. "Don't get me wrong. I know marriage is a two-way street. We rushed into it. I think I was in love with the idea of marriage. I won't make that mistake again."

"What mistake?"

"Marrying. The year before Derek died I felt like I had to guard everything I said. I even went to the doctor because I was so anxious. I would cry at the drop of a hat. I was always so tired, and it wasn't from work like it is now. My husband didn't want me to work after Kip was born. I agreed with him." *To keep the peace.*

Gideon covered her hands with his. "You'll feel different with time. It hasn't been that long since he passed away."

She nodded. "Fifteen months. But I don't think time will make a difference."

"You're a great mother, patient with your sons even when they test you. You might want to marry again, have another child. Your mom told me you once said you wanted six kids."

"I was fourteen. When did she tell you that?" She was going to have to keep an eye on her mother. Next she would be bringing out her baby pictures to show Gideon. She knew what her mom was up to, and she needed to put a stop to it.

"When she was quizzing me about when I was going to start a family. I don't think your mother knows the meaning of the word subtle."

"I'm finding that out lately. Don't mind her. She thinks the answer to my problems is a man. She doesn't understand a man got me into the mess I'm in." The second she said that her cheeks flamed, heat radiating down her neck. "I mean…"

His hold on her cupped hands tightened as he shifted toward her. "Shh. I understand perfectly."

In the soft glow she could barely make out his face. But she couldn't read the expression on it. Which meant he couldn't read hers. Relief trembled through her because embarrassment still heated her cheeks. The cool breeze flowed over her, but it did little to ease the warmth suffusing her.

"This past week you and your family have kept me sane. You have given me a purpose at a time when I haven't been feeling so useful. You have to understand I'm a man of action. That came to a grinding halt with the accident."

She opened her mouth to tell him she was sorry again, but he covered her lips with his fingers.

"Not a word about you causing it or I will leave."

"Do you always threaten friends?" She tried to school her voice into a serious tone, but laughter leaked through.

"I'm not answering that on the grounds that it might incriminate me." He cradled her face in his large palm. "When do you go back to the hospital?"

"The day after tomorrow. I think we'll be back on our regular schedule soon unless something further happens. How about you? When do you report to headquarters for desk duty?"

He groaned. "Don't remind me. In two days, but I guess it's better than doing nothing."

The feel of his skin against hers momentarily robbed her of speech. She frantically tried to put together a coherent sentence, but every inch of her was aware of the man sitting next to her, so close his breath fanned her chin. "You call what you've been doing nothing, and you've been doing it with only one arm. I certainly have appreciated all your hard work around here and at the cottage."

"I'm glad." He bent a few more inches toward her, their mouths only a breath away.

Her pulse accelerated. Her throat went dry. Her stomach tightened.

His hand ran down her jawline until he took hold of her chin and tilted it up toward him. Her lips parted as she inhaled deeply.

Chapter Eight

All evening Gideon had wanted to kiss Kathleen, so when his lips touched hers, it felt right. Better than right. He wound his arm around her and drew her to him. His mouth settled on hers as he deepened the kiss, pouring into it all the feelings he'd experienced whenever he was near her. Earlier, he'd watched her mouth move as she talked, smiled or frowned. He'd wondered what it would feel like when his moved over hers. Now he knew.

But in the back of his mind he heard Kathleen's words again. She didn't want to become involved with any man. She'd been burned by her deceased husband. She had been warning him. And he needed to listen.

When she slid her arms around his neck, he pulled back, his ragged breath sounding in the sudden quiet of night. "I'd better be going."

Pushing to his feet, he hovered over her. She peered up at him, but he didn't want to see her expression. He wanted to think she enjoyed the kiss, at least some. But he also needed to remember she didn't want to get involved with a man. He had lost too many special people in his life. There was no way he would go through that kind of pain again. So he had to back off before he fell in love and ended up hurt.

"Good night. I'll see you tomorrow." He descended the remaining two steps, wanting to stay and pursue the feelings rampaging through him, but needing to go because of those feelings. He pivoted and started down the sidewalk.

"Gideon."

He stopped and turned but he didn't say

anything. No words would describe the conflict raging in him.

"I— Thank you for your help today."

"Anytime." This time he rotated around and hurried away.

Kathleen watched Gideon almost flee from her. What just happened?

She ran her fingers across her lips. *I was kissed by a dynamite, caring man. I was...*

She didn't know what to think. Instead, she sat there letting her feelings dominate her—no, overwhelm her. From her hammering heartbeat to the tingling awareness of everything about Gideon.

What made him stop and pull away?

Did I do something wrong?

Derek's rejections the last year and a half of their marriage mocked her. Would she ever be free of those memories?

She stood, pulling in deep breaths over and over to calm her. She hadn't come to Hope to find a man. She didn't believe, like her mother, that a man was the solution to her problems. A man had put her into debt, attacked her self-confidence. No, she would be fine by herself. She would put her family back together.

But still she had wanted that kiss to continue. She'd wanted to bask in the feeling of femininity it had brought out in her for a while longer.

The next evening after spending the day at Miss Alice's and then at the cottage picking through the rubble, Kathleen helped her mother put together soup and sandwiches. The back door opened and in came Jared.

"Did you two invite Gideon to dinner?" her mother asked as she put the soup onto the stove to heat.

"Yep. He's going home to wash up and feed Butch. Kip went with him."

"He did?" Kathleen needed to say something to Kip about bugging Gideon too much.

"He wanted to help with Butch." Jared's gaze lit upon Miss Alice sitting at the kitchen table.

"Whatcha doing, Miss Alice?" Jared

plopped himself down across from the older woman, put his elbow on the tabletop and settled his chin in his palm.

"I had to do something. Your mom and grandma didn't want me to help with dinner so I'm playing solitaire."

"Can I watch?"

"Sure, if that floats your boat."

"Floats my boat? I don't have one."

Miss Alice laughed. "If that makes you happy."

"Nana plays solitaire sometimes, but it doesn't look like that."

"There are hundreds of different kinds of solitaire."

"Why don't they have different names?"

"Solitaire really means any card game you can play by yourself."

"Oh."

"Why didn't you go with your brother?"

"I don't know." Jared shrugged. "I guess 'cause I'm tired after working all day."

"You did good."

Jared beamed. "I did?"

"Both you and Kip really helped Gideon.

I heard him say so. I just wish I could have done more."

"But you're an old lady."

"Jared!" Kathleen closed her eyes and waited for Miss Alice's reaction.

"And proud of it. I've seen and done many things." A chuckle accompanied her declaration.

"Like what?" Jared moved around to the seat next to Miss Alice to watch her play the card game.

"I've ridden a camel in the desert and an elephant in India. I've dived with sharks, and I've climbed some of the tallest mountains in the world."

His eyes grew round. "Weren't you scared the sharks would eat you?"

"Tell you a secret." Miss Alice leaned close and whispered something in Jared's ear.

Kathleen didn't think her son's eyes could get any bigger. "The first time! How many times did you swim with them?"

"Half a dozen times. I'll show you some

of my pictures when I can get back into my house."

"I'd like that."

"Now let me show you how to play this version of solitaire." Miss Alice shuffled the deck and laid the cards down in a pyramid, telling Jared what she was doing as she did it.

When Kathleen heard a knock on the front door, she merely continued making the sandwiches. Her mother looked over at her and said, "That must be Gideon. Would you answer the door?"

Kathleen thought about refusing her mother's request, but that would start a whole series of questions she didn't want to answer. Besides, she and Gideon could be casual friends.

She finished cutting the last turkey and Swiss cheese sandwich in half, then hurried into the foyer. Gideon stood on the porch. A picture of him kissing her the night before flashed into her thoughts—along with an image of him ending it suddenly and leaving right after that. All day she had avoided being near him and now she was face-to-face with him, only two feet from him. Way too close for her peace of mind.

He had kissed her and found her lacking. The insecurity she experienced reminded her of Derek that last year of their marriage. He had hardly ever touched her.

"Where's Kip?" Her voice cool, she stepped to the side to let him into the house.

"Butch needed walking, and he wanted to do it. I said okay. I hope that's all right with you."

"That's fine."

She swept around to go back into the kitchen, but Gideon grasped her hand and stopped her. "Is something wrong?"

Yes. His warm touch only reinforced his rejection. "No, everything is fine."

"I'll go get Kip. I shouldn't have let him do it." He released her hand and started to open the door.

"Leave Kip. I said it was fine. I know how much my children love animals."

"Then this must be about last night.

You've hardly said two words to me today. I know I shouldn't have kissed you. I was presuming something between us that's not there."

Being punched in the stomach would be better than what she was feeling right now. She backed away. She gritted her teeth and tried to think of something elegant to say. Nothing came to mind except all the hurt his words produced.

"I'm not explaining myself well. I mean—"

"Please, you've made yourself quite clear. Now, if you'll excuse me, I need to help Mom get dinner on the table."

This time he didn't stop her from leaving. Thankful he hadn't, she fought the tears jamming her throat. All she wanted to do was get through this evening without saying or doing something she would regret.

In the kitchen, her mother studied her for a few seconds then went back to setting out the paper goods they were using so they didn't have as much to wash. "Dinner is ready." She looked behind Kathleen. "Where's Kip?"

In the doorway Gideon replied, "I'll go see what's keeping him." Then he disappeared down the hallway before anyone could say anything.

The sound of the front door opening and closing filled the quiet.

Miss Alice swung her attention from Kathleen to her mom, then rose and asked Jared, "Will you help this old lady to the restroom to wash her hands?"

Jared jumped up and held Miss Alice's arm.

"We'll be gone for a few minutes," she announced as she and Jared left the kitchen.

Her mom leaned back against the counter. "Okay. What's going on? I noticed all day you didn't say anything to Gideon. Are you two having a fight?"

"That would imply there was something between us."

One of her mother's eyebrows rose. "And there isn't?"

"No, we're barely friends."

"Oh, I see. So you two did have a fight."

"No, we didn't and I don't care to talk about this anymore. I'm starved. I worked up quite an appetite today."

"Ignoring your feelings will not make them go away. Since you and Gideon were getting along so well yesterday, I guess something happened after I went to bed last night. Today you wouldn't even think y'all knew each other. What happened?"

The tears fought to be released. Kathleen swallowed again and again. "On second thought, I'm not very hungry. I have to be at work at seven tomorrow. I'm turning in early tonight." Biting her lower lip to keep from crying, she headed for the hallway.

"But, honey, it's only six."

She ignored her mother's words and rushed up the stairs before Gideon returned with Kip. She didn't want to run into him. She didn't understand what she was going through, but she was determined to get a handle on it before she saw him again.

In the safety of her bedroom, she closed the world out and sank onto her bed. What happened last night was a good thing. It reconfirmed that she didn't need to get involved with anyone. Maybe after her children were grown up, when what occurred between her and a man would only affect her. Her sons didn't need to be subjected to a volatile situation as they were the past few years no matter how much she tried to protect them. Jared and Kip needed stability. That needed to be her focus.

A rap at her door startled her. "Who is it?"

"Gideon. May I talk to you?"

No, she wanted to shout, but instead she closed her eyes, fortified herself with a lungful of air and rose. Her pace slowed as she neared the door, and when she opened it, she still wasn't prepared to see him. Nor the angry expression on his face.

"Can I come in?" Steel accompanied each word.

She backed away and let him into her bedroom.

She opened her mouth to speak, but he cut her off. "I asked you if there was anything wrong and you kept telling me everything was fine. Friends don't do that to each other."

"Friends. Is that what we are?"

"Yes." He paused and averted his gaze for a moment. "At least that was what I thought."

"And so friends kiss each other like we did last night?"

"I knew it. I knew I shouldn't have kissed you. I've ruined everything, and I didn't want to do that."

"Wow. That certainly makes me feel better. You regret kissing me."

"I never said that. I shouldn't have kissed you because it led to complications, and I don't want to lose your friendship."

"That's nice to know."

"Sarcasm doesn't become you."

She closed the space between them, her own anger surging to the surface. "Tell me why you kissed me last night. What were you trying to prove?"

"All day I'd been thinking about kissing you, and I thought if I did, that would be it."

She sucked in a ragged breath. "I guess I should appreciate your honesty." But her self-confidence had taken a beating the past couple of years. She hadn't realized how much until he'd pulled away and left so quickly the night before.

"You want honesty?" He got in her face.

She stood her ground. "Yes."

"After you said that you weren't interested in getting involved with anyone, I had decided that was fine. I could respect your wishes. Then before I realized it I was kissing you, telling myself that at least I could satisfy my curiosity then let it go."

"I'm so glad I could accommodate you. Now you won't lose any sleep over that."

A humorless laugh escaped his lips. "I wish that were the case."

"What do you mean? You pulled away and left in such a hurry I wasn't even sure what had happened. I figured you regretted—" She stopped, realizing what she was revealing.

"If you were going to say I regretted kissing you, you're right."

Her anger dissolved into hurt with his declaration.

"And you are wrong."

"What do you mean?"

"I mean that kiss was amazing, but after what you said I shouldn't have done it. I should have respected your wishes and not complicated our relationship. I'm sorry I didn't communicate that well to you last night or earlier this evening."

"The kiss was amazing?"

He looked at her for a long moment then grinned. "Most definitely. Everything I anticipated and more."

The words washed away the hurt and lifted her spirits. "I thought—"

He held up his hand. "No more speculation. If something is wrong, we need to talk it out. That is what friends do. You and your family have made my medical leave bearable, and I appreciate that more than you can know."

"I guess this isn't the time to point out I was the reason for the medical leave."

A stern look descended. "This is the last time I am going to speak of this." He rapped his knuckles against his hard cast. "I forgive you. Totally. One hundred percent."

Kathleen chuckled. "Okay. I believe you. I promise."

"It's about time. Because I didn't know what else I could do or say to convince you. I guess I could have had my friend write it in the sky for the whole town to see."

"Don't you dare." Laughter overtook her as she pictured the words. *Kathleen, you are forgiven. Gideon.* "That would set the tongues wagging in Hope. I probably wouldn't be able to show my face. Of course, it would take everyone's mind off the hurricane."

"Well, then I'll do that."

She punched him playfully in the arm. "You'd better not."

"I won't. I don't want to get on your bad side again."

A shriek and barking reverberated through the house. Kathleen started for the door. "Kip brought Butch back here?"

"Well, not exactly."

"I'm not sure I want to hear what you mean by that."

"That will depend."

Kathleen opened the door and stepped out into the hallway at the same time a small brown wiry-haired dog ran down it with Cottonballs on its tail. Kip raced after the pair toward the living room.

"*That* is what it depends on?" Kathleen gestured toward the dirty dog.

"Yep. How do you feel about adopting a homeless dog?"

Kip skidded to a stop at the end of the corridor and swept around toward her. "I found him hiding under a bush. He was scared, shaking and whining. He's lost. I had to bring him home." Then before she could reply, he hurried down the stairs after the fighting animals, drawn no doubt by the racket the mutt and Cottonballs were causing in the living room.

"I'm not sure this is the best time. I never got to have a dog when I was younger. Mom didn't want any pets." Kathleen entered the living room to the picture of Kip kneeling by the couch and trying to coax the dog out from under it while Cottonballs stood next to him, tail puffed out, teeth bared and giving off a banshee cry that made *her* hair stand up.

Miss Alice, Jared and her mom came into the room from the kitchen.

Kip lifted his head, looked at Kathleen and said, "Mom, he is so scared. Do something," then went back to trying to soothe the animal.

"Jared, can you get Cottonballs and take him to the laundry room for me?" Miss Alice moved slowly toward the sofa while Jared darted around her and scooped up the cat that continued to hiss and scream as he took him away. Miss Alice trailed after Jared.

Her mom stepped over to the sofa.

"What's going on here? What is under there? Another cat?"

Gideon inched closer to Kathleen and whispered, "Kip brought the dog in through the front door and was taking him upstairs when Cottonballs sensed his territory had been invaded and went on the defensive. I didn't have a chance to say anything to your mom."

Kathleen stooped next to Kip and leaned down until she saw the mutt cowering in the back. On closer inspection the dog appeared underfed. His ribs showed, and that sight squeezed her heart. "Maybe if we moved the couch, he'll come to you, Kip."

"What's going on?" Ruth asked again. "What's under there?"

Kip peered up at his grandmother. "I found a dog that needs a home. Can I keep him? Please."

"I don't know if that is such a good idea. I'm not a pet person."

"But, Nana, he's homeless. We can't turn him away. We've got Cottonballs here. He's a pet, and Gideon had Butch here during the hurricane. Pretty please."

"But that's the reason why. We do have Cottonballs here. One pet is enough. Look what nearly happened with Bubbles."

"No one will know he's here. I'll keep him in my room. Feed him. Bathe him. Walk him. Besides, Miss Alice will be leaving soon when her house is fixed up."

Her mother sent Kathleen a beseeching look.

"Honey, let's get him out from under the couch first. Gideon, will you help me move it?"

"Sure. Kip, be ready to snatch him if he makes a run for it."

Kathleen stood on one end of the sofa while Gideon took the other. "One, two, three. Lift."

Positioned to grab the mutt when the couch was moved, Kip lunged forward and scooped up the medium-size dog, skinny with his ribs showing. "See. He's been homeless for a while and he has no collar."

"It's dirty." Her mother wrinkled her nose

and backed away. "He needs to be outside. We don't have enough water yet to bathe him."

"I can't keep him?"

"Certainly not in this house until he is clean. No telling what he's brought in here. Fleas. Ticks." Her mother folded her arms over her chest.

"I don't have to drink any water. He can have my share."

Kathleen's gaze fastened onto the dog's sad face as he laid his head on Kip's shoulder. The animal's brown eyes latched on to hers. "Mom, why don't we keep him in the garage for right now? At least for the time being while we decide what to do with him."

"Please, Nana. I promise he won't be a problem."

"Fine, for now. But you have to do everything for it. And you have to keep it away from Cottonballs. I thought an animal was dying in here."

"Thanks. I will. You'll see."

Gideon scratched the animal behind his

ears. "C'mon. I'll help you set up a bed for him. We'll make him feel right at home in the garage."

Kip rushed past his grandmother as though he was afraid she would change her mind.

Which given a chance, she might. Kathleen closed the gap between her and her mother. "Thanks. This means a lot to Kip."

"It stays only as long as it isn't any problem. We don't know what kind of diseases it carries. It's so mangy looking."

"I think some food will help with that, and I'll have a vet look him over. The dog must have been on his own for some time. Probably before the hurricane. He looks like he hasn't eaten much lately."

"So what do we feed him? I don't have any dog food here."

"I'll talk with Gideon. Don't worry." She hugged her mother then headed toward the garage.

Kip found an old comforter in the Goodwill bag her mother kept and put it down near the door into the house. When he set the dog on it, he stroked the dirty fur on the animal's back and murmured, "You're all right now. I'm gonna take care of you."

"How about food?" Kathleen asked as the dog curled into a ball, laying his head on Kip's leg.

"I can get some of Butch's dog food. I stocked up when the hurricane was coming. He'll need a bowl of water, too."

Kip grinned up at Gideon. "Thanks. He needs a lot of it."

"I'll find a bowl and fill it with water." Kathleen snagged Gideon's attention. "May I have a word with you?"

He nodded and backed toward the door into the house.

"Mom, tell Nana it's my share of the water."

"We'll find a way for everyone to have water, even your dog. I think the water will be restored soon anyway, so we'll be fine."

"See, I told you everything would be okay." Kip put his arm around the mutt and rubbed his face against the matted, dirty fur.

Kathleen hurried inside before she threw herself between the dog and her son. *Boys like to get dirty. Boys like to get dirty.*

In the kitchen she shifted toward Gideon. "Which vet do you take Butch to? I hope he can see Kip's dog tomorrow."

"Dr. Anderson. Let me see if his clinic is set up to receive patients. The area of town it's in didn't get hit as hard as some. When are you off work tomorrow?"

"I should be home by four."

"We can do that, then stop by the beach afterwards."

"Why?"

"It's not the most ideal bathtub to bathe an animal in, but it's better than nothing."

"Good thinking."

"I'll have everything set up tomorrow for the dog. You can go to work and not worry about it."

As he left the kitchen, Kathleen began searching for a bowl for the water. When pulling down a plastic dish to use, she stopped in midmotion. In a short time she was beginning to depend on Gideon, to turn to him for help with certain problems. She had to put a halt to that or she would fall right back into the role she had in her marriage where she'd let Derek run everything. She really had only herself to blame for the situation she'd found herself in. She'd never insisted to be informed about their finances. Their marriage had never been a partnership, and she just now realized she was partially the reason it hadn't been.

Chapter Nine

Kathleen surveyed the live oak that remained standing guard near the old white lighthouse on the Point. From what she understood, the historical tree, more than two hundred fifty years old, would live in spite of the fact the hurricane had stripped off all its leaves. Seeing it gave her hope that the town would revive and be better than ever. The Peace Oak, as it had been known through history, had been where a treaty had been signed between the French and the Indians in the area.

Gideon came up behind her and stopped next to her, staring at the lighthouse. "It

makes me feel good to see these two landmarks here after the surge of water covered
most of the Point."

The past two weeks she and Gideon had
seen each other in passing and a couple
of times had stopped to talk but that had
been all. With the power and water back
on, most of the neighbors had retreated to
their own houses to repair what they could.
She missed the camaraderie of working on
a team. "The lighthouse definitely needs a
fresh coat of white." Four feet up the structure all the paint was gone and above that
band the rest was dull from years of wind
and weather.

"That's one of the projects we are tack-
ling today. If we can get the park back into
some kind of order, then we'll be able to
decorate it for Christmas."

"So they'll still turn the holiday lights on
Thanksgiving evening?"

"Yep, twelve days away. That's why we're
here. The powers-that-be want the holidays
to be like every other year."

"Actually, that's a smart move." Kathleen

pointed toward the Peace Oak. "Now if we could glue the leaves back on it, it would be like every other year."

"Gotta find those leaves first."

"They're probably somewhere around Jackson." She turned away from the tree and lighthouse and scanned the beehive of activity all around Broussard Park that was one of the favorite spots for the townspeople. "So what are you doing here today?"

"Helping rebuild the playground. Zane Davidson is donating the new equipment along with some help setting it up." He nodded toward a large truck pulling into the parking lot. "In fact, he's here with it now. What are you doing?"

"Helping to lay gravel for the playground."

"Ah, so we'll be working together. Since Miss Alice's house, I've missed that."

For the past two weeks she had been pulling double duty at the hospital, coming home and helping her mother repair what they could or going to the cottage to dig through the debris for anything of hers or her sons'. "I'm almost through with the cleanup at the cottage. The city should be around at the end of the week to pick up the trash."

"Where are Jared and Kip?"

"Coming later with Mom and Miss Alice. They're contributing lunch for the volunteers."

"Good. I've arranged for your sons to tour Station Two next Saturday. I want to tell them today, but I want your okay first."

"They'll enjoy it."

"How's Rocky doing?"

"The second Kip was able to give him a bath he started bugging Mom about letting him come in and stay in his room. I think he's been counting down the days until Miss Alice goes back to her house. Davidson's Construction Company will be starting on her home Monday. Do you know Zane is only charging her whatever the insurance company gives her to repair her home? She won't even have to pay the thousand dollar deductible. When Zane told her that, I thought for a moment Miss Alice was going to do a jig."

"Now that I would have liked to see."

"I went to school with Zane, and if you had told me he would be doing so much for Hope, I would have scoffed at that."

Gideon's forehead crunched. "Why? Since he returned to Hope, he's been doing a lot for the town."

"When he was in high school, he had quite the reputation of being the bad boy. He rode a motorcycle way too fast and drank. But when I saw him at Miss Alice's house yesterday, I hardly recognized him."

Gideon waved at a tall, black-haired man talking to the driver of the truck.

"You know him?"

"Yeah, this past year he's been coming to this park to play basketball with my youth group."

"What's going to happen to Hope Community Church?" She glanced toward the church across the street from the park. All that remained of the front building was the bell tower. The older original church that had stood behind the newer part was still intact, not having received any water damage because it sat on a rise that had protected it from the flooding.

"We have plans to restore the worship area in the original church. The pastor hopes to have it complete by Christmas Eve services, even if the rest of the church restoration hasn't been done. It amazes me how the building built a hundred and fifty years ago withstood the hurricane but not the one built seventy years ago."

"Have you ever wondered why certain things happen while others don't? Like the church or the tree falling on Miss Alice's house. It could have fallen on Mom's."

"That's why I've always felt being prepared for everything is better."

"But you can't always think of everything. Events occur out of the blue that throw your life into a tailspin."

"Is that what happened when your husband died? He had to be young."

She nodded. "Thirty-five. That's young for a heart attack, but he had been under a great deal of stress. He'd tried to hide the trouble he was in, and it had taken its toll on his body."

"What kind of trouble?"

"Financial. He got himself into debt. He took a second mortgage out on the house. When he died, I couldn't make the payments. The bank foreclosed on us. I tried to stay in Denver for the boys. So much had changed in their lives, I didn't want to move away from what they were familiar with. I sank deeper into debt. Finally, I came home."

"And now with the hurricane, you've lost what you had when you came back to Hope?"

"Yes. Some pieces of furniture and boxes of possessions were still at Mom's, but most of what we owned was in the cottage. I hadn't gotten renter's insurance yet. All we have from the cottage fits in two boxes."

He moved close and took her hands. "But you and your sons are alive."

"Yes, and my car was at Mom's so it wasn't a total loss."

"Many people are in the same predicament. We just have to pull together. One prayer is good, but when it can be many, that's even better."

As before, Gideon's nearness sent her pulse racing. Her senses became attuned to him, everything else fading into the background. As far as she was concerned, they were alone in the park. The breeze from the Gulf carried the scent of the sea. The warmth of the sun canceled out the slight chill in the wind. It was a perfect day, a day to enjoy a picnic, like when she was a child.

"Mom!" Jared ran across the parking lot toward her.

Life intruded. Kathleen tugged her hand from Gideon's and stepped back, turning toward Jared and smiling. This wasn't a day to enjoy a picnic. It was a day of work, a day to remember what happened in Denver with her husband. A day to remind herself not to rush into anything, to be cautious.

"I helped Miss Alice and Nana with the sandwiches. Kip didn't. He was playing with Rocky." Jared skidded to a stop in front of her. "Nana told me to tell you her and Miss Alice are setting up over by the bell tower." Facing Gideon, he stood at attention. "What can I do? I'm here to help. Nana said we have to if we want a playground."

Gideon clasped his hand on Jared's shoulder. "Let's go see what we can do."

She watched her son walking off with Gideon, both with casts on their left arms. The sight thickened her throat. Often when she was working and Gideon was off, her sons spent time with him, helping around his house or a neighbor's. Butch and Rocky had become "best buddies" according to Kip.

Jared stopped and whirled around. "Aren't ya coming?"

"Yes," she answered, noticing Kip helping her mother carry the food to the church.

If she could ignore the damage all around her, she could for a moment see a glimmer of hope. Jared and Kip had settled in at her mother's. She had a good job, which would help her get back on her feet. She was surrounded by family and friends who cared. But she knew this moment would never last. Worry nibbled at her composure. She kept waiting for the other shoe to fall.

Zane approached Gideon. "You're determined to ignore that cast on your arm, aren't you?"

He laughed. "I keep trying to get my captain to ignore it."

"Obviously desk duty isn't setting well with you."

"Would it with you? You own a large construction company, and yet I see you often working at one of your sites. How come?"

"I enjoy it. Hard work makes me feel alive."

Gideon stared at his friend he'd met while trying to put out a grass fire threatening the pine forest along Interstate 10, all because someone had thrown out a lit cigarette. "It's scary how alike you and I are."

"That's why I want to know what is going on between you and Kathleen. I knew her in high school. She was a freshman when I was a senior. Nice girl."

"She's a nice woman."

Zane cocked an eyebrow. "Don't tell me you're abandoning me. I thought we would go into old age as confirmed bachelors."

"How did you get *nice woman* to mean marriage? I think all this hard work is going to your head."

"In all the years I've known you, I haven't heard of you dating a woman longer than a couple of weeks. Long-term isn't in your vocabulary."

"And it is in yours?"

"No," Zane said with a chuckle.

"For your information, three years knowing me isn't that long. I've dated women longer than two weeks."

"Who?"

Gideon stuck up his forefinger. "One is Missy Collins, two is…" He could hardly even count Missy because they were more friends than anything else.

"Two?"

"Okay, I haven't found the right one yet."

And most likely wouldn't since he wasn't looking for any long-term commitment.

"So this makes Kathleen special."

"Of course she's special, but we haven't even gone out on one date."

"From what I've heard from Pete, you're always over at her mother's. He said something about arranging a tour of the station for her sons. I just saw you a while ago having an intense conversation with her. It looks serious to me."

Gideon released a frustrated breath. "You're not going to rile me. Since when have you listened to gossip?"

"Pete seemed to think it might be something."

"Since when have you listened to Pete?"

"Since high school. Why haven't you gone out on a date?"

"Hurricane Naomi. Did you forget about that?"

"Not all dates are at a restaurant, the movies or something like that."

"Now you're giving me dating advice?"

Zane clapped him on the back. "Someone's gotta help you. That's what a friend is for—giving you unsolicited advice. I'm quite good at it."

Gideon gestured toward a worker. "I think one of your men needs your unsolicited advice."

"I think I've treaded on a touchy subject."

"Bye, Zane."

His friend's laughter as he strode toward his worker grated on Gideon's nerves. Why would he risk getting hurt after Kathleen made it clear she wasn't interested? But Zane was right. They didn't have to go to a restaurant for a date, and friends could go out together. Kathleen deserved something special. She'd been working nonstop since the hurricane. Maybe he could do something about that—as a friend.

"Hey, Gideon, we're taking a break. Wanna shoot some hoops?" Kip approached him with a basketball under his arm. "I got this from the church. Nana said it would be all right to take it so long as I put it back."

"Sure. Let's see if we can get some other boys and maybe a couple of dads."

Kip turned in a slow circle, going from one father and son to another. A frown creased his forehead.

It didn't take much for Gideon to figure that Kip was missing his dad. He could remember the first few times after his dad had died and he'd seen a father and son together how much it had hurt him to realize he would never have that. He'd gotten really good at avoiding situations where that might take place. The hurt had faded but never totally went away.

"Trust me," Gideon said the next Friday and turned Kathleen away from him. "Close your eyes. I'm putting a blindfold on you."

"Blindfold? Why?"

"It's a surprise and I don't trust you will keep your eyes closed."

"Do you hear yourself? You ask me to trust you and yet—" The feel of the cloth over her eyes interrupted her train of thought. Actually it was more the close proximity of Gideon and the lime-scented aftershave she smelled that affected her thinking.

He leaned near her ear and whispered, "And yet I don't trust you to keep your eyes closed? Sometimes life doesn't make sense."

"More like you don't make sense," she said in response to him but was amazed she managed to utter those words when she still felt the tickle of his breath on her neck. She pictured him nibbling on her lobe and nearly melted into her mother's front lawn.

He chuckled. "I've been told that before. Now quit complaining and relax. You've been working too much lately."

"And you haven't?" He took her hand and led her to his Jeep.

"I have called in a few favors to pull this together so I want you to sufficiently appreciate my efforts."

"But there is so much to do."

"I agree and it will be there tomorrow.

Have you taken any time for yourself in the past three weeks since the hurricane?"

"Are you kidding? With the cleanup and the demands at the hospital? Just yesterday a man came in who was trying to repair his own roof and fell off. He broke several ribs, and one punctured his lung." She relaxed back against the seat while he pulled out of the driveway.

"When the power came back on, we had several electrical-caused fires. It's bound to happen with all the damage."

"We take for granted electricity until we lose it. So much of what we use is run by electricity and without it, we become lost."

"One good thing was the hurricane was late in the season and the temperature wasn't as unbearable as it can get in the summer."

"Or cold like in Denver, even in November."

Gideon slowed down then made a right turn. Kathleen tried to figure out by the direction he drove where he was taking her, but she wasn't as familiar with Hope as she had been growing up and with the hurricane, detours were necessary in some places. Sections of the road along the coast were still closed off because of extensive damage to the pavement.

When he stopped, he opened the door and said, "Stay right there. Don't take off the blindfold. I'm coming around to lead you to my surprise."

She was tempted to peek but then decided to give in to what Gideon was doing. He'd gone to some trouble to do this, and she didn't want to disappoint him. He'd done a lot for her family. Jared and Kip were constantly making excuses to go down and see Gideon. She'd even found herself trying to come up with one, especially since the day at Broussard Park. Seeing Gideon playing basketball with her sons made her realize how much anger she still had toward Derek. It should have been him, but he'd chosen a destructive path. He'd wanted possessions over his family.

When Gideon opened her door, he clasped her arm and assisted her out of the Jeep. A light breeze blew, carrying the scent of the sea. Only three weeks ago that same water had raged against Hope. The shrieks of the gulls echoed through the air, and the noise of waves washing onto shore soothed her even more. She loved that sound.

As he led her toward his surprise, she asked, "Can I take off the blindfold now? I know we're on a pier."

"But where is the pier?"

"On the Gulf. Not too far from Mom's. It didn't take us long to get here."

"Hope isn't a huge town and traffic was light." Finally, he came to a halt and reached behind her to untie her blindfold.

When the cloth fell away, she faced a twenty-foot sloop, bobbing on the water. "Is this yours?"

He shook his head. "It's Zane's. I learned how to sail when I came here. Zane lets me borrow it when I want to go out on the sea and be truly alone."

"How did it survive the hurricane?"

"Zane took it out of the water."

"Do you sail alone often?"

"I get the hankering about once a month." He hopped down onto the sloop and held his hand out to help her. "My trip is well overdue."

"But if I go, you won't be alone." Stepping down onto the craft, she came up against him as the boat rocked.

He steadied her. "I know, but I thought you could use this time away. I love getting out on the sea, listening to the waves lap against the hull, feeling the sun on my face and the salty breeze powering the sloop to parts unknown. No agenda. Just sailing."

"You've sold me on it. Let's go." She settled herself on the sailboat. "But I've got to warn you, although I grew up on the Gulf, I never learned to sail. I went sailing with friends, but never took lessons. Always too busy doing other things."

"No worries. I've done this many times. This is my gift to you. Enjoy the sun and sea, and don't think about what has to be done when we get back. Okay?"

She smiled as he untied the sloop from the dock. "I like that."

He steered the sloop away from the pier and headed out into the Gulf. "Are you still trusting me?"

"Yeah," she replied slowly, wondering what he was up to.

"I have a destination in mind."

"And you're going to tell me?"

"Nope. You'll figure it out soon enough." He adjusted the mainsail. "I'm curious. What kept you so busy while you were growing up here that you couldn't learn to sail?"

"Two things—dance and cheerleading."

"Neither of which I would have guessed."

"What do you think I did in high school?"

"National Honor Society, Science Club."

"Why?"

"Your mom told me you were valedictorian."

"What else has my mother told you?" She was going to have a word with her mom when she got back home. Every opportunity she got she invited Gideon to come eat with them. On several occasions Kathleen had caught her mother and Gideon laughing over something, but the second she came into the room they would go quiet.

"Just that."

"I did those, too, but my passion was dance."

"Which kind?"

"Ballet."

"Like Swan Lake and the Nutcracker?"

She nodded. "Have you been to a ballet?"

"No, there isn't much opportunity around here."

"True. What did you do in high school?"

"I tried to stay out of trouble."

"No wonder you and Zane are friends. That about describes him."

"I was an angry teen until my last foster parents dragged me to church. At first I sat in the pew determined not to hear anything the pastor was saying." He hitched up one corner of his mouth. "That didn't last long. Once I began listening I realized all that anger at the world was only hurting me. Yeah, I got a raw deal with the death of my parents, but that didn't have to define who I was. So the spring of my junior year, I went out for football."

"You were a jock. That doesn't surprise me."

"Football taught me the importance of being on a team. From there when I graduated from high school, I decided to do something to help others not go through what I did as a child."

"So you became a firefighter."

"It was a kind of therapy for me. I faced what I had feared for years and came out on top."

Had he really? By his own words he kept people at a distance—just like her—afraid to risk getting hurt again.

"What made you become a nurse?"

"Actually, I wanted to be a doctor, but I met Derek and not long after we got married, I became pregnant. My plans changed."

"Why?"

"It didn't seem to fit our future. I loved being a mother and wanted more children.

The cost was too much to do it all so I remained a nurse and gave up my dream of being a doctor. I didn't work much though after Jared came along. Derek wanted me to stay home. He never liked the idea of me working." And she had agreed because she had enjoyed being a full-time mommy, but once her sons started school she'd wanted to go back to work. She and Derek had fought a lot over that. In the end it was easier to volunteer her time than disrupt her family.

"It's not too late."

"Yes, it is. I have a debt to pay off. There's no way I could afford med school."

"Where there is a dream, there is a way."

"Sometimes dreams have to change. Reality has a way of doing that." She shielded her eyes to look out over the glistening water, so tranquil now.

"True. I know that better than some. The day my parents were killed changed my dreams and my reality."

"What was your dream?"

"At eight I wanted to be a firefighter or police officer."

"Then you're living your dream."

"Not exactly. I wanted to grow up to be just like my dad. He was a great father. He wasn't a firefighter, but he was a police officer. My dad would have been so disappointed in me as a teen. I rebelled every chance I got."

With the sails completely up and catching the wind, the boat glided over the smooth water. The shoreline faded the farther out they went. Kathleen relished the beautiful day—the peace, the sense that all was right with the world, that a hurricane hadn't plowed through her hometown.

But on the sloop emotions churned. The past lay exposed between Kathleen and Gideon. She decided to share more of hers. "The disappointment I faced was from my husband. I could never do anything right. I'd made a commitment to him and was determined to make our marriage work, but it was getting so hard. My self-confidence felt attacked from all sides. I questioned everything I did. Then he died and I learned the extent of his betrayal. He kept so many secrets, but right after his funeral they began to come out. By the time the will was read, I realized there was no money, and I most likely would lose the house that meant so much to Derek."

"I'm sorry, Kathleen. That couldn't have been easy."

"The day the bank foreclosed was one of the lowest in my life. I felt a complete failure. My sons were so upset. Their father's death totally changed their lives, and they were groping for stability. That's why I finally decided to come home. That's what Hope has always meant to me." She gestured toward the distant strip of shoreline. "We're here for seven weeks and a hurricane strikes, totally disrupting Hope. Even moving here hasn't been the stability that Jared and Kip need."

"Maybe you're looking for the wrong kind of stability."

Squinting, she stared at Gideon. "What do you mean?"

"Objects and places don't really offer true stability. They are temporary as we in Hope have found out lately. It's something that happens inside you, a sense of yourself, a peace with yourself." He laughed, little humor in the sound. "Of course, it took Pastor Michael to show me that true stability comes from faith."

Instead of turning away from her faith because of her struggles, should she have turned toward the Lord? Was Gideon right? She did know firsthand how possessions were fleeting. First in Denver and now in Hope, much of what she owned had been taken from her and her sons.

"We're almost to our destination."

Kathleen shifted forward and gazed across the calm sea to an island. She hadn't been paying attention to where they were going, only where they had come from. Much like her life of late. "Which island is this?"

"Dog Island. Zane is one of the owners, and he asked me to check out what the hurricane has done to the place. I told him I would be glad to. He has been turning this island into a refuge for certain species of animals like the different types of eagles. There's a cabin in the heart of the island. He didn't know if it made it or not. He hasn't had time to come out here."

"It sounds like I'm not the only one working too much."

"There is so much to be done rebuilding Hope, and that is what his company does the best. I'm glad he took on Miss Alice's house for cost of supplies. I've heard he's been doing that a lot." Gideon guided the sailboat toward the center of the island to what remained of a pier, a couple of pilings sticking up out of the water.

"The dock is gone."

"Yeah, I was afraid it would be. We can bring this sloop in close. You might roll up your pants and take off your shoes. We'll wade into shore. It shouldn't be too deep."

"Speak for yourself. You're over six feet. I'm only five-two."

"Don't worry. I'll take care of you."

A few minutes later, after Gideon had

tied the boat up to the piling nearest shore and thrown an anchor overboard to keep the craft in place, he hopped into the water, holding their shoes and a towel in a bag. "Here, take this." He gave her their belongings. "I'm carrying you to the beach."

She glanced at the water lapping against the bottom of his jean shorts and thought of that foot difference in their heights. "Won't it be hard with your cast?"

"I'll manage." His grin rivaled the sun.

She eased into his arms, conscious of his cast on the left one. He nestled her against him, with the bag clutched to her chest, then waded toward shore but didn't stop until he was up the rise of the beach where the sand was firmer. Then he set her down near a log from an uprooted tree, probably during the hurricane.

"We should wear our shoes. No telling what is hidden in the sand or ground on the island." He sat on the log, leaving her enough room to do the same.

She did, then took her footwear from the bag and passed it to Gideon who used the towel to dry off his wet feet before putting on his deck shoes. After tying her tennis shoes, she glanced up at the area around her. It looked a lot like the beach area in Hope. "I'm not sure this place fared very well."

"At least the island looks like it's intact. Remember the hurricane that split Ship Island into two parts?"

She nodded. "But Fort Massachusetts remained."

"Ready? We'll walk to the cabin before I show you the other side. The waves are a lot bigger on that side. The boys would enjoy swimming here in the summer."

"So you've come out here before. How many times?"

"A few times a year. Sometimes by myself, sometimes there is a group of us to make improvements." He rose, took her hand and tugged her to her feet. "We can't stay too long. I'm just checking to see what will need to be done later."

"I didn't know you and Zane were such good friends."

"We both want to preserve the Barrier Islands and the habitat on them. Most are a part of the park system. This is one that isn't. He didn't want to see it fall into the wrong hands so he got a group together to buy it."

"Zane certainly has changed. Back in high school my best friend's cousin had a crush on him and he hurt her. They dated for a while then he just stopped all of a sudden. He left that summer after she graduated from high school. She didn't know where he went or why. I can still remember listening to her cry in her bedroom."

"People change from when they were teenagers. I certainly have. If I had kept up doing the things I was doing, I would probably be dead by now. I took chances I should never have taken."

She'd changed, too, from having a direction to not having one. From having a dream to living one day at a time with no purpose but to keep her family together, even if it meant losing herself in the process.

"Let's go. Evening will be here soon enough. This will be a whirlwind tour, but I promise I'll bring you and your sons back here to explore the island leisurely, maybe ride the waves."

"Please don't say that to Jared. He'll want to do more than that."

"He's been really good lately. No risks."

"Wait until his cast comes off. I think he has been biding his time."

Gideon waded through the debris and downed tree limbs scattered about the island. "I know that feeling."

"How many more weeks?"

"I go back in four weeks. I've starting doing what Jared does—marking off the days on the calendar."

"But before that there's Thanksgiving and my mother's ambitious plans to celebrate it."

He paused in the path and cupped her face. "She has risen to the occasion as well as you. I'm continually amazed at her ability to organize it. It will be the best Thanksgiving ever."

"Leave it to my mother to find the way to show our thanks and involve hundreds of people."

His warm palm against her cheek rooted her in place. In spite of how the kiss ended the last time, she wanted him to kiss her again, but she would never make the first move. And she didn't have to. Gideon dipped his head toward hers. She dissolved against him, her fingers entwined behind his neck as his mouth settled over hers. For a moment she felt that peace he'd talked about earlier.

Chapter Ten

Next to the lone bell tower at Hope Community Church, Kathleen's mother stretched her arms out wide. "Thank the Lord for this gorgeous day. We have been blessed. This will be the best Thanksgiving ever."

How could her mother say that? There were so many people in need. Kathleen's gaze shifted to the tall pile of boards and debris off to the side of the destroyed newer church. The town had finished the initial trash pickup from the storm and was just starting its second round. It would take more than a few rounds to clean up Hope.

"Why did you want to serve the people here?" Kathleen asked her mother as Gideon pulled up with Jared, Kip and Miss Alice, who had wanted to ride with him.

Sweeping her arm out, she rotated in a full circle. "Look what we have accomplished so far. Broussard Park is ready for our kickoff of the holiday season tonight. Even the church is coming along. It should be ready for Christmas Eve service in the original church. The Point was one of the hardest hit and after a month, it's beginning to show signs of restoration. That's due to the townspeople."

"You should run for mayor, Mom."

Kip, carrying two sacks of groceries, came to a stop between her and his grandmother. "Mayor? You're running for mayor, Nana? Neat."

"No, please don't say that to anyone. What would I do as mayor?"

"Motivate the town. You're a great organizer. Our current mayor has decided not to run again. In fact, I hear he's thinking of moving away from Hope." Kathleen caught Gideon's gaze as it skimmed down her length, leaving a warm trail where it touched. "What do you think, Gideon. Should my mother run for mayor in the spring?"

"I'd vote for you." He set his paper bags down next to Kip's.

"Me, too." Miss Alice joined them with Jared.

"How did we get from feeding the people who lost their homes to me running for mayor?"

Kathleen shrugged. "But it is still something you should seriously consider."

"Let's get through today first. I think we should set up the tables in the park instead of the church's meeting hall. It's just too pretty to be inside and the park looks great after last week's cleanup. The kids can enjoy the new play equipment."

"Yes, I think we should try it out. Come on, Jared." Kip didn't wait for his little brother. He raced across the park to the new playground.

"Miss Alice, do you need me to bring the

rest of your pies?" Jared asked while his gaze strayed to his older brother.

"No, I can manage. You go check out the equipment. We wouldn't want anyone to get hurt if there was a problem."

"Yeah, you're right." Jared gave Miss Alice the two pies he held, then sprinted toward the playground.

Miss Alice laughed. "I didn't have the heart to tell him no. Wait till you see the pie Jared helped me make."

"Should we serve it?" Kathleen remembered her son coming back from Miss Alice's with flour all over him yesterday evening. That had been the first day she'd been back in her mostly repaired house. Zane and Gideon had made it a priority.

"Most definitely. He baked an apple pie and did a great job." Miss Alice winked. "With some assistance from me."

More cars arrived with helpers that her mother had solicited to set up the big Thanksgiving feast she'd planned. Zane stopped to talk with her sons while Pete, his wife and two children joined them with their contribution to the meal—deep fryers for the turkeys. Pete and Gideon went to work setting them up and preparing the birds for the oil. The last of the volunteers—Mildred, a couple of firefighters, her cousin Sally and some of her mother's friends from the ladies group at church appeared with their food and willing hands.

Kathleen's mother asked Gideon to whistle. He put two fingers into his mouth and let out a shrill sound. Everyone turned toward him.

Ruth ascended the steps of the church halfway then turned toward the crowd. "We have three hours to get everything set up. Let's make it special for the folks who have lost most of their possessions."

Kathleen sensed someone approach her from behind and slanted a look at Gideon. The kiss they'd shared last week on Dog Island had haunted her since it occurred. She couldn't seem to get it out of her mind. "Thank you for taking Jared and Kip to the fire station. I wanted to come, but one of the nurses had an emergency and I agreed to fill in for her."

"Did they tell you about the tour?"

"Oh, yes, I heard about it all evening when I got home. Kip's favorite part was the slide. But then I don't know if he enjoyed doing it the most because he truly liked it or because Jared couldn't go down the slide with his cast. Kip made a point of telling me over and over about pretending he was called out to a fire and having to slide down the pole."

"That's okay. I let Jared sound the siren."

"I know. I got dueling stories after that. I went to bed with a headache and those stories running through my mind." But not as much as the kiss she'd received a couple of days before that from Gideon.

"I'm sorry." He circled around in front of her and cut the distance between them. "I didn't mean for you to lose sleep over it."

"I didn't exactly lose sleep over it as much as I had a weird dream with Kip sliding down the pole over and over while Jared sounded the siren continuously. Kip said something about going back again. Are you sure?"

"We have an open house every Christmas. A lot of the kids come and get to play firefighter for a little bit. One year we had to leave because of a fire, and instead of being a disappointment to the children, they were excited to see us in action."

"Kids have a way of turning something around and looking at it from a different view."

"Are you all coming tonight to the Lights On Celebration?"

Kathleen nodded. "We may just stay here until it gets dark. With the church open, we have all the comforts of home. Zane has been busy."

"Yeah, he's finished the structural restoration of the original church. Now all that is left is the interior makeover."

"Not a small task."

"After church in the meeting room on Sunday, some of us are staying to work on the chapel and classrooms. If you don't have to be at the hospital, why don't you stay and help?"

"Unless an emergency occurs, I should be off."

"Great."

"Hey, you two. We could use some help over here. You can chat later."

Kathleen glanced toward her mother. "The general has spoken. Maybe we should say the mayoral candidate has spoken."

"Do you think she'll run?" Gideon started toward the stacks of tables that Zane had delivered for the people to sit at.

"I hope so. Mom needs a purpose. She was getting too caught up in her soap operas and The Weather Channel. There isn't anyone who knows Hope better than her."

"Everyone needs a purpose."

"Since coming to Hope, I've looked forward to getting up in the morning. The last few years of my marriage, I felt at such a loss, aimlessly going through life."

Gideon hefted one end of a folding table while Kathleen took the other end. "I've been to that place and don't care to go back there."

Kathleen set her part down and flipped the legs out then looked toward Gideon. He stood perfectly still, staring toward the water, his eyebrows slashing downward.

"Gideon?"

When he didn't respond, she said in a louder voice, "Gideon, what's wrong?"

He jerked around, said, "It's Kip. He was by the water and now he isn't. Something's wrong. It doesn't look right," and then began running toward the edge of the Point overlooking the Gulf.

Kathleen heard Gideon and the concern in his voice but for a few seconds the meaning didn't register in her brain. When Gideon was a hundred yards across the park, she raced after him, all the while her heartbeat thundered against her skull.

Gideon reached the edge of the ten-foot cliff, whirled toward her and called out, "Get help. The ground has given way and he's buried under the dirt. There's his ball cap."

Bracing himself with his good arm, he

went down the incline. Kathleen hesitated for a breath, wanting to continue toward Kip but instead she hastened back toward the crowd, homing in on Zane and Pete.

"Gideon needs your help. The ground over there—" she wildly waved her hand toward the cliff "—gave way and Kip is buried in the dirt."

Zane was already moving toward his truck before Kathleen had arrived. "I've got some shovels."

Pete and a couple of other firefighters headed across the park toward the water. Kathleen followed. When she reached the men, Pete and their captain clambered down the incline to help Gideon. She started after the pair.

The firefighter left on top stopped her. "Let them take care of it, ma'am. It's a closed-in space and the tide is starting to come in. They need to get him out before that. I've called 911. We'll get him out before they arrive."

She tried pulling away, everything in her screaming for her to be down in the hole created by the ground giving way, but the man clasped her to him. Zane, along with a crowd of people, arrived. He ducked around the firefighter and Kathleen and started down into the hole.

"I need to be there," Kathleen said, watching Zane disappear with the shovels. "Kip needs me."

"They need to get him out first."

The firefighter's calm voice didn't appease the terror building up in Kathleen. The man handed her off to her mother and Sally then corralled everyone back from the edge.

"Get back. The ground has been undermined, probably by the hurricane."

"Mom. Mom. What's wrong with Kip?" Jared clasped her around the waist, fear on his face that matched what she was feeling.

She had to hold it together for both her sons. They would get Kip out, and he would need her then. *Please, Lord, save him.*

Gideon tore at the dirt with both his hands as Pete and his captain joined him.

"He's under here and the water's coming in." His tennis shoes sank into the mud at the bottom of the cliff.

As the water rose, the dirt turned to mud, making their digging more difficult. Zane slid down the incline with two shovels and a spade.

Gideon grabbed the smaller tool. "We'd better not use the shovels. We could hit Kip."

"I'll work from the edge inward, carefully." Zane propped one shovel against the bank of dirt behind him while grasping the other one to use.

"I found something!" Pete shouted and scooped up another handful of mud. "A leg."

Gideon and the others concentrated in that area. Kneeling in the water coming in, Gideon estimated where the boy's torso and head would be. Soon he felt Kip's shoulder and increased his speed, working to uncover the child's face while his captain removed the pressure from Kip's chest.

Gideon removed the last layer of muck

from around the boy's mouth and nose, then his eyes. Finding his thready pulse at the side of Kip's neck, Gideon released his bottled-up breath. "He's alive." As more of the child was unearthed, Gideon looked up. "Call 911."

"Taken care of!" someone shouted from above.

Wound tight, Kathleen paced in the hall-way outside the waiting room. She couldn't sit still while waiting for Kip to come out of surgery. "A collapsed lung, internal in-juries. He was standing on the cliff looking out into the water and the next moment he is being swallowed by the ground. Why didn't anyone check the stability of the cliff after the hurricane? Children play in that park. The town is having the Lights On Celebration tonight."

"Not anymore. The mayor has called off the celebration until the park can be checked." Gideon leaned against the wall.

"If you hadn't seen him going over there, he might have disappeared. He could have died before we found him. He could…" She couldn't get the rest of the sentence pass the lump in her throat. She swallowed several times, but it was still too painful to speak.

Gideon pushed himself away from the wall and stepped forward. Drawing her into his embrace, he whispered against the top of her head, "He's all right. They will patch him up and in no time he will be back playing with his friends and Rocky."

"I know the things that can go wrong. What if—"

He pressed his forefinger over her lips. "Have faith he will be all right. Believe it, Kathleen."

"I wish I could. When are things going to stop going wrong?"

He backed up slightly and looked down at her. "Want the truth?"

She nodded. Her throat burned, her stomach roiled.

"Things will never stop going wrong. That's part of life. Problems and complications happen."

"To me," she said. "But why Kip? He's a little boy."

Her mother appeared in the waiting room doorway. "Jared is awake and needs you."

She'd left her younger son on the couch when he'd nodded off a while ago. Before that, he'd been so quiet she'd known he was trying to process what had happened to his big brother. He had rebuked her attempts to talk with him. Now Kathleen hurried to the couch where Jared sat, his shoulders slumped, his hands twisting together. When he lifted his head, a bleakness seized her heart and squeezed.

"Hon, Kip is going to be all right." She had to have faith, as Gideon had said. The alternative was not acceptable.

"He was mad at me for hogging the tire swing. He stomped off. That's why he was at the cliff. He wouldn't have been there—" Her son burst into tears and flung himself into her arms. "I'm sorry. I'm sorry."

"Jared, you did not cause what happened to your brother. It was an accident."

"But it's got to be bad. They're operating on him."

"To fix him up." She placed her finger under his chin and raised it toward her. "He'll be fine. Good as new. You two will be back to arguing in no time."

"Nope. I'll never argue with him again." Tears continued to leak out of Jared's eyes. "Dad had an operation and died a few days later." He clasped himself against her. "What if the same thing happens to Kip?"

His question stole her breath. She gasped for air and tightened her arms around her son. Kathleen closed her eyes, and when she opened them a few seconds later, Gideon stood in front of her, the concern etched into his expression threatening her composure. Jared needed her to be strong, and she didn't feel very strong at the moment.

Gideon knelt and laid his hand on Jared's back. "We can pray for Kip."

Jared's sobs quieted. He pulled back and peered at Gideon. "You think it will help?"

"Yes. God can always help."

Jared shifted toward her. "Mom, can we?"

"Of course, honey. Gideon has an excellent idea."

Gideon reached out and took both Kathleen and Jared's hands, then bowed his head. "Father, we place Kip's care and recovery in Your capable hands. Be with him during this time and surround him with a protective shield. In the name of Jesus Christ. Amen."

The surgeon appeared in the doorway, spied her and crossed the room. "Mrs. Hart, Kip is in recovery. The surgery went well. We were able to stop the internal bleeding, remove his spleen and repair the lung that was punctured."

"Can I see him?" Kathleen rose.

"Yes, you can stay with him in recovery, then we'll move him to his own room."

"Can I see him, too?" Jared hopped up.

"Just your mom right now, but it won't be long before you'll be able to see him," the doctor replied.

Gideon interjected, "While your mom is with Kip, why don't you, me and your grandmother go get something to eat? We didn't get a chance to eat our Thanksgiving feast so let's check out what they have in the hospital cafeteria."

As Kathleen walked toward the exit right behind the doctor, Jared called out, "Promise me you'll come get me the second I can see Kip."

She turned and smiled. "You will be the first one."

"Kathleen, I'll let everyone know about Kip."

"Thanks, Mom."

When she found her son in the recovery room, his eyes closed, his breathing even, she collapsed in a chair near the bed and finally cried. *Thank you, Lord.*

"When can I go home? Rocky has to be missing me." Kip lay in the hospital bed with his IV still in him, his face pale, his eyes dull.

But for a few seconds Kathleen glimpsed a sparkle in his gaze. After five days, Kathleen saw an end to his hospital stay. His chest tube had been removed after the lung re-expanded. He wasn't on as much pain medication from the abdominal surgery and he was complaining. Always a good sign with Kip. "Tomorrow. This will be your last night in here." And mine. She could certainly understand Kip's impatience to be out of the hospital. She'd spent most of her time here with him except when her mother or Gideon relieved her to go home to see Jared and shower.

The door opened, and Jared charged into Kip's room. "I've got more get well cards from your class. After school Amanda gave this one to me and made me promise you'd read it first." He plopped the stack on Kip's bed. "I think she likes you."

"We're friends. That's all."

"What about Ginny? She follows you around on the playground." Jared positioned himself next to Kip as close as he could get.

"Who brought you?" Kathleen asked before her sons got into a fight over girls.

"Gideon."

"Where is he?" She smoothed her hair, hooking it behind her ears.

"I got on the elevator before him and the door closed. He'll be here. He's way too slow."

At that moment Gideon entered the room, carrying a duffel bag that was partially unzipped. A yelp sounded from it.

"What do you have?" As tired as she was, it was so good to see him.

"A surprise." Gideon placed the bag on the empty chair near the bed and lifted Rocky out.

The grin that spread across Kip's face endeared her even more to Gideon. But still... "Dogs aren't supposed to be in here."

"Shh. Don't tell anyone." Gideon passed the wiggling pet to Kip but kept one hand on the animal. "We can't stay long, but he has been missing you."

Kip buried his face in Rocky's fur. "I've missed him, too."

Jared puffed out his chest. "I didn't say a word about the dog to them."

Gideon ruffled the child's hair. "I appreciate that." He stepped back, allowing Jared to pet Rocky, too.

The dullness in Kip's eyes was replaced with a twinkle. Two patches of red colored his cheeks. The sight of Rocky had done more to lift his spirits than anything else.

"Thanks for doing this, although I should report you to hospital security," Kathleen said.

"I talked with Kip's doctor to make sure it was all right. I'd never do anything to hurt him."

She looked into his gaze. "I know. That's one of the things I like about you." Although Derek had never harmed his sons, those last few years he had been emotionally distant. He stopped doing things with Jared and Kip, and they hadn't understood why. She hadn't either—until she'd discovered her husband's money troubles.

"I gave him a bath so he would be as clean as possible. I figured with Kip coming home tomorrow, Rocky would be all over him then. I didn't think one day would make much difference."

"One day has made a difference. He has been moping around here all day. Even complained there was nothing on TV to watch." She nodded toward the bed where the two brothers were talking civilly and loving on Rocky. Both the boys grinned from ear to ear. "That's a big difference."

"Miss Alice and your mom are planning a small homecoming celebration tomorrow. People have been asking about Kip in the neighborhood. The mayor told Ruth this morning he's waiting to have the Lights On Celebration so Kip can throw the switch on the lights."

"Usually it's a town dignitary. I'll talk with the doctor and find out how restricted Kip's activity will be over the next couple of weeks. So they have reopened the park?"

"Yes and different groups are decorating the whole area. Before it's over with, it's going to look like a Winter Wonderland without the snow. The fire department is taking care of the lighthouse, and we're not sparing anything. It's going to be the best

Christmas lighthouse this town has ever seen."

"That's nice," she said while watching Jared open the cards for Kip to read since her older son was hugging Rocky against his side.

"Nice? It's going to be spectacular. I'm in charge—a desk duty I don't mind."

Kathleen chuckled. "Jared gets his cast off at the end of next week. What about you?"

"The fifteenth of December and I'm counting down the days."

"That evening let me make you that dinner I owe you from way back before the hurricane."

"Sure, I can come to your mom's."

"No, I'm coming to your house. The dinner isn't a family affair."

"Oh, then you've got yourself a date."

"Yes, a date." Ever since that kiss on Dog Island, they had been dancing around each other—friends and yet more.

"That's the best news I've heard all day." Gideon winked then made his way to the bed. "I hate to break up this reunion, but I promised the doc I wouldn't tire you out. Rocky will be waiting for you at your house tomorrow. Jared, can you get Rocky?"

As her son scooped up the dog, Gideon opened the duffel bag. When the animal was inside, he zipped it partway. "I don't want others to get the idea that they can break hospital rules so mum's the word."

Jared paused at the side of his brother's bed, then suddenly he bent down and gave Kip a hug. "See you tomorrow. I've been taking good care of Rocky for you."

"Is something wrong with Jared?" Kip asked, staring at the door as it closed behind his brother leaving.

"I think he blames himself for what happened to you."

"Why?"

"He said something about a fight you two had over the swing."

"Oh, that. That had nothing to do with the cliff giving way."

"You left the playground and went over

to the edge. He thought it was because you were mad at him."

"Not really. I was tired of playing. I like watching the water. One day I'm gonna get myself a boat. I saw one I liked and went over to look at it as it passed by."

"You might say something to Jared about that."

"Why? I think I'll let him suffer a little more. It's kinda nice not arguing all the time."

Kathleen stuck her finger in her ear and wiggled it. "Say that again. I don't think I heard you correctly."

"Oh, Mom. I'm growing up. Fighting is for babies."

"I see. I'll remind you of that when you fight with Jared again." Because as the sun rose each day, she was sure they would fight again.

The next afternoon, before taking Kip home from the hospital, Kathleen had gone down to the office on the first floor to make arrangements about the bill. With the length of stay and the surgery, even with the insurance she had, her part would be thousands of dollars she didn't have. She still hadn't paid for Jared's broken arm. The woman she'd met with had given her a rough figure—worse than she had thought—but had said not to worry about it just yet until the insurance company settled their part of the bill.

Pulling into her mom's driveway, she switched off the engine and tried to paste a cheerful expression on her face as she turned toward the backseat where Kip was. "Ready? I understand Miss Alice baked you a welcome-home cake. Your favorite—chocolate fudge."

"Really. How did she know? Nana?"

"Yep. There are a few people here to see you, but the second you're tired let me know. I'll clear them out. I don't want you overdoing it."

"Mooom, quit babying me. I'm almost ten."

She climbed from her car and opened the back door. "I've got news for you. I'll always be concerned about you even when you are a grown-up and living on your own."

Jared slammed open the front door and ran down the steps, barely managing to stop before barreling Kip over. "You're home. I'm starved, and Nana said I can't have any cake until you're here."

Kip rolled his eyes. "You'll survive."

"C'mon. You get the first slice. Miss Alice said so." Jared pulled on Kip's arm.

"Jared Taylor Hart, let go of your brother's arm. He will be inside in a second. How about you come over here and help me take our stuff inside." Kathleen swung the small suitcase out of the back and handed it to Jared, then faced the house. "When did you all put up the Christmas decorations?"

"Yesterday afternoon. Gideon helped me and Nana. We've got the tree up but no decorations on it yet. We were waiting for you to come home. Maybe we can do that later today."

"Slow down, Jared." Kathleen grabbed the sack of items she'd been given at the hospital for Kip. "I doubt we will tonight. Maybe tomorrow."

"Do you know Miss Alice doesn't put up any decorations? She told me it was too much effort for just her." Jared walked ahead of her and Kip toward the porch, jabbering and not caring they weren't keeping up.

At the front door, he finally stopped and waited for them. "So what do you think?"

Kip scrunched his forehead. "What about?"

"Decorating Miss Alice's house for her. Our gift to her. Wanna help me?"

"Before you go planning your brother's life, I think you need to realize he will be restricted for the next several weeks while he continues to heal. He won't be able to do a lot of what he used to. Recovery from surgery takes time."

"Sure, Mom." Jared opened the screen door then the main one. "But he can help me with Miss Alice. That shouldn't be a lot of work."

When Kathleen, Kip and Jared entered

the living room, she came to a halt, taking in the sea of people crowded into the small area. This was not her definition of a small celebration.

Gideon moved to her side. "Glad you're here. I didn't know what we were going to do with Jared."

"We need to use the same dictionary. In mine, this wouldn't be defined as small."

"Well, it started out that way, just a few friends and family. Then the firefighters who helped rescue Kip wanted to come. After that, one neighbor after another asked if they could drop by and see how he was doing. They all dropped by at the same time."

Stunned, Kip scanned the people in front of him, his gaze pausing on several of his classmates, especially a pretty young girl with long brown hair and blue eyes. Amanda? Ginny? Kathleen peered at her son. His cheeks reddened, and he looked down at the floor by his feet.

She turned and whispered into Gideon's

ear. "It looks like my son doesn't care who is here so long as that pretty brunette is."

"Ah, Amanda, the one who decorated his card with glitter and hearts."

"I thought that might be her."

Her mother climbed up on the coffee table, nodding to Gideon. He gave a loud whistle and the room quieted, except for a few whispers and giggles. "Mayor Thomas has a few words to say before we cut the cakes."

Kathleen leaned toward Gideon again, taking in a whiff of his lime aftershave lotion. She immediately thought of her favorite pie—key lime. "I thought there was only one."

"When your mother saw all the people showing up, she had me go buy a couple more, along with some drinks and ice cream."

"You'd think this was a birthday party."

"The ice cream was Jared's idea. He went with me. Guess what kind I have."

"Vanilla."

"Yep. I tried to talk him into chocolate,

but he told me he didn't like chocolate. What kid doesn't?"

"My son. He's never been a big fan of it. But give him a bowl of ice cream, so long as it isn't chocolate, and it will be gone in no time. Takes after his mother."

"What flavor do you like?"

"Cookie dough. I never got many cookies baked because I ate half of the dough. Got sick a couple of times when I ate too much. My mother didn't take pity on me. How about you?"

"Chocolate. I do like chocolate in any form."

One side of his mouth quirked into a grin that flipped her stomach. He was totally focused on her, and her knees went weak. She gripped his arm to steady herself. "Sorry. I haven't slept much the past week. You know it isn't easy sleeping in a hospital unless they knock you out. Too much noise and people."

"Yeah, you would have thought you had that figured out since you work in one."

"Didn't think about it until I had to stay

five nights. When my husband was in the hospital, he didn't want me to, and I needed to be home with the kids."

The mayor made his way to the sturdy coffee table and joined her mother. "This is a great time for me to ask Ruth if she will run for my office. Don't y'all think she should?"

Her mother blushed beet red. "When you said you had a few words to share with the crowd, I didn't think it was about me running."

"I've been hearing rumors and I thought it was time I tried to talk you into running for mayor."

Everyone cheered, Kip and Jared the loudest with Gideon whistling.

"See. They all want you to be our next mayor."

"I have no experience."

"Have you lived in Hope all your life?" the mayor asked her mother.

She nodded.

"You know everything about Hope and probably just about everyone in town.

C'mon, let's hear it for Ruth as our next mayor."

Ruth raised her hands to calm the roar of approval. "Why don't you run again?"

"Because I've been mayor for eight years, and it's my time to step down. I'm retiring."

"I've already retired from one job. I don't need a second one."

"You might not, but the town needs someone who cares. That's you, Ruth. Look at the Thanksgiving feast you organized."

"We had to postpone it because of the accident."

"Just the celebration part. The food was distributed to the people who needed it." Mayor Robert Thomas took her mother's hand. "We've been friends for a long time. Since elementary school. You're what this town needs now. Promise me you'll think about it."

"I—I—" Her mother stared down at their clasped hands. "I don't know what to say."

"All I'm asking is you think about it." The mayor's face lit up like a Christmas tree.

"He knows he's got my mom," Kathleen whispered to Gideon in the silence that enveloped the room. She lowered her voice even more and bent close to Gideon, saying, "I heard that once they were an item before my dad came on the scene. You would think he had proposed to Mom in front of the neighborhood the way she is acting."

Gideon laughed, breaking the quiet. Suddenly, the room was filled with chatter and cheers.

Her mother extracted her hand from the mayor's and stepped down from the table.

Robert Thomas raised his arms and signaled for silence. "My other reason for being here is to welcome Kip Hart home from the hospital. His accident only reinforces how cautious we need to be. We're still discovering all the effects of the hurricane on Hope. We don't want any more children hurt."

Jared took Kip's arm and tugged him through the crowd toward the dining room. "I don't know about you guys, but I'm starved. Time for cake and ice cream."

A sprinkle of laughter rippled through the group, neighbors parting to allow Jared and Kip through.

"They know it's dangerous to get in the way of a child and cake and ice cream." Practically plastered against Gideon, Kathleen moved away from him. She released a long, slow breath. "I'd better go rescue Miss Alice and Mom."

"Those ladies don't need rescuing." He grasped her hand and drew her toward the front door. "You need to rest."

Before she could say anything, Gideon had her on the porch and sitting in a white wicker chair. "What just happened?"

"I'm rescuing *you*. You're tired. The past week has worn you down."

She cupped her face. "I look that bad?"

"No, but I can tell something is wrong. Did the doctor say something today?"

She shook her head, wishing that she didn't always have a hard time hiding her feelings. "Kip will be fine in time. By Christmas he'll probably be chasing Jared around the house."

"Then what is it?"

"Quit being so perceptive."

"I haven't been accused of that before."

"It's really nothing. There is just so much to do. I can't believe Christmas is weeks away. I started thinking of all I need to do, and I got tired."

He scrutinized her for a long moment, his eyes boring into her as if he were trying to read her thoughts.

She stiffened, determined not to squirm under his probing.

"As you know, I have a fairly normal schedule until after I see the doctor on December 15th, so what can I do to help you?"

"You've already done enough."

"That's not the point. The point is you need help. How can I help you?"

Don't press me about what's wrong. She couldn't tell him she was even more in debt than before in spite of having health insurance. Twenty percent of thousands was still a lot of money—money she didn't have. She would have to figure out something when she wasn't so exhausted.

She had to say something to Gideon. The expectant look on his face told her he wouldn't let it go until she did. "You could come tonight and help us decorate the tree. I don't think Jared will rest until the tree is fully up. We usually do it Thanksgiving weekend. One of our long-standing traditions."

"That's all?"

"Well, it's a start. If I can think of anything else, I'll be sure to say something. Truthfully, you being here is nice."

"Nice?" His smile grew. "I guess that is better than okay."

His infectious grin spread through her. "That's all you're gonna get. We'd better get back inside. I want some of that ice cream. I know where my mom's stash of caramel sauce is. That goes great with vanilla ice cream." As she pushed to her feet, she prayed that Gideon dropped the subject of what was wrong. Her problems were hers—not his.

Chapter Eleven

"Mom, where's the hot chocolate?" Kip sat on the couch putting hooks on the ornaments.

"Hot chocolate? You want that? It's fifty-eight degrees outside." Kathleen took another Christmas ball from her son and found a space on the eight-foot artificial tree.

"Yeah, it's a tradition. We've done it *forever.*"

"That was in Denver where it's cold."

"Please."

"I don't have the ingredients for hot chocolate." Her mother handed a homemade decoration, one Kathleen had made in grade school, to Jared to place near the top of the tree.

He climbed the stepladder and reached up to hang the ornament on the fake pine. "You can go get some. I'm with Kip. We can't decorate the tree without hot chocolate."

Kathleen peered at the nearly finished work of chaos standing in front of the picture window in the living room.

"I'll go get it. What do you need?" Gideon asked.

"Tell you what. We'll take a break. You need to rest, Kip. Gideon and I will go to the store and get the ingredients. Then after we've had our hot chocolate, we'll finish the tree."

"I'm on a roll. I don't need to rest." Jared hooked another ball on the same limb as two others. The artificial limb drooped.

Ruth sat in a chair near the tree. "Tell you what, Jared. Why don't you go see if Miss Alice would like to share some hot chocolate and leftover cake with us?"

Kip laid his head on a sofa pillow and closed his eyes. "Hurry back."

Jared went out the front door with Gideon and Kathleen and raced across the lawn to Miss Alice's.

"Let's take my car. It's right here." Kathleen dug into her purse and retrieved her keys, then tossed them to Gideon. "I'll even let you drive."

When he tried to start the vehicle, a loud cranking sound echoed through the interior, grating on her already frazzled nerves. She held her breath when he attempted it a second time. Dead. Now what?

"I don't think it's going to turn over this time." Still, Gideon turned the key in the ignition again.

She heard nothing but the choking noise of a dying car. She didn't have any extra money—not for Christmas, not for the hospital and certainly not for car repairs.

"Let me get my Jeep and use that. Pete knows about cars, and I'll have him come over and take a look. It could be something simple he can fix." He opened the door.

With the interior light shining in the darkness, he angled toward her. "Don't worry about it tonight. We'll make hot chocolate and sit around and pretend we are in front of a fire."

Tears tightened her throat. *Don't cry. Don't ruin this evening.* It wouldn't change the fact that the car would need an infusion of cash to get running.

Gideon sat there, his gaze fixed on her. "Are you okay?"

Her emotions screamed for release. She wanted to rile, to yell, to cry. "Fine," she said. Averting her face, she fumbled with the handle to open her door.

His hand on her shoulder compelled her to shift toward him. "I thought so earlier. Something is wrong. Sometimes talking about it helps."

"No, it won't. I'm tired. That's all. Don't make it out to be something it isn't. Lately a few things have gone wrong. Haven't you had one thing too many happen to you and you just want to give up?"

"Sure, but Kip is on the mend and the town will recover."

Tears crowded her eyes. Why couldn't her body do what she wanted? Frustrated, she balled her hands, fingernails digging into her palms. "I'll be much better tomorrow after a good night sleeping in my own bed. Hospital cots aren't the best place to sleep." She hurriedly thrust open the passenger door and exited before he asked any more probing questions. The money was her problem, and she'd never been comfortable sharing her problems with others. She'd learned in her marriage to keep them to herself.

Standing back in the dining room doorway, Gideon finished the last sip of his delicious second cup of hot chocolate, watching the last of the decorations being put on the tree by Kip, Kathleen, Jared and Ruth.

"I declare that is the most unusual Christmas tree I've seen in a long time. There is a pine tree under all those ornaments, isn't there?" Miss Alice staked her claim on the chair with the stool in the living room.

"Somewhere under there," Ruth said with a laugh, moving back to get a good look at the overall picture. "We do have a lot of decorations, an accumulation of many years of collecting Christmas memories."

"Jared, you might go a little to the left then reach up a few inches. There's one blank space left without anything on it." Miss Alice pointed toward an area on the tree.

"Oh, yeah, I see. Thanks." On the stepladder, Jared glanced over his shoulder at Miss Alice at the same time he leaned to the side.

The child wobbled. Jared flapped his arms to get his balance. The sequined ball went flying across the room as he finally grabbed hold of the nearest object—the Christmas pine—to steady himself on the ladder. But instead, he kept plunging downward to the floor with the tree tumbling with him.

Gideon shot forward but all he caught

was air. He looked down. Jared lay in the middle of a mountain of ornaments, some broken, with some green pine poking out. The look of confusion on the child's face evolved into horror as he took in what happened. His eyes became round like perfectly drawn circles.

There was nothing but complete silence for a few seconds until Jared struggled to get up and crushed several more decorations under him. Gideon offered the child his hand, which he took. Gideon lifted him free of the mess and set him a couple of feet away.

Jared opened his mouth to speak. Nothing came out. He snapped it closed.

Finally, Ruth began laughing. "Well, that is one way to weed out some of the ornaments."

Kip chuckled, followed by Miss Alice.

Gideon's attention riveted to Kathleen, who stood frozen, shock on her face.

"Are you all right, Jared?" she finally asked, a taut thread woven through her words.

The child nodded.

Kathleen's stunned expression melted into relief, and she sagged back against the windowsill.

"I think we can salvage this." Gideon stooped and grasped the trunk then hoisted the tree to an upright position.

Some of the loose ornaments fell to the floor, a couple shattered among the shards of other broken ones. Gideon made sure the pine was stable, and then he backed away. "In answer to your earlier question, Miss Alice, there is a tree underneath there."

Kathleen shoved herself from the window ledge. "More hot chocolate anyone?"

Everyone quickly said yes.

"I'll help you get it." Gideon quickly trailed Kathleen into the kitchen while the others discussed how to clean up the mess.

Kathleen covered the distance to the stove where a pan of hot chocolate was still on a burner. "Poor Jared. He's going to be so upset with himself." She slanted a look at Gideon. "Mom really did have too many ornaments, but she never would get rid of any of them. She has been collecting them from before I was born. She always insisted the boys make her something for the tree as her present every year."

A memory invaded his thoughts. The boxes of Christmas decorations stored in his childhood home in the attic. All burned up—gone forever. After that he hadn't collected many—only a handful given to him by friends over the years. The small two-foot tree he put up at Christmas had a lot of bare places on it.

As Kathleen poured the drink into the mugs, he came to her side, inches from her. The sound of laughter drifted from the living room. He smiled. "This could have been a disaster."

"Next year all those bare places on the tree now will be filled with new decorations. It was an accident. The topping on a difficult day. I figure I need to cut my losses and go to bed."

"That might not be a bad idea. I'll help your mother clean up the mess. Go on.

You're right. This past week has been hard on you."

"But what about the ornaments that have to be put back on the tree?"

"We'll take care of it." He captured her hands and turned her toward him. "Go. Rest. You deserve it."

"But this is my…"

"What?"

"My family. I can't ask you to fill in for me."

"You aren't asking me. I'm volunteering. No, I'm insisting." He cupped her chin and lifted her head so he could look into her eyes. He grazed his forefinger across the top of her cheek. "I see it there. You're exhausted."

"I can't let you do my job. This is my family."

"Why not let me? I'll borrow yours for the rest of the evening. Tomorrow you'll be better rested."

"You know when I agreed to decorating the tree tonight, I'd forgotten how much work it could be, especially a second time."

"I saw that when all you did was sink down on the windowsill and stare at your son when he fell."

"Yeah, I didn't have the energy to react. He has his share of accidents, but this was a doozy. I'm glad Mom took it so well."

"Ruth goes with the flow."

"That's something I'm still learning from her," she said in a voice that reflected the world crashing down on her.

He brushed his lips across hers, then urged her toward the door into the hallway. "C'mon. Off to bed with you." He watched her walk toward the stairs, her shoulders slumped, her step slow.

She bent over the banister to look at him. "Thank you."

"You're welcome."

As she disappeared from his view, he remembered bits and pieces of their interaction throughout the day. Something was wrong. Kip's accident had been traumatic, but there was something else going on with Kathleen. He'd given her several opportunities to confide in him, but she hadn't.

Frustration churned his gut. He was falling for her, and she was putting up barriers between them. He needed to shore up his own walls, protect himself, but he was afraid he was too late.

"Kip wanted to know where the hot chocolate—" With glitter sparkling in the light on his jeans and shirt, Jared paused in the entrance from the dining room and panned the kitchen. "Where's Mom?"

"It was past her bedtime."

"She doesn't have one."

Gideon crossed to the tray with the full mugs and picked it up. "She was tired, and I told her I would make sure everything was cleaned up from your little disaster."

Jared yawned. "You know, I'm tired, too. I think I'll go to bed—after my hot chocolate."

"Sorry, I'm not buying it." Another yawn made Gideon chuckle. "Still not. You're stuck on cleanup duty."

A grin spread over his face. "Oh, well, at least I get to stay up past my bedtime."

"When is it?"

Jared leaned to the side and peered at the clock on the wall behind Gideon. "In ten minutes."

"Guess you're gonna miss it."

"Yes." Jared pumped his arm in the air.

Gideon carried the tray into the living room and passed the mugs around to everyone, except the one who requested the hot chocolate. Kip lay on the couch asleep.

"Should I wake him?" Gideon set the tray with the last mug on the coffee table in front of the couch.

"Young man, don't you know you never wake a sleeping child? Wait, maybe that's a sleeping baby." Miss Alice sipped her drink.

"Where's Kathleen?" Ruth put the lid on an empty ornament box then sat with her hot chocolate cupped between her hands.

"She went to bed." Gideon looked back at Kip. "I can take him up to his room."

"That would be great if you think you can with your cast." Ruth took a swallow from her cup.

"Sure." He thought about the time he'd

carried Kathleen to the beach on Dog Island. He'd enjoyed the feel of her in his arms.

Squatting by the couch, Gideon carefully scooped up Kip and rose. The boy snuggled against Gideon and draped one arm over his shoulder. His eyes closed, Kip murmured something Gideon couldn't understand and settled against him.

A few minutes later, he laid the boy on his bed and covered him with a blanket. He stared down at the child and wondered what it would feel like being a father. When Kip had fallen last week, his heart had plummeted and a gripping fear had taken over as he'd never experienced. He'd rescued children before, but that had been different.

When he returned to the living room, Miss Alice sat forward, then stood. "I'd better be going."

"Let me walk you home." Gideon started for the foyer and opened the front door.

"Good night, y'all. Thanks for sharing this with me. It's been years since I've participated in decorating a tree." Miss Alice shuffled toward Gideon, a softness in her expression that a month ago hadn't been there.

He offered her his arm, and they descended the porch steps.

"Those boys are good kids, but they need a father." Miss Alice's declaration broke the silence between them halfway up her sidewalk to her house. "If you're not interested, maybe one of your friends. That Zane fellow is nice. I like him. He did a good job fixing my house."

"I don't think Zane is looking for a wife."

"Are you?"

He nearly faltered on the stairs leading to the porch, quickly grabbing hold of the railing. "I hadn't really thought about it."

"You'd better stake your claim fast. She needs a good man to take care of her."

"Why do you say that?" Gideon stopped at the front door, shifting from foot to foot.

"She's sad. I see it in her eyes. From what Ruth has told me and what I see, I don't think her path has been easy."

"What has Ruth told you?"

Alice dug into the pocket of her sweater and pulled out her key, then inserted it into the lock. "That, young man, is something you will have to ask Ruth or Kathleen. I don't gossip. Well, occasionally I have but not in this case."

"Good night, Miss Alice." He turned to leave.

He descended the steps when Miss Alice said, "Don't end up like me—alone all your life. It isn't all it's cut up to be."

He glanced back at the woman, but she went into her house and shut her door. As he walked back to Ruth's, darkness surrounded him with a hint of a chill in the air. Could he risk his heart with Kathleen? Miss Alice's words about being alone pricked his heart, threatening his belief that he was better off not caring too much for others and going through life more an observer than a participant. This past month he hadn't been. Was it because of the hurricane or Kathleen that he'd gotten more involved than he usually did?

When he reentered Ruth's house, he found Jared and her in the living room with broom and dustpan, cleaning up the pieces of broken decorations. "I thought if I stayed gone long enough you two would have this all taken care of."

Jared giggled. "I should have asked to take Miss Alice home." He moved the dustpan away, tilting it forward enough that its contents spilled all over the floor again.

"Jared, pay attention." Ruth's loud sigh conveyed her annoyance.

Gideon bridged the distance between them and took the broom from Ruth. "I'll help Jared in here."

She gave him a grateful look. "Then I'll take care of cleaning up the dishes we used." After gathering the tray and mugs, she strolled toward the kitchen.

"I didn't mean to dump the pieces." Jared's mouth drooped in a pout. "I don't mean to cause trouble."

"I know. Sometimes it just happens. Here, hold the pan while I sweep it up again." As he worked, he saw Jared's sagging shoulders and tight mouth. "What happened tonight reminded me of a time when I was eight and couldn't wait until Christmas Day to open all the presents under the tree. My parents were getting ready in their bedroom to go out. I decided to sneak a peek when they weren't in the room. I wheedled my way under the tree, wanting to get my hands on the big box in the back. I wiggled the wrong way and the tree came down on top of me."

"You did? What did your parents do?"

The memory was seared into his mind as though it had happened yesterday. "They heard the noise and came running. When they found me, they must have laughed for five minutes before they got the tree off me. I didn't understand why they weren't mad at me. It had taken us hours to decorate the tree, and I had destroyed it in seconds."

"They didn't do anything to you?"

"Oh, they did. I had to clean it up all by myself and put everything back on the tree without their help. They decided not to go out that evening and instead sat there on the couch watching me, talking to each other and ignoring my whining." He wouldn't trade that memory for anything. It made his parents seem so real to him for a few minutes.

"Where are your parents?"

"They died years ago."

"My dad did. I miss him every day."

"I miss my parents every day."

"Everything is so different now."

"How so?"

"Mom has to work a lot. She's always worrying. Nana told me worrying only makes the problem worse."

Grinning, Gideon finished sweeping the last pieces into the pan. "She's right. But it doesn't stop me from worrying."

"Why doesn't it?" Jared kept his gaze fastened onto the pan as he lifted it and walked slowly to the trash can, then dumped the contents into it.

"I've never really found that worrying about a problem solves it. It just makes me stressed over it, but for so long it has been a habit of mine I'm trying to change."

Jared cocked his head to the side. "Yeah, you're right. I worried about Kip when he was in the hospital. But that didn't really make him get better. I think my prayers helped. Nana and me prayed every night he was there."

"That's great. You're a good brother."

Jared puffed out his chest. "Yeah, I am."

Ruth reappeared in the living room. "This looks nice. You wouldn't know you toppled the tree."

"Except there aren't as many ornaments on it. Maybe Kip and me can make some to put on it this weekend."

"I'd like that." Ruth hugged her grandson.

"How about you, Gideon? Will you help us on Saturday?"

"Sure. I can't think of a nicer way to spend the day." As he said those words, he realized he had meant every one of them. When he had kidded Kathleen about borrowing her family for the night, he hadn't realized how it would affect him. He wanted a family for himself.

Kathleen sat at the kitchen table gluing sequins on a plain gold ornament while Jared and Kip glued paper rings together to make a garland for Miss Alice.

"Did ya get it?" Jared asked the second Gideon came into the room on Saturday.

"No *how are you?*" Gideon bent down and rubbed Rocky behind his ears.

"Hi. They've been wondering what was taking you so long. They wanted me to take them to the store to find you," Kathleen said with a chuckle. "I had to remind them my car is being fixed and they would have to walk. They decided to wait a little longer."

"Miss Alice is gonna be so surprised." Kip used the scissors to cut some more red and green strips of construction paper.

"How big is the tree?" Jared dabbed some glue on the end of the ring to hold it together.

"I got a live tree in a pot. It's about three

feet high. Then if she wants me to, I'll plant the pine after Christmas."

"To replace the tree she lost. I like that." Kip paused and leaned down to pay attention to Rocky sitting by his chair.

"Where's Ruth? I thought she would be in the middle of this."

"She's getting ready to leave. We decided Nana should take Miss Alice out shopping while we decorate her house. That was my idea." Jared patted his chest.

Gideon took the chair next to Kathleen across from the boys. "How are we going to get into Miss Alice's house?"

"She gave Mom a spare key when she moved back into her house. I guess with everything that has happened, she has decided that might be for the best rather than us breaking down her door if we think she's in trouble." She'd missed Gideon the past few days, working at the hospital as much as possible to make up for taking off while Kip was there.

"How long do you think we'll have?"

Gideon scooted his chair closer to the table, his arm brushing against Kathleen.

"An hour, probably, so we need to be finished with these decorations when Mom leaves."

"We're almost done. Look at this." Jared, with Kip's help, held up the long paper garland for Miss Alice's tree.

"That ought to go around all of it." She slanted a glance toward Gideon who made a design with glue then sprinkled red glitter on the plain gold ornament. "What time are we going to the Lights On Celebration at the Point?"

"Six. With Kip throwing the switch we want a good place to see it. Wait until you see what the fire department did with the lighthouse. We went all out this year. Y'all might want to bring your sunglasses."

"At night?" Jared wrinkled his nose.

"You'll see what I mean in a few hours."

"The hospital did the Christmas tree." Kathleen began gathering the decorations in a box to take to Miss Alice. "I helped some yesterday afternoon after work."

"I wanted to come, but Mom wouldn't let me. She said I needed to rest. That's all I've been doing. I'm getting bored with watching TV and sleeping." Kip put the last ring on the garland.

"I don't want you to overdo it."

Purse in hand, Ruth stopped in the entrance into the kitchen. "I'm going to get Miss Alice. Give me ten minutes then go on over. We won't be gone more than an hour. She wants to rest before tonight's celebration."

After her mother left, Kathleen placed the paper garland on top of the ornaments. "Let's clean this up. We won't have a lot of time when we come back here before dinner."

"Mom, I think someone needs to keep a look out for Nana and Miss Alice leaving. I'll do it." Jared hopped up from his chair and raced toward the living room.

Kathleen opened her mouth to tell him it wasn't necessary, but he'd fled so fast she'd barely formed the first word in her mind.

"I've got to harness some of his energy. I could use it."

"I'd better help him." Kip followed his little brother from the room although at a much slower pace.

"We're alone at last." Gideon waggled his eyebrows. "I thought they would never leave."

Kathleen laughed. "And what did you have in mind?"

He bent toward her and kissed her quick on the mouth. "That. I'd been thinking about it since I first came in here." He started to pull away.

Kathleen stopped him with a hand on his arm. "Hmm. I don't call that a kiss. Maybe a peck, but certainly not a kiss."

He locked his gaze on her lips. "You're mighty picky today. What is a kiss in your book?"

She smiled, one that came from the depths of her heart, and wound her arms around his neck, tugging him toward her. Her mouth connected with his, and she poured everything into it until she forgot to breathe and finally had to step back to take a deep gulp of air.

"Ah, I see what you mean. We might need to practice some more later." He moved back quickly as the sound of footsteps neared the kitchen. "When we're alone again," he added in a whisper as Jared and Kip burst into the room.

"They're gone," both boys said at the same time.

"Let me get the key. Jared and Kip, carry one of the boxes of decorations. I'll bring the large Christmas card you two made for her." Kathleen crossed to the desk and pulled out the drawer where Miss Alice's house key was.

Jared examined the kitchen table. "You two didn't do a good job of cleaning up. The glitter is everywhere, paper on the floor. What were you all doing?"

Kathleen wasted no time coming up with an excuse. "I decided to leave some for you and Kip while we wait for the pizzas to be delivered."

Kip punched Jared in the arm. "Why did

you go and say that? When are you gonna ever learn to keep your mouth shut?"

"I was just wondering." Jared stuck his tongue out and hastened from the room with his box.

When Kip went after his little brother, Gideon blew out a breath of air. "Quick thinking."

"If we aren't one step ahead of our kids, we get trampled. Not fun in the least."

Gideon grabbed the pot with the small pine. "Sounds like you've been trampled a few times."

"I wish it were only a few. I lost count way back."

An hour later the four of them finished with Miss Alice's living room, confining their holiday decorating to that one room she spent most of her time in. On the front door the boys hung their three-foot-by-two-foot card with the outside displaying a huge fir dripping with ornaments and lights and packages beneath it.

With Kip on one side and Jared on the other, Kathleen stood in the middle of the living room. Voices from the front porch announced her mother and Miss Alice's approach.

"We should hide like a surprise birthday party." Jared scanned the area. "I can, behind that chair."

He started for his hiding place, but Kathleen grasped his shirttail and halted his movement. "I think she'll know something is up with that huge card on her door. Besides, we don't want to give her a heart attack."

Cottonballs whined and weaved in and out of their legs as the knob on the front door turned.

"Let me put this sack down and get my reading glasses on. Who would leave me such a big card?" Miss Alice moved into the foyer and caught sight of them in the entrance to the living room. She gasped, dropping her sack and splaying her hand over her heart. "Oh, my, what are y'all doing here? Y'all scared the—" Then she took several more steps until she saw all the decorations. Her mouth fell open.

While Miss Alice remained rooted to the floor, Jared came up to her and pulled on her arm. "Something's leaking all over the tiles."

Miss Alice blinked and swept around, her hand covering her mouth. "My eggs. They're broken."

Kathleen skirted around the woman and stooped to clean up the mess. "I'm sorry. I'll replace them. We wanted to show you how much we care about you and give you a little bit of Christmas." Gathering up the egg carton, she placed it into the torn sack while taking out the other grocery items. Thankfully, none of them were broken.

A suspiciously shiny sheen to her eyes, Miss Alice surveyed the living room, saying, "Don't worry about the eggs. I can't believe y'all did this for me. No one has done..." Her voice cracked, and she lowered her head, pulling a tissue from her coat pocket and dabbing at her face.

"It was my idea," Jared piped in.

Kip stepped forward. "No, it wasn't. I

thought of it and talked to you about it. I came up with the big card on the door."

"No, you didn't." Jared sent his brother a glare.

"Boys, that's enough. Let's say this was a cooperative idea between Jared and Kip." Kathleen walked toward the kitchen. "I'm throwing these away. I don't want to come back in here and see you two fighting."

She strode to the trash can and dumped in the sack and carton of eggs, straining to hear what was going on in the living room. All she heard were murmurs. She rushed back to find Miss Alice seated in her recliner, tears streaking down her face.

"I'd forgotten what Christmas was about until this year. You couldn't have given this old lady a better gift."

"We made everything in here." Kip beamed.

"Well, except the tree. But everything else." Jared stood next to his brother, his grin as big as Kip's.

"I'll never forget this. And you two can play soccer in my front yard anytime you want." Miss Alice swiped the tissue across each eye, then stuffed it back into her pocket.

While Kip brought Miss Alice the Christmas card from the front door so she could read the inside, Kathleen watched their neighbor interact with her two sons. A warmth flowed through her. Her sons still bickered, but for this project they had worked side by side with little fighting. In the past week they hadn't said once they wished they were in Denver. Hope was becoming their home. At least one thing was working out as she'd prayed. If only the rest of it would.

At the front of the crowd at Broussard Park in a semicircle around the lighthouse, Kathleen huddled in her light jacket, not having expected the wind to be as cold as it was, blowing off the water. She hugged herself and tried to focus on what Mayor Thomas was saying.

Next to her, Gideon drew her close to him, wrapping his arms around her. His warmth spread through her, alleviating the chill some. She cherished the feel of his embrace, the sense of being protected from the elements. "The temperature is dropping. A front must be moving through. It's always a little cooler here, which is great in the summer."

She turned her head and whispered, "Some people came better prepared than I did. I'm looking forward to a cup of hot chocolate."

Gideon's face, only inches from hers, threw her heartbeat into a fast tempo. The cold fled completely as the mayor finished his little speech about the future of Hope.

"It's time to turn on the lights. A beacon of hope in the dark. Ships passing by will be able to see our little light display. Hope may have been hit six weeks ago, but we aren't down. There will be a new Hope rising even better than before. Kip Hart will flip the switch this year on our Lights On Celebration. Kip, are you ready?"

Nodding, her son positioned himself next to a big red button.

"Okay. Ten. Nine," the mayor said with everyone as usual joining in the countdown. "Eight. Seven. Six. Five. Four. Three. Two. One."

Kip pressed the button and bright lights flooded the park—thousands and thousands of them, glittering and dazzling.

But Kathleen's gaze fastened onto the lighthouse the fire department had decorated. Red, white and blue lights covered the whole surface of the white structure as though the building was wrapped in an American flag. "Stunning."

"I'm glad you like it. It was my idea. A tribute to our soldiers and citizens who continually fight to make this country better. All I have to do is look around at the people in this crowd."

The warmth of his breath tickled her neck. She shivered.

"Still cold?"

The crowd began to clap at the display not only on the lighthouse, but on the ten-foot Christmas tree standing tall at the edge of the cliff as if it defied the sea to take it down as it had so many others in the hurricane. The park's pines, live oaks, stripped of their Spanish moss, and magnolia trees left from the storm were lit up in white like stars glinting in the night sky.

Kip made his way through the people surrounding the mayor. "Mom, what did ya think?"

"You did great."

"The mayor told me they found a few more areas along the cliff that had to be shored up. That I prevented others from being hurt. I helped save some people."

She was glad some good had come out of the tragedy, but it didn't make it any less painful.

"I'm hungry. Can I go get some dessert and hot chocolate?" Jared wedged himself in front of Kathleen.

"I was thinking that very thing." The church would block a lot of the chilly wind. A much better place to enjoy the treats her mother's ladies' group had fixed. "If we hurry, we can be first in line."

Jared shot forward, nearly knocking into

a young woman in his haste. Kip trailed his brother at a more sedate pace, still not up to his usual active level.

"I probably shouldn't have said that. But then with everyone who turned out for the celebration, it would be nice to be at the front of the line."

Gideon glanced around. "I think others have the same idea."

"At least we'll be out of the wind."

Gideon waved at Pete and his wife. "We could break in line."

"You're such a rebel."

"Your mom said something about making divinity."

"She makes the best in town. Probably the state. I don't know how I'm going to carry on her tradition. Mine isn't nearly as good."

"Y'all have a lot of traditions at Christmas."

"Yeah, passed down from my grandmother. There is a comfort to them. Kip and Jared will feel right at home here because we've done the same thing since they were born. We were a little late with the tree because of the accident, but tomorrow we're all going to make Christmas cookies and take them to Hope Retirement Home along with Mom's homemade eggnog. Now that, I have mastered."

"Even when my parents were alive we didn't have any traditions other than going to church on Christmas Eve."

"You're welcome to take part in our traditions. Miss Alice is going to help tomorrow with the cookies and go with us to deliver them."

"I wish I could, but I promised Pete I would help with some of his repairs at his house. He still has quite a bit of work to do on his place."

"Somehow I can see you doing that more than baking cookies," Kathleen said with a chuckle. "It's a lot of fun, but the real work starts after the cookies are boxed up and ready to go."

His forehead furrowed as he slowly moved forward in the line. "Taking them to the retirement home?"

"No, cleaning up the mess my boys make. Sort of like a mini hurricane blowing through the kitchen. You know flour goes everywhere and in places you don't want when you start throwing it at your brother."

"Interesting. I would never have figured that." His laughter filled the air.

Kathleen loved hearing him laugh. It invited her to join in on the merriment. She was falling for him, and she didn't know if that was a smart move. Her marriage problems were still so fresh in her mind. What if she made a mistake as she did with marrying Derek? She had more than herself to consider in this. As she reached her mom behind the first table of goodies, she shook the dilemma from her mind. She wasn't going to let worrying over it ruin her evening.

"Thanks for carrying Kip up to bed again. All this activity is wearing him out. It's hard to restrict him at this time of year." Kathleen opened the front door for Gideon.

He headed up the stairs with Jared following.

"Why does he always get to be carried up the stairs? I should have fallen asleep in the car on the way home, then you would have to carry me, too. Except I would like you to do a fireman's carry with me."

Gideon bit the inside of his cheek to keep from chuckling at the continual one-upmanship between the two brothers. At least he finally heard from *his* brother overseas. He would be returning to the United States in the spring and wanted to meet Gideon after all these years.

He had vague memories of times spent with Zach as children. Lighthearted, fun times. When he was living at some of the foster homes he'd been at, the atmosphere had been anything but lighthearted. Not all but a few—enough that he always watched his back and guarded his words.

Gideon placed Kip on the bed and covered him as he had the night they had decorated the Christmas tree. The simple action connected him to the child. He backed away, his emotions swelling in his chest, closing his throat.

"I'm going downstairs and probably fall asleep on the couch," Jared said at the doorway. "Remember the fireman's carry if I happen to fall asleep."

Gideon strode behind the boy. "Okay, but didn't your mom say something about getting ready for bed?"

He whirled around and began walking backward toward the stairs. "I didn't hear that. I'm not tired a bit."

"Well, then I guess you won't fall asleep on the couch."

He swung around and faced forward, grasping the banister. "I can get sleepy real fast."

"Okay, I'll keep that in mind."

Downstairs, Jared ran toward the den where the sound of voices was coming from. Gideon paused in the living room and stared at the tree. True to their word, the boys had filled almost all the blank places on the tree. He could hardly see the pine beneath all the decorations.

"Hi, I thought maybe you had gone home." Kathleen came up behind him and put her hand on his arm.

The touch zapped him with more feelings of wanting to belong to a family. "I wouldn't leave without telling you goodnight. Besides, I have a sneaky suspicion that Jared is going to fall asleep on the couch in the den, and I'm going to have to carry him upstairs using the fireman's carry."

"You are? So now all I have to do to get him to sleep in the future is to have you here, ready, willing and able to carry him up the stairs over your shoulder. You're hired for the job."

He tweaked her pert nose. "It's a freebie." Hooking his arm around her, he pulled her close. "I enjoyed tonight. I've gone every year to the Lights On Celebration, but this year was special."

"Because we're celebrating more than the beginning of the holiday season. We're celebrating our comeback."

"I can see that you were a cheerleader in your youth."

She laughed. "I'm gonna take that as a compliment. Someone has to cheer people on. I'm very good at standing on the sidelines and doing that."

"Not participating?"

"In this case I guess I did. I still have paint under my fingernails and probably a splinter or two still in my hands."

He grabbed one of them and turned her palm up. "Where? I'm very good at taking out splinters. Show me and I'll get a needle and alcohol."

She snatched her hand back. "I think I'll take care of it. I still have one in my hand from when I was a little girl. It would take surgery to remove it now."

"I'm a trained paramedic. I probably could do that, too."

She snuggled closer. "Don't forget our date on the fifteenth. This is your chance to tell me what you want me to cook for you."

Enjoying her close to him, he looked over her shoulder and up. "Hmm. Let me see.

Lobster and T-bone sounds great. Or..."
He tilted his head, pretending to be in deep
thought. "Actually, surprise me."

"No lobster and steak?"

"Nope. Although I do like seafood, lobster isn't my favorite."

"I think I have the perfect recipe in
mind."

"What?"

"You wanted me to surprise you so I'm
not telling you."

"That day I'll be at the doctor late. Do
you want to use my kitchen earlier?"

"Probably would be better than me cart-
ing all the dishes to your house."

"Are you working that day?"

"No, and I will need all afternoon to prepare my feast." She grinned. "But that is all
I'm telling you about what I'm preparing."

Their easy repartee only reinforced how
comfortable he was with Kathleen. Her
smile encompassed her whole face, joy
radiating from her. He couldn't take his
gaze off her mouth. Inviting. Tempting.
He had to taste it.

He slowly lowered his head. "Thank you for this evening."

Her lips parted slightly, and he swooped in to kiss them. He pulled her against him, their rapid heartbeats matching tempos, and put everything into the merging of their mouths.

From afar, someone clearing her throat intruded into his dazed mind. He didn't want to end the kiss, but Kathleen disengaged and stepped from his embrace. She shifted to the right.

"Jared is asleep on the couch. He told me when he fell asleep I was to get Gideon. That he'd know what to do." Amusement laced Ruth's voice.

Bereft without her in his arms, Gideon nodded his head and clicked his shoes. "Duty calls."

The urge to tickle Jared was strong, but Gideon resisted it. He bent down and hoisted the child over his right shoulder. He weighed next to nothing considering some of the equipment he had to haul in a fire. Mounting the stairs, he sensed Kathleen's gaze on him. That awareness of her heightened an electric sensation that charged his nerves.

Then she was behind him, following him up the steps. What would it feel like to carry his own child to bed, to have his wife accompany him and them both put him down to sleep? The way his life was going, he'd never find out unless he was willing to make a change and risk getting hurt again.

Chapter Twelve

As Kathleen sliced up the red pepper for a salad, her hand shook. Finally, she lay it beside the cutting board and gripped the edge of the counter in Gideon's kitchen. How was she going to find the money for the medical bills for Kip? She was still paying off her husband's debt. The doctor's bill had arrived this afternoon, and it was worse than she thought. She didn't even have the energy to call the doctor's office to talk with someone about what she owed. All her mistakes from her past were crushing her, and she didn't know how to get out from under them.

She forced herself to pick up the paring knife and finish making the salad. The scent of shrimp gumbo saturated the room with its spicy seafood aroma. The repetitive motion of dicing the pepper up into small pieces didn't soothe as it usually did. That was one of the reasons she enjoyed cooking—she could forget her troubles for a while. But not this time.

Gideon would be home soon and ready to celebrate after having his cast removed today. And that was the last thing she felt like doing. She wasn't even sure how she was going to get enthusiastic about the holidays. She had purchased a couple of gifts for her boys before Kip's accident and the car repairs. That would have to be their Christmas. Although she was already working some extra shifts at the hospital, maybe she could find another nursing job. She didn't have anything else she could sell to raise money. Most of her possessions were gone in the hurricane. The more she thought about her mounting debt the more her movements slowed until she couldn't even lift the blade.

Tears blurred her vision, and she closed her eyes, setting the knife on the counter. She didn't have any answers to her problems. She'd thought about filing for bankruptcy, but she didn't want to do that if at all possible.

The sound of the front door opening then closing underscored she wasn't alone anymore. She needed to get her composure together. This was her problem, and she didn't want to burden anyone else, even Gideon, with it. She straightened, wiped the tears from her eyes and picked up the knife to complete the salad.

"Honey, I'm home," Gideon said as he came into the kitchen. "Now does that not sound like one of those shows in the fifties like *Leave It to Beaver* or *Father Knows Best?*"

She forced a smile to her lips and turned toward him. "I think, Mr. O'Brien, you've had way too much time on your hands."

"I beg your pardon. I've been working at a dull desk job."

"Which must have given you time to daydream."

"I did find myself drifting off every once in a while, but don't tell the captain." He held up his cast-free arm and waved it. "Now that I'm back on rotation, he'd have me doing twice the work."

"Poor guy. You can't have it both ways. Either desk duty or firefighter. Which is it going to be?" She began dicing the rest of the pepper.

"No contest—firefighter." He closed the distance between them and drew in a deep breath. "Ah, that's a great smell. Shrimp gumbo. How did you know that's one of my favorite dishes?"

"A little sleuthing on my part. I called Pete, and he told me."

"And he didn't say a word to me. I didn't think Pete could keep quiet about anything."

She smiled at him. "This time he did."

"Can I help you with anything?"

"You can put the French bread into the oven at 375 degrees. Everything else is done."

"Want me to set the table?"

"I already did. In the dining room."

Gideon gave a low whistle. "You are going all out."

"That's the only way to do something. I even brought two of Mom's china place settings."

"I'm feeling pampered, and all I had to do was go into a burning building and do my job."

She caught him watching her reaction to his words. "For your information I have forgiven myself weeks ago about my part in your injuries. You have convinced me I wasn't responsible."

"Good. I was ready to launch into my spiel again if I had to." He put the bread in the oven then moved toward the dining room. "I have one final touch to add to the table."

"What?"

He swung around at the doorway. "You

are not allowed in here until it is time to eat."

"Okay. But that's not fair. This was my evening to do for you."

He headed out of the room. "Who said life is fair?"

Fair? No, it wasn't. Since before Derek's death, it had been one problem after another. When something went wrong, she didn't even have time to recover before another crisis occurred. The tears threatened again. She swallowed them away, but her throat burned.

"All done. I had to lend my finishing touch to the table."

She picked up the bowl of salad. "I'm done, too. I'm going to put this on the table—"

He plucked it from her hands. "Your ploy won't work. I'll take the food in."

"While you're in there, bring the bowls for the gumbo. The bread should be done in ten minutes."

"Great. I'm starved." He stopped in front of her by the stove and grasped the wooden spoon to stir the pot's contents. Bending over the heat rising from the gumbo, he inhaled and held the breath for a long moment then released it slowly. "I love that smell. I've been wondering all day what you were going to cook and was regretting telling you to surprise me. I don't like surprises normally."

"Neither do I." She threw a glance toward the dining room.

"You only have a few more minutes to wait." He inched toward her. "I can think of a couple of things we could do to pass the time until the bread is done."

His eyes gleamed as they roved over her face. He reached up and brushed her hair behind her ears, his gaze glued to her mouth. Her heart plummeted. His smoldering look spoke to her feminine side, urging her to give in to the feelings he generated in her. She couldn't, shouldn't.

When he sought her mouth and touched his to hers, she knew she needed to break it off. Her heart refused to listen to common sense that said she should get her life under control before even thinking of becoming involved with a man. She surrendered, giving him a part of herself she didn't have to give.

When they broke apart, their breathing ragged, Kathleen quickly tried to recapture that elusive part of herself—her heart. She couldn't risk it right now. She could never ask another to take on the kind of debt she had. It was *her* problem. No one else's.

He framed her face between his hands, his eyes leaving a heated trail where they roamed. "This wasn't exactly how I pictured telling you this. I wanted something a little romantic. But here goes. Kathleen Hart, I love you. I have never said that to another woman. Ever. In these past two months you've become so important to me. I hope one day you'll agree to be my wife. You don't have to say anything right now because I know you need time, but please think about it. I want to be a father to Kip and Jared. I want to be a husband to you."

Each word seared into her. *No. Don't. I can't.* She stared at him, seeing the sparkle in his eyes slowly fade, the smile transform into a look of puzzlement. Still, she couldn't say anything. It wouldn't be fair to Gideon. Her problems weren't his. She couldn't…

She backed away. "You know how I feel about marriage. I had one bad marriage and that was enough. I never want that again."

"To be married or a bad marriage?" His terse voice sliced through the air.

"Both. Not now." She whirled around and started toward the doorway into the dining room. She needed to get out of here.

He stopped her with a hand on her arm and rotated her toward him. "Stay. We can talk about this."

"No, enjoy the gumbo." The scent of burning bread permeated the kitchen. She gestured toward the oven. "You'd better take the bread out."

When he dropped her arm and turned toward the stove, she fled, hurrying past the dining room table. A gorgeous bouquet of flowers—lilies, carnations and others she didn't recognize—infused the air with their sweet fragrance. On a plate was a present in a small box. Its sight spurred her to a faster pace.

This wasn't the time to give her heart to another—not with all the complication in her life. *He'll thank me later.* But as she left his house, that thought didn't comfort her one bit.

Gideon yanked the burning bread from the oven. In his haste, one of his fingers touched the hot pan. He dropped it and jumped back. Staring at the bread on the floor, he stood rigid from the emotions bombarding him as if he were being hit over and over from all sides.

She doesn't want to have anything to do with me. She might as well tell me to get lost.

This was the reason he didn't put himself out there. Anger vied with his hurt. He wanted to be mad at Kathleen. He needed to be. Otherwise, the hurt would win, and he would be back to how it had been after his parents' deaths. He wouldn't go there again. He'd fought to get where he was today.

Lord, what do I do?

After a long day putting in overtime, all Kathleen wanted to do was put up her feet and do nothing. But tonight was the time she'd set aside to finish baking some goodies for her gifts to family and friends. It was all she could afford to do. When she entered the kitchen with her two bags of groceries, she found her mother at the table with her two sons painting the Christmas plates the goodies would be placed on. She'd wanted to help with that part, too, but when the overtime opportunity came up, her mom said she'd love to assist Jared and Kip. It would be a treat for her.

"It's about time you got home, Mom," Kip said, holding up his work of art. "What do you think? This is for Sally."

In the center of the white plate, he'd painted a green Christmas tree and then put ornaments on it and lots of presents under it, much like the front of Miss

Alice's huge card. "Beautiful. She's going to love it." Her cousin was still living with her mother at least for a few more months until her apartment building was rebuilt.

"I'm doing one for Gideon. What do you think about mine?"

All she saw was Jared's big grin as he showed her his plate with green rolling hills and a night sky with a brilliant star shining in it. "You've done a great job."

"That's the star the Wise Men followed. I remember Gideon telling me about it when we put the star on our tree." He tilted his head and furrowed his forehead. "Why haven't we seen him lately? He hasn't been down here in a week. I had to visit him to see him without his cast."

"Yeah, Mom, is he mad at us or something?"

Kathleen locked gazes with her mother. "I know he isn't mad at you two, but now that he can work as a firefighter again, he has needed to focus on that."

"I asked him to go to church with us on Christmas Eve." Jared set his plate down among the others they had painted. "He said he couldn't. It's sad he doesn't have a family to share Christmas with."

"Yes, it is," she murmured and turned away from her children before she started crying in front of them. She'd made such a mess of everything.

"We could be his family this Christmas," Kip said.

"That looks like the last two plates you need to do." Her mother glanced at the clock on the wall. "You said something about watching that Christmas movie on TV tonight. It'll be on in five minutes. You need to wash up and get into your pajamas. It'll be late when the movie is over and time for bed."

After her boys left the room, her mom approached her. "Are you all right?"

"No. Everything is falling apart. I—" Kathleen couldn't find the words to tell her mother how much she'd missed Gideon the past week. She glimpsed him once leaving his house, and it had taken all her willpower not to run after him and beg his forgiveness.

"I haven't wanted to pry—okay, maybe I have—but talking about what happened between y'all last week might help you."

"I had just gotten the final bill from the doctor and hospital for Kip's accident that day I made dinner for him. When he told me he loved me and—"

"He loves you! Why didn't you tell me? That's great. That's—" Her enthusiasm waned. "Is that the problem? You don't love him?"

"I do love him. I didn't want to fall in love, but this whole week he's all I thought about. I miss him terribly and yet, Mom, how can I ask a man to take on my debt, especially now that thousands more have been added to it? I can't. It's not his problem. It's mine."

"Did you talk to him about it?"

"No."

"Why not? He at least deserves to know you care about him, and why you don't

want to see him anymore. You aren't being
fair to him."

"I believe he told me life isn't always
fair."

"That's a cop-out and you know it." Her
mother sighed. "He's good with the boys.
They deserve someone like him in their
lives. From what you told me, their own
father didn't pay much attention to them
in the last few years before he died."

"Yeah, and both Jared and Kip have
drunk in Gideon's attention."

"Did you think they wouldn't ask why he
wasn't coming around?"

"I didn't think. I just reacted to him tell-
ing me he loved me. I got scared. I still am.
What if I make a mistake like I did with
Derek?"

"Gideon is a good man. He is nothing
like Derek. Whether he is for you is another
question and one only you can answer. Do
you want Derek to control the rest of your
life? He will if you let what happened between you two dictate how you live now."
Her mother took her hands. "Honey, you

shouldn't be having this conversation with me but with Gideon."

"Have I told you lately how much I love you?" Kathleen hugged her. "I don't know what I would have done if I hadn't come home. I was a mess after Derek died. I should have come back to Hope right away."

"I tried to get you to."

"I know. I thought I was giving Jared and Kip what they needed. Stability. When what they needed was here all along."

"Go rest. You look beat. I'm going to make some brownies and divinity for your goodie plates. Then if you want to add anything besides the lemon bars you did last night, that's fine. The kitchen will be all yours."

Kathleen dragged herself up the stairs to her room where she was sure she would go to sleep immediately after falling into bed. But fifteen minutes later, she punched the pillow and flipped over onto her back. As she stared at the ceiling, she turned to the Lord for guidance. She needed help untangling the mess her life was in. He was the only one who could help her.

"Gideon, a lady is here to see you," Captain Fox at Station Two said as he came into the living area on Christmas Eve.

Through the open doorway, Gideon spied Kathleen standing in the bay where the fire trucks were parked. Wearing a red and green plaid dress, she looked beautiful. His heartbeat responded by kicking up a notch, and his stomach muscles cinched.

I don't want to see her. Who are you kidding? It's taken all you have to stay away from her. Not to storm down to Ruth's and demand she love you.

Gideon shoved to his feet and covered the distance to the exit, aware of his fellow firefighters looking on as he left, intense curiosity in their expressions. A woman didn't usually come to the fire station unless she was a wife of one of the firefighters on duty.

"Thanks, captain," Gideon said as he passed him.

When he emerged into the large bay, a cool breeze blew through the large open doors. Beyond Kathleen, Christmas lights shone in the darkness. He stopped a few feet from her.

Her smile transformed the tired lines of her face into a look of radiance. "I didn't realize you were working tonight. I'd gone down to your house to talk to you and see if you would go to Christmas Eve service and discovered you were working."

"I'm filling in for a guy who has a young family. He should be home tonight and to-morrow. I don't have anyone."

"Jared and Kip will be disappointed, but I can certainly understand."

"I'll be off tomorrow night. I'll come and see them then. I have some gifts for them. Is that where you're going now—to church?"

"Yeah, I'm going to meet Mom and the boys there. I told them I needed to come see you first."

"Why?"

She took a deep breath. "I had my speech

all planned. That was why I had gone down to your house. But when you weren't home, it threw me off."

"You don't go with the flow much, do you?"

"I'm still learning." She turned toward a table to the side and picked up a plate with goodies covered in plastic wrap. "Merry Christmas. The boys decorated the plate, and Mom and I made the sweets."

"Thanks." He didn't know what else to say to her. He'd gotten her a heart-shaped necklace the day he'd gone to have his cast taken off. It still sat on his dresser, a constant reminder of the risk of falling in love. But he hadn't been able to bring himself to return it to the jewelry store. The couple of times he had tried he hadn't been able to do it.

Silence descended. Gideon took a step back. Kathleen looked out toward the street.

Seeing her only made him want to talk some sense into her. Or to drag her to him and kiss her senseless until she gave in to the feelings he knew she was beginning to have toward him.

"Well…" He searched for the right thing to say. "Tell the boys and your mom Merry Christmas for me. I'll be sure to drop by tomorrow evening." He backed away some more.

"Don't leave yet." Her chest rose and fell several times. "I—I was wrong with what I said the last time we saw each other. From the beginning I've been afraid of my feelings for you. After Derek's death I'd decided I didn't want to get married again. That I would focus on Jared and Kip. Then I met you and you changed everything. I love you, Gideon. I have no doubts about that."

He clenched his hands at his sides. "Then why did you say what you did?"

"Because earlier that day I had found out the extent of money I would owe for Kip's accident. Thousands of dollars added on top of the debt my husband left me. It was too much to process. I still don't know exactly what I'm going to do, and I certainly didn't want you to be drawn into it."

"Haven't you learned by now that it's okay to ask for help? The Lord didn't intend for us to go through life alone. It's taken me years to realize that. In fact, until I met you I didn't fully realize how alone I was. After my parents died, I lost hope of finding that connection I needed to fulfill my life. You and your family gave me that hope."

"And then that night I shattered it. I'm so sorry. I was afraid. Still am, but I had a long talk with God. I think He brought me here to Hope and to you because He wanted me to heal. I've been emotionally alone for many years, even before my husband died. I need you."

He closed the space between them. "I can help you. Together as a team we'll work it out. As a firefighter I've learned to be a team member. It hasn't always been easy because I kept those walls up. But this town, these people have helped me to break those walls down." He clasped her hands and drew her toward him. "You have. Let me be a part of your life. Fully. I'm in this relationship one hundred percent."

She wound her arms around his neck and dragged him down for a kiss. "How can I turn down an offer like that?"

He smiled and hugged her close to him. "I'm hoping you won't." He wouldn't be alone anymore. He had a family to care for and love.

Epilogue

The next evening Gideon arrived at Kathleen's mother's house with his arms full of presents. Jared and Kip were speechless as Gideon handed them their gifts. "Open them," he said as he sat next to Kathleen on the couch and took her hand.

Both boys tore into the packages, unveiling clothes and other items they had lost in the hurricane.

Glimpsing the joy on Gideon's face, Kathleen leaned toward him. "You shouldn't have. But thank you."

"They needed the clothes. I had so much

fun shopping for them. And I threw in a couple of treats for them, too."

Jared held up his rock tumbler. "Yay! I have some rocks I've found that I can put in here. Can I tonight?"

Kathleen chuckled. "Somehow I figured you would say that. We'll set it up in the garage so the noise doesn't drive us crazy."

When Jared and Kip had finished, sitting among the boxes and wrapping paper, beaming, Gideon rose and drew Kathleen up next to him. "I have one more surprise for you two."

Kip looked around. "Where?"

"On the porch." Gideon started for the front door.

Jared and Kip peered at each other then went after Gideon. Kathleen took up the rear.

Out on the porch sat two boys bikes— one red and the other blue. Her sons' eyes bugged out, both Kip and Jared rooted to the cement.

"The red one is Kip's and the blue,

Jared's," Gideon finally said when they still hadn't moved.

Suddenly, they surged forward, clasping the handlebars of their bikes. "Thank you. Thank you," Kip said, then Jared.

Kip swept around and hugged Gideon. "Mom, can we go for a ride?"

"Yes, but only on the sidewalk. You can ride down to the end of the block and back."

Gideon helped Jared and Kip carry their bikes to the sidewalk, the Christmas lights from the neighbors giving off enough illumination for them to see where they were going.

When they took off, Gideon moved back next to Kathleen to watch, slipping his arm around her. "I haven't forgotten you." He drew her toward the steps where the porch light glowed and handed her a wrapped box lying on the wicker chair. "This is for you."

She carefully removed the paper then the lid, and lifted a gold chain with a heart dangling from it. "This is beautiful. I love it."

"You have my heart. I wanted you to have one to wear close to yours."

"Will you put this on for me?" She turned her back to him and lifted her hair so he could.

His fingers on her neck sent a thrill through her. After fastening the necklace, he bent forward and whispered, "That isn't the only surprise for you."

She glanced over her shoulder. "You're spoiling me."

"I want to spend the rest of my life doing that very thing." He turned her around and kissed her. "The mayor heard about your medical bills and wants to help. A fund has been set up to help you pay for Kip's accident."

Words refused to materialize in her mind. She stared at Gideon for a long moment, trying to comprehend what he told her.

Gideon shifted her toward him. "Are you all right?"

Thank You, Lord, for sending Gideon to me. "I'm more than all right. After all, I'm in love with a wonderful man."

* * * * *

Dear Reader,

His Holiday Family is the first book in the A Town Called Hope series. Hope, Mississippi, is a small town on the Gulf Coast that faced a hurricane. The series is about how a town rebuilds after a hurricane and grows stronger from its trials. I lived for many years on the Mississippi Gulf Coast and faced several hurricanes that hit my town. This is a tribute to all the people who assist people back on their feet after a tragedy.

I love hearing from readers. You can contact me at margaretdaley@gmail.com or at P.O. Box 2074 Tulsa, OK 74101. You can also learn more about my books at http://www.margaretdaley.com. I have a quarterly newsletter that you can sign up for on my website or you can enter my monthly drawings by signing my guest book on the website.

Best wishes,

Margaret Daley

Questions For Discussion

1. When tragedy strikes, who do you turn to? What do you do to solve the problems that arise from the tragedy—ignore it, figure out what steps you need to do or wallow in self-pity?

2. Kathleen began to doubt that the Lord cared about her. She'd prayed for help and didn't think she was getting any from Him. Have you ever thought that? What did you do?

3. Gideon lost so many people important in his life that he became a loner. He felt if he didn't care about others, he couldn't be hurt. Have you ever dealt with someone who emotionally kept his distance? What, if anything, did you do to break down his walls?

4. Who is your favorite character? Why?

5. What would you do if a hurricane (or any other tragedy) struck your home and took all your possessions?

6. Gideon learned as a firefighter to be a team player. Do you prefer doing things solo or with a team? Why?

7. Both Kip and Jared were not happy being moved to Hope. They were angry with Kathleen because they missed their friends and home in Denver. Did you have to move as a child? How did you adjust? What helps a child adjust to a move to another town?

8. Kathleen didn't feel she could accept help from Gideon. After her bad marriage, she thought that would be saying she was weak. Is it easy for you to accept help from people? If not, why do you have trouble with that? What are some ways people can get over thinking they have to do everything themselves?

9. What is your favorite scene? Why?

10. Kathleen had to learn to believe in herself again. She was afraid to trust her feelings developing concerning Gideon.

Instead of letting herself care, she pulled away. She denied her feelings, thinking she was better off by doing that. Have you done that? Did it work? Why or why not?

11. Kathleen felt guilty for causing Gideon's injury. She had been conditioned and didn't know how to work her way through her guilt. It was one of the reasons she had reached a crossroad in her life. How have you dealt with guilt?

12. Kathleen and her family had certain traditions they did at Christmas. Are traditions in your life important to you? What are some that you and your family do?

13. Kathleen had a large debt to pay because of her husband's spending. She felt overwhelmed and wasn't sure how to reduce the debt. Have you faced money problems? What are some steps that could help Kathleen get out of debt?

14. When Gideon's house burned down as a young boy, he grabbed his baseball card collection that he and his father had collected. He treasured it because it reminded him of his father who died in the fire. What would you grab if your house was burning and why?

15. Kathleen rejected Gideon's love and hurt him. Gideon had never told another woman he loved her. It took a lot for him to do that. Sometimes we can't avoid being around people who have hurt us. What are some things we can do to deal with people who have hurt us?